Tales of Bristeria

The Knight and the Leviathan

By: Brooke Smiley

CLC Publishing LLC
An Innovative Author-Friendly Publisher

Published by CLC Publishing, LLC, Mustang, OK

ISBN 978-0-0000000-0-0

Fiction/Fantasy

Lies... aka labels. First, they are hurtful. Then quickly embedded. Then habitually thought on. And last... They are believed. Before we know it, we have become blind and can longer see the real us. We become what we believe. So I encourage you all to lift up your eyes. Don't look down to where all you will hear are lies. Look up!

CHAPTER 1

Annalise

I blinked my eyes open to the sight of Tailya tending to a cut above my left eyebrow. Sitting myself up in order to rub the ache on the back of my neck, I mumbled, "W- where am I?"

Needless to say, I was still a little out of it. Tay gently placed her warm palm over mine. Looking into my eyes, she soothingly told me, "You are in my house." "And mine!" David blurted. It was obviously clear that he wanted me to know he'd also done his fair share in

rescuing me as well. Tailya looked annoyed. She glared at her brother and hissed, " Yes David. If you would let me finish, I was just about to inform Anna that

it was you who saved us. Geez." Then she rolled her eyes.

"Well, you sure were taking your time about it," David scoffed. My head started to spin as they bickered back and forth. My mouth widened into a deep yawn and then I lost all vision as my head went fuzzy again. Feeling dizzy, I had let my body sink back down into the pillow, hoping to ease the twirling. I started to taste the acid from my stomach on the tip of my tongue and feel the bubbles in my throat rising. "I'm going to be sick!" I shouted, causing them to quiet their quarreling. They raced across the room to my bedside to check on me. David looked at Tay worried. Tay grabbed the towel from the water bowl and rung it out then gently placed it around my neck. A few slow deep breaths later, the nausea dissipated which calmed my nerves.

David and Tay glowered. "Sorry for our disruptive actions," they both said in unison with their heads sunk low. "We didn't mean to cause you any more illness. Are you alright?" Both my friends were fidgeting and wouldn't look at me. The sloshing in my brain finally ceased, and my dizziness was also gone. My body felt a little flushed after the symptoms lifted and I knew it was time for some more rest. "Yes, yes, I am better," I answered. My tired body began to weaken, and I started to doze. Before I went under fully, I could hear the two of them chattering about something that had to do with Fawn's letter and retrieving what we had left behind in that enchanted world we'd just escaped. I tried my best to hang on and listen to them a little longer, but my fatigued ears wouldn't let me. Their voices became muffled and then whispers followed by silence. I passed out. It felt endless on the time It was taking me to heal. I was on the verge of going bonkers having to be stuck in the bed. Time went by slowly as I healed. About three weeks later, my body was completely back to normal. All that was left behind were scars. I didn't mind the looks of them, not even the bright red stripe on my chest. They were my warrior wounds. A reminder of being brave and doing what was right. Even though Tay and I lost to the Queen and Kedron, there was still something inside of me that felt liberated. While putting on my shoes, I stared at my bedridden cage. I was thankful to be rid of it and happy to walk again. The thought of being stuck in that thing for one more minute, made my insides churn. I was ready to leave. Ready to go find my brother, Brighton and save my family.

Being able to pick myself up off the floor, I realized I was happy that I could now stand without the usual twitching of my legs. Reaching for the door handle about to leave the room, my eyes became transfixed on a peculiar painting that was hanging on the wall to my left. " I can't believe I've never noticed this before", I thought while taking a closer look. As I stared at the picture, it began to rub me the wrong way.

It's as if I was getting drawn in. The image gave me goosebumps which caused all the hairs on my arms to rise. A woman getting sucked into darkness with no way of being set free. The poor lady was trapped and looked to be in anguish. My heart pinched at the thought of her pain.

The more I gazed into the woman's eyes the more I felt I was catching a glimpse of her soul. "Creepy," I said aloud, as I opened the door to go find and join Tailya and David.

As I began traipsing down the hallway, I noticed pictures of Tailya. " Huh?" I thought as I leaned in for a closer look. " Strange", I mumbled. There weren't any photographs of her and her parents, none of her and David, not even one with the family all together.

All of the portraits only had Tay in them, and she was holding a cake. Well except the first one, in that photo, her face was planted into that cake. "Anna!" I heard Tailya calling me from a short distance. "Yeah?!", I shouted back. I waited for a response but got nothing. " Where are you? This entryway is never ending!", I yelled. There were so many pictures on each side of the walls that I felt like the hallway would go on forever.

"We're down here and to your right," Tay shouted. I peeled my eyes away from the memorabilia distracting me and followed the sound of my friend's voice until we were face to face. "Hey. There you are, ``she shouted. Excited to see me, she asked, "Are you rested up and ready to go? My eyes narrowed and I shook my head, " No. Not until you tell me what the plan is." I wanted to ask about the hallway, but instead, I kept quiet. David came from around the corner, stuffing his face with what looked to be a turkey leg. "Oh, come on Annalise. Don't be like that. Haven't you ever wanted to do something without knowing the outcome?" "Yeah, what he said," Tay chimed in. I rolled my eyes. Nonetheless, my friends made a good point in their wheedling . It probably would be exciting to go on a journey of the unknown. On the other hand, what I had just faced chained me to the fear of anything and everything I didn't know, and I was nowhere near on board with their enthusiastic proposition.

My little brother, now a man, tried to kill me, and the evil inside the Queen, my mother, was not stopping at any lengths to destroy me. Not even healed for a month, and the tormenting in my mind was already resurfacing. I would like to say, "Go away and let me regain my strength in peace, geez." At least that's what came to mind. I wanted to share it out loud, but I knew I probably shouldn't. Tay and David might think something was wrong with me if I started to talk back to the notions in my head.

Keeping quiet with the answers to myself was probably the best thing anyway. I knew the silent treatment would not be able to last much longer. My eyes wandered from wall to wall around the room until Tay stepped into my view. "Annalise. What are you doing?! Why is it, you can't answer a simple question without drifting off into space every time?!" Needless to say, I've annoyed her again. Irritating Tay was starting to become a bad habit, and I didn't care for it.

I stood there. David smiled and walked toward me to clap me on the back only it wasn't a big thud like usual. This one was a soft pat instead, and his normal boyish friendly gesture now made me feel a little awkward... "Get away weirdo!" I blurted while swiftly jerking forward away from his random act of kindness. "What?! I was only trying to comfort you. Get over yourself Anna," David scowled.

Drawing in a deep breath, he lowered his gaze from mine and moped away. I felt nothing. I knew I wounded him somehow, but I didn't seem to care. "What is going on with me? Why did I not apologize to David?" Asking myself these questions on the inside still didn't help my outside actions. I couldn't even form the words to say, "I'm sorry." It was as if something was holding my tongue, keeping my lips from parting.

"Annalise! What is your problem? My brother was only trying to help!" Tay stomped over to address her anger toward me by slapping me on the arm. "Now look at what you have done."

I turned to see the poor boy burrowed up in the corner brooding. As I stood there watching him, hands and knees tucked together, it didn't give me one sense of emotion. I shrugged.

Tay went over to console her brother. I heard her telling him it would be alright, and to get up and show me it didn't 't bother him. Then, she said something that I thought could be true. "Maybe there is something wrong with her brain. That beam blasted her real good, remember?" Gasp. That's right, my brother's staff. I forgot how I almost died. David. It was he who saved Tay and me. My memory was coming back full speed and I was starting to feel an inkling of regret, followed by a hint of Deja-vu.

Walking over to David, I dropped to one knee and placed my left hand on his shoulder. While feeling the red stripe on my chest I said, "David, I think your sister is telling you the truth. My mind is still trying to recap the empty spaces lost." He swiped his hand in a fast-paced motion across his face. I think he didn't want me to find out he was angry crying. "Come on Anna, let's go pack while David gathers himself." Tailya grasped my fingers and took me away. Pacing back down the hall, I squeezed Tay's hand. "I really am sorry for my outburst on your brother." I wasn't though, I was lying straight through my teeth. But I didn't want to fight with my best friend, so I told her once again what she probably wanted to hear.

Something awfully bizarre was lurking and more and more I was starting to feel like somebody or something else.

Tay and I made it to the room. She started grabbing all the shoes and clothes we could fit into this big brown bag that she had hidden underneath her bed.

Right as Tay began to tie up our luggage, David barged into the room. "If you think for a second, I will let you two go without me, then clearly not one but both of your brains are fried!"

Tailya rolled her eyes. I just sighed and shook my head. "This boy is clueless," I thought. He stood in front of his sister and me like a king's guard, ready to protect and serve. I turned my back to muffle a giggle. "What is it you think you can do if we were to find ourselves in trouble, huh?" Tay taunted.

David narrowed his brows. In that moment I realized, I didn't want to hear their squabbling throughout our travels. Looking at them and trying not to sound harsh with my words, I said, "You know you two have been so great, but I don't want you to come with me. I need to do this on my own."

My tone must not have been pleasant because my answer back from them was a couple of glares that gave me the heebie-jeebies. "What…?" I stared blankly. Silence from both of them continued. I shivered. The air was thick and intense. Tay threw her arms up. "You are not going anywhere without us! Don't even think about it for one more minute! Plus, you need us, Anna!" Tailya was strong in her speech. I sighed. Knowing that I wasn't going to win this battle, I stared both my friends down while crossing my arms tightly. "I was worried for your safety, not my own. Just try to stay out of trouble, okay? I don't want you two to get yourselves killed." Both scowled at me as they gave me a slight head nod. We gathered up the rest of our essentials and formed a plan to stay on track. I sat there listening to Tay describe the whereabouts of where we needed to go. "What?!" I cut her off when I heard my home, Bristeria, mentioned. It was frightening to think we might run into Queen Cheylenna and Kedron again. "Calm down, will you? We are not going through there. It was just a thought," Tay's words infuriated me.

Crossing my arms I retaliated, "A bad thought Tailya! Really. Your worst ever!" Nervousness caused a rupture from my lungs as I ended the last part of my sentence.

My friend huffed and then drew in a deep breath. I thought I saw a tear trickle down her cheek, but my blood was still boiling for some odd reason, and it caused me not to care. She stood, picked up the bag, and glared at me as she walked out of the room.

David's eyes told me he was shocked and why wouldn't he be. My behavior was way off. I rolled my eyes just knowing what was about to happen. He was about to give me his two cents. The moment he parted his lips I shouted, "What?!" A fight. That's what I wanted. There was so much anger building inside of me and I needed to release it all or at least let some of it out. Instead, what he did threw me for a loop. The boy just stood there offering me his right hand in complete silence with a goofy grin. He leaned further down and said, "Stand up." "What?" I said baffled. He caught me off guard. His calm yet firm approach told me I wasn't going to get my fight after all which made my insides cringe.

Taking David's generous hand, I let him help pull me up to my feet keeping the hostility to myself. His hand was sweaty, and I could see he was nervous. "What's the matter?" I stomped one foot after the other on the floor below me hoping to get out a bit more steam that didn't seem be going anywhere anytime soon. I puffed out a huge deep breath. All he did was smile bigger and run a hand through his sun kissed blonde locks. "Yeah, the boy is timid," I thought. Answering back with a devious grin, I contemplated what fun scheme I could torment him with.

My hand was still attached to his clammy fingers. Eye to eye we stood there in silence. Knowing that I was eye candy to him, I planned to play off of the feelings that he had for me. I started batting my lashes while twisting side to side. I watched and waited for his stare to soften. "Now is my chance. I thought. I bet I can get him to do whatever I want." The wicked contemplations just kept flooding in. I began to ponder on them until I realized I was now biting my lower lip in anticipation. After that, I started to confess under my breath, " This isn't a good idea at all, and it more than likely won't end well.

"Okay. Good, it sounds like there is still some kindness left in me ", I thought as I reassured myself with a much-needed exhale of relief. "Okay. Take in a giant amount of air. Anna, take as much as your lungs will allow." David's method seemed odd, but I did it anyway. Anything to get my mind off of my malicious thoughts.

I parted my mouth. I sucked in so much air that it felt like my heart was going to implode. I think fainting was in the cards for me because David gripped my shoulders screaming, "Let it out! Anna! Blow it out!" Whoops, brain lapse. I don't know why I held it in for so long. What was I thinking about? I couldn't retrace my last notion. It completely vanished. I gasped. I was beginning to think something, or someone was trying to control me.

"Are you alright, Annalise?" David had no clue of my thoughts, but he could tell something was definitely troubling me. "Were you ever going to exhale?!" he loudly questioned. My friend grabbed the back of his neck and began rubbing. "Crapes girl. You had me concerned over your life there for a second. I didn't think you were ever going to breathe."

"Yeah. I know me too. Strange, huh?" I chuckled trying to play it off like nothing was wrong. David of course gave me a faint smile not wanting to press the issue. I fluttered my lids once more and said, "Come on. Let's go find Tay. Isn't it time for us to head out? I know she is probably tapping her foot right now wondering what is taking us so long." Dropping his hand while motioning with my head to have him follow behind, I assured," When we find your sister I will apologize, and all will be forgiven. You'll see."

Both of us left the room. Rushing down the hall I tried to think of what I was going to say to receive Tailya's forgiveness. "Yes. That's it! That is what I will go with." "Huh?" David replied looking puzzled. "Good night. Here I go again blurting my thoughts out for all to hear," I huffed. Reaching the front door, I swung around to tell David, "Oh.

You know me. Just talking to myself." The boy smirked as he opened the door for me.

CHAPTER 2

Brighton

I had always wanted nothing more than to become a knight, but the hour had come, and I knew the time was upon me to wear the crown. Figuring this because I am the eldest and Kedron was only five. There was no way for Lissy either since she was a girl and a lady can't become king. No. It had to be me. I didn't want to leave them again, but I had to get out. Suddenly a hard swallow formed, and I slumped down into my seat staring at my empty glass that was strangely just full of ale.

I didn't want the crown. I wanted to be a knight. I was ready to spread my wings, ready for an adventure. I wanted to go search for the serpent in the sea my friends had told me about, not become the next king.

Becoming a soldier would teach me how to help destroy it. They said the powerful monster was wreaking havoc, and sailors and knights would go out into the water to catch fish but never return to be seen again.

Sitting in the tavern and wondering what was taking the wench so long to refill my mug, a friendly voice sounded above me. "What's got you so locked in the cave bud?" I looked up from out of my stupor. "Well, well if it isn't my old pal, Willy. What brings you here? Weren't you in Egladon training Pegasi?" I said with a mischievous grin followed by a chuckle.

Willy glared at me and guffawed mocking me in return. "White horses with wings," I said as I shook my head. Surely my friend was pulling my strings when he wrote to me. I knew of the serpent from the guys here in Bristeria, but I had never heard of Pegasi. Just the thought of it had me baffled.

Willy raised his voice to get my attention. "Hey! Brighton!" Squeezing my eyes and rubbing them, I cleared my throat and straightened. Looking at my friend I asked, "Do you want to hear what I found out about Egladon?" His lids widely expanded as he sat down in his chair across from me.

"Okay. So I was reading your letter"- "Okay, and?" Willy interrupted. " Do you want to hear this or not, man.?" I replied sternly. He bobbed his head, so I started again

" As I was saying, I was in the middle of reading your letter and I would have finished it too if it weren't for Trevor, Kevin, and Tristan rushing up to me like a pack of wild hyenas. Their rambunctious behavior caused me to lose focus. All three of them were chattering at the same time. Most of it I couldn't even make out but what I did hear intrigued me to run home and grab one of my father's books. When I got there, I saw it in the study sitting upright on the shelf in plain sight .A story of the horrible legendary sea beast that killed millions. Anyone who ever lays eyes on the monster didn't live to tell about it."

Willy was hooked. He sat there squeezing his fists together in anticipation. "Go on!" he shouted. I told him how the book spoke of one lowly man who had seen the vicious creature from afar on a mountain top. Also how I spoke with my father about the story and how my father, King Cyrus laughed and didn't have much to say about it.

"My king only shared one thing. The book was written by my grandfather, but he didn't want to tell me any more than that. I think it was because he didn't want to tarnish the memories I had of grandfather. I could tell he wanted the memories of his father to be known and remembered about more than just the wacky tall tales he was mocked for. Father said he loved hearing them and the look of excitement that came from grandfather's face when he was telling them. But he said that was when he was a young lad. As he grew older, they soon became childish stories to him." At the end of my tale, I realized I had just done to Willy what my father did to me when I asked about grandfather's book. Remembering my King distinctly ordering me not to go off chasing folktales from a mad man's mind. I cleared my throat while placing a hand on my friend's shoulder. "Forgive me Willy for the Pegasus pun." He shrugged. I placed my palms down on the table. "So. White-winged horses, you say." My friend coughed while lifting my mug to the wench for a repour and one more glass.

"Tell you what. When she makes her way over you get us a pitcher of that ale and I'll inform you on everything I know about the flying chargers in Egladon." Willy said. I shook his hand. "We have us a concurrence." Both of us sat there waiting trying not to become impatient.

After listening to Willy tell me about the pegasi and how he'd flown on the back of one I found myself in a childlike fascination. I wanted to set off foot as soon as possible to Egladon. I was eager to see these winged horses with my own two eyes. I could not wait to become the world's best-trained knight. Willy and I poured out the last of our pitcher. Clinking our mugs together with only having a swallow left, we ended the evening.

"Get plenty of sleep for our journey," Willy kept repeating, "We start at sunup. Don't forget, Brighton. We start at sunup." I chuckled. Seemed my buddy needs more sleep than I do.

We met up the next afternoon. Apparently, Willy needed more sleep time. At least that is how he so actively put it when he chucked a shoe at my head for trying to get him up on time. The sun was high, and it was starting to become humid. I had just finished untacking Nico and Willy's horse and packing their food when he finally traipsed up. He scratched his head while yawning. I shook my head. "My mistake. Clearly, you're not awake yet. It's not as if it's noon." I couldn't help it to not torment him a little. After all, he's the one that was adamant about the time we were to leave. He overslept, not me.

I gave him a sarcastic glare, but Willy didn't pay me any mind. Instead, he stretched his hands over his head and laughed. When he was through with his guffawing, he searched me from head to toe. "Umm… You need to bulk up a lot before we travel anywhere. Otherwise, you won't last two days in Egladon brother." Right as Willy finished, I thought , " I don't know who's leg you're trying to pull, I have more muscle than you buddy." I squared my shoulders allowing my pride to show. Then I huffed, "Well. You aren't much bigger than me, so what's your excuse?!". Willy glowered. "It's my asthma," he said under his breath. Creasing my eyes, I yelled "Huh-speak up mute! I can only hear your mumbles!"

While shouting, I noticed Willy was clenching his jaw and that I had struck a nerve. He shot his daggers at me while saying, "they said I can't join the ranks because of my asthma. I am only able to be a server for the knights. Over the years I've watched all of their techniques on how to become stronger and swifter so I know I can help you."

Then he hawked and spat right near my shoe in frustration.

I immediately regretted my words and my tone. I was too harsh.

Clapping my friend on the back to ease the tension, I said my apologies.

"I thought- well, I really can't grasp what I was thinking. My mistake Willy."

He took in a vast amount of his inhaler. Blowing it out he said, "Come on. The quicker we start, the faster we can get there."

The riding in silence was agony and forced me to wallow in my deep thoughts. Kedron and Lissy came to mind. I missed them. A twinge pricked my heart as their names sounded in my head. I could hear Lissy's giggles as I pictured her riding on her new horse, Ghost, and Kedron in front of me jumping up and down overzealous to show me one of his magic tricks he mastered.

I could feel the burn trying to form in my eyes. Not wanting to break, I let my lungs take in a lot of air and then slowly released while sharply twitching my head to regain focus.

"Hey man." Willy jerked his head around to face me. From the way he examined me, I noticed my voice had a squeaky sound when I spoke. My emotions were trying to hold on strong. Not wanting my friend to either worry or mock me, I straightened and coughed to clear my throat, "Where are we going?"

Willy pointed forward, but there wasn't anything in front of or in the back of us. Nothing. It was a never-ending dirt road. Not one tree or bush in case I have to relieve myself. "Willy. Hey man, you aren't trying to leave me for dead somewhere, are ya ?" My friend chuckled and pointed his finger forward again. "Keep your leg linens on. We're almost there."

"Well, we better get there soon because there's something awful brewing on my insides and I ain't going off to find a hole to do my business in. A man demands some privacy." Willy snickered.

Out of my anxiousness, I hawked and spat while kicking myself subconsciously. "Man., I wish I wouldn't have had a second helping of those nuts and berries," I said, as I clenched my stomach while puffing out my cheeks.

Looking up ahead, I saw Willy take another dose of his breathing medication. Focusing on the mechanism and how it worked, it looked irritating. "Poor Willy", I thought. The whole thing was odd. This amber glass bottle looking thing with three ends to it carried the means of his lifeline. I noticed two out of the three ends hold the medicine which looked like water. The third end was for my friend to place his mouth around in order to suck out the medication. "What in the saints", I thought while watching him. ?" The guy was always puffing on it. As many times I caught him, I started to wonder if this contraption was even helping him at all.

After exhaling he said, "I wouldn't be here if it wasn't for this stuff." I nodded blankly I was going to ask a couple of questions to pique my curiosity but the look on his as he put it away made it clear he didn't like talking about it, so I didn't speak a word. I guess he thought it made him look ailing or something. However, I suspected he was really brave and smart for always being prepared.

"How much longer?", I groaned. The pinches in my gut were getting stronger and stronger. All I could do was focus on taking deep slow breaths. "About three more miles!" Willy shouted ahead. Then I thought, "Oh crapes." A little way forward I could read a sign that said "Welcome. You have arrived at Camp Herculean".

"Willy, you lied to me!" He gave me a toothy grin. Throwing my arms down to my sides, I balled my fists. "It's all fun and games until someone loses an eye. Now, where's the blasted privy." My growl made Willy gasp and he hastily pointed toward a small brick hut down the pathway from the entrance. I took off as fast as my squeezed legs would move.

Finding my way back to the gate, I saw Willy standing under the sign waiting for me I'm guessing. The board above my friend's head read "Welcome to Camp Herculean Where we turn sissies into sol-diers' '. After reading the whole banner I became so mad that I could have spit nails. Willy considered me to be puny. My ears were burning, and it felt like smoke was steaming from each one. I spat. A soldier made his way from the tree post inside the gate. "Woo-wee. Look here, boys. Fresh meat!" Before Willy and I knew it, men were pouring out from everywhere. I started to tremble. Through my chattering teeth I said,. "Hey Willy, I think they were waiting for us." At that mo-ment I realized I was a bit of a chicken. My head lowered and I dropped my shoulders.

Startled, Willy had to take a deep breath of his medicine again. "I-I brought my friend here to train with you. He needs to be granted safe passage to Egladon." The soldier's face was stern as he stared Willy in the eyes. The man started marching toward Willy and just when I thought he was done for, the soldier smirked at him. "I'm just joshing you guys. Yeah, we're up for the challenge." He turned to his brothers. "Right men?" They all shouted "Sir!" in unison.

Willy and I relaxed. The soldier clapped my friend on the shoulder while looking at me from head to toe. I spread my feet and squared my shoulders. The man and his crew took one look at me and started guffawing. When they were finished, the soldier said to Willy," Haha ha. Well, my boy you have brought him to the right place."

He straightened and it was as if he had grown about two feet taller. Clearing his throat he said, "I have to warn you lads there is only blood, sweat, and pain expected here. No wimps and no whining allowed." Both of us stuck our hands out to form a firm agreement. After we signed me up, we were shown our living quarters and I thought to myself, "How long do I have to stay here?"

I have to admit that I was a little shaky coming into contact with Godzilla standing in front of me. I mean the man looked to be eight feet tall with bricks as arms and bulky legs. Also the man had a chest I'd never forget It was as if he had cement poured all over it, nothing was busting through this giant. I thought, " Anyone who wants to take this guy on is nuts." His head was even shaved. The man had no hair. "I'm not cutting or shaving my hair," I said aloud to myself while running my hands through my strawberry blonde locks.

"You will if they tell you to brother.", Willy said sternly. I gulped. I forgot I wasn't alone. Looking at my friend worried I asked, "Willy. Do you think I will have to cut my hair?" Before my friend could answer, he was cut off by the soldier that entered our cabin. "No son you don't have to cut off your hair. This was a choice, not a requirement," he said pointing up to his bald head.

"Well thank the saints man. I thought yours was mandatory." The soldier chuckled. "No. All is well lad. From now on though you will address me as sir or my name, Sir Hammon." I nodded as he left. Dropping my head, I huffed. "Willy. Where have you brought me ?!" He stood up straight and spoke to me as if I were a bug. A tiny little bug. "Brighton. Listen, you need to be here. You are nowhere near in shape or strong enough, wait. I don't even think you're brave enough to face what is in Egladon. These men will teach you to become fierce and master brute strength. Trust me, man. You need this." Then he gave me a stern look.

I spat.

"Willy, I don't belong here! Wait a minute. What did you mean when you said I am not brave enough? I mean I know I'm a bit of a scaredy cat but come on man, you don't have to be so blunt. What is it you're not telling me Willy?" Now I was the one doing the glaring.

My friend took in a puff of his medicine. When he was ready, he proceeded to tell me his story. "Okay. So, you know the other night when you were telling me of the sea serpent monster?" I crossed my arms. "The one in my grandfather's book. Yeah, I remember." He sat down on his cot. "Well, I already knew about it. It's the reason I left and came back to Bristeria." I gasped. "So, have you seen it? Far away I mean. Have you seen it?"

He shook his head, and I couldn't help but ask, "Why are we going there then? Why all of this, if you ran away?" He puffed out his feeble chest. "I didn't run! I-I. Well. You would have to if you heard the things

I heard. Enough of all this. You want to be a knight to help slay it, don't you?" "Yes!" I growled.

Willy stood up. "Then let's get you prepared and both of us will have to pique our curiosity when we get there. Deal?" He spat in his hand. " Deal.", I said as I did the same. Then we connected our saliva and shook on our agreement.

CHAPTER 3

Annalise

Walking out of Tay's house, I started to wonder how we were even going to find my brother. Tailya looked at her brother who was closing the door behind him. "So. Did you tell her?" David shrugged. "Tell me what?" Tay ignored me and stared at her brother. "David. You were supposed to tell her!" she growled. Crossing my arms and gritting my teeth, I said," Tell me what!"

The girl finally acknowledged me. "Yeah. It's me, Annalise. Remember? I'm still here!" Tay smirked and I blew out a strong breath of air. "Where are we going? Why are you two hiding something? Come one. Cough it up." I held my gaze strongly, hoping one of them would crack. Tay's face dropped. She was about to spill it. I took a deep breath. She started talking and then I heard it.

"What?! Bristeria?!" David's eyes lowered and he shook his head. Tay sighed. "Yes, Anna. We have to go there. In the forest near your home is the only place I know how to get back inside that world." I raised my voice. I was so agitated. "And how in stars do you plan on getting through the portal? We're no longer fairies! We have no magic. We couldn't even save my king!"

Tailya reached out to me. I was huffing and puffing. Probably even blowing smoke from my mouth like it was the dead of winter when the sun was still visible but puts off no friendly heat.

"Calm down Anna, geez!" Now Tay was mimicking me. So, I bit my tongue. Steam had to be coming out of me from somewhere because my eyes were stinging so bad, I had to rub them. Not knowing if these were tears of anger or fear of having to travel back to where I almost died and where my father is still held captive was taking its toll on me. I felt bile rise from stomach and up into my throat.

I wanted to scream and maybe even hit something, but the only thing around us were trees, and I had just healed. I wasn't trying to break my hand on any tree barks. I looked at Tay and David with a glare. "So... how far is it to Bristeria then?"

Tailya's eyes widened, and she screeched out, "Well, you see Annalise-

I cut off the sound of her voice when my mind began drowning with "She called me Annalise. Oh no. Okay, this must be serious." When I focused back it was on her last word "Bristeria". My body cringed.

"Why is it when I hear the name Bristeria, my home, I get all shivery?" I thought as I creased my eyes. "What about Bristeria, Tay?" I asked. "Did you not just hear anything I said?" she hissed. Crossing her arms and walking right up to me, I felt the frustration pouring right out of her by the hot breath on my face which forced me to take a hard swallow.

'We are in Bristeria!" she shouted. Right after she said Bristeria my eyes popped out as my mouth flew open. An overwhelming touch of fatigue washed over me. I felt my eyes start to roll into the back of my head. Then they crossed toward one another and suddenly it was dark.

Foggy sounds chimed in my ears as my lids started to squeeze. I blinked my eyes open, only to see the sky above me. It was odd to not feel any pain. "I could have sworn I fainted", I thought. Then I felt each of his hands under my arms.

"There you are. We thought we'd lost you. Are you okay, Anna?" Lying in his arms I looked up into the boy's eyes while thinking, "He caught me. My friend, David, caught me. He saved me from hitting the pavement and for that I made myself muster up a smile to thank him". When I felt his chest rise deeply under my back, I awkwardly coughed. "Okay. I'm alright now, David. You can let go of me now." He hoisted me straight up and then with a shy look on his face he scratched the back of his head.

Tay grinned. "You two," she said while shaking her head. When I could finally catch my breath, I asked, "So exactly how far are we from the castle?"

I gazed deep into her eyes. Not one blink of relaxation was going to be offered from me. I was done with the both of them beating around the bush. I turned to David but all he did was gulp. When I turned back to Tay her eyes were shooting daggers at her brother.

"Enough! You two had very well better fess up! I mean it! Right now!" Livid as I was, I couldn't stop shouting. That was until Tailya's face went pale. White as a ghost even. My anger intact, I shouted, "What?!"

Both her hands gripped my shoulders. While gritting her teeth and cocking her head to the side, she said very quietly, "Anna, can you please calm down? Look over there." "Over where?" I whispered. She jerked her head swiftly. It looked like she was losing control. She wouldn't stop twitching. So, to humor her, I glanced to the side. "Holy mountain!"

My body froze from head to toe. I couldn't believe my eyes. My heart sank like a poor flower when it has been given too much water. There she was cackling with Kedron, walking straight up to our path. I couldn't move, couldn't even blink. I was like a snowman waiting for the sun to come out and melt me away. Before I could comprehend the fearful thoughts trying to plummet my mind, I was yanked up off my feet by David and all three of us rushed over to hide behind the bush near their front door.

Peeking between leaves, I could see them getting closer. "She looks the same. Nothing about her is different", I thought. My mother hadn't changed one bit. Even though terror was upon my head , the thought of my father, King Cyrus, being locked up while these two didn't have a care in the world made the acid in my stomach boil. I sat in silence biting my tongue. Not long after, bile started to rise up into my throat. I began to taste copper which seemed to be also mixed with a hint of salt. I wasn't even aware of the tears trickling down. I guess I was too afraid and angry to notice.

All of us held our breath and covered our mouths so they wouldn't hear our heavy breathing. I glared at my mother and brother as we watched them pass by the bush. I couldn't have been more relieved the moment they left our sight.

Getting up off the ground, we all dusted the dirt off of our knees. I thanked Tay for the heads up and then turning to David I stuck out my hand to give his a firm shake while saying , "Thank you for being such a great friend." His shoulders dropped as did his smile. "What is it?" I asked while our hands were still connected. When he looked at me, he said something I wasn't expecting. He let go of my hand, crossed his arms, and planted his heels. "Annalise." My eyes widened. "Yeah?" I tried fluttering my lashes to ease the tension, but he didn't soften. David gave me a hard stare. "Annalise. You really ought to toughen up more. You could have gotten us killed! You can't keep freezing up every time something scary comes along!" When he'd finished scolding me, I made a pact with myself to not be a little weakling anymore. It's time to strengthen up and put on a hard shell that can't be cracked.

While we were walking, I was making all of these promises to myself. When I looked up and saw we had arrived in the forest, the freak out came back.

"Nope! Huh-uh! Not ever going to happen!"

Tay grabbed my hand. Her soft voice tried to soothe me. "Come on, Anna. This is the only way we are going to be able to find your brother, Brighton."

David grabbed my other hand. I didn't notice it at first, but they were dragging me up to a very tall tree. Looking all around I started to grasp that it was by far the tallest in the forest. "How come I haven't noticed this before?" I thought to myself.

Tailya and David's hands tightened around mine when the tree split to form a door. "At least I'm not the only one rethinking this," I said aloud. They both gulped then smirked at me.

Tay glanced at her brother and nodded. David dropped my hand and lifted me off my feet. Then he threw me over his shoulder like I was a sack of potatoes being hauled off from the village market.

The blood was starting to rush to my head, and I could see spots. "Put me down!" I shouted. David chuckled. He wasn't paying me any mind. So, I glared at Tailya. "Tell. Him to put. Me. Down!" She looked at her brother and panicked. "Put her down. Put her down." As soon as the blood went back down, I shouted, "What in the stars is wrong with you two?! You know I would have been just fine holding both of your hands and stepping through!" Tay pressed her palms up and down toward the ground. "Whoa. Whoa. I thought this would have been easier for you. I 'm so sorry, Annalise." "Sorry- Sorry," I spat. I shot my eyes at David as I shouted, "Your brother over there was crushing my ribs!" I was also wanting to lay into him. But when I finished yelling at her and actually took the time to stop and look at David, I could see it written on his face that he didn't mean to hurt me , so I decided to just take a deep breath and let it go.

Looking at both of my friends, I saw the sympathy in their eyes. It caused me to weigh out my thoughts on what was more important. Was it being a chicken or wanting to find Brighton? Needless to say, I picked the latter. We all joined hands and stepped through the glimmering door that was in the split of the tree.

CHAPTER 4

Annalise

The crossover seemed different. This time we could see each other and everything around us were places Tay and I had been to. However, there was one place I stared at that felt fairly familiar, almost like I could remember being there in that garden. I started to let my mind drift, but I couldn't seem to scratch the surface. Nothing came to mind.

Letting it go, for now, I started to think of how Brighton was going to react when he saw me. After all, I was nine when I ran away. Now I am sixteen going on seventeen. My thoughts swayed off to Ghost. "Ghost!" I shouted out loud from my flashback. Regret was weighing my heart down. The thought that I might not ever get another chance to ride him again caused water to well up in my eyes.

I closed them tight, blinking away my tears. I could still remember the smells of the forest in the spring. Being up on Ghost was like sitting on top of a high hill with nothing and no one around taking in scents of honeysuckle and pine from the air and the feeling of the sun, bright and beautiful, shining on my face.

Also how the sun split through the trees just enough to give us light to trot safely through the trail and avoid the gloomy shadows that gave me the creeps. Ghost's coat shimmered like snowflakes when the rays from the sun hit him just right. Thinking back on all of this, I felt one small tear fall down my cheek and I quickly swiped it away.

"Annalise!" I heard someone say my name very faintly. Looking down at Ghost, I say, "That's strange. Hey boy. Do you hear that?" There was no one else in the forest with us. "Annalise." Ah. There it was again. "Ghost?" He lifted his head and shook it as he let out a whicker. "Come on Anna. We're here. Snap out of it!" Tay pulled me from my flashback. I opened my eyes and sighed with deep regret. Here we are, back in the world where we defeated the witches, I muttered. I let out another sigh noticing that this was what my life had become.

Tay was flustered until she saw the sorrow in my eyes. I let her take my hand and guide me out of the gateway. Her kind eyes were telling me that this wasn't how my story ended. I turned to see David smiling at me. His empathetic grin caused me to straighten up. No way was I going to let him pity me.

Oh no no no. There it was, just as we'd left it. We could see the mountain with the waterfall, the meadow, the stream, everything. Only it was different from before. The water was brown, not crystal clear and you couldn't see down to the bottom anymore. There was only one sun in the sky this time, and it made the enchanted world that was once so beautiful look like a dark shadow had come through and made itself a home .

It was as if we'd killed all the beauty of it by destroying the witches. "What happened to this place?" David questioned with his mouth gaped open. He was in shock just as I was . "It slipped my mind that this had been his home for years and that he was a unicorn for most of his time. At least, I think. Let's face it. I'm not sure of how all this warping through worlds and our age changing really goes." I scratched my head at the thought.

As I began to try and puzzle it all together, I realized it was only making my head hurt, so , I left it there implanted for another day. Squeezing Tailya's hand a little tighter than necessary, I said, "Why are we here?" "Ouch!" she screeched while yanking her fingers out of mine. I think she noticed the reason behind the actions of my hostile clench.

David groaned, "Uh. If you two are finished messing around, can we please go get it now?" I jerked my head toward the tall blonde headed boy standing beside me. "Go get what? Tay, what is he talking about?" I crossed my arms and glared. "I'm not moving another muscle until you tell me why we're here!"

I stomped my foot on the cliff. That's where the passage had landed us this time. On a blazing cliff. "I mean stars. Talk about some-thing wanting me gone from existence. If I fell here, there would be no way of knowing who I was when you reached the bottom. The moun-tain rocks would have mangled my whole body on the way down."

When the thought crossed my mind, a piece of the cliff was forming a crack underneath my planted foot. Then I started to wobble as it began to crumble beneath me. "Tarsus! It's happening! My thoughts are coming to pass!" I screamed aloud.

My friend wrapped his giant boy arms around me and pulled my whole wobbling shaking body into his. "Geez, be more careful, will you? You almost got us all killed!" David was frustrated and who could blame him. I was throwing a tantrum like a little kid in a candy store. You know the one where your parent says no to the lollipop and the kid collapses onto the floor kicking and screaming. Yeah, that was me. It was making me so angry to know that they kept hiding things from me. So little did he know but his feelings had nothing on mine.

My eyes started to burn, and I could feel the heat of my rage. Also the looks I got from the both of them were not pleasant. Looks of discretion and oddly enough, fear, which caused them to take about five steps back. Their faces were screaming, telling me that something serious was going on with me.

Exhaling and softening my jaws, I gave both of my friends a small, almost faint smile. As I watched Tay's shoulders drop in relaxation, I thought, "Stars. I wonder what they saw. I mean, I'm mad but I don't want them to be afraid of me." I puffed my cheeks and blew out the hot air hoping it might cool my insides.

I asked them once more why we were there, which caused the both of them to just stand there with blank stares on their faces. Gripping my head with my hands, I shouted, "Tailya! David! Why. Are. We. Here?!" I honestly didn't care about scaring them at this point. It was time to get some answers.

Tay's mouth started to move, and I thought, "Finally."

"Annalise. We came back here for the wand and spell book. We need them if we are to bring your mother back from the evil that's swallowed her soul."

Tailya's voice was soft and gentle, so I knew she meant well. It dawned on me that she probably never wanted to step foot in this dreadful place either. Although David didn't seem to mind. Staring at the boy who saved me, I thought, "What's his real story? Is he really Tay's brother? There weren't any pictures of him on the walls. What is he hiding? I am going to keep a close eye on him and make it my personal mission to crack his code." He shot daggers at me. "What are you looking at Anna?" he hissed. I just smiled and batted my lashes.

After playing Sherlock in my head, I took a deep breath while looking at both David and Tailya. "Okay. So, what is our play?" Geez. After I said it, you could almost see the excitement clear in Tay's eyes. "First, let's head over to Yurika's old tree and make sure we didn't miss anything. Maybe there's something we didn't notice before. After that, we'll all go get what we need from Fawn's hut."

Tay's idea of retracing our steps back to Yurika's place frightened me. Apparently, it looked as if I wasn't the only one. When looking over at David, his eyes and mouth were popped wide open. I knew we had to be in sync with our thoughts and feelings about the whole thing. It was strange to see him act this way. I thought to myself, "He must be putting on a show, to keep his true identity hidden. Which means... Is Tay still brainwashed?" Brainwashed. The theory kept rolling around and around in my head. That was until he looked at me like he knew I thought something was off.

I gulped and looked away quickly.

"I wonder if we still need this letter of Fawn's," I thought. While looking up at the sky and wiggling the note with my toes that was tucked away in my shoe. I grabbed Tay's arm only now with no underlying wrath. This time it was with an understanding of her plan.

Tay glanced back and forth at her brother and me. She noticed the fret in our expressions. Empathy in her eyes told me I didn't have anything to worry about. Turning around to face David, I was hoping he had got the same message. We didn't need to be anxious about anything. Yurika and Fawn had been sent back to where they came, and I knew those witches weren't able to hurt anyone ever again.

I couldn't seem to get over my thoughts. Standing there, I watched Tay and David quarrel like usual. I pondered on if the witches really were gone for good. "Is it true? I mean. We only witnessed them disappearing. I don't even remember there being a trace of any bodies, only dust", I thought. Rubbing my temples from the dull pulses penetrating through my head, I closed my eyes hoping for a small ounce of relief. After taking in a few calming breaths, I opened my lids to a crease and peeked through. I noticed Tay glaring at me and David was staring up at the sky. Opening my peepers a little wider, I could see the sweat droplets on my friend's forehead.

"What?" I hissed. "No Annalise, we're safe. Now can we please get a move on? I don't know if you've noticed but we aren't fairies anymore and David is no longer Starbeam the unicorn."

Tay blurted out her words loudly and the tone of her voice let me know I had spoken my inner thoughts out loud once again. No wonder David was staring at the sky. Tailya wasn't finished with me yet. I could see the frustration in her eyes, as she started wagging her finger in my face.

"We are no longer who we were. We have no magic, no tricks, and no spells to help us this time, which means this journey is going to take longer because now we have to walk the grounds. When we could all fly, it only took half a day but now, it might take us three days to get to Fawn's house. I for one do not want to stay here and turn any older. Do you?!" Her voice was stern and hollow on the last question.

Looking at my friend's squared shoulders, I shook my head. When she turned to her brother, I frowned and then blew out a heap of air.

Letting out my breath, I knew she was right. I sure didn't want to age faster than I was naturally supposed to. If I did Brighton might not recognize me.

I started twirling my hair around my finger. Before fully zoning off, I caught David eyeballing me like I had lost my marbles or something. "Do you mind?! I huffed. He smiled of course, like he always does, and I couldn't help myself from letting out a bashful snicker. I mean let's face it, the boy's boyish charm could have me smitten if I let it. "I was just thinking about my brother and if he would know who I am. I've changed so much. He might think I'm a stranger and with him training to be a knight I don't see that going over so well."

I was expecting friendly words of reassurance but all he gave me was a nonchalant head nod. I caught myself looking at him for approval when it's my brother's acceptance I wanted.

Making the hard choice to let go and push aside the thoughts of reconnecting with Brighton, I redirected my thinking on the plan at hand and put my focus back toward getting out of here as fast as possible.

Grabbing Tailya and David's hands, I intertwined our fingers.

"Let's get what we need and get out of this life-stealing nightmare." They squeezed my hands tight to concur.

Step after step, we cautiously made our way down the giant rock tower and stood on land that was once so enchanting.

When the three of us finally set foot on the ground we quickly became overwhelmed with sorrow. The land as we remembered was gone. Now it was a world of decay. As I stood there staring at the ugly bristled points sticking out of the ground around our shoes that was once a breathtaking emerald green, my heart sank in despair. Our charming land was dying.

The grass had changed to a reddish brown yellow mush. It was now embedded in the mud making it look like we were about to have to trek our way through some animal droppings. "Eck, Look at this. I'm not going through that.", I protested. David guffawed. "Don't be such a princess. "I closed my hands tight into a ball and glared at him.

Tay didn't pay us any mind. "Come on you two, we need to hurry." Grabbing both our hands, she swiftly pulled us through the muck. Right then I was grateful Tay had given me shoes to wear. If I had to feel the sludge on my bare feet I would have probably thrown up. I shivered at the thought.

After beating our feet across the wet soil, we had made our way to the grey stoned bridge. It didn't look the same either. There were cracks were forming and it looked like it had been chipped because there were missing pieces everywhere. Looking over it, I gasped. The sparkling dream was now a dank-smelling swamp. "You can't see anything," David said. All I could do was shake my head.

The water was so murky. It was impossible to scour through it. While I'm standing there trying to grasp the newness of this world, I hear an annoying sound of chomping teeth and smacking lips in my right ear. David was eating a chocolate chip cookie. "What are you doing? How can you eat with this smell?" I grumbled.

Pinching the tip of my nose, I watched him wipe cookie residue from under his bottom lip. "I don't smell anything Anna except the other cookies." He eyed Tay's bag and when he started walking toward it , she snapped at him. "One!" His eyes widened. "What?... Oh, come on." Tay straightened. "Just-one- David!", she scolded ,pointing her finger sharply at her brother. The poor boy was left on the bridge to brood.

Crossing over the once clear blue pond with Tay's death grip on my hand, I started to think about how truly magnificent it all really was. You could see straight through to the bottom. When we first stepped through the portal there were all kinds of colorful frogs leaping across the lily pads. A pinch in my heart made the liquid start to fill up in my eyes. Looking back over my shoulder, I knew not only would I never see them again, but this place will never return to what it used to be.

CHAPTER 5

Brighton

Sir Hammon made me start right away on my training. I thought for a second, he was out for blood. I was surprised he still had a voice from all his yelling. "Get up that rope boy! Now over the wall! That's not fast enough! You're not fit to be a knight! Go back home! Camp Herculean isn't a place for sissies!"

I made it to my tent and even though my exhausted aching back wanted my bed at home, the cot was going to have to do. The top part of my body fell forward first as my bottom half hit part of the cot and half onto the floor. I felt some pressure on my face, but I was too out of it to care.

Waking up to Willy smacking on an apple, I tried to chuck my boot at his head. He chuckled when it landed in front of him. "Man, be quiet. Did you see what I had to go through yesterday? I'm sore all over. I don't think I can even move." My friend stood up over me, tossed his core in the trash, and said, "Brother, this is why I brought you here. Look at ya . One day, not even a full day, and you're ready to throw in the towel and leave. At his rate, you'll never be a knight."

I chucked my other boot at him. Willy shook his head as he kneeled down. "Brighton. You aren't dead. That means I know you can do this. Now stop wimping out and get up. You need to eat and gain some strength for today." I watched my friend exit as I laid there sulking a couple of minutes longer while thinking to myself that I had never been this sore, not even after mucking out stalls all day back home.

Finally rolling myself off the cot, I picked up my boots, put them on, laced them up, and readied my sluggish self to go join Willy in the dining quarters. Right as I stuck my hand through the opening, I heard Willy say, "Good, you're up. Here, drink this. It will help heal your muscles while you eat."

Listening to my body yearn for some relief, I chugged it down. I spat, "What in all the horses was that?!" "I don't know brother. One of the guys gave it to me, told me it would help ya." Willy couldn't stop laughing as I stood there spitting the nasty taste from my mouth.

"You should be right as rain by mid-day," he said.

Burying down my anger, I just kept telling myself over and over, "It's worth it, It's worth it. It builds character." Reciting the commander's words in my head started to make me forget how much I wanted to lay into Willy for bringing me here.

The next morning, I awoke to my friend clanking two pots above my head. "Geez, Willy. You couldn't have just shoved me back and forth a couple of times?! Did you really feel the need to give me a heart attack instead?!" I growled while clenching my chest.

My buddy's eyes popped wide open. I glared at him, saying, "Look, Willy. I'm going to count to two and you better be far out of my reach!" The boy fled like his feet were on fire. After I'd finished lacing my boots, I heard Willy by the tent. "All finished, Brighton? You know every day may not be good but there's something good in every day. Now come on and get out here brother." I sat there shaking my head and contemplated on whether I still wanted to give him my fist or just grin and bear it .

"Brighton! I'll stand out here all day if I have to. Trust me I know a lot of melodies!" He raised his voice as loud as possible and started singing.
"Oh I, could tell you why, you will never make the cut. It is because you are being too much of a butt so, please quit pouting and leave this hut." As I walked out, he was still mocking me with his made up song. Two men walked by and awkwardly stared at us, so Willy started whistling the tune instead.

"Are you finished?" I couldn't help but laugh at his sense of humor . "Well, well. Look who decided to grace me with his presence.", He teased. I smirked. "Now you're just trying to get a rise out of me. Come on let's get going, I'm famished." My friend crossed his arms and stood tall. "That's more like it. You know the commander doesn't take kindly to tardiness." Giving him a toothy grin, I smacked him on his arm. "Well, we better get a move on then don't you think?" The poor guy huffed and puffed then shook his head. I knew he was still in good spirits though, because there was a huge smile forming on his face and he was doing the best he could to try and hide it from me.

The bell sounded. It was time for the first meal. Willy and I took off in a mad dash toward the eating quarters. When we arrived, all the men were lined up awaiting their nutrition for the day. . A couple of them turned around and stared at me because my stomach had let out an untamed rumble.

One of the men clapped me on the back. "Gracious lad. Don't worry there is enough for all." The other soldier smacked me across my arm and guffawed as we began walking down the line. Willy was snickering behind me, and I felt like the color of my face looked like a giant red tomato.

Finishing up with our meal, Willy and I went to return our trays then headed out toward the training grounds. Sir Hammon was addressing the soldiers about today's agenda. I nudged Willy with my elbow. "It's a good thing I wasn't tardy." He slightly turned my way so I could see his response.

He moved his lips and jerked his head side to side while repeating my words back to me. A huge chuckle rose out of me. There wasn't any way I could hide it. Commander Hammon pulled out of his announcement, turned to me, and said, "Ah. Look, boys. Look who decided they wanted to speak. Well. Come out with it Brighton." He glared.

Bowing my head, I quieted my mumbling. Willy whispered with a smirk, "Oh you're in for it now." I slapped him in the gut. "Yeah. Well, you're the one that made me lose it."

Both of us stood there laughing through our teeth. We sounded like two snakes hissing. That was until Sir Hammon put himself right in front of us. Our snickers quickly left us, and we gulped in anticipation of our punishment.

"Five laps Brighton. Willy, you go help clean the eating area." I glared at my friend, sighed then took off in a sprint. About the third time around, my feet were starting to feel heavy. I began to drag a little. My feet were starting to stick to the ground and trip over one another. "Brighton! Pick up the pace, son . We don't want to be here all day. Look. Your comrades are getting testy!" Commander Hammons shouting gave me the boost I needed to finish, but when I settled back in line, I gulped at all the hard glares the soldiers were putting off toward me.

I felt bile rise from my stomach. I couldn't pin point where it was coming from, fear or nausea from running nonstop, either way my breakfast was coming back to show its face. After hurling, it was time for us to start the drill. The men were agitated with me because they didn't get to start on time. They had to wait till I finished running. Trying to think about anything else other than my comrades' hostile daggers shooting at me , I focused on my groaning in my head. "Man., I have sweat in places I didn't know was possible to perspire in. Seriously. What is the meaning of all this running, jumping, and climbing? I thought I was here to train to become a knight. They ride horses and have swords and shields. They aren't track stars."

In every jump and every climb, I was getting more and more angry.. My thoughts were causing me strife and I caught myself clenching my teeth. When I came out of my head and regained focus on my training, I heard the Commander's and the men's shouts and mocking's towards me. They were tired and hungry, and my out-of-shape body was taking forever to finish. Pushing through the burning in my chest, I picked up my pace as much as my lungs would allow.

"Come on. Just a little further. You're almost there. Feet don't fail me now." I was trying to encourage myself but revving myself up didn't help. As I tried to push forward my feet failed me, and my legs followed along buckling beneath me.

"This is stupid!" I spat. Sitting there wallowing in self-pity, I watched the Commander, and all the soldiers turn heel and head to enjoy their second meal.

I was lying on the ground when Willy came running up. "Come on brother. It's not that bad." I spat to my side while he offered me a firm hand to lift me to my feet. I patted my friend on the shoulder. "I'm going to bed. I'll see you in the morning." Willy grabbed my arm before I started to walk. "Come on brother. I know you're flustered but you need to eat. Plus, it'll get easier."

A deep thunderous growl rose out of me. I am flustered, Willy!" Flustered?", he repeated, confused. I glared at him. "Yes. You brought me to this blatant camp! Do you have any idea what all I've done today?! First, I had to run till I puked, two, I had to listen while all the men and Commander Hammon made fun of me! And C, when I tried to finish strong, well you saw the gist of that when you pulled me up!" I spat.

Willy knew there was no cheering me up, so he left me there to sulk in my frustration. I felt a little torn watching him trek away. I knew he was only trying to help fulfill my dream. Still, I was hurting, exhausted, and hungry. He was right though. I was beyond hearing anything that would try to cheer me up.

Taking in a deep breath and blowing it out hard , I trudged off in the dark to our sleeping quarters.

A week had passed, and Willy started to notice that I was now the first one to always arrive at the eating quarters. Every morning now I have a table with both of our meals ready. Poor Willy, his never stays hot enough for him to enjoy because now he was the one who had been running behind schedule. My porridge on the other hand was gone in seconds of me sitting down.

Usually about ten minutes after my meal, I wait for Willy to pop in. Finally, he walks in, and I wave him over. He grabbed a chair and scarfed down his almost frozen porridge. "Man. That's disgusting! How can you even eat this?"

Willy's groanings of his breakfast are the same today as they have been for the last week. The words never changed. I began to think I might be in some sort of time laps, but it wasn't that at all. I think my friend was just getting bored of the same food and routine as I was.

After Willy had finished his milk, he tried to make small talk. "Morning buddy. How'd you sleep?" I looked down at the empty bowl in front of me and with a small smirk, I shook my head. "Man., I don't have time to shoot the breeze with you. It's time for training. Maybe tomorrow you'll actually get up on time. I know you'd at least enjoy your breakfast, and we just might be able to have an actual conversation." Standing up, I patted him on the back chuckling as I went to join the soldiers outside.

Fooling about waiting on Willy almost made me late. I lined up just in time for Commander Hammon's instructions. "Alright men. Today starts week two and we're going to change it up a little." He cleared his throat and began to give us our specifications for the whole week.

"Men. I am going to time you on your obstacles. The soldier with the fastest time today will get to have a rest day tomorrow."

I stood there listening to the men all around me hoot and holler. It quickly took my mind to the time when my father, King Cyrus, took me and Lissy to a jousting tournament. Lissy of course was too young to remember, she was a just a little babe. I, on the other hand, could recall everything. It was one of the most exciting places I've ever been. Watching two knights full speed on horses charge one another was incredible. The anticipation was endless.

Thinking about fond memories made a small smile appear, but then I heard Sir Hammons shout, "Understood?!" It broke me out of my flashback and all my brothers around me shouted back, "Yes, Sir!" One by one they started to break off around me. When I moved my head from side to side, I could see I was the only one left standing there. Sir Hammon saw it too. He turned back and started pacing my way.

I gulped.

I didn't hear anything he had said. Too busy reminiscing. The huge giant stood there, brick arms crossed, and tapping his foot. At that moment I was wishing I was a chameleon. Able to change color and hide from my predator.

Gritting my teeth and breathing deeply through my nose, I decided to stay put and let him drill me. I needed to know the instructions no matter the consequences. Planting his feet and squaring his shoulders, he asked, "Brighton. What are you doing still standing here? The other lads have already started their training."

His hard stare was intimidating but I stood my ground. I coughed out my words. "Well. You see sir..." The commander didn't take his focus off me. "Yes. Come out with it." I cleared my throat.

"Commander Hammon Sir. I didn't hear your orders, Sir. I was too busy off in la-la land Sir."

The Commander tipped his head back and guffawed while I stood there taking in air so I could breathe again. Oddly, Sir Hammon wasn't as scary as the men made him out to be. After laughing hysterically, he gave me my requirements for the week, and I took off to start my new training.

CHAPTER 6

Brighton

"I'm done. I'm done!" My body was about to give out but screaming those words in my head out of anger wasn't doing me any good. Our new task was to run for one hour, climb the ropes one hundred times, jump the brick walls one hundred times, and flip the heaviest boulder we could find. If that wasn't enough then our last obstacle was to climb the treetop lookout. All of it was timed.

In the middle of my twenty-fifth climb up the rope, I heard the men below booing. "Someone must have finished," I thought while fighting my way to reach the top. I sighed at what was still ahead and kept climbing. By this rate, since I was the last to start, I'd be lucky to be finished by dinner.

I had just flipped my boulder when I saw Justin shaking Commander Hammon's hand and heading out for dinner. I learned his name from Willy because he was one of the men laughing at me in line when we first arrived. We became brothers shortly after our scoffing with one another. We quickly decided we were both buffoons and one wasn't better than the other.

The sun was beginning to set as I watched him leave to go eat. Moping with a heavy head hung low, I made my way to the last obstacle. Inhaling deeply, I began to climb. Halfway up I witnessed all the men leaving to go enjoy their second meal and my insides started to growl at me. "Hurry up. I'm starving!" I bet that was what it would shout at me if my stomach could talk.

I thumped my gut and said, "Quiet you. I know you're hungry. I'm almost done. Now pipe down and behave." I smacked my head up against the tree. "Saints. I'm losing it. Pull yourself together man."

About a fourth up from the ground, the lights in the meal room went out. "Stars!" I spat. "Hey, watch it." I looked down to see Willy standing there with a bowl in his hands. I never scurried down a tree so fast. Plummeting to the ground crossed my mind for me to slow down , but I was thankful, and I was starving .

Yanking the bowl out of Willy's grasp , I shoveled the cold meal into my mouth. It was only potatoes, but it would have to do for the night because the kitchen was closed. I thanked my friend with a mouth full and watched him laugh as bits of potato splattered out of my mouth.

Forcing down the last lump of buttery goodness, I grabbed Willy's shoulder. "My energy is sapped. I'm going to turn in. Thanks for the sustenance." He nodded his head and said, "Let's go rest up." My legs were as loose as a stripped screw getting ready to fall out of its hinges.

Willy looked back to see me traipsing behind, so he offered an arm for me to lean on, and we made our way slowly back to our sleeping quarters. After what seemed like forever, we finally reached our tent. Drawing back the flap, my eyes transfixed onto my cot. My head grew heavy, and my sight grew dim as I eased myself down for the night. Before closing my eyes, I thought to myself, "Man. I thought week one was difficult." I nodded to myself outwardly as I said , "Yep. I'm going to die here." Then I allowed my lids to shut for the evening.

Waking up, I rolled myself off my gurney. I know I had a dream, but I couldn't seem to remember it. I looked down and noticed I had left on all my attire. It was a good thing too because I again was running late, and it felt like day one all over. .

Bolting out of the tent, I passed right by Willy. "Hey. Where are you going?" Looking back over my shoulder I shouted, "I may be late, but I'm not missing the first meal!" My friend started to chortle after he caught up to me.

"Hold on. Sea biscuits, you're fast." He took a giant puff of his inhaler. "Geez, Brighton. Eating quarters don't even unlock the doors for another ten minutes." My mouth dropped open. Shockingly I said, "Are you telling me I'm still on time?" He rubbed the back of his neck. "Well, yeah. Why? Did you- "Wait," I cut him off. "What in the stars is a sea biscuit?"

Willy doubled over in glee. "You'll hear it soon enough. It's a catchline from a lad named Mason in Egladon. Did you think you were running behind again? Is that the reason for the dust behind your tail?" I chuckled. "Yeah. I noticed I still had everything on, so I bolted out of our sleeping quarters trying not to miss our rations. I need them if I'm going to last up to dinner. What the Commander has us doing this week is brutal."

Willy and I ambled next to one another toward the feasting area as I told him about the new tasks for the week.

Day three flew by like a flock of birds flying south for the winter. I was becoming faster and stronger. I could feel it in every part of my body. I now realized what Willy meant when he said I needed this.

Week three was a breeze. More running but the same obstacles with more counts. I didn't meet the time requirement for a rest day the last two weeks, and it's a good thing too because if anyone needed this training it was me. . There was no doubt in my mind I would've lasted a day with the knights in Egladon if it weren't for Commander Hammon and the rest of the soldiers.

I was halfway down the tree when Commander Hammon shouted, "Two more hours lads." Planting my feet on the soft ground, I took off in a sprint toward Sir Hammon. His eyes bugged out when he saw I was the second to finish for the day. Justin was of course the first. He was always first. "There's just no beating this guy." I thought while catching my breath.

The commander bestowed a respectful nod toward me. "Well done lad!" Hearing those words come out of his mouth was by far better than winning first place. I gave him a small grin. "Thank you, Sir." He still had shock written across his face as I walked away content and without a care in the world. I was finally becoming a soldier. My confidence once more was being restored and I had to admit I was also feeling a bit prideful.

Weeks five, six, and seven went by quick. I was excelling in all of my training. Commander made me Captain over the group. Justin wasn't too happy about that, but I didn't care. I told him when I leave, he could have his spot back.

Sir Hammon started to teach me the basics of weaponry tactics and skills. I soon knew how to handle a sword but when it came to the javelin, crossbow, and halberd, I didn't have the slightest clue how to use them.

In the midst of sparring with Commander, I told him how I liked the sword the best. Our blades clanked and he grabbed my arm. Before pushing me away, he said, "If it's the sword you can only handle well, then stick with it. That means it's your most skillful weapon." I nodded and then he pressed me back to return to our fencing lesson.

Putting my sword away for the day, I remembered Kedron and me in our sword fight playing days. It has only been seven weeks since I had last seen the little lad, but it felt a lot longer. I sighed at the thought of his little self-showing me a magic trick.

I went back to polishing the blades, wiping away an unwanted tear, and pressed down the sorrow. I knew my little brother had Lissy and she'd do her best to keep him busy. Plus, I knew I would see them again.

Week eight was finally here. Willy and I were gathering up our belongings and saying our farewells. It was time for us to head to Egladon.

Commander Hammon was pressing us to stay one more week. He gripped both of our shoulders and sat us down on a rock near the obstacle grounds. "It would be wise for you two lads to stay and train another week. Captain Brighton, you haven't mastered the crossbow yet, and I do say that's what I think you'll be using it the most."

I gave the man a friendly nod. "Sir. I am very appreciative of your camp. Camp Herculean has been greatly educational on strength, endurance, and weaponry. I know everything you've taught me has prepared me for this trip so thank you, Commander Hammon. Don't worry sir. I will practice the crossbow more in Egladon."

The poor guy looked puzzled. He didn't understand my eagerness to leave but he shook our hands anyway and bid us goodbye. The whole reason I joined this camp was to prepare for becoming a knight. I accomplished this mission, and I was ready for the next. With my sword in hand, I waved off to the commander and soldiers as Willy and I untacked our horses. Nico was getting fat and stout. "What have they been feeding you, boy?" I questioned while I moved my hand up and down his mane.

As I was saddling Nicodemus, I saw Willy feed his horse a carrot. "Hey. Where did you get that? And do you have one for my horse as well?" I had to ask seeing as Nico was nudging his face into me and whining behind my back. My friend chuckled and moseyed over to Nico. I don't think I've ever seen a horse eat a carrot that fast before. "It's like he didn't even chew," I thought as I scratched the top of my head.

"Nico! Slow down some." There was no doubt he was laughing at me with all his neighing. Willy joined in, slapping me across my shoulder, and said, "He's laughing at you brother." I crossed my arms and raised a brow at Nicodemus then I smirked and patted him on his side. "I missed you too buddy. Come on, we have a long trip ahead of us," I said while leaping up onto him.

"Are you ready brother?" Willy still had two feet planted on the ground. Looking back to see him give me a slight nod forward, I took that as him giving me the ok. . Once again, we said our goodbyes in waves as we passed through the gate putting Camp Herculean, Commander, and all my new brothers behind us.

It was time to start my quest. Time to become a knight. "Onward to Egladon!" I shouted with zest while thrusting my fist to the sky.

CHAPTER 7

Brighton

Three days into our journey, and Willy distinctively forgot to mention we were going to have to stop by my castle. "We have to go through the forest to get to Egladon, brother." He said . I did my best on trying not to shoot him daggers through the back of his , from the fire that was rising up inside of me.

"Sorry, Brighton. I forgot to tell you." He murmured under his breath, but I still heard it, so to myself, I mocked him in anger I didn't want to go back home. Back to the crown that I had fought so hard to escape. "Willy. I hope I don't see any familiars otherwise it's your funeral." I threatened. My friend's Adam's apple sunk down slowly in his throat. Then he quickly took a puff of his medication. I felt remorse for my harsh words. "I'm just jesting but seriously. The reason I was at the tavern that night when you ran into me was because I wanted to escape Bristeria, not go back to it. I don't want the crown. I want to become a knight. Maybe when this is all over, I can hand the kingdom to my little brother, Kedron."

Willy nodded as he understood. He reached into his satchel and pulled out an old cloak. "Here. I too know what it's like to want to escape. Now put this on and be quiet."

I threw the thick heavy cloth over my head while Willy took hold of Nico's reins to guide us through the village. "It's like death under here!" I groaned in a whisper. Willy threw what felt like a pinecone or something else just as hard at me to get me to pipe down. "We're almost there. Now be quiet or this lady passing by might hear you." I was too busy wiping sweat off my brows to care about my friend's heeded warning. I needed air. I felt like I couldn't breathe from the heat, and it was starting to get wet and sticky under there so I lifted my head slightly. I wasn't fully trying to rebel against Willy's warning, but I needed to feel some kind of coolness on my face for the fear of passing out from heat exhaustion.

When I lifted my head, my eyes nearly popped out of my skull. The lady beside us was my mother, the queen.

I gasped.

Rushing my head back down, I held my breath as we passed by. I was afraid she might sense me. When we had our backs safely toward her, I shot my head over my shoulder to see what she was up to. I wasn't surprised when I lifted my head and saw his sign. Then I knew where my mother was headed. "She still hasn't changed," I said under my breath as I watched her go inside Renard's store. I let out a huge sigh. Guess it was loud enough for Willy to hear because we stopped. Then I heard him ask in a quiet voice, "You alright brother?" Moving the blanket with my head gave him the reassurance he was looking for and we started to move again. "We're just about there," he said. Hearing those words, I brushed off what I had just seen. I couldn't stress myself with the Queen's engagements any longer. "She'll be judged for her actions one day," I thought to myself.

"Whoa. Whoa, boys. Easy. Easy boys." Willy was calming the horses to stop. "We're here, Brighton. You can take it off now." Lifting the cloak up off my head, I could feel the shade of the trees and then the breeze that followed. In the midst of my cooling off, Willy started to pester me about my mother. "Hey, who was that lady? Why did you get so upset when you saw her?"

I scratched my head. "How did he know? He must've been keeping an eye on me, making sure I was following orders," I thought as I stared at him with dumbfounded eyes. "Huh? Oh. That was Queen Cheylenna, my mother," I sighed. "She's up to no good as usual," I sighed again.

My friend got quiet after that and didn't ask any more questions. We dismounted our horses and began walking through the forest. Passing by the opening where I could see the castle, I saw Lissy and Kedron playing our favorite game chase in the meadow.

I closed my eyes as my heart sank into my chest. I was going to miss those two silly babes terribly. I opened my saddened lids only to find them two were getting closer to the part of the forest Willy and I were standing in.

Panicking, I quickly let go of Nico's reins and yanked on Willy's hand. With one foot in front of the other, we made haste to our destination.

Willy and I stopped in front of a ginormous tree. "Where did this come from?" I thought. "I can't recall ever seeing this tree before," I said aloud. "This is it, Brighton. We're here." Willy was excited and anxious while I on the other hand was smacked in the face with confusion.

I stood there watching him fiddle with some of the branches thinking to myself "Okay. He's lost it." Then I saw him lift up on the stray twig that was covered in leaves on the ground.

I lost sight for a split second as light shone through the bark of the tree. The beaming had me squeezing my lids shut for it was brighter than a star in the pitch black sky at night.

My mouth gaped open as I witnessed the tree in front of us begin to split in half , creating a passageway for us to enter. I began to breathe heavily while pointing at the tree and moving my feet backward. Completely shaken, my body swayed back, and I fell flat on my tuchus causing my friend to laugh at me.

Quickly he gave me a hand and pulled me to my feet. "Don't be such a sissy, Brighton. This is the only gateway to get us to Egladon. Now come on. Pick yourself up and let's go, man."

Knowing Willy was speaking truthfully, I let him continue to grasp my wrist and pull me toward the bright in between . A huge gulp came from me as we both took our steps into the nothingness.

What looked like a bright hole from forest tree in Bristeria was actually another world on the inside of this very bizarre passage. I couldn't believe my eyes. This place was unreal.

Willy interrupted all of my racing thoughts. Swiping me across the shoulder, he said, "Brother, everything you've ever heard, read about, or even imagined is all true." Right after he spoke those words to me, a flashback picture from my grandfather's book appeared. I gasped when it became clear. This tree was the same one in the story. My eyes wandered back and forth over this enchanted place as all of grandfather's stories ever told to me came alive right before me.

Darting my focus to my left, there they were. The two unicorns he had talked about. Beautiful snowy-looking beasts. "Quite intriguing," I blurted. Just as I was starting to become mesmerized by these creatures, I let my eyes drift to the right, curious to see what the dark shadow was in my peripheral vision. I shivered. A dark and gloomy tree hut was off in the distance as was also a bright flicker of light that looked like a flame from a burning fire. I blinked vigorously, trying to gain more focus but as my vision began to adjust, it vanished. I shook my head and forcefully thrust my palm against my right temple, thinking this had to be some sort of weird dream. Willy caught me hitting myself. "What are you doing?" He quickly held up his hand and asked me to count his fingers. Guess he thought all of the sudden I had lost my marbles. I chuckled, "Eh. I'm fine. I'm fine," I repeated while swatting his fingers out of my face and still laughing.

An expeditious blow hit my arm. "Saints, Willy! That one stung!" "Well, aren't you just remarkable? Gather yourself and let's go. It's time to get to Egladon."

After Willy finished scolded me , I nodded, and we started walking toward the bridge as I rubbed out the ache.

Willy started to tell me where we were and what this place was, but his voice became muffled when she appeared right before my eyes.

Gulp.

I grabbed my friend's shirt collar, stopping him mid-sentence, causing him to choke. "What in all the saints, Brighton?" he roared as he turned around.

Savagely yanking his garment, I whispered, "Do you see her too?" A stunning blonde-haired beauty was standing right in front of us. Her presence was overwhelming, and I couldn't seem to look away.

The enchantress grabbed my hand causing me to yeep like a little school girl. Needless to say, I freaked out, tuck-tailed like a scared animal, and ran back to the entrance. She giggled at my reaction.

I paused in terror when I saw that the gateway had sealed itself and I'd come to the realization that there was no escape. Slowly circling back toward Willy and the mysterious woman who apparently still had a hold of my hand, I gulped once more. After a few deep breaths, my heart slowed, and my nerves were starting to calm down. I lifted my head and took another glance at the beautiful blonde woman that had appeared out of nowhere. I seemed to be making a fuss over nothing, seeing as she wasn't even scary. On the other hand I fear if I were to stare into her eyes to long, I might become hypnotized.

"Geez Brighton. Get it together, man." I said under my breath as I thumped myself in the head. She smiled and bowed as she led Willy and me into the direction of the tree hut.

Clearing my throat to sound like my manly self again and not a pansy, I asked, "So where are you taking us, my lady?" Her response was a giggle and a nod, which didn't reveal anything remotely to my question. I turned to Willy to witness him smirking and shaking his head at me.

I bet he thought I was trying to court her, but I was really just curious about where we were headed.

Shrugging at my friend's assumption, I stared back ahead at the beauty to ask again. This time she placed a finger to her lips and calmly said, "I'll explain everything soon." Her voice was soft, almost like a whisper in my mind. "Wait a minute." I scratched my head. She stopped suddenly and I could hear her telling me to relax, but her mouth didn't move. "Please be silent until we get there, she might hear you."

Gulp.

The enchantress was talking to me in my head. Then I started to wonder who else she was referring to. Who is the other she? How is this possible? Have I really come face to face with a real witch?

I was starting to get a headache when she said, "I am not a witch."

Gasp. "Now, just breathe and try to quiet your thinking please." I nodded so hard I thought I had cracked my neck. "This is weird," I said aloud. "What's that?" Willy said, staring at me, eyebrows raised.

The lady looked at both of us as she lifted her luminance. We could finally see her clearly. Her hair was the color of the yellow sun back home. Her eyes were sky blue like the water in Bristeria. Her face shimmered like a diamond does when catching the beams of sunlight. She was breathtaking and my eyes wouldn't peel away from her. In all my life I had never seen such...

"Thank you."

"Huh. What?" She looked at me and smiled. "Everything you just thought of. Thank you."

Embarrassed, I coughed out, "You're welcome." Then I scurried toward Willy. He didn't seem taken away at all by this enchanted being. I wonder if he had been here before. We had finally reached the odd-looking tree hut and Willy was the first one up the steps. My suspicion came to an end. He had indeed been here before.

The lady smiled while opening the door. Lifting her arm, she gracefully invited Willy and me inside. The door closed behind us, and she spoke, "I'm surprised Willy didn't tell you about me." I turned to Willy to glare at him, but he wasn't there. Seconds later I found him across the room near a table full of treats. He, of course, was stuffing his face.

Giving me puppy dog eyes he said, "Om sor gungmt broth gungmt." "What?!" I growled. "Willy. Finish swallowing. I can't understand anything you're trying to tell me with your mouth full!" Feeling a little annoyed, I dropped my head and shook it.

"I'm sorry, brother. I wanted to tell you, but I didn't think you'd believe me. You made fun of me when I told you about the pegasi ." His pleading stare brought out a remorseful sigh. I gave him a ruing nod. "I'm sorry, Willy. You're right and I did lose it when you appeared in front of us." I said, turning my attention toward the enchantress.

The lady's eyes shimmered, and her cheeks rose as she let out a chuckle. "So many questions young Brighton. If I am right, you will make a great king one day."

My eyes widened and I could feel my chin drop. "How did you? Where did you? Huh...?"

She softly placed one of her hands on my shoulder. "You are safe." I looked across the room at Willy and got a reassured head tilt. Turning my eyes back on her, she smiled. "My name is Fawn. I have been watching over you and your family for quite some time." My mouth sank even wider. Fawn giggled and continued.

"I know your mother. Queen Cheylenna. You see it was my job to protect her from the others, but I believe I have failed." She knelt her head in disdain and all I could do was stand there frozen and con-fused. My mind started to race. "Who is this woman? How does she know about my family and me? Oh, wait. Can she hear my thoughts right now?"

Once again, she answered every question in my head. "Brighton. My name is Fawn. My lord placed me over you and your family. Yes, I can hear you and everything you think."

Gasp!

"Don't worry little king, I am of no harm to you." I cleared my throat. "Oh. Umm. I didn't mean to offend you, my lady. Forgive me but this is just way out of my element. I'm going to need some time to process."

She took a deep breath, relieved that I was willing to still listen. My guess was she didn't want to lose another person from my family.

CHAPTER 8

Annalise

There it was. The tree where I first met David, "aka" (Starbeam) and Yurika. "How could such a beautiful creature turn into a witch?" I stood there in deep thought. "Annalise, look!"

Tailya spotted up in the tree what seemed to be Fawn's wand. "How do you suppose it got there?" Tailya was stumped. I just shrugged. It was the only answer I could give. I was over here baffled with my own theories, and I didn't have the slightest clue myself. All I could do was stand there, move my shoulders, and tilt my head.

"Hey, sis. What's wrong with her? Has she gone silly or something?" David asked while tapping Tay a couple of times on the arm along with an odd glance my way.

"No! I haven't went crazy!" My outburst scared David so bad that he fell back and smacked into the tree. I bent over with my hand on my stomach. "Wait. It hurts. It hurts." I couldn't stop laughing. "Geez, Anna. Warn a guy first, will you?" Watching him stand up and dust himself off, I started to laugh again. "Yeah. Ha. Ha. Ha. You just wait. We'll see who gets the last laugh in the end." His glare had a chill to it and my guffawing came to a halt, when I heard his last words " In the end" .

Though I wanted to stand there and ponder on his threat, I shook it off for now because we needed to retrieve what we came here for.

"Oh. Get over it. You big sissy." I said as I slapped his arm.

He smiled at me and left it at that.

Focusing my vision back toward the wand in the tree, I started to remember the moments Tay taught me magic. Making that baby bud grow, finding my grandma Mesha, all of that. I hope she doesn't blame me. After all, I was only doing for her what I thought was best. A small sigh left my lips.

As I stood there in memory lane, I could see my grandma standing there beside a little boy. "But who could that be?" I thought, bringing my finger up to chin and tapping it . In the midst of my flashback, I started to bite my lower lip, really trying to think about why he looks so familiar. "Annalise" I heard my name softly and it snapped me back.

Looking at Tay and David not knowing who it was that called me, I just eyed the both of them. "What?" I asked.

Tay rolled her eyes and shook her head. I guess she already knew. "How is it that girl knows I'm daydreaming before I'm even aware of it myself?" I thought, flustered. David touched my forehead. "Are you feeling, okay?" His palm was sweaty and two small worry lines formed above his eyebrows.

It was sweet how much he cared. When I lifted my gaze toward his and our eyes met, a small tingle tickled my belly.

Quickly, I swatted his hand off from my forehead. "I'm fine", I replied. "Just thinking about our last time here. I thought one of you called me, but I must have heard wrong." He sighed in relief, then gave me an awkward grin. I waited for him to walk away before I puffed out my cheeks and blew out a huge amount of air.

"Annalise." There it was again. I started looking around while David and Tailya were going over how to climb the tree. "Annalise. Over here." I walked over toward a stray bush. I don't remember this being here, I thought as   I tilted my head. "Annalise." This time I followed the voice around the shrub.

"Fyra!" I yelled so loud it made me cough. "Oh, how I missed you!" I said still a little congested. Her talons began to prance in place, and I stood there in awe of my beautiful golden-eyed creature. I raced over to stroke my hand across her feathers. She began to bury her beak into my hair. I felt guilty for leaving her here all alone.

Running my fingers over her pillowy soft chest, I wondered how long it's really been. "Many many sunrises." She answered. I hung my head. "Sorry girl." She leaned down to me. "It's alright my friend. It seemed like you were trying to figure out how long it has been since we have last seen one another. I only wanted to help answer, not make you feel any certain way."

Slowly exhaling, I let go of any guilt trying to attach itself to me. "I'm so happy you've learned to adapt." "For a moment, I was under the impression you wouldn't be able to. I really wish I could have taken you with me." She bowed and pushed her head into my face. "Come on girl. Let's go for a ride. What do you say?" Fyra's wings moved up and down in excitement. But I froze when I noticed him. He was hiding under her right wing.

"Wait." I said . She stopped and looked at me in concern. "What is it, Annalise?" I pointed at her right-wing and she lifted it. "Oh right. I completely forgot. Sorry. But you remem - "Wesley." The boy said sternly. The once crying little lad cut her off mid-sentence. When he stretched out his hand for me to shake, I backed away in shock. I thought Tay and I were the only ones who got older here. "What in the stars?", I mumbled . While staring I thought to myself, " This boy has to be my age or a little older now." Then I continued to search him over.

A burden of culpability washed over me, and I felt the water start to race down my cheeks. I wasn't able to control them, not for this, nor did I want to. No. This time I would let every single drop flow freely. I lifted my palms to cover my face. Sniffling through my wet fingers, I pleaded for him to forgive me.

When I didn't hear anything back, I wiped my eyes and looked up only to notice Fyra was watching me. "Wha- Where did he go?" I asked confused. "He left a while ago. About the time you covered your face." She replied. "Oh." I sniffled.

"Fyra. Grandma Mesha asked me to return him to his mother. He's not from here, he's from my world, and I absentmindedly forgot about him. What should I do?

Grapes! How could I be so careless, so thoughtless, so... ugh." I smacked myself in the head with my hand. I wondered how long it was going to take to make it up to him.

"Fyra. I'm so sorry. We'll have to go for a ride next time, girl. I need to go find Wesley and make this right." I squeezed her tight and allowed more tears fall. I knew there wasn't going to be a next time, but she didn't, and I couldn't bear to tell her the truth.

Waving goodbye to my beautiful bird, I went back around to Tay and David. They were still standing there going over how to climb that silly tree. When I got up close to them, they both had scrapes and cuts on their arms and knuckles.

"Did you guys start climbing without me?" I said. Tay crossed her arms. "We thought you were off in the sky with that bird." I gasped. Swallowing my spit hard, I thought to myself, "they know everything." Tay stared at me. "Yeah, we heard Fyra. So, David and I just figured you left us and went on a ride." I exhaled. "Good. That's all they heard. They don't know about Wesley", I said to myself. Clearing my throat, I spoke out, "Well, just look at you two. Glad you didn't kill yourselves."

I changed the subject from my meeting with Fyra and my run-in with Wesley. They didn't need to know anyway. "Oh no!" I thought. No- no- no. Quickly, I swayed the mean thought from my head. I needed their help if I'm to reunite Wesley with his mother.

"Okay. Now that I'm here, how can I help?" Tailya walked up to me and slapped my shoulder. "I've got a great plan." She winked. I gulped. "No. Seriously, it's good. I promise." She said. I couldn't hide my uncomfortable giggles. What was this girl up to?

"David. This includes you too. Get over here." Tay shouted. Both of us ambled our way over toward her. "What's the grand plan, Tailya?" David posed. My friend was so lost in thought that I didn't think she was even paying any attention to him.

As I watched David raise his hands, I flinched and raised my shoulders to my ears. I just knew what was about to happen. When his hands met together it sounded like a huge crackle of thunder. Tay quickly came out of her stupor and started yelling at him. I guess his effort to bring her back to reality was more unsettling than he thought. I started laughing as Tay scolded her brother.

"Hey! What's the big idea? You clapping your hands hard like that? Really? Are you trying to scare me half to death?!" David clenched his stomach. "Ow! Come on sis, I was worried you might have been hypnotized or something." Her balled-up fist and heavy panting said that that wasn't the case.

She went on reprimanding him, shouting," I was trying to figure out a way for us three to get the wand out of the tree. When… or if I need help with brain loss, you'll know!" The poor guy flinched as his sister walked up to him again, only this time she placed a hand on his shoulder, gave him a corky smirk, and said, "Now. Do me a favor. You and Anna stack up on top of one another so I can climb up onto your backs and retrieve the wand."

I stopped laughing. It wasn't funny anymore. Marching over to both of them, I looked Tay square in the eyes. "You want us to do what?" David snorted. "Yeah right. Are you crazy?" He protested. She tightly squeezed her hand again, causing David to retract. "Alright. Alright. Come on Anna. You can be on top, so I don't squash you. I guess Tailya's okay with the loss of her brother if you crush me." That last part he mumbled under his breath, but I still heard it. The boy's groaning caused something clearly inevitable and uncontrollable. A belly bursting laugh. "Just get on!" He hissed. Not wanting to poke the bear, I flashed him a cheesy grin and a quick wink before climbing up. "Fine by me.", I mocked while lifting up my right knee first to start my way up his back. With every movement, I could feel him shaking his head. I reached down and pinched him on the cheek. "Cheer up. It'll all be over with soon." His body started to move beneath me. When I saw the side of his mouth turn up and I heard a titter, I thought, "Well, at least I made him laugh." Thank the stars something good was happening out of this ridiculous plan.

Finally balanced I said, "This isn't so bad." Then I giggled while patting my friend on the head. I heard him huff and puff underneath me. It gave me great pleasure to know I could annoy him, and a small smile spread across my face in accomplishment. I braced myself as Tay started to make her way up my back. "Wow. How much does this girl weigh?" I thought. Clenching my jaw and squeezing my eyes closed, I focused on keeping my body centered instead of the gut-wrenching pain she was causing from her thin pointy kneecaps and her bony palms pressing into my lower back and shoulder blades. "Geez. I wonder if David felt this way when I first climbed up." I thought. This was unpleasant in so many ways.

I looked underneath me to see how David was holding up. "Hey. Are you alright down there?" I asked. If I was anything like his sister, there was no way he wasn't feeling the same as me right now. I suddenly felt a wave of vibration through my kneecaps. David was growling at his sister. "Tailya! Will you hurry up already? My body's starting to go numb!" Just as he finished, I felt our human tower start to sway. Then it happened. There was no gaining control on this .

Tay and I started to scream, while David guffawed under us. Our bodies moved side to side causing gravity to take its place. I guess he didn't want me to get hurt or his sister for that matter because I quickly felt him roll to the left to catch me then he shoved me far to the right to break Tay's fall. After the huge catastrophe, we laid there glued to the dead grass and muck stuck to our backs and legs. We stayed there for a minute panting and staring at one another.

I rolled on my side to face Tay. "Well, that worked like a charm." She grabbed a handful of mud and chucked it at me. Both of us were in a stare-down, that was until we blinked and blew air between our lips. We rolled back and forth sounding like a couple of first-time trumpet players. David joined in shortly after.

All three of us laid there laughing uncontrollably. David broke it up by deciding to taunt his sister. "So, what do you suppose we do now, oh knowledgeable one?" Her laughter vanished and she glared at her brother. I could see the tension starting to build up between them. "Oh, great here we go again, another round of tweedle dee vs tweedle dumb." I mumbled as I rolled my eyes and sighed.

Thinking of some way to diffuse the flame so I myself wouldn't get burned, I pointed at the big log across the way. "Hey, guys! Stop fighting. Look. We can use that to climb up." Tay shook her head. She had David and I completely thrown when she lifted her left hand in the air and said, "No need.", along with a huge white toothy beam of pride and satisfaction draped across her face. "Well, why in all the stars did we just go through all that then?" I asked.

My friend started to giggle, and it was again becoming contagious. I could feel the small bubble inside of me trying to make its way out because the flutters of glee and excitement were rolling around in my belly. But I didn't act on it. Instead, I stood there, mouth wide open and occasionally blinking in disbelief. The stick was in her hand this whole time. "How in the...?" I said with a small squeak.

At that moment, I realized being in this weird place was messing with my head. I thought, "Maybe this wand can help keep these evil thoughts at bay. I don't want to have another bad thought about my friends. Since we stepped foot back here, I haven't been left alone at all. Tailya caught me scratching my head in deep thought. She glared as she strode up to me.

Gulp.

I screeched, "Oh no! I did it again." "Huh." She replied, clearing her throat, not taking her eyes off of me. "Sorry!" I said as I focused on my feet. "Honestly, Annalise. Sorry is for the flies. Now stop daydreaming." She hissed. "But I wasn't. I was just so deep in thought that I didn't hear a word you said." At least that's what I wanted to say. Unfortunately, I just nodded in compliance.

Still prideful as she was, David and I watched her toss the wand from one hand to the other. "I was counting on it to still have magic. One down, one to go." She smirked as her cheery self-began to playfully point it at her brother. "Now then, tell me David, if you're truly my brother why aren't there any pictures of you on the walls at home?"

My eyes widened as I had wondered the exact same thing. While we were waiting to hear his answer, David instead counteracted the question with a temper tantrum. He raised his right hand and swatted at the wand. "Get away from me with that thing." Tay shrugged. "Oh well. I thought it was going to be something good, but I'll just ask father when we get back."

I watched David's shoulders drop and I could see a bit of worry across his face.

Fawn's wand was back in our possession and this time we were prepared to use the powerful rod for good. "Time to save my family, free my father, and rid my mother of the evil that haunts her." My determined thoughts brought a faintness of hope to my heart. Faint because my fear had more of a hefty latch on me. "Would I succeed? Am I strong enough, brave enough?" I bit my lip in deep alarming thought. Then it hit me. The torment was back. "What is going on?!" I cried on the inside.

CHAPTER 9

Brighton

A dusty chair invited me to sit, rest, and try to cerebrate everything I've just heard and witnessed. But as I sat down, Fawn kneeled beside my leg. Apparently, she had more she wanted to tell me.

"Your mother and I met when she was very little". She spoke. "She was in the corner of her room crying after dabbling with a book and a candle she had found in her mother's room. Your Queen at the time couldn't have been more than nine or ten years old. I could tell she needed some guidance in lighting the black glim in front of her, so I snapped my fingers and made a flame appear from the wick. Your mother's eyes dazzled at the sight." A self-satisfying smirk shaped her lips.

I shifted my hips further back into the chair. I couldn't believe what I was hearing. "Wait!" I thought. She paused. "Saints, she heard that- Saint's she heard that too." I coughed. "Something wrong, little king?" "Huh? No no. Please continue." "Geez, that was close". Saints, Brighton, stop thinking!" "What was that?" she asked. I put my knuckles to my chin and leaned forward. "Nothing, please go on."

The lady creased her eyes. I knew she wasn't buying my act of seriously paying attention, but I didn't care. I had to stop thinking so she couldn't read or hear any more of my thoughts. I gave her a boyish grin. She blushed, covered a giggle, and started again. "You see, back in that time, I couldn't be seen. I wasn't pow-" She paused, cleared her throat, and searched my eyes deeply for some form of apprehension from me as to what she'd just said. When I smiled, she relaxed. "What I was saying is that I couldn't be seen back then because my master wouldn't allow it."

Standing up, I looked across the room at Willy. He was still stuffing his face. "Ah- thanks my lady, for all your hospitality, but I think we should get going now."

I looked over at my friend and shouted across the room.

Willy! There should be more food where we're headed. Am I right?" The poor guy swallowed his whole muffin and I felt bad when I saw his Adam's apple move swiftly up and down as liquid fell from the corners of his eyes. Then he started coughing. "Sorry man. I just think we should get going soon." I apologetically said.

I narrowed my gaze, and he grasped my indicated notion. When he nodded and grinned, I turned back to Fawn and thanked her one more time. "Wait." She pleaded. The strange enchantress desperately grabbed my arm not wanting us to leave, especially me for that matter. There was a chill that crept up inside me but on the outside, I played it off with a graceful bow, saying, "Yes, my lady."

Sitting back down, I focused on the open window that I couldn't remember seeing when we first arrived. Fawn knelt back down to tell me the rest of her story, but her voice became muffled when my eyes transfixed on something completely impossible.

"What in all the stars?!" Fawn stopped talking immediately when I sprung myself out of the chair and raced over to the window seal. "Young king, I wasn't finished." I dug my fingers into my eyelids and jabbed myself in the head a couple of times. "Is that? I mean... No, surely not." I let out an awkward chuckle.

My mind was beside itself. I opened the glass to see if I could hear the three of them talking. "That looks just like-" "Ha. Ha. Ha. Young Brighton don't be silly." "Ann-" At the almost mention of my sister's name, I knew she'd again been reading my thoughts.

I decided to throw this witch for a loop and speak directly to her. "How do you know Lissy? And who are those other kids with her?" I didn't let up on my hard stare. I wanted to make her nervous. It worked but only for a moment. She actually looked taken away by my decision to speak and ask questions out loud. But when Lissy and the others- "At least I think it's Lissy...", I paused in thought.
When they were getting closer, she lightly placed her hand on my arm and moved me so she could close the window. Then, she pulled the curtain. "I don't believe that is who you think it is," she said while softening her gaze and smiled.

I didn't trust her though. It had to be her. We even locked eyes for an inkling of a second. I'm not injudicious, I know what my sister looks like. "But was it really her?" I rubbed the back of my neck. "She looks older, like maybe a woman now." Perplexed, I shook my head and thought about the last time I saw Lissy. It had only been about four to six fortnights. Surely-

The enchantress chimed in again. "Brighton, I really don't think that's her. Please. I need to finish what I've been trying to tell you. Then, I need to see you and Willy off, quickly."

Sighing deeply from lack of knowledge, I let it go. I mean I really didn't have a choice in the matter. It seemed that way to me anyhow. I tried to focus on her words as she started again. "Like I was saying. Your mother and I became best friends. She learned how to do so many incredible things. I taught her well." I rushed my hand over my mouth to cover a yawn.

I was starting to feel myself doze off from boredom. Her voice had become a dull tone in my ears. Leaning in toward her like I was in all honest paying attention, I decided to try and get some different information.

"Excuse me, my lady, but earlier you were telling us on the trip over here to keep quiet. Why was that?"

"Young king, I've been trying to tell you." She answered back, then sighed.

"Your mother, the queen is magical." That word woke me up. Sitting up straight in the dusty chair, I realized maybe I should hear this mystical hag out. I caught myself nodding to her every word. "A young woman came from the flame of the black candle, and she started to dance. That's when I saw your queen's body start to fade in and out before my eyes. Becoming pleased with her quick learning skills, I granted her one of my very own chanting books."

Moving from side to side in my seat, my eyes flickered. I couldn't believe what this enchantress was trying to do. Does she actually think she can intrigue me with this mumbo-jumbo story? I know what I saw when I was little was real. Everything out of this witch's mouth was prideful lies. I really thought my mother was just sick in the head or something, but now I know the cause of why she became the way she is.

After the enchantress finished and seemed quite pleased with herself, I cleared my throat and stood to my feet. "So, what you're saying is, my mother, the queen, has been taken over by some dark cloud or something?" The lady grinned and it felt like a spider was crawling up my back.

Fawn walked over to a stick of wax that apparently this whole time had been laying on the little table across the room. Her eyes got really big as she muttered, "Watch closely." With the snap of her fingers, she lit the candle, and I now began to witness the strange creature dancing inside the burning flame. My eyes began to widen as I stared at the thing that lured in my queen, and I could feel the compulsion coming off it.

The whole thing was creepy.

The enchantress had some kind of hold on me. The outside of me was being drawn in and wanted to see what was going to happen next while my inner voice was screaming "Look away- Look away!" My head was starting to get heavy, and my palms were becoming sweaty. Then, I heard it. "Curiosity killed the cat, Brighton." The voice was so faint, I almost couldn't make it out but there she was saving me once again with her nagging. My childhood friend, Jenny. She was my caution guard on everything. Her warning gave me the strength to be able to blink and turn away.

I don't know why or even how Jenny's voice popped in my head at that precise moment, but I was unquestionably thankful.

"Uh- That was neat, my lady." With what had just happened, it was all I could think to voice out. Fawn snapped her fingers again, this time the candle disappeared before my eyes, and I noticed the disturbing mannerisms coming off of her. There seemed to be a hint of fear rolling off of her as well. It didn't matter how I felt I just knew I was ready to get as far away from this place as possible. "Well. Thanks again my lady for all of your kindness but we must get going this time. Willy. Let's go." I said as I looked at her with my boyish charm and gave her my biggest toothy grin. "Uh. So how do we get to Egladon?"

She let out a snicker and began to speak when Willy crossed the room to grab my arm, leading me to the back of the hut. Excited, he said, "This way through Fawn's room. You're ready then?" I was about to show my compliance when I heard, "No, wait! That's not where-" Fawn's screeches were calling me to stay, but my friend had introduced to me a way out and I'd be wooden-headed if I didn't take it.

Willy still had a hold of my arm and without a second thought, I let my friend drag me into another world.

CHAPTER 10

Annalise

"Annalise." I looked up to see that neither of my friends' mouths had moved. I tilted my head to the side and began smacking myself in the ear, a couple of times like I was trying to drain the water out after swimming, and I finally gave in, allowing myself to go ahead and listen to whatever it was whispering to me. I needed to get these two's attention so I could disappear for a moment without making them worry. "Hunt- hum." "What is it, Anna?" Tay hissed. She and David were quarreling again. "I just wanted to tell you I'm going around the bush again for a second. I forgot to say goodbye to Fyra and because I know we'll be leaving now that we have Fawn's wand, I want to spend a little more time with her." "Go, go, go," she flicked her hands, shewing me away like I'd suddenly become a nuisance. With a slight nod, I made my way around the shrub.

It didn't sit well with me that lying was now becoming so easy, but in order to be able to listen for this voice, I needed to be somewhere quiet. "Annalise." There it was! "Yes, I'm here. What do you want? Do I know you? How is it you're only in my head? Where can I find you? Sorry, I rapidly spout out inquiries when I'm nervous."

Still no figure, but I heard a faint chuckle.

"My child, I wouldn't have you any other way." The kind words relaxed my built-up anxiety. I could feel my stomach untightening when I slowly let my feet take baby steps away from the bush. "Follow my light and I will direct your path." the voice said. The second sun appeared out of nowhere in the sky, looking like a huge ball of fire. When it lit everything in sight, I noticed I was standing in front of a house that surged in flames. "Oh, no!"

Rushing toward the burning building I looked around for something, anything I could get my hands on to put the fire out with. Then, the still voice made its way through my hasty notions. "Do not be troubled, Annalise. It is I who is in control of this fire." My thoughts eased and I became aware that I was standing in the flames. I looked down at my feet "Wha...?I don't feel a thing!" Somehow without any recollection, I had already made my way inside the gate.

Astonished and spinning in circles, pretty much until I became nauseous, I laid my eyes on the most beautiful garden I had ever seen. Bright green grass, like spring had never ended. My eyes were lost in all the wondrous flowers surrounding me. The sweet taste of Bristeria's baker's gingerbread bear cookies suddenly danced on my tongue. I felt like I never wanted to leave. Letting my view drift over one flower to the next, I noticed a particular bud that was all by itself.

Gasp!

Is that the baby rose I cast a spell on? What in the stars is it doing here? "You aren't meant to do sorcery, Annalise. I did not create you for such things." "Huh? Oh, wait. It's you again. Are you ever going to show yourself to me?" "You will find me when you seek me, child." "Uh… Yeah okay, whatever that means." In the air around me, I heard a crackle of thunder but on the inside, it sounded like my father's laugh. "How strange." I thought. I pondered for minute on what the voice had just spoke. "I did not create you for such things" "Well good Galatians. What in the sapphire did that mean?"

I put my hands on my hips, confused, staring off into space. Just then, a beautiful ray of light flashed before me, but all I could focus on were its torched eyes. It was like staring into the amber of a fire. When it spoke, I could hear the sound of a symphony playing. The melody was so delightful. I tried my hardest to focus on his words, but the instruments were bombinating so loud that all I got was , "You will come to realize this very soon my child. But I say to you, above all else guard your heart, for everything you do flows from it."

I stood there blinking rapidly. Just as the aureate beam began to fade, a pudgy scraggly brown-headed boy took its place. "Chris-Christopher Robin?" Completely overthrown Intensely started rubbing my palms against my eyes. "Leaping leopards, is this real?" I said aloud. I was standing face to face with one of my brother, Brighton's childhood friends. Sticking out his hand he said, "Annalise. There is nothing to be frightened over." "H-How did you? Where did you? Huh?" I must've leapt back about three feet. "Name's Ferguson," he said while boldly offering out his hand. "Well for all the stars. I thought you were someone else." Slowly, I walked back toward him. "Wh-Who are you? Wh-What are you?" The boy smiled. "I told you already. My name is Ferguson. I was sent here by my omnipotent to watch over you." "Oh. Why do you look like someone I used to know?" I asked, while connecting my hand into his, standing there dumbfounded. He slowly shook my wrist and answered, "To make you less uncomfortable. If I showed up in my real form first, I'm afraid that you might would have fainted." "Uh huh…" I replied, watching my hand move up and down as slow as molasses. Standing there observing this new being, I started to ease up a bit and I finally smiled at him.

After exchanging pleasantries, my watcher decided I was ready for his real form. "Okay. Fear not now, Annalise. Remember this is still me." I took a deep breath in, closed my eyes, and blew out the air.

Popping open a lid and letting the other follow, I was now staring at humongous soles, like what is on the feet of calves. I followed his straight legs up to his waist. Covering him were a set of ginormous wings. "Wha!" My eyes froze in place when I noticed he had four sides to him. Man's hands lay rested all around him. "This is incredible! An astronomical being is towering over me right now!" Ferguson laughed but this time I felt uneasy because what I heard was the roar of a lion, the squawk of an eagle, a man's chuckle, and the roar of an ox all in one.

"W-W-What was that?" He looked down at me and I saw four faces staring back, with lots of eyes. I jerked my hands to my face so fast that I smacked myself hard enough to fall backward a step or two. "I didn't frighten you, did I?"

I straightened and locked my shaky knees. "N-no." My screech wasn't convincing to him at all. "I-I can get used to it," I said. "Your talons on the other hand." I looked down to see one of his claws tapping, making a hole in the dirt. "Geez. You have to be like three thousand feet tall, Ferguson."

Another roar sounded. "Don't be mad, Annalise. I'm at least five." He lowered himself to my eye level and it felt like I was in an illuminated room. Light shone all around me so much as if it were just him and I in some kind of magical dome. "Ferguson. This is too much for me. Can you go back to being a person? I can't see anything. It's like we left the world behind us or something."

"Apologies, Annalise. Sometimes I get carried away. You can open your eyes now." Seeing that he was the figure of the boy I once knew and played with, I grabbed my watcher's hand and smiled. "Thank you. Now did I see correctly? Do you really have four faces, four wings, and all those eyes?" I screeched again when I said eyes.

He snickered at my flabbergasted inquiries. This time I didn't shudder. He was a boy again, so his laugh was that, just a normal boy-ish laugh.

Gaining some ground, I started to ask him again about his unique qualities. When he stopped his chuckling, I finally was able to get a word in. "Ferguson. When you laughed earlier in your true form, why was it I could hear different sounds? It kind of startled me."

My watcher smiled. "I have three faces of animals. That's why you heard an odd sound. Nothing to worry about." I nodded. "Oh, okay. What about the other two wings of yours that go higher than my eyes can follow?" "Can't say I have the answer for that one. Suppose that's just how my all-knowing created me. I don't ask many questions, you see. I only do as I'm told."

Looking at him, shaking my head on the outside, but not com-ing close to understanding a thing on the inside, I wouldn't dare to ask about his many eyes. Instead, I decided to grill him about Omnipotent. "Ferguson. Who was the figure before you came? Do I know him? Why did he sound like my king Cyrus? How was I created? I thought it was from my king and queen but when he said, " I did not create you for such things", now I'm not so sure. And why did Omnipotent send you to watch me?"

The poor overwhelmed boy took in a giant amount of oxygen, but he wasn't letting it go. Oh no! I bugged him so much the poor guy didn't want to go on. "Breathe!" I screamed.

His air was hot on my face. I thought I was going to start to perspire or at the very least melt. When Ferguson started giggling uncontrollably, I began asking myself, "Wait. Does he even need to breathe?" "Ferguson." He was still guffawing.

Raising an eyebrow, I jerked my hands to my hips. "Ferguson!" Silence. I achieved my goal or so I thought. A gut-wrenching glare is what came after my outburst and suddenly I was fear-stricken. "There is no need for that tone, Annalise." His words were stony, and I found myself wondering where my attitude all the sudden came from.

Coughing in order to clear my throat after being scolded, I tried to say sorry.
But once again the words wouldn't form across my tongue. He met my eyes, and I couldn't say anything, just swallow hard.

While letting him stare me down, I went off into my assumptions as to why I all of sudden changed. "Why did I act out like that? He's so nice and cheery. Why did I yell? What's wrong with me?"

A bile taste entered my mouth. I wished I could retract what had just happened, but I couldn't. So, I let him stare while I stood there feeling compunctious and frustrated.

Finally, I relaxed. "Feeling any better?" he asked. "How? What did you do to me?" Meeting my eyes kindly, he said, "It wasn't I, but Omnipotent that silenced your rage." My belly fluttered, my heart eased, and I was able to muster up a small grin. "Ferg-" He cut me off. "Annalise to answer your questions earlier all will be revealed soon. Where you're about to go with those two, I shall not follow but if you need me speak with your eyes closed to Omnipotent and ask for him to let me come back to you."

In the blink of an eye, he changed back to his original form. I watched him fly straight into the air to where my sight could no longer follow. Just like that, he was gone. I pondered on Ferguson's words. "Where are you going, I shall not follow." Where am I going? How does he know about Tailya and David? Where are we going that's so bad, he isn't able to come with me? I sat on the ground picking flower petals in silence. I took in a deep sniff of the aroma from all the flowery fragrance. "It's so quiet here." The calming thought made it all the more difficult for me to want to stand to my feet and head back to Tay and David.

After plucking the last petal, I crossed my left leg over my right in order to straighten myself. I took in a heaping amount of air deep through my nose as I left the astonishing garden and sauntered my way outside the gate. I turned back for one more glance at the serenity and a tiny sigh was all I could leave behind.

Making my way back to my friends, an inkling puzzle piece of my memory kept replaying in my mind. I was walking into a bush, it was pitch black, and I couldn't see anything. Then, a light appeared. Suddenly a small voice. "Hmm..."

Smack!

I was so lost in trying to piece it back together, that I walked straight into Wesley. "Ouch. Why don't you watch where you're going?" he huffed, glaring at me and rubbing his forehead. "So-sorry, Wesley. I was overthinking and not paying attention." "Well, I'll say." His words were cold, forming a chill straight to my heart. "Excuse you! If I were you, I'd watch where you're standing!" I shouted the last part. It was like I couldn't stop myself from the outburst. I glanced him over while trying to calm down. The poor guy looked like he had grown up without proper attire also with very little food and drink for that matter. His t-shirt had a rip in the sleeve like he had been attacked by something. His leg coverings were high above his ankles and there was a visible cut just below his right eye. His red hair was scraggly as well.

Remorse was sinking into my soul fast as I focused on his bony arms and wrists. What has this guy been through? I wondered about how long it had been since he'd last eaten. Softening my stare, I asked, "Umm. Hey, Wesley? Would you care to follow me back to Tay and David? We packed food and snacks in case you're hungry."

When he finally made eye contact with me, something mystifying coming from his gaze made my blood run cold. In my frozen state, I witnessed bright green eyes. For a brief second, I could think of nothing but rage. All my childhood memories came racing back through. Every single horrifying event.

I felt my body trying to give in to the temptation even though the other half of me was screaming in torture. Then, he smiled and what I saw stilled me to my very breath.

Yellow gunk surrounded his teeth, and I knew it wasn't Wesley I was standing in front of anymore. It was the darkness. It was- "Y-Y-Yur-ika." My vocal cords tightened, and I could barely force myself to speak. My feet were planted there like I was trapped in quicksand not being able to move just sink further and further down into the hole until there wasn't a single piece of me left.

She formed an accomplished grin across her devious demented face and suddenly I felt defeated. It was as if I had been shackled to some giant silver cuffs with a long heavy chain that no one can burst out of, not even the so called strongest man from Bristeria.

Drops of salty liquid fell down my cheeks as I closed my eyes. I heard her laugh, and while I was crying for help under my breath she decided to speak. I quivered when I felt her hot breath come close to my skin. "Please. Somebody, anybody, help me." I wept fearfully on the inside. Then she maliciously cackled, only this time it wasn't her voice. It was a growl. A deep dark growl like a wolf does when it's getting ready to attack its prey. "Don't be afraid, little girl. Give into it. Give in to that rage. You will be amazed at the things we can do together. We'll get vengeance on all who have hurt you. I'll make you queen over Bristeria, and Queen Cheylenna will fall at your feet."

The growl turned into a hiss, now sounding like a snake slithering through my ears. I opened my eyes to see Yurika still standing in front of me. Just about to compellingly take her hand, Ferguson suddenly descended from the clouds in his real form. "Annalise. No!..." He roared while snatching me away and straight out of the pit that was trying to overtake me.

My watcher's yell killed any of Yurika's constraints she had me under and I could not have been more thankful. If it wasn't for him, I'd probably be enslaved and blinded. I looked up and noticed he was girded with a sword now and all of his wings were now down to his sides. He lowered himself to my level. "Wait here. I need to destroy that dark spirit." "Huh?" I replied completely at a loss for words.

CHAPTER 11

Brighton

Willy seemed to be glad he had returned home. My friend slapped me across my back as I feasted my eyes on this new world. "Beautiful, isn't it? – he said, smirking and pointing out over the land- "I told you you'd love it. Come on, let's go meet Lord Timious."

I rubbed my eyes trying to take in this amazing view. "Give me a minute, will you? This place is- is, well, what a girl would say, breathtaking. Nothing even remotely the same of where we just came from. And that's saying a lot."

Willy stepped back. He was allowing me the chance to take it all in, the magnificent beauty he called home, Egladon.

"Whoa, Willy, this is where you're from?" I couldn't keep my mouth shut. I didn't want to. I let the gaping hole form away while thinking I never wanted to leave this place.

The land definitely had an exotic look to it. Colors of mint, bright red, dark amber, and coral covered the whole island from where we were standing. Below the cliff, I could see a creamy white shoreline. The bright rays of the sun made the deep blue sparkle. "I don't know if I need to see anymore brother. The view from up here makes everything else seem self-explanatory."

Willy's lips curled into a satisfied grin. It was clear he loved my keenness of Egladon. "Wait until you see it at sunset. You think the view is amazing now." He threw his arm around my shoulders and shifted my body with a side bear hug. "Come on, I'll show you around and after we're finished getting you enrolled, we'll come back to this spot, and you will see just what I mean about the view."

We headed down the mountain top and I got to witness more beautiful eye-catching landscape. "Whoa… What's with all of this red hue?" Willy guffawed. "Those are butterflies, man." I spun myself about. "There's so many! It almost looks as if they've taken over all of Egladon." My friend laughed again at my exaggerated exaltation of his home, but I couldn't help myself. I had never seen so much beauty from bugs. I mean the cherry-colored wings on those things were inconceivable. I nudged Willy on the arm. "What are they here for? Why are there so many? Are they friendly?" The frail guy chuckled and shook his head. "They are for the pegasi. Some would say they keep them in a state of peace." I squinted my eyes and tilted my head. "They do what? And how in sea monkeys can they do that?" I couldn't keep my composure any longer, so I continued to shout. Needless to say, my curiosity was getting the best of me.

Willy fervently blinked and then cleared his throat. "Brighton. I don't know everything, man. And yes" -he let out a boisterous laugh- "the fluttering insects are cordial" –then he paused for a moment and scratched his head- "that I know of."

I vomited out all my racing thoughts. "You mean to tell me these alicorn beasts are kept happy from the butterflies? "Yes." he answered. "What do you all use them for, anyway? "Man."-he said, agitated, while rubbing the back of his neck- " You'll get your answers when you meet Lord Timious." "Geez, Willy, if they have to be stabilized, why in flippin flippers are we training with them? Will they try to eat us if they become upset?" My friend looked down and shook his head.

Turns out my panicky outburst had some carry to it. I seemed to have drawn the attention of more than just Willy's ears. Two other men were bent over, bellowing, one hand rested across their stomachs, while waving the other in air.

It's safe to say I was feeling very sheepish right then. Also, a little annoyed from their mocking guffaws. One man made his way up to my friend. They began bear hugging one another and shooting the breeze while I stood there waiting for introductions.

Finally, I coughed. "Ahem." When they turned to me, I was rolling forward and backward on the balls of my feet. I even looked up at the sky and whistled, you know, trying to be nonchalant. Willy said his apologies for not introducing me right away and the new guy stuck his hand out for me to greet. "Good on ya mate. They call me Mason." He seemed convivial enough, so I returned his welcome. "Name's Brighton." I replied, our palms still in acquaintance. During our pleasantries, he said, "She'll be right, mate." I had no clue what he was getting at with those words, but if I had to take a guess, I'm guessing he was trying to console me, seeing as he had the look of empathy in his stare, but the name pegasi still weirded me out. I don't even know what they look like and that right there gave me the willies as well.

I turned to Willy cocked my head, then turned back toward Mason. The odd stranger was still smiling at me. Feeling awkward and still a little embarrassed, I raised my brows and gave him a- "yea, okay, I know, you're odd"- kind of grin. At least that's what I was thinking. So, I believe I smiled back, I hope, I don't know..., he was still grinning, so I guess that was a good sign.

I cleared my throat and let go of his palm. "Have you ever ridden one of them?" I asked, hoping for an answer to help calm my nerves while also trying my best not to sound like a coward. After all, I am a man, and men were supposed to be strong. I looked over Mason's head, which was not hard, seeing as he was probably only "five foot six" or "five-seven". I on the other hand am at least "six-two" or "six-three" It was clear I tower over the poor guy. I caught myself staring and sizing him up. He had short stubbly black hair growing off his chin, a head of black hair that was spiked, the way a soldier would wear it, and dark brown eyes reminding me of wet chopped wood in the forest back home. Good for him that he's stocky otherwise he might get mistook for a young lad. It must have been a slack day off because he wasn't wearing anything remotely to what a knight would. His tunic was plain white, and his shorts were dingy blue with rips in them. On his feet, he wore worn tan leather sandals.

"Crikey, mate! Ya been staring long enough, don't ya think?" His outburst brought me back to the present and out of my thoughts. He placed a couple of fingers on my back. "Ya come a long way, haven't ya? They ain't that bad, days maybe weeks and they'll trust ya. Ya got my guarantee." I snickered at the way he talked then I shrugged.

"There they are!" I shouted looking over Mason's head again. Willy looked toward Mason saying, "They're actually out in sight, who would of figured" "I know mate, ain't it somethin?" Mason replied with a huge cheese. "Those things are huge!" I yelled in Willy's direction. Halfway slapping him across his arm, I said, "You didn't tell me there were so many and in different colors! They have wings! Willy, you didn't say anything about flying!" "I did" -he sucked in a deep puff from his breathing contraption- "I said horses with wings. Come on brother, put two and two together."

I myself had to inhale a heap of air. I felt like the oxygen in my lungs was running scarce, even though I knew it was just my nerves and theories about the whole thing. Besides Willy and Mason kept reassuring me that the flying beasts were friendly.

"Ha ha ha." Mason and Willy were laughing at me. They both clapped me on my back. "No worries. She'll be right, Brighton." "Uh. Yeah, what Mason said." Willy responded. Mason gave me a brotherly punch to the arm. "Come on, it's almost time for brekky."

Willy licked his lips like he could already taste the food. "Yes, let's go. I'm starving." I tilted my head and gave him a dumbfounded stare. "Breakfast, brother, he means breakfast." I was a little vexed, because I had no understanding of Mason's lingo.

Mason started shouting to the other men a ways down from where we were. "Brekky, don't wait on us mates." Then he looked at my friend and I, saying, "Best get a move on if we goin to get full up for s'arvo!" I just gave him a friendly nod. I still had no clue what he was saying. Guess I will learn the longer I am here. Although Willy seemed to understand everything the man was saying. Why wouldn't he, he is from here after all. He was even able to converse right back. I followed behind them, listening to the two chat it up like a couple of maidens walking home from their studies. I was becoming envious like any third wheel tag along would. Needless to say, I was feeling left out.

All three of us finally reached the food line. I was so hungry that when the aroma from all the different foods hit my nose, my stomach rumble. I shyly looked around, hoping I was the only one who heard it. In front of me were all types of edibles. My nostrils began to flare at the scent of sweet rolls and cinnamon custard. The custard was for dipping the bread in. I licked my lips in pure bliss.

To my right was your usual complimentary eats. The hot steaming trays were filled with eggs, cabbage, fish, and brown bread. On my left, there was food I had never seen before. Thankfully they were all labeled so I would know what I end up liking and what to stay away from because it was disgusting.

I grabbed a trencher, started reading the names of the entrees, and began filling it up with sweet rolls. "I will remember this smell for a lifetime", I thought as I took a giant whiff. I continued with the cinnamon custard, patties, which were just labeled meat, marzipan, and then to top it all off , I added some strange-looking berries. I thought while grabbing the first one, " Surely these are not harmful to eat." They were the only dish that didn't have a label. When my meal was complete, I went to find Willy.

Willy and Mason found a table in the very back of the eating hall. I made my way through the crowd to join them. Noticing neither one had touched their food yet, I was grateful to see that they had waited for me. The first thing I had to try was the odd-looking berries, each one was a different color. The one that caught my eye was dark purple, which intrigued me. I bit into it and when I reached the middle, I chomped down on a giant seed that almost chipped my tooth.

Willy clapped me in the middle of my back. "Easy, brother. Go easy on the fruit." I held the side of my mouth, saying, "Willy you may call this fruit, but I think it should be called the purple teeth cracker. That way I'll remember never to let it enter my mouth again." I made Mason laugh so hard that he sprayed his sweet rolls all over the table. Willy knew me and how much I overreact on things, so he just shook his head.

"Next time I'll stick with the creams, wafers, and rolls. I like those." I said aloud and then blew the huge seed and all of its particles out of my mouth. I didn't notice how strong my breath was until I witnessed it fly across the room, hit the wall, ricochet, and graze a poor maiden across her forehead.

Quickly springing out of my seat, I rushed over to check on her, making sure the seed didn't draw any blood. The dining hall didn't have one empty seat which made it difficult to make my way through. Every time I passed a chair, I heard a small snicker. The lads were laughing under their breath.

Finally, I made it to the poor girl. "Are you alright, miss?" I asked as I dropped to one knee and took her hand in mine. She blushed.

I glanced over to where Willy and Mason were sitting, and both were giving me a dead stare with wide eyes and food dropping out of their traps. Mason yelled out, "Streuth! What are ya doing? Don't be a drongo mate!"

I turned my focus to Willy who was still wide-eyed and now had saliva running down the corner of his mouth. I knew it was from leaving it open this whole time. I dropped my chin and shook my head. The maiden looked down and softly questioned, "What are they saying, kind sir?".

My head raised up so fast that the poor thing almost got a headbutt from me. "Saints. That would be assault number two, way to go, Brighton, make the lady scared to be near you." I hissed to myself. Clearing my throat, I followed with an apology. "Forgive me, my lady, but my eyes yearned for a view of the face that this beautiful, sweet sound to my ears belongs to."

Her still soft voice was like a calming whisper that I never wanted to fade away. I knelt there thinking, "I could listen to her speak forever". I became bashful as electric shockwaves began to pulse through my body. It started to cause the not so charming side of me to erupt. Feeling uncomfortable, I burst out a laugh only, it sounded like a little girl's squeak, which startled her.

Letting out an awkward cough, I moved my hand toward her forehead. "Nope, no blood, just stand up, let go of the nice girl's hand and step back slowly". Agreeing with my thoughts, I gave her a coy smile and bowed gracefully. Standing there I continued to think, " I bet I look like a prat. I hope my laugh didn't make me come off like a mad man. Saints Brighton."

I couldn't even answer her question. My voice had left me the moment I gazed into those heart-stealing eyes. It was as if I was staring into the heart of the ocean. Her color of topaz with specks of white sparkled and caught me by surprise. All I wanted was to get lost in them.

I tried clearing my throat again. "I..." Nothing. Just one syllable was all that would come out. Even though it made her giggle, I found myself embarrassed. My cheeks felt hot, and I just knew they were turning bright red, so I tipped my head, smiled, and quickly turned heel to head back to my table. I needed to wallow a bit in my shame.

Sitting there, not even trying to look at those two, I gave myself a side smack to the head. "The most beautiful girl you have ever laid eyes on, and you couldn't even get out one full sentence. Come on, Brighton!" I screamed on the inside while swirling my spoon around in the cinnamon custard.

After deriding myself and spooning what was left of my cold meal, I looked up to see that the one who stole the words from my lips was nowhere to be found. She had left. I sighed. My head lowered back down to the leftover grub, and I finished my meal, listening to my two friend's carry on while wondering if we'd ever meet again.

Willy and Mason finished up shortly after me. Wiping his chin Mason said, "So, are ya goin to tell us why ya jumped up so fast to introduce yourself to that wild sheila?" Then Willy palmed my shoulder. "Yeah, Brighton. What were you thinking, going up to her like that?" I just gave them a blank look.

Willy seemed more panicked than Mason, but I couldn't grasp the understanding as to why. "Brighton, don't you want to know who she is?" Willy asked under his breath, leaning in toward my left ear. I threw my arm around his neck, giving him a playful wink and said, "No, not from your perspective, but I'm sure you're going to tell me anyway. So come on. Out with it. Who is she then?"

My friend grabbed my face and smushed it between his two palms. "She's master Patroklos' sister!" Removing his clammy hands, I followed with, "And that means?" I still wasn't getting the gist as to why talking with this woman was such a big deal and why Willy was so nuts against me wanting to learn more about the captivating maiden that took my breath away.

"Honestly brother, do you not remember anything I have told you over the years? I know I've mentioned her a time or two. She's the mad maiden."

The last part, Willy gritted through his teeth. Suddenly all of his letters about the mad maiden, Milaya of Egladon rang a bell. He gripped my shoulder but when he saw the disappointment written in my stare he said, "Sorry brother. There will be others. I will introduce you to some that aren't mad in the head."

My friend was loyal and all he wanted to do was look out for me, this I knew but I still couldn't get mad- I scowled at the thought of almost coming into agreement with these two's name for my mysterious lady. No. I wouldn't call her that. I'll refer to her as the maiden of my dreams. I'll call her Lady Milaya. A yearning sigh left my lungs, and I was dying to get to know my dream girl.

CHAPTER 12

Annalise

I stood there watching Ferguson slash and thrash the form of what I thought was Yurika. Hot flashes began to take hold of my body. Something was happening and I couldn't seem to shake it. My eyes started to burn. Then, I felt a pinch in my chest. "Give in." There it was again. The hissing, only now it was enticing my every nerve.

Shaking my head, trying to ignore its attraction, I placed my focus on the battle at hand. I watched their swords cling and clank back and forth. Every move between the two was like a life-ending dance.

My heart raced, causing my chest to rise high and sink in. Suddenly breathing was not an easy thing to do. My eyes widened at Ferguson's fist connecting to Yurika's right cheek followed by a slice to the stomach by his sword. The darkness recovered quickly, almost as if it didn't even phase it.

My stomach rose into my throat as I watched the nightly shadow retaliate. Tears seeped down until I tasted salt as I witnessed the evil being sever my watcher's left arm. Wickedly it threw in another slash almost connecting with Ferguson's head, but my watcher ducked, fiercely connecting his heel to the dark one's face. I gagged when I saw it spit gooey black tar from its mouth.

They circled, kicking, punching, and slicing one another. Worrying about the outcome was causing my stomach to tighten and my heart to race even more. I felt faint so I began to take slow deep breaths, as much as my lungs would allow in order to steady my nerves. Concentrating on continually blowing them out, I watched the final scene. Ferguson quickly dashed to the right avoiding the shadow's sting of its sword.

A sense of solace swept over me as I observed my watcher's divine steel impel through the obscure black force's gut, slicing from navel to nose. Ferguson dropped his head in sorrow and began to walk back toward me. I watched his severed arm grow back as he changed back into his human form. I stared at the huge cloud of black smoke as it floated toward the sky. It evaporated before my eyes, and I kept wondering to myself how all of this was even possible. "This time I hope that witch is gone for good," I thought.

"Annalise." I was being shaken out of my stupor with both of his hands planted firmly on my shoulders. "Annalise, it's over. You're safe for now." My eyes flickered and I was able to get out "For now? What do you mean for now?" Ferguson dropped his hands. "My dear child you are being tempted by the adversary. It has come to steal your good thoughts and replace them with evil ones. The darkness wants you to think what is bad is actually good and what is good is really bad. You cannot allow yourself to give in."

Huh. There they were again. Those two alluring words "give in". Staring deep into my eyes he said, "Yes. You cannot give in Annalise." "Uh-huh," I answered, moving my head slowly up and down. I started to walk back and forth in a straight line. What in all the stars is happening? How will I know and how am I able to resist? I couldn't even enable myself to turn away this first time. The overwhelming notions hovering around were no comfort at all and I must have had this look of defeat on my face because my watcher showed some compassion toward me by placing his hand gently across my back.

"Annalise. Do you remember why you came to be here again?" I pursed my lips, beginning to reply but for some strange reason, I lost all recollection of what my quest was for. My answer turned out to be a routed head shake as my eyes lowered to focus on the dirt beneath my shoes.

Ferguson cupped his left palm around my cheek then placed his other one on the top of my head. "Close your eyes and all will be as it was." I furrowed my brow awkwardly looking back at him. Knowing I am at a loss, and I have the slightest clue as to what any of this all means, I decided to trust him and do as he commanded.

The moment everything darkened, sounds of crying and anguish started ringing through my ears, but it wasn't coming from the outside. No, this was all happening inside my mind. All of the sudden, pictures were transforming and were being connected to the mourning's. The first image that became clear was me running through my forest back home. I looked to be about nine. I was scared, maybe even terrified. I turned my focus onto the rest of the clips that were not yet visible.

"I remember," I said to Ferguson while putting the puzzle pieces together. My heart sank and the corners of my eyes formed heavy tears as I watched my queen portray so much evil toward me. The last image wafted in front of another. Anger pulsed through every ounce of me when I witnessed my king, old and imprisoned.

Opening my eyes, I grabbed Ferguson's hand, hung my head and wept bitterly.

After my melt down, I gathered myself and dried my tears by roughly wiping my face with my palms.

The action of how I felt must have been showing through because Ferguson said, "No, Annalise. Don't give in. It's your choice, remember my words, it's your choice. Don't listen, it's what it wants." I could hear the eerily caution from every one of his directives, but he was too late. The indignation from my memories I welcomed all of it in.

The burning in my body started to flare up again and my eyes started to sting from the heat. I felt like I was on fire. It was as if I was becoming a human flame and anyone who comes near me would get scorched. A small smile rose upon my lips and Ferguson seemed alarmed at the way I was handling the once lost information.

"Oh, Annalise, my child."- He let out a deep disturbed sigh- "Looks like I need to stick by your side for a little while longer." Then he concerningly dropped his head and shook it. There was a part of me that yearned for his divineness, but the biggest half wanted more feelings of anger to pour in. Finally, I said, "Ferguson, you can go. I don't think I need anything from you. Thanks for the recap. I know what I need to do now."

My watcher gave me a stern glare. "That's pride, Annalise. Try to fight it." Stepping back two beats, I raised my hands to my head. It was pounding and sounded like lightning and thunder were striking each other in my brain. "What- what's going on? Ferguson, I can't think, I can't focus, I need"- "No, girl, stay angry, remember we can do great things. Pride, think power, think queen, think"-

I began strongly rubbing my head. I felt wetness fall down my face and I was just about to close my eyes but before they shut, Ferguson stretched out his hand and flicked me right between the middle of my brows.

The heavy whisper and affliction were silenced . I grabbed my protector's hand and squeezed gratefully. "Ferguson. How did you? What was that?" His gaze into mine was soft and still, almost as if he was speaking to me through our connection. My chest rose high as gratification passed through my relieved heart. "Thank you, Ferguson." His response was a graceful head bow. We stood there in quietude. I don't know what he was thinking but I was reflecting on everything that had just happened, wondering how I was going to survive the next attack.

At the end of my reflecting, I made it a point to later ask Ferguson more about Omnipotent but for now, I wanted to return back to my friends. They were probably worried about me, and I am sure I was going to get the third degree from Tailya.

"Ferguson. I need to get back." I could see he was displeased but if continuing this journey was the only way to save my king and rid my queen of her bondage of evil then so be it. I carefully took my watcher's hand. "Ferguson. You don't understand. I have to choose this way because it's the only solution in destroying what has a hold of my mother." He began to pull from my grasp. "Annalise, child," he sighed. "Since this is what you choose, I'm afraid I cannot be here to guide you. I will not follow you and I have no choice but to leave you now." Within his words he fully let loose of my hand, and I watched him descend back up into the clouds.

I became cold all of the sudden, and the warmth that I felt before he left was no longer around for comfort. Letting out a deep exhale, I gathered my thoughts and set off to return to the journey at hand. Along every step, I wondered about the timing of my disappearance from Tay and David. I also became curious as to why they never came to look for me.

Making my way up to the bush, Fyra was sitting there waiting for me. I walked up to stroke her chest. "I wish I knew how to change you back, Fyra." I buried my head into her feathers, closed my eyes, and welcomed every droplet to fall freely. It felt as if more pieces of my heart were being chipped away. She didn't ask to become this way, taken from her home to be turned into some sort of enchanted flying beast.

Pulling my face from her and wiping the salty liquid from my eyes, I sniffed out a farewell. When I started to turn heel, she spoke. "My dear friend, please live well and do not worry about me. I am able to fend for myself. If you ever return to this place I will be waiting."

I gazed into her beautiful vibrant golden eyes one last time. We both bowed toward each other and then I fully spun myself about. Finally reaching around the shrub, Tay and David were just as I left them. "You two are still at it?" Sarcastically, I shook my head. Tailya enigmatically gawped at me. "What are you talking about, Anna? You just left us."

Stumbling back a couple of steps, I looked up toward the sky cogitating on the fact that time was different from where I was. "Are you okay? Is something wrong?" David asked, concerned. I also picked up a hint of curiosity in his tone.

Swallowing my thoughts, I replied, "Yes, I think so. I am learning that there's something very perplexing about this place." The last part I said to myself. Pushing away my theories, I followed with, "Are you two ready to leave? I don't believe we need the book." Tay laughed. "Then tell us, Anna, how do you plan to save your kingdom?" Standing there completely out of thought, I realized she had a point. "I don't know. Can we not just use the wand? Do we really need to go all the way to Fawn's hut?"

I sighed after asking the inevitable. I knew the answer, but that didn't mean I wanted to hear it. Plus, I wasn't really looking forward to reuniting with Wesley even though I was supposed to send him home. He didn't act like he cared for me much, so I knew it would be hard to get him to stay put long enough for Tay to send him back.

"Anna, what's going through that head of yours now?" Tay huffed, walking over. "Tailya, do you remember Wesley?" Her stare was blank, and she began tapping the side of her head, so I continued to try and jog her memory. "Think back to the time we freed my grandma Mesha and then the boy. Can you recall?" My friend's eyes widened as she realized what I was saying.

Clasping my hand strongly and staring, she said, "Have you seen that little boy?" I nodded slowly, my eyes now in shock. "Anna, that kid was meant to stay a bug. He isn't real. Did he say anything to you?" The dismay in her voice sent up red flags all around me and I was beginning to feel very uneasy.

My first word came out in a squeak as I replied, "He's not a boy anymore and yes he did but it was cold and cruel. I think he might be our age or a little older." She looked distraught when I was saying all of this to her. She rose her fingers to her mouth, stuck one in and started to chew on her nail. "We have to find him!" she blurted. Furrowing my brows, I gave her a stern bob, then we turned our focus back to David.

"David, stop eating our food!" Tay huffed. She stooped herself down to his eye level, giving him a mean headbutt. "Did you hear anything we were saying?!" She did it again and the poor guy fell back rubbing himself right below his hairline.

"Crapes, sis, that hurt! Yes, I heard you two, but when you and Anna conspire it usually takes forever and well, I was hungry!" he argued. Watching those two bicker back and forth stirred up some laughter and enjoyment that I most definitely needed. I copped a squat under a tree nearby and continued to watch the show while treating myself to the last baked good we had, a piece of bread.

I was on my last bite and nearly choked it down when David rushed up to his sister, shaking his fist, eyes pinched like he was about to hit her. "Why do you always have to assault me when getting my attention?!" he yelled. "Few he didn't touch her, that was close." I said to myself, letting out a gruntled sigh. Tailya propped her hands on her hips, creasing her glare. "If you would pay more attention to us instead of your stomach, I wouldn't need to feel the reason to attack you. Besides, it's fun to ruffle you up." She snickered and David's eyes looked like they changed to a different color.

"David, your eyes!" I shouted, hoisting myself off the ground, and making my way over to break them up. My friend turned on his heel to hide his newly transformed orbs. Tailya hastily stretched out her hand in an attempt to keep her brother from leaving. "Let him go, Tay. There's something seriously wrong with him. Did you see his eyes?" I emphasized, gripping the hand meant for David.

My friend pursed her lips, giving me a hollow stare. "I don't know what you're implying Anna, my brother is just fine. I probably made him cry. It's that or I made him extremely angry to the point of tearing up."

Viciously jerking her hand out of mine, she yelled, "Stop trying to make up unnecessary accusations about my brother!" I felt conflicted for her and myself for that matter. "I mean, I know what I saw but how come it was only me who witnessed it? Is Tay trying to cover up for him or protect me? Is she scared of him? Does she know something? After all, she does live in the same house, so I'm sure she'd notice no photos of him on the walls as well."

I was standing there deep in thought, staring and tilting my head while Tay rolled her eyes at me. "There you go again. What tales have you incorporated now?" she hissed. Was I though? Did I really see something or was it just my nerves playing tricks on me? My theories were just that, made up presumptions of my own analogies. Still, I didn't care for her odious way of speaking toward me. Ignoring Tay, I decided to focus on the other imperative matters. David's eyes and what made his eyes turn. I found him just a ways from the meadow. He was taking his frustrations out on a helpless tree trunk.

The bark had red splotches and I could see it was from the cuts on David's knuckles. "Hey, stop! What are you doing? You're going to break your hands!" I shrieked, running up to him. "Go away, Anna. I need to calm down." I grabbed his arm just before another blow. "David, your eyes- what's wrong with your eyes?"

He fiercely jerked his head from my gaze. I knew it was to keep me from staring, then he aggressively yanked his arm from my grasp. "I told you to leave! Go!" The oxygen in my lungs quickly fled and my chest was beginning to tighten.

Rapidly sucking in air, my head started to feel fuzzy. My eyes crossed, which was making it unbelievably hard to see. Right when nausea kicked in, I knew I was done for. I called out to him, hoping he'd stop my hard fall. "D-D-Da-Dav-" My lids sealed, and I felt a hard thud before falling away into a pitch-black hole of nothingness.

CHAPTER 13

Annalise

"Anna!" Everything around me was muffled. I couldn't even hear my heartbeat. "Annalise!" I began trying to stand up. Placing my right palm in front of me, I pressed myself high enough to be able to stand. "Rats, not much strength with one arm, Anna," I thought. This time using both hands I pushed my body off the black ground below, only to plummet back to my original position. I kept trying and one after another I collapsed.

My eyes popped open finally and in my face was David. "Anna. Annalise! Annalise, can you hear me? Wake up, Anna!"

My poor body felt weak from being shaken back and forth. "Yes, David. I'm fine. Will you please stop shaking me?!" I hissed. He helped me to my feet and searched me over. I guess I hit the ground pretty hard because I could see the perturbation in his stare.

Shoving him off, I crossed my arms. "Crapes, what's with you? I'm fine, really I am." David glowered at my response to his kindness. "Geez, Anna. Your body was jerking up and down. I thought you were seizing." "Huh? No, I was trying to stand up. That's all." Examining me over, aching a brow, he huffed, "Well it didn't look that way. Your whole body convulsed, and your eyes were rolling around under your lids."

Focusing on the poor guy's look of concern , I thought, "I will give him a handshake. It was the least I could do for him since he stayed beside me during my spell of fainting,"

Clearing my throat, I stuck out my hand. "Thanks for-"

Gasp!

The boy tugged me with so much force that my forehead went flying into his chest. I couldn't even finish my sentence. All I could say was "Ouch!" He pushed me back on my heels to look at me. Then wrapping his hand around my face, he rammed my head back in for another embrace.

Placing both my hands under my squished body, I pressed my-self away from his tight hold. I began brushing myself off like I had dirt all over me, only I couldn't comprehend why I even started to do that in the first place. I glanced toward him, and then coughed out an awk-ward thanks.

The whole thing felt funny to me and not in the laughing ha-ha- sort of way. Looking at him, he had a faint grin pursed upon his lips and now I really felt odd. "Uh, I think we should get back to Tay. I'm surprised she hasn't found us, that is if she's even been looking."

Absentmindedly I grabbed his hand. "Come on." His smile didn't leave out any teeth. Gulp. I threw the poor boy's hand down and hastily dropped mine straight-lined to my side.

Rocking back and forth on my feet, not knowing what to say now, I just lifted my hand in the air and pointed my thumb behind me motioning for us to go. He replied with a slight nod. We finally made it back to Tailya. She was crossed-legged on the ground, nibbling on what looked like berries.

Rushing toward her, leaving David to eat my dust, I laid my focus on the round purple balls in her hand. "What are they?" I asked while licking my lips. I was so hungry I felt like I could eat a thousand or more.

Tay clenched her hand, hiding her rations from my sight. Closing her eyes and shaking her head, she hissed, "These are mine; you can't have any. If you want some, go get your own. They're over there by the tree in that bright green bush." I looked over to where she was pointing, and I saw them.

I spun my head back around to my friend. She was enjoying her edibles again. "I thought everything here was dead and gone. You know, withered like the ground and leaves on the trees. Even the bush where Fyra was at had been touched. Its leaves had almost all fallen off."

"Beats me, I wasn't going to ask her any more questions. It's there, I'm hungry, so I grabbed some." What she said made sense, but I was still skeptical about why that was the only living shrub we had come across. As I knelt down beside her, she closed her hand a second time. "Don't worry, I'm not going to take any. I think I'll pass on these." She shrugged. "Suit yourself," she said while standing to her feet and wiping off her berry juice remnants.

Trying to stand up with her, my foot popped out of my shoe. I reached down to put it back on and there it was lying on the ground, Fawn's letter. Picking it up while putting my heel back into my shoe, I stood up.

"What do you think? Should we take a look?" I asked, dangling the paper in front of her face. I was hoping it would provoke her enough to want to read it. "Let me see it." She snatched the note out of my fingers. "Grapes, sis, I'm sure Anna would have given it to you if you had asked. Why so hostile?" David asked as he moseyed his way over. I creased my eyes, flattened my lips, and gave her a swift nod.

Tay smirked at my disgruntled reaction to her brother's opinion. Shoving the handwritten message into my face, Tay shrieked, "Anna, look! There's stuff about Queen Cheylenna on here!" "What did you just say?!" I yelled back while ripping the letter from her fingers. The girl's peepers popped wide open along with her mouth. "What does it say?" David questioned while bouncing up and down on the balls of his feet. "Shh, quiet. Let me read!" I hissed.

Shuffling my view over every other word until I found my mother's name. I read about Fawn's plan to take down Yurika. Halfway through the note, there it was, My mother's handwriting.

Gasp!

My name, penned down in bold print, was all capitalized. Queen Cheylenna must have known what she had encountered when meeting Fawn. This wasn't information about the witch, no, this was a goodbye missive. Tay and David both reached out for my relic, but I quickly turned my back while lifting an elbow to shrug them away. This was the first nice thing I had ever received from my queen, and I was going to be the first to read it.

Ambling away from my friends, so I could read in peace, I focused on every beautiful caring word while brushing stray tears off of my cheeks.

My precious Annalise Chelynn , you are growing so fast. I can't believe it's already been six months since your father, brother, and I found out there was going to be another female in the family. My heart fluttered every time I thought of who you might resemble more. Would you have your king's nose and chin? I'm quite fond of them. Or would you have my eyes and hair?

I had to look away from her message to unblur my vision. She had never spoken to me so gently before and it was hitting every one of my heartstrings. Rubbing my eyes trying to get all of the moisture out, I focused back on the letter. I noticed a dry droplet of water in the crease. I knew it was old because it had changed the color of the paper only on that one spot.

A couple more tears fell from my eyes when I thought to myself that she might have been crying while writing this. I quickly swept them away off my cheeks and continued back to my mother's memoir.

Dear sweet precious girl, if I could have seen the future, I would have stayed far away from this evil woman. I never realized how blinded decisions could be so damaging and life changing. I've put our beautiful family in danger, and now I have to live with the outcome of never getting to have a relationship with my only daughter. Annalise, something has overcome me. Something so dark I can't control it. I have horrible night terrors now. When I close my eyes, I'm in some other world and there are two of me. One is me as a little girl, sitting alone crying, while the other is me now, but I have dark circles under my eyes and a weird grin on my face while looking down at my child self. I watch the adult me start to chain up the little me and then everything starts to go black, and I begin to suffocate. Then I wake up sweating.

Every one of her kind words kept playing over and over in my head. When I read the last thing she wrote, I felt fragile like a porcelain doll. Every single one of my emotions were on edge. If someone pushed me over right now, I'd shatter.

I'm sorry, my daughter. Please forgive me for what I might put you through.

Another dried tear spot at the end of the letter concluded my theory. She really was crying while writing this. I clenched the only good memory I now had of my mother to my heart before folding it back up and putting it into the sole of my shoe for safekeeping.

When I thought back on the last time I saw her, bile began to rise from my stomach. I mistook her for the evil that was actually the one calling the shots all this time. I even tried to end her. Everything around me started to spin.

I dropped to my knees and began staring at the ground in deep thought. So many notions were going all at once, but only one stood out.

Gasp!

"Has my little brother, Kedron always been evil?

I shook my head hard to the impossible thought. He had so much joy when he was a boy; I would have noticed something strange, plus a person can't be evil and also filled with joy, it just doesn't make sense. At least, I think-

No. I certainly would've been aware.

In the midst of talking to myself, I heard footsteps crunching the dry grass behind me. I twisted my body and saw David.

My friend knelt beside me. "Anna, Tay sent me over to check on you. Why are you on the ground? What did the letter say? Come on, let's get you up." He stood first brushing the dirt from his pants. Looping his arms through mine, he jolted me to my feet. "Thanks. I don't want to talk about the letter. Let's just get back to Tay." I said brushing myself off as well.

He let go of the fact that I didn't want to talk about it which made me feel relieved. Tay on the other hand, I needed to think of something to say to keep her off my case.

"David, where are we going? Where's your sister?" I stopped walking, planting my heels, and crossed my arms. Turning around to meet me, he laughed. He marched up, smirked, grasped my left wrist undoing my arms, and began to pull me, "Tailya went on to Fawn's hut. I was supposed to come get you, and then we are to go meet her on the way. Now come on, let's go."

"Oh," I muttered. "Geez, Anna, what am I going to do with you?" He made a clicking sound with his tongue as he directed me. I felt like my ears were on fire and my eyes started to burn. Jerking my wrist from his hold, I hissed, "Let go! I am very capable of walking my-self. I don't need a leash!" David froze with his mouth wide open. I had left him dumbfounded and it was my turn for some amusement.

My friend furrowed his brows and squared his shoulders, huff-ing, "Why is it whenever I take the initiative to help you, you always become so moody?"

I didn't answer. Instead, I crossed my arms again, saying, "Just lead the way." The poor guy turned from me and sighed while shaking his head. I followed from a short distance behind.

Why do I get so flustered around him only? Then I thought, "No. It isn't just him. I've been like this with Ferguson and Tailya, but for some reason I only feel bad acting like this in front of my watcher.

I looked up toward the clouds wondering if Ferguson could hear my thoughts or if he could sense my iniquity.

David shouted ahead. "We're almost there!" "I guess Tailya's already made it, seeing as we haven't run into her!" I shouted back.

He didn't reply and I started getting angry again thinking he was ignoring me. The hissing sound started up again. "You know he's not paying attention. You aren't important to him. That's why he didn't answer."

"No, Annalise. He probably didn't hear you. Don't hold a grudge. It's not good for your heart." Another voice sounded and it was like I had two people speaking to me subconsciously.

"I've lost it. I have hit bottom. I am having a conversation with myself in my head," I thought.

Finally, we reached Tay at Fawn's tree hut. She was waiting by the steps. The inside of my ears itched when I heard, "See, your best friend doesn't even want to wait for you. She only cares about herself and the magic she'll be able to do." Listening to the voice, I gritted my teeth and pressed my lips together, shooting daggers at her.

Just as I was about to march, I heard my name in a whisper. "Annalise. Don't listen, it's not true, it's a lie." The gentle breeze through my ears sounded so familiar like I had just heard it not long ago, but I couldn't seem to recall from where or when.

Frustrated from not being able to have a thought to myself, I tightly squeezed my lids and screamed at the top of my lungs. "Stop!" Opening my eyes to see Tay and David with dropped chins and gaping holes, I knew I didn't yell in my head like I had wanted to.

I busted out in anger. "Can we get the book and get out of here?!" Tay snapped back. "Well, you're the one that took so long to get here." David of course had to put his two cents in. "Annalise, my sister has been patiently waiting for us. What's your problem?" "Nothing!" I hissed.

"Don't be so rude, Anna!" Tay huffed while standing to her feet. I rolled my eyes and sighed. The inside of me felt like I was being ripped apart as I watched Tay and David make their way through the door.

My heart stung from the way I had just treated my friends. This voice I was subconsciously listening to was starting to overpower me. A teardrop trickled down my face when I heard "Just give in." I suddenly came to know just how it felt to be my mother as a little girl in her nightmares, chained up, having no way of escape.

I dropped my head in defeat and followed my friends inside.

CHAPTER 14

Brighton

"Come on mate. You can stare at the unknown later. It's time we all got to our jobs. Catch ya guys later." Mason clapped Willy and me on the back and then took off to shore with a sailor to hook some fish.

"So, I'm thinking he's maybe seen the leviathan, hmmm?" Willy's eyes widened. He stared deep into mine which started to give me the chills. "What, did I say something wrong?" My friend wouldn't stop his gaping. It was like my question froze him and he couldn't speak, blink or move.

"Willy!" I shouted while clamping my fingers together. It sounded like I was breaking sticks. He still didn't reply. "Hey, brother!" I continued to shout.

Right before my fist rose to his cheek, he caught it and shoved my balled-up hand back to me. He scowled, "What were you thinking, meaning to hit me like that?" I coughed out an apology. "Well, brother, you were stunned, and I was just trying to help. I called out your name twice. I shouted and still couldn't get your attention. I was ready to knock you out of whatever stupor you were in."

He dropped his glare and calmed down. "Don't ever bring up that wicked creature around here. The men will throw us in the sea for fear of bringing it to land."

Befogged, I scratched the top of my head. "But I was under the impression that's what I came here to train for. Become a knight and help the others slay the sea monster." Willy nodded slowly, gripping his hands on both of my shoulders.

"It is, brother, but we never speak of it. We instead say we're here to train with the pegasi. Anyone who speaks of the evil creature and goes out to sea, I'm afraid to say they never return."

There was a scared, serious look in his eyes almost as if he'd seen the wicked beast himself and hasn't told anyone. I couldn't keep from staring at the poor guy. I just knew those eyes were hiding a breaking story and I was the only one who was going to be able to get it out of him.

I felt a little discontent when my untamed tongue caused Willy to drop his head and let out a deep breath. "Come on brother. We don't want to be late," he said with no emotion. Willy's tone of voice told me to relinquish the conversation for now. I didn't want to make my friend feel more burdened with his secret. So, I forced out a quick bob followed by a half-smile. "Okay, I'll resist the urgency of the truth for a little longer, but I expect you to inform me of what you're hiding soon. Got it?"

My friend lifted his focus back to mine and clapped me on the arm. "Okay. Let's go meet your first ever pegasus." My stomach clenched as my mouth flew wide open when it all of the sudden dawned on me, I was about to come face to face with a flying horse. "After we've finished for the day, I'll take you to that tavern over there on the hill by the cliff." "What's it called again?" I asked while gripping him in a side bear squeeze. "Egladon's never-ending ale," he muttered quietly, almost as if he were trying to whisper it.

I clasped my forearm a little tighter in excitement. "Yeah, that's the one! The place will be loud, and all the men will be talking amongst themselves so you shouldn't feel any pressure to spill it."

I stared my friend down. "You're going to tell me everything," I thought to myself, never letting him out of my gaze. The guy furrowed his brows and snickered.

My eyes darted to the side as I quickly figured out that what I was thinking to myself, I had actually spoken out loud. When I focused back, Willy's brows were no longer furrowed. Now his eyes were wide open, and he was glaring at me. Locking down his cold stare, he chuckled and shrugged his shoulders.

Through his guffaws I could already read what he was thinking. It was infuriating to know that the guy was mocking me to himself. When his smile widened even more, I shouted, "No, I am not a march hare!" He used to call me that in school before he moved here. My sudden annoyed outburst caused Willy to belly over in laughter. I stood there and watched as my friend poked fun at me. At least he didn't take what I said to heart. I thought, trying not to become more irritated.

After he'd finished, he said, "Brighton, brother, there's no dull moment with you, is there?" Crossing my arms and squaring my shoulders, I grimaced. "Oh fiddlesticks, just get over it and come on!" I huffed.

He straightened himself right and sucked in a huge breath of breathing medicine. Then, he jerked his head toward the keep. "Alright, alright, let's go meet the master and introduce you to your very own winged horse." He yanked my arm, and we took off in a high step.

"Wait, Willy look!" I stopped us dead in our tracks. Blinking uncontrollably as we both panted like two exhausted dogs, I saw her. "She's here!" Willy looked at me with wide eyes and gasped. "Oh wow! "Yeah, there she is, isn't it amazing?"- He cupped his left palm on ,my shoulder- "Now come on!" he scoffed.

My poor friend wasn't pleased in the slightest that I'd become distracted once more by the woman they called mad. In my opinion, she was too beautiful for me not to stop and enjoy the view.

Honestly, I really couldn't see what they were talking about. "These guys are blind," I thought to myself while still gaping.

"Brighton! Quit gawking so we can go and get to work. We have to go meet the master, remember? Come on man." I let my angel leave my sight for the time being and continued to follow Willy to the knights' training grounds.

"How much longer man?" I pressed Willy. It felt like we were traveling from one side of the island to the other, and my poor feet were beginning to drag against the dirt like heavy cement blocks.

Willy swiped a hand through his hair. "Brighton, I mean this in the nicest way possible. You brother are the biggest bellyacher I know." Then he sighed. I smirked, annoying him was starting to become a little amusing. "I'm just saying, I don't want to miss my chance to become acquainted with her."

"Huh?" Willy stopped, rubbed the back of his neck, and shook his head. "For the love of snails man. Can you get your mind, right? We're almost there, geez!"

I laughed and my heart thumped as I thought about my beautiful angelic lady and of course the pleasure of driving Willy to insanity.

"Calm down. I'm perfectly capable of focusing on both my lady and my training." Willy slapped his forehead. "Yeah, okay sure." Just as I began to grin and bob my head in agreement, the frail guy backhanded me in my gut. "Not!" He blustered as he retracted what he thought to be a playful gesture. It wasn't.

I gritted my teeth letting him know his smack was no help at all. "Hey, brother. Are you okay? I didn't mean to slap you that hard." He pleaded. I bit down on my tongue, squinted my brows, and slowly nodded my head with a fake smile.
"M-hmm, m-hmm." That was all I could give him at the moment.

I couldn't let go of my vexation. I wanted to pop him one right back. Shaking my fist I said, "If you ever hit me-" I got cut off. Willy decided to imitate me. "If you ever hit me," he copied. I took a deep breath in. Hold your tongue. Hold your tongue, Brighton. He's just messing around. No, you don't want to kill him. He's your friend. Repeating these words over and over in my head helped me calm down and I was able to form a chuckle.

His sarcastic sense of humor after all did come from me. Both of us guffawing at one another changed the mood immensely. "Okay, Willy. Let's get to work," I said while grasping the back of his neck and wiggling it from side to side.

What felt like a fortnight's journey finally ended. We made it to the knights' quarters and as we stepped through the gate, I set my eyes on all the different colored flying horses. I spun in place on my heel wanting to capture everything that was around us only to come face to face with the master of Egladon.

"Good afternoon, gents. I am Lord Patroklos. Willy, this must be Brighton. Is it?" he asked, stretching out a firm hand to greet me with.

I humbly obliged as I thought to myself about his appearance. He was shorter than me yet had a stocky broad stance showing good character and a firm grip. This man was not to be tried, that's for sure.

I cleared my throat. "It's good to finally meet you, my lord," I articulated with the deepest sound of my voice. He tittered then looked at Willy. "I trust you'll report to me all of his training accomplishments." My friend gave him a strong nod. Then, he turned his gaze to me. "Brighton. I can't wait to hear about all of your great achievements. Willy's already told me so much about you. I trust that you'll work hard and not give up." I clenched my eyes tight and jerked my head. "Good, I'll look forward to more meet-ups with you. You two go on ahead now. Willy, take him to meet his pegasus."

I watched the ruler of Egladon stride away while lowering my chin in respect before turning back on my heel to have my first encounter with this magical beast. "Wow. Willy, there are so many. What's with all the colors? Oh, look! Their eyes are different colors as well!" My friend chuckled at my excitement. " That isn't all. Look closer, Brighton. Their eyes form different shapes."

I squinted my focus to get a clearer view. He wasn't jesting me at all. One was white with ice blue wings. Its eye color was grey like a cloud before it rains. The beast's eye shape looked exactly like an icicle.

I turned to my right and saw another that looked like it was covered in soot. The creature's wings were huge, and they reminded me of the snowy white trees during winter back in Bristeria.

A small exhale escaped me as I thought of my family. I focused back on the horse beast's eyes. It was like I was gazing into the tip of a flame and became mesmerized with every glisten. The shape of this one's eyes had what looked to be sharp-edged points. I got a little closer. "Wah! Willy look! This guy's eye shape are swords!" I blurted out in astonishment.

Just when I had thought surely that was the most amazing thing I had ever seen, I turned to my left.

"Woah! Look at this one!" Willy guffawed. I was acting like a tike picking out his first hunting bow and I didn't care.

His body color made me thirst for a glass of fresh-squeezed cherry juice. I licked my lips as my mouth watered for just one taste.

The enchanting colorful winged creature made contact with me, and its eyes caused me to drop my chin. As the wide hole formed, I once again found myself looking like a codfish.

I was in aww staring into its lead-painted eyes. They were the shape of twin Sai's. This one's wings made you feel like you were sinking straight down into the bottom of the ocean.

These three miraculous beasts were unforgettable and seeing them made me all the more eager to meet mine. We continued to make our way down the stony entrance, and I was wowed by all the rest of these creatures. Willy clapped me on the arm. "Well, Brighton here he is. Your very own pegasus."

Here, I thought to myself I wanted the one that was to my left but when I gazed upon this guy, everything silenced around me.

"What are you going to name him?" Willy asked with a big grin knowing I had become still of breath.

I shrugged off his giddy taunt while I stood transfixed on my very own flying horse.

His jade body glistened like a crystal hanging in the sunlight. His violet wings reminded me of the flowers my sister Lissy would have in her hair after playing in the floral garden near our forest back home. My chest rose high from the happy memory. His eyes were crystal clear just like the pond in the world where I met that strange enchantress lady named Fawn. They sparkled when he looked at me. The shape of his eyes were horseshoes making me miss Nicodemus all the more.

"Well don't just stand there brother. What do you plan on naming your beautiful new creature?"

After hearing my friend's second outburst, I started thinking Willy was a bit more anxious for me than I was. I was so overcome by his stunning appearance that a name didn't even come to mind.

"Uhh… How about-" "Geez Brighton, can't you sound more excited? This is your first pegasus!" I pursed my lips and creased my forehead. "Give me a second. I'm thinking." My friend chuckled then crossed his arms while tapping a foot on the ground.

"Okay, I got it." I walked up to the beast and gently stroked his feathered purple wing. "What do you think, boy? Do you like Arkimedes?" My guy suddenly tipped his head and creased his eyes. It looked like his eyes were smiling at me. "I believe he concurs." Willy grinned, and in knowing this magnificent creature belonged to me, I followed my friend and gave Arkimedes a big toothy smile.

After getting acquainted with my pegasus, Willy and I got straight to work. I thought our job would be to take care of Arkimedes only, but it turned out that everyone took care of each other's pegasi.

Willy and I reached out a hand each to rub Arkimedes on his chest, then we bowed our heads and exited his stall, making our way to the end of the chain line of men.

We had our work cut out for us. The job required us to muck out stall after stall, groom them from head to hooves, feed, and even brush their teeth. You had to climb a ladder to reach their head and the top of their bodies. I saw Willy take two puffs of his breathing inhaler. Guess the job was tiring him out.

He wasn't the only one and here I thought Camp Herculean was tough.

We finally made our way back to Arkimedes' stall. I told Willy to sit down and take a break while I worked on my guy. He seemed happy to see me again. My beast was nodding his head and ruffling his wings when he gazed at the brush in my hand. I laughed at his enthusiasm.

There had been a ladder already set up in front of him. "Have you been taken care of yet, boy?" I asked. He shook his head and I gasped.

"Can-can you understand me?" I stared deep into his horse-shoe crystal blue eyes, waiting. Only, I didn't really know what I was waiting for. I was just being a simpleton. "Horses can't talk, let alone flying ones," I thought to myself. A bubble of laughter shot out of me as I shook my head and made my way up the ladder. The theory was ridiculous.

Midway up, Arkimedes' mouth moved. I began to shake as I had never had an animal speak to me before. My body shook so hard in terror that I lost my grip and fell backward off the ladder.

Right before I could let out a yell, Arkimedes caught me on the rim of his face. I looked down to see Willy all wide-eyed. "Did you see that?!" I screeched.

All Willy could do was peer at me and nod. I gulped glad to still be alive.

Clearing my throat and grasping my bearings, Arkimedes slowly placed me back on the ladder. When our eyes met, I could feel the instant connection.

I reached the top and pressed my head to my new friend's fur thanking him for saving my life or at least from broken bones since I didn't die from the fall.

CHAPTER 15

Annalise

The moment I stepped foot inside, the voices started back up. This time they were telling me to grab both the book and wand then leave Tay and David behind.

A self-satisfied smile ran across my lips as I began to listen. Still, something inside me said that would be wrong and you know it.

The sitting room put off a darker vibe this time undoubtedly like someone had died or something. David walked over to pull back the curtain on the window that was covering the light. "Somebody has to liven this place up." he said aloud.

"Th-This place gives me the trembles. Can we get out of here?" David saw my body twitch as I spoke out with a little stutter. He snorted at my shivering sound. I rolled my eyes, spun on my heel toward Tay, and whipped my hair hoping to get enough momentum to smack him in the face. "Ow!" David groaned.

Yes! Direct hit! I was jumping up and down with laughter on the inside but on the outside, I just turned toward him and gave a huge toothy grin.

"You two stop messing around. I have the book and there's the exit. Let's go." Hearing Tay hiss at us, I could see she was just as ready to leave this world as I was. Turning my head back toward her, I gave her a thumbs up with a great big smile plastered on my lips.

I was so ready to get the stars out of there. It felt like I had aged more. I was really starting to hate this life-sucking world. "Come on, let's go!" I shouted aloud as I began to march up to the portal.

"Wait, Anna! We have to lock hands, or we might get separated into different worlds," Tay protested, grabbing my wrist, and yanking me a couple of steps back away from the inviting way out.

I huffed listening to her then I took both David and Tay's hands. Tay led the way through the passage. I was the last one to walk in, and behind me, it sounded like Fyra was trying to tell me something. Shrugging my shoulders thinking I was just hearing things I let my friends pull me into Egladon.

Everything around us was pitch black. I didn't care for this part of our journey. Clenching David's hand with all my might in fear of being split up, I started to hear screams of agony all around me.

A weird sound started to ring in my ears as if someone's teeth were chattering and the person was right beside me. My body jerked hard, and I couldn't hold my composure any longer. I let out a hella-cious shriek causing David to almost let go of our locked palms. "No!..." I cried. A shiver ran up my back when I heard its deep cackle, and my insides froze like solid ice the moment I felt the sting of its hot breath against my face. The shock of horror brought water to my eyes.

Just at the point of losing my marbles, we had come to an exit. "Finally, there was a trace of light!" I shouted so thankful to be out in the open somewhere.

Tay turned around and peered her eyes into mine, mouth dropped, and shaking her head slowly, the poor thing was speechless. "What's wro?"- My query to Tay got cut off by a woman's loud shrill. All three of us shook with terror. I looked at Tailya and she was trying her best to answer me. "I-I think we've been here before, r-remem-ber?" She replied wide-eyed frantically moving her head up and down, still not being able to speak clearly. Her words were all jumbled and hard to understand.

Looking up I notice the sky was dark red with traces of smoke embedded through. I gulped. "Go back!" I screeched knowing now where we were. The instant we had all turned on our heels, I saw that the portal had sealed itself shut. Panic consumed my whole body as I had come to the realization that the only way out of here was to travel through this nightmare and find another gateway.

"What's the big deal, you two?" David was trying to be all non-chalant about the whole thing even though Tay and I both heard him gasp loudly, twice. "Oh, stop pretending like you're the macho man and nothing can scare you." I hissed; hands planted on my hips.

Our tiff was cut short the moment we heard someone yelling for help down below us. "Tay, did you hear that?" David's yeep was even more girly than my own and I couldn't hold back a laugh. My friend just shook his head while following along with a glare to shut my trap. I covered up another giggle.

Tailya marched up to us with a finger pressed to her lips. Her eyes were creased as well. She looked worried and I already knew the reason why.

This place was not to be taken lightly. There was burning hot lava everywhere below with flames shooting out into the air. People were crying out and pleading for us to help them. We couldn't even if we wanted to. They were all in a lake of fire and brimstone. There was no way to get to any of them.

My eyes began to water, and it was taking all of my self-will to stay sane in here. I wondered how Tay and David were holding up. Every time I glanced up, they were looking all around for a way out.

It was a little unnerving that they seemed calm and not as frantic as me. I shrugged my shoulders at the thought.

"Hey, can you help me?" A little girl's voice chimed in my ears softly almost like a whisper. I lifted my head to get a look at her but there was no one there. I was still walking behind David with our hands locked as Tay led the way.

" Hey David, did you hear that little girl?" I jerked my friend backward causing poor Tay to stumble. "Anna, what's with you?!" Tay shouted. Huffing and puffing, she stomped her way right up to my face. Nose to nose she began to give me the third degree.

"Honestly Annalise,-" Uh oh, my full name, the girl is angry- "David and I are trying to get us out of here. Why in the stars are you stopping? And for what? A voice you just happened to hear. Don't you know where we are? I mean it seems like you are content. Maybe we should break our hold and David and I leave you here! Since you are so relaxed and all."

My poor friend, I knew she didn't mean it. I could see she was just as anxious to leave this world as me. I kept quiet and nodded waiting for her to finish and take a breath.

"Help me." I stared at Tay wide-eyed. "There it is again! Did you hear it?!" The voice was no longer faint. It was loud and clear like this little girl was speaking right into my ear.

Tay's brows lowered causing her forehead to crease. The look of distress was written all over her face. David just stared at me blankly. Neither one of them could hear the voice. David grasped my hand a little tighter. "Don't worry, Anna. We'll get you out of here." "I'm not crazy!" I protested. "I really do hear someone!" All three of us started walking again and I did my best to ignore all the voices ringing through my ears. So many please help me, whimpering, moans, and groans. I clenched my teeth together, breathed in deep, and tried my best not to listen but they were becoming more and more overbearing. "Ahh!" A terrifying scream from a woman penetrated my ear drums causing me to brake my hold and squeeze the life out of David. He grabbed my arms, pulling them away from his body to spin around and look at me. His brows raised as he began to search me over.

"Look!" Tay shouted from a distance. David dropped his gaze and shot up his head. He let loose of his grasp, gripped my right hand again, and almost yanked my arm out of its socket as he pulled me. "Anna, there it is! Let's go!" So, there it was. The escape we were all hoping for. It finally showed itself. Our one way ticket out of there just a few paces away. My two friends and I couldn't wait to leap through the gate.

As I laid my eyes on freedom, the temperature in my body started to rise. Little beads of sweat began to run down my forehead and into my eyebrows. I reached up to rub my lids and it felt like my skin was on fire.

"Hey. Tay, David, is it just me, or are you two drenched from head to toe like I am back here?" Tailya gave me a small shrug, but David decided to turn his head to see what my groaning was about.

"Geez, Anna!"

At a loss for words, the boy's grip over my clammy hand began to tighten. He continued to squeeze out of shock and my poor fingers were paying the price.

The prick of my pinkie nail wedging its way into the skin of my index finger forced out an uncontrollable squeal I was trying to keep hidden inside. I followed it with a pop of my left hand to the side of his head. Then, using the back of my palm I ran it across my hairline and eyebrows to keep the salty liquid from trickling down into my eyes.

"Leaping lizards, David! Loosen up a little, would you?" I watched my friend's forehead wrinkle as his stare grew cold. He slit his eyes my way.

I continued to watch the display from my action completely baffled as to why I still didn't feel even a lick of remorse.

David caught me raising both shoulders to my ears and sticking out my bottom lip. "What are you doing?" He asked eyebrows slanted down with his lips awkwardly pursed.

The boy probably thought my brain had gone to goo. Huh, so that was the reason for his kindness. The thought made me giggle under my breath. The smile left behind quickly faded when I felt the need to apologize but couldn't get the words to roll off my tongue.

David unwound his tight fingers and I could feel the cool air make its way through the separation of our palms.

"Wait! We can't let go, remember?" David's eyes widened as I locked my fingers onto his. I figured it was a better hold, easy to break again if I needed to.

Tay had the same thought apparently as her brother and I heard her yell, "Don't break the chain! We're almost there!" "No, we aren't!" I angrily shouted back. It seemed everything out of my mouth lately was nothing but spite.

Tay bounced me off like I was a piece of rubber in that rubber and glue witticism I used to hear from my brother Kedron when he was little. A small flutter tickled my heart at the thought.

Lowering my head, my stare left my friend. Thinking of how innocent he once was, I took a quick moment to myself.

"Why are you thinking of him when he's thinking of ways to end you the next time you meet? No, don't reflect on these empty meaningless memories. Focus on me. Listen to me. I'm going to make you powerful. You don't even need these two. Why are you still with them? Let go… Let go. Come child… join me down here. I'm at the bottom waiting for you. Together we can be unstoppable".

Each one of my fingers left their nooks from in between David's. I could feel my whole body react as I began to listen to the snake voice slithering through my mind.

Its constant hissing was clouding over any good notion I had and was trying to hold on to. David clenched down onto my palm staring at me with concern. I wanted to cry out for help, tell him he could break my hand if it meant not unsealing our bond, but my tongue froze, and I couldn't speak.

I felt like there were two of me. One wanted nothing more than to escape the awful world while the other me seemed a little too eager to relish and make this home.

My wicked grin alarmed Tay. She started to shout out something, but her voice was muffled from the thunderous flow of the lava. I tried my hardest to read her lips, but they were moving too fast.

It was as if some kind of strong force wanted to take over my body. I could feel my self-control slipping away. The strenuous wriggling of my hand caused David to grit his teeth. I could see the determination in his stare. He was not letting go. The guy must have been using all of his strength to hold on because there were little drops of sweat hitting the black rock beneath us.

"Annalise, please. Don't tell me you want to stay here." He pleaded. A part of me didn't. My friend's sad gaze didn't trigger anything in my heart. I had no feelings. I had become completely cold to him blankly transfixed over the lava pit.

Tailya huffed and puffed, marching herself right between her brother and me. "Anna, whatever you heard or think you heard, it's not real, okay. Don't give it one moment of your attention."

Her strong words would have been encouraging if I hadn't already fallen victim to whatever the hissing voice was coming from.

"It's too late sis. I think we've lost her," David said with no hope left in his tone.

"Yeah, Tay. The boy is right!" My sharp remark made David drop his head low to the ground. "Oh. You don't think I can do anything, huh? Well, I'll just have to use this!" Tailya pulled Fawn's wand from her back pocket. David shot his head up so fast that you could hardly see his hair move.

Both my friends' eyes were lit up with aspiration. Tay firmly gripped the magical stick and launched it into the air. She began to twirl her wrist and chant.

Whatever was trying to control me wasn't having it. All of a sudden, my right foot hoisted off the ground. My heel explosively connected to David's stomach causing him to fly back into his sister. My kick sent them straight toward the exit.

I stood there grunting like a zombie with no words listening to them scream and plead. "Annalise, no...!" That was the loudest I had ever heard David yell. "Annalise, Annalise, we'll come back for you. Just hold on!" Tay shouted right before they were sucked through the gate, leaving me all on my own.

I felt a jolt of energy go through me. My body shook and I fell back a pace or two. Nothing. I saw nothing and suddenly all of my emotions were present.

They became overwhelming. Every one of them was so intense I dropped to my knees and began rocking back and forth.

"Well done…, well done…. Welcome to Abaddon , little girl Mua ha ha ha, where you will never leave. Hahaha-muahahaha."

The evil impish gloat kept playing over and over in my head. I felt like I was starting to lose my mind.

"It's not real. It's not real," I said out loud, now sitting and hugging my knees to my chest. My eyes were sealed shut and I was still swaying back and forth.

"Oh, but it is real, little girl. Open your eyes and see. We are all real down here and we are waiting for you."

The devilish voice had me frozen solid like a glacier. I wasn't melting anytime soon. Everything went quiet for a moment, and I could focus on my thoughts. "Okay, Anna. Open your eyes. Think, how far away from the gate are you?"

I unclamped my lids only to find that the door had vanished. Streams of water were now leaving the corners of my eyes. There was no way out.

"He told you." The hissing started to slither through my head again, so I decided to answer it. Sniffling twice and rubbing my eyes, I struck up a conversation with this so-called snake.

"He, who is he?" Swiping my hand underneath my nose, I listened as the snake voice began to answer. "Why, the master of this world of course. Come on, he's down there ready to meet you." "I don't want to meet him." "Oh, but you do. Trust me."

Standing to my feet, still not able to see what was talking to me, I looked around. "I don't see anyone." "He's down there, you see." Frustration set in; I was now becoming annoyed with this invisible dark being. "Where?! There's nothing but hot lava down below."

The voice laughed and it felt like something was tickling the inside of my ears. Out of nowhere, my feet started stepping toward the edge. I was now looking over the cliff. I had listened too long and was now losing control of my body again.

"Go ahead. He's waiting." I could feel the compulsion taking over as my eyes closed. Both of my feet moved in unison causing me to free fall into the pit of fire and brimstone.

CHAPTER 16

Brighton

Willy rushed up to the ladder. "Brighton, man, are you okay? Want me to take over? Do you need to rest?"

I couldn't help but chuckle a little from his vigorous amount of questions. "Yes, Saints, Willy, I'm alright. Arkimedes saved me, you see." I turned back to my new loyal beast and thanked him again.

After I had finished grooming, I made my way down the ladder. I noticed on the last step that Arkimedes' legs were chained. "Hey, Willy. What's the deal with these chains? How come no other pegasi we've seen were in shackles? Why is my Arkimedes the only one?"

At this point I was testy, and, in my frustration, I snapped out my last question. Poor Willy stepped back from me. "Woah, calm down there Arkimedes." I shook my head hard. "Arkimedes? Huh? No, Willy, I'm Brighton. Are you feeling, alright?"

My frail friend took a seat on a chest underneath the ladder while reaching in his pocket to grab a couple of puffs from his breathing mechanism. I thought to myself " Yea my friend it looks like you need that" as I watched his chest puff out. Turning my nose up to look at Arkimedes, he twisted his head from me, giving out a snort blow.

It's the sound Nicodemus would make when he got frustrated or bored. As I kept listening, I was starting to get the feeling Arkimedes wasn't bored.

Walking toward Willy, I tapped him on the shoulder. "Breathe, buddy. Are you calmed now so we can talk?" He slowly stood to his feet and lifted his view to my pegasus who still had his head pointed away from us, but Willy still decided to address Arkimedes

"Now that you've relaxed a bit, I'll inform you about the chains." He said shaking his finger. Arkimedes' ears moved in Willy's direction. Both I and my beast were eagerly waiting for his answer. Suddenly I felt a wave of electricity jolt through me as I heard " I'm waiting".

Tilting my head, I raised my index finger toward my right ear and poked the ear hole. I shook it up and down thinking to myself, "Pshh, that's impossible." Just then Arkimedes turned and looked down straight into my eyes.

The saliva in my mouth began to dry as I took a hard swallow. Bumps were forming on both my arms causing the hair to stand. Looking at my new found friend, I thought to myself, or at least I thought I had been talking to myself in my head, but it turned out I had spoke out loud, "This is real." My pegasus closed his eyes and nodded. Staring at Willy with no emotion, completely astounded, I felt my chin drop to the floor.

He chortled. "Guess you've figured out that you two are more than just connected with your minds." I blinked rapidly with my mouth still gaped open.

Arkimedes neighed and it made Willy smile. He cleared his throat. "Now as I was saying. All of the pegasi are secured in their stalls until they have a master. It's nothing personal my friend."

Arkimedes blew through his nose again, this time without aggravation and I could sense his understanding of Willy's words.

"Now that that's all out, let's get these shackles off," I said, bending one knee to the floor. "You need the key to unlock those. I'll be right back." Willy said as he left in a hurry. Stroking Arkimedes' legs, I noticed Willy's inhaler on the chest. It must have fallen out of his pocket before he rushed out.

"Surely, he'll be fine for a few minutes without it," I thought, scratching my head. I didn't want my worrying to make me anxious since Arkimedes and I were linked. So, I decided to sing in order to subside my thoughts. It always seemed to do the trick.

"Da da da- God is my strength and power and He makes my way perfect. He makes my feet like the feet of deer and sets me on high places. He teaches-" "You have a beautiful voice, sir," she said standing over me batting those smoky dark brown eyes of hers.

"My lady," I choked out, knowing my face was probably about as red as a cherry tomato.

"Thank- huh ehm," I cleared my throat to get rid of the girly squeak trying to come out. Once again, speechless by this beauty, all I could do to greet her was display a giant toothy grin.

She giggled at my loss for words. I bet to her I looked like some kind of prat knelt there on the floor. Arkimedes blew through his nose, and I just knew he was laughing at me.

"Come on. Get it together, Brighton," I said to myself while watching this fair lady take a trip around Arkimedes. She looked to be fascinated by every one of his features.

The beauty started to speak again, and it was like beautiful strings of music through my ears. "I promise what they say about me is untrue." Huh, I wasn't even thinking about that riffraff the guys were pouring out to me. "Please, keep singing. Don't stop on my behalf."

My angel made her way back around to me, still speechless but now locking eyes, I asked myself, "How could someone with so much grace and poise be called mad?"

"I'm back. Ready to get these chains off Arkimedes?" Willy asked entering the stall and not a moment too soon. I stood to my feet, dusting off my knee.

Puffing out my chest, I bowed to the angel in front of me. "Lady Milaya." It was like Willy being back pulled out the man in me and I had something to prove.

She stuck out her hand and my lips went down to it like some kind of magnetized force was trying to suck them in. Quickly I lifted my hand to greet hers. She sighed under her breath and Willy chuckled. I turned and gave him a solid glare. It didn't faze him any though, he still grinned while coughing out laughs.

I turned back and Lady Milaya was staring intently into my eyes. I wondered what this stunning young maiden could be thinking. Standing there rocking back and forth on my heels, hands in my pockets, she broke the silence.

"Sir, would you please join me on the hilltop this evening? Say about half-past sundown?"

Arkimedes whined and pranced as I blurted out, "Yes!" I gave my new friend a side glare along with a scowl. He blew out from his nostrils, pleased with himself.

My poor maiden fell back a couple of steps from my overbearing assent. The uncontrollable bobbing of my head eased her tension. She smiled once more and said, "Seven on the chime, don't be late." Then she left and I watched her raise a hand to cover her shy giggle. My heart started beating remarkably fast, a feeling I could undoubtedly get used to.

"Uh, Brighton?... Come in, Brighton!" Willy was waving his hands in my face trying to get my attention, pulling me out of my love stupor. I sighed like a girl with a crush as he said, "Arkimedes is waiting. Come on."

Wily had brought back two keys with him. He gave me one and made his way to the back of Arkimedes' legs, leaving me to unshackle his front.

Just about to place the key into the second lock, when Willy and I hear someone yell, "Hey, help!" Hurriedly I undo Arkimedes' last chain and tell him to be good before racing with Willy out of the stalls.

My friend's head frantically twisted side to side, looking for the one who was in distress. "Heeelp!" I looked at Willy. "The shout came from over there." I shouted anxiously as I pointed my finger in the direction of the sea.

"Somebody! Anybody! Can anyone hear me?!"

This time Willy and I recognized the soldier's voice right away. Our muscles tensed as we turned and peered at one another. Then we croaked, "Mason."

Swiftly our feet took to the ground as we shouted for all the men working to come follow. All but one came racing down toward us. The last one moseyed his way out of the stalls yelling, "What's the big idea?" One of the men standing beside me stuck his arm around my shoulder. "Aaa, don't worry about Rufus. He's always a grouch. I'm Fryer, Fryer Greasebucket." "Eh, nice to meet you," I said looking at him strangely while sticking my hand out. His enthusiasm made me feel like I was about to lose one of my arms.

"Hey!" This time we all heard Mason yell. "It's coming from down there!" Willy shouted while pointing. We all dashed toward the shoreline to meet up with our terrified brother.

When we got there, the soldier's face was drenched in sweat, and he was hovering over a fisherman's half corpse. "Woah, what's that smell?" One of the men asked while using his two fingers to pinch his nose shut.

"Man, that's ripe," another soldier uttered. All at once, it became too loud for Willy or me to think, or even speak over. Every soldier gathered around Mason asking him what sounded like a million questions.

Finally, he left his shell of shock, turned to us, and noticed that Willy and I were patiently waiting to hear his tale of horror.

Even though I was curious to find out what all of the commotion was about, I couldn't help but think about how long this was going to take and if it would run into my time meeting up with Milaya.

My nerves started to tighten at the thought of not being able to see her. Climbing my way up to a tall rock, I stood over all the men awaiting to hear Mason's story.

I could sense Mason's tragedy was going to take longer than I wanted. So, I raised my voice to get their attention. Clearing my throat, I asked, "Who here is a knight?" All but ten raised their palms high in the air.

Relief washed over me. There were only about thirty men, not including Mason, the corpse, Willy, and me, on the shore. So, twenty leaving was already making it more bearable for my next question.

Eyeing all of the knights, I asked, "Do you think Lord Patroklos would be beside himself if he knew you all left in the middle of training?" One of the knights turned to the others and said, "The lad's right men. We'd best get back." Turning back to me, he shouted, "Let us know if you all need anything, lad." Then, he and the others marched off.

I waved farewell and stared down at the remaining soldiers, raising a brow. "Any of you finished unchaining and grooming your pegasi?"

The men chattered amongst themselves, uttering words under their breath as they rose up their fists, shouting, "Nae!" They treaded off muttering. I smirked, thinking to myself, "Don't worry, fellas. I am sure Mason will tell you all about it later."

Pleased with my cunning self, I rubbed my palms together. My fellow brothers were disappointed, but I didn't care. The only thing on my mind was helping my friend and meeting up with my dream girl. "The one that stills the very words from my lips", I thought while lifting my eyes toward the sky.

After watching all of the men leave, Mason worked on catching his breath and recapturing in his mind everything that had happened. Willy and I waited in silence. We watched as Mason took one last look at his charge before he wrapped his headless body.

The man controlled the salty droplets trying to form by spitting and wiping his eyes. Turning toward us, he asked, "Are you two ready to hear about the beast that roams these waters?" We nodded. Alright then, come and help me load him into the boat."

Willy and I walked over to our friend. Helping him, all three of us placed the fisherman onto the boat, pushing the poor guy out to the sea to rest in peace.

"Courage man, you did your best. I'm sure of it," I said while gripping Mason's shoulder. "Yeah, Mason. What he said," Willy agreed.

Our friends voice shook when he thanked us. We sat down under the crag, wide-eyed in suspense, waiting for Mason to collect his thoughts and stop shuddering so we could understand him.

The poor guy took a deep breath and made his way over to us. He just sat down when Willy blurted, "Well, go on Mason." Our brother grimaced. I knew I was eager to get to Milaya, but Willy was just a little too impatient about the whole situation.

Mason finally spoke. "Mates, do I have a gruesome story for you." I squeezed the sand between my fingers in anticipation and listened for him to continue.

He cleared his throat a few times then went on. "Drake and I were sailing, that's his name, Drake." I watched him focus on twiddling his thumbs around one another trying not to get choked up. Willy and I nodded in unison when he looked up at us and started again.

"Drake and I were sailing toward the middle of the sea, even though we knew it was dangerous. But the reason why was because we couldn't seem to catch anything here by the shoreline."- He ran a hand under his nose.- "When we stopped at what looked to be a good spot, Drake told me to drop the anchor while he cast his net out the other side. We felt the boat start to sway. Excited that the mesh might be full, Drake hollered for me to help pull it in."

CHAPTER 17

Brighton

I looked at Willy and we locked eyes like we could read what the other was thinking. Both of us were wide-eyed and turned our attention back to our friend who was wiping his nose again, only now with his shirt, while still telling us the story.

"After reeling in the fish, we began to reach down and pull up the anchor, until our eyes saw a smokey shadow under the water. It was coming straight towards us."

He took a deep swallow, causing Willy and I to do the same. "My charge said it was just a shark and not to worry. He continued grabbing the rope and winding up to sail, but the grey under the water began to turn darker and grow bigger, still not surfacing for us to see a fin. Drake almost completed reeling and was just about to pull in the anchor when I noticed the shadow was now swarming around the entire boat. The grey shadow had turned jet black. For the first time, mates, I was afraid."

I heard a noise in my left ear. Turning to look at Willy, I saw my friend's fear-stricken body was frozen, his teeth were chattering, and his fingers dug into the sand for dear life.

Nudging him with my elbow, I whispered, "Saints, man, get control of your teeth. Mason's terrified enough as it is. You're making me have stirrings myself."

I huffed the last part but lowered my voice so Mason wouldn't hear. Refocusing my attention back on the poor guy, I noticed he never stopped talking.

"Drake and I were ready with the oars about to head back when a dark grey cloud appeared above our heads. You guys, I'm telling ya I heard that cloud chuckle! The vessel started to sway again, only this time we were certain it was going to tip. The shadow figure turned black above us and was covering the light from the sun. It was as if day turned into night in an instant."

Mason's story was starting to sound more and more like what I had read in my grandfather's journal back home, and I started to have the feeling that this was the exact same creature he had warned about in his story all those years ago.

"Ouch!" Willy bit his tongue. Turning to check on him, I saw that the guy's eyes were watering. "He must have taken a good chunk of it out," I thought.

Mason stood up tall, shoulders squared, and fists clenched tight as he continued. "The dark shadow around us went under the boat. We thought maybe it left and it was time to take a sigh of relief, but instead we choked on our breathing when that thing savagely shot straight up into the sky, causing water to spill over and fill up the boat."

Mason's eyes widened like he'd seen a ghost. "Brighton, Willy, this creature was taller than any castle I'd ever laid eyes on, and it was staring at me. Two black holes for eyes piercing through the pupils of my orbs. I thought I was a goner at that moment, mates. I promise ya that beast smirked at me right before it hovered over Drake. My knees were shaking, and I lost control of some of my bodily functions." "Wait, huh?" Willy blurted, cutting Mason off confused about what he was implying.

"He let it go, Willy." I informed. Poor guy still wasn't getting it. "Saints man!" He peed himself", I popped my clueless friend on his knee, looking down at the sand shaking my head. "Oh…," he said sheepishly.

Willy squirmed in his spot on the rock. "Sorry, Mason. Please go on."

"Where was I? Oh, right. Mates, its body hovered straight over Drake. I watched as the beast's ginormous mouth open. All you could see were teeth shaped like needles. I turned to look at Drake and the guy was blubbering, knowing that it would be the last day he'd ever see his family and in an instant, the sea creature's mouth dropped down over Drake's whole body devouring his very existence.

There was nothing I could have done. Mates, I couldn't even scream. Then, the vicious beast spoke to me." "It spoke to you?!" I shouted, now wondering what in the stars was behind this thing. "Yes, mate. It could talk. Drake's blood was dripping from the sharp pointy edges of its teeth, and I knew I saw some pieces of Drake's skin dangling from its slit nostrils. In a flash, it swallowed him up and I knew I was next. I began sweating profusely. I wasn't ready for my demise. Not until I have lived a little, maybe even settled down with a nice sheila, you know?" he protested. Willy and I watched him thrust both his fists in the air. "Guys, the serpent-looking monster dropped to my eye level. The air left my lungs and I felt like someone gut punched me. Then, right as I lay fixed on its pit of despair, soul-sucking eyes, it felt like they put me in a trance. Mates, Mates! I swear it smiled at me just before spitting out Drake's body. A squeal came out of me when I saw that his head had been the only thing eaten. Then it said with its hot reeking sardine breath, "Not to worry, Mason. I am not here for you, though I do have to admit your friend sure was delicious. For an afternoon snack anyway. Now go and be sure to tell all that these waters are mine." Mates, the length on this beast, and all those teeth, and, and-"

Our poor friend had finally told us his whole story. I was afraid but not nearly as terror-stricken as Willy. He was hugging his knees to his chest and the poor guy's teeth were chattering uncontrollably again. Mason just sat there staring ahead. Disappointment started to set in because of an affliction. I might not be able to see my lady. I knew that if Mason were to go off and tell the other men about what he had seen, the people of Egladon would go awry.

"Mason, Willy, I think we should keep this under wraps right now. If you go and tell others, I'm afraid the soldiers would gather together, go out to seek this sea serpent, and end up losing their lives. Then there would be more casualties and we don't want that, right?"

Both gawked at me confused about my reasoning. Willy scratched his head. "Yeah, but there'd be more deaths if we don't say anything."

"Yeah," Mason agreed. "More fishermen will go out to cast nets and get eaten if we stay silent."

I could hear the disgruntlement in Mason's voice and also noticed the confusion written all over Willy's face. "Brighton, mate, don't you think we should be gathering up our men to hunt this thing instead of hiding it?" Mason asked, glaring my way. "Yeah, brother. Why in the name of sea turtles would you want to keep this quiet?!" Willy shouted with crossed arms and now scowling at me.

I sighed. Neither one was trying to understand where I was coming from with this. It was like listening to a broken record with these two. They just kept repeating the same thing over and over.

Twiddling my thumbs, I decided to come clean about why I was wanting to keep it hidden. "I have a date with Lady Milaya."

My friends leaned closer toward me, squinting their eyes and moving their ears right up to my speaking zone.

"We can't understand your mumbling, mate," Mason said with his ear almost pressed right against my mouth.

Shoving him back, I shouted exasperatedly, "I have a date with Milaya, and I like her! Okay?"

Both Willy and Mason were dumbfounded. I leaned back waiting for one of them to say something. Willy spoke his peace first.

Guffawing, he said, "You mean to tell me, we're keeping this from our men all so you can make googly eyes with the crazy girl everyone here warned you to stay away from! That is the most hair-brained nonsense I've ever heard!"

My frail friend was so upset he had to take two puffs from his inhaler.

Mason stood up to drop in his two cents. "I have to say, mate, I agree with Willy." "Ugh, fine! At least give me until this evening before you both say we're under attack, can you?"

Staring both my friends down hoping they would grant me some bit of sympathy, I thought about what I was going to bring with me to our outing.

No compassion.

I thought at least Willy would cave in, but not even a "sure buddy" came from him. Neither of them cared about my meet-up with the lady of my dreams.

Standing up, I raised my chin high toward the sky and turned on my heel to march away from the two non-empathetic men I called friends.

"Go ahead and tell. I am going to get my evening with my maiden. I don't care," I mumbled to myself while climbing up the hill, listening to their guffaws in the background.

I had lost all essence of time, arguing my case with those two. When I reach the top of the hill, I was afraid she wouldn't be there, I'd have been too late, and I knew I would have missed my chance.

"Come on Brighton. Almost there. Just a little bit further," I said with clenched jaws, trying to encourage myself and take my mind off the fact of how bad my calves were burning from the hike.

Finally, I took my last step with my legs feeling numb like that jiggly stuff my brother and sister loved to eat. Suddenly, the taste of strawberries and oranges danced upon my tongue. I missed them greatly.

Shaking away that emotion, I came to see that I was not too late. I was right on time as I watched my lady love. She was lifting a cloth in the air to place neatly on the grass for us to sit on.

Walking toward her, swept completely away by her beauty, I watched, mesmerized by her every feature as she carefully pulled out each dish from a brown wicker basket.

She looked up and we locked eyes. The organ in my chest palpated so fast that I began to sweat under my arms and on my palms. My heart was beating so fast now that it sounded like there was a drum set playing in my ears.

Lady Milaya giggled, batting her eyes. She spoke in a gentle voice. "Well, are you going to join me?" Digging my heels firmly toward the ground, I squared my shoulders to keep my knees from knocking into each other. Then, I cleared my throat so a squeak wouldn't be able to force its way out.

"I probably looked like a ninny, but it was better than sounding like a sissy," I thought, trying to not give off an awkward smile. My heart continued to race as my eyes swept over her. My angel was perfect in every way. She had pink cheeks, a little nose, silky brown locks, and a petite stature. I could pick her up with one arm, no problem.

I nodded on the outside listening to my prideful thoughts. Milaya smirked then covered her mouth to hide another giggle. Pretty sure I had —"Warning, boy who has no clue how to talk to a girl is about to sit down"- planted across my forehead, or at least that's what it felt like when she looked up to smile at me.

Those big brown eyes with a hint of gold specks peered up at me and I kept swallowing hard like there was a lump stuck in my airway.

Milaya shifted over to the left side, patting the open space for me to join her. She offered again. "Sir, won't you please join me?"

Her beautiful smile could light up a whole banquet. It certainly took my breath away. I grinned big and nodded to the conversation in my mind.

My lady stared and I could see I had made her uneasy. Kneeling down, one bent knee after the other, I softly smiled, hoping it would ease her thoughts a little.

"Brighton."

Milaya tried to hide her bashful rosy cheeks from me. Guess I made her shy when saying my name to fully introduce myself.

Her ear-to-ear smile caused me to encounter some stirrings I wasn't quite familiar with. I lost myself in gazing into those enchanted twinkling eyes. A sigh left my lungs as I stared at her thinking I could stay right here in this moment for the rest of my days.

(Milaya)

______"He speaks! Calm down. Calm down. Okay, so yes, he's per-fect and yes, I can see myself getting lost in his...

"Ugh, those sweep me off my feet, I'll give you the moon, riveting green eyes." I got lost in thought, whining to myself as I bit my lower lip. "Milaya! Wake up, you don't even know him!"

My inner shout caused my eyes to blink, breaking away our deep gaze. He suddenly became nervous, grabbed my hand, and searched me over.

Timidly, I pulled my palm away from his with a faint smile forced upon my lips. "Brighton." "Say it again," he pleaded, touching every piece of my heart with his request.

"Sir Brighton, honestly I didn't mean to startle you, it's just that, well,"-

Oh just spit it out, Milaya!- I screamed on the inside.

"Sometimes I talk to myself and answer the questions and opinions in my head."

The words rolled off my tongue faster than I could control, leaving me panting like a hot and thirsty animal. "Is that all?" the soldier asked, his broad chest rising high and low.

I couldn't pull my view away. Watching his shirt tighten and then loosen over and over again, I had become like a statue, never moving from my post.

My soon-to-be knight chuckled. "Uh, hello? Lady Milaya? Up here."

"Huh? Oh, sorry. What were you saying?"

Pulled out of my blissful daze, I met his gleaming viridescent eyes.

His coy smile sent tingles through my whole body, melting me like wax falling from a burning candle. I couldn't seem to find any flaws in him whatsoever. Contentedly, I giggled, staring away into those emerald breath takers.

Breaking the silence between us, he said, "I don't think this food is going to eat itself, but I am willing to let it go to waste if you will allow me the pleasure to sit here and stare at you all night."

He fluttered his lids, mocking me. Both of us bellied over laughing hysterically.

CHAPTER 18

Annalise

The steam from the scorching obsidian came up to meet my fall. I could feel my body burning and it felt like pieces of my flesh were starting to ooze off.

I dared not to open my eyes for fear of my thoughts turning into reality. They seemed to be my own at this moment. So, in meeting my demise I decided to think about as many positive memories I could recall.

Images of Brighton sneaking me some of the cook's pastries before bedtime, Kedron's rosy cheeks and bright twinkling eyes when he learned a new magic trick, watching my father, King Cyrus play his pianoforte while I sang along with him to the melody, Queen Cheylenna and I eating our delectables in silence, and my animals.

My heart pinched when my last reminiscence was how Sampson, Ghost, and Fyra were doing. I hoped Brighton would rescue Sampson from home now that I wasn't able to go back myself to get him. I wouldn't be able to save my mother and my little brother. I took one last deep inhale before turning into flames. The air in my lungs was forced out by a hard thud. "Am I dead?" I wondered, still not wanting to unclench my eyes.

"It's alright now Annalise. You can open your eyes. I've got you." The voice was encouraging and sounded very familiar. "F-Fyra." I coughed out, still trying to take in enough air to catch my breath.

"No! Get back here!" The vicious roar pierced straight through me. My whole body went into shock as I clung tightly to my rescuer's feathers.

I could feel the air getting cooler on my face, so I forced my eyes open to look around. She had flown me up into the red sky. The clouds smelled like burnt flesh. Now I knew these weren't just any ordinary clouds. They were the vapor of lost souls. I shivered at the thought. I almost became Abaddon's next victim.

"Yes, there it is." Fyra's voice rang through all of the commotion in my head. Grateful to hear her speak and get rid of the what ifs playing over and over in my mind, my nerves calmed, and I was able to converse telepathically with her.

"Fyra, I'm scared. How are we going to get out of here?" "Look. Just ahead, there's the gate. It keeps disappearing and reappearing. I think your friend is having trouble keeping it open with that wand."

Her wings picked up speed when the portal showed itself straight ahead of us. "Annalise, when we get close you must jump into the shimmery light."

I buried my face deep into her frill. "But what about you? Fyra, I want you to come with me." I felt her feathers puff out underneath my legs. "We're almost there. Okay, ready Annalise?" She wasn't answering me, and I knew it was because she wanted me to keep focused. But I cried out anyway while squeezing her neck, "No! I'm not going without you." My beautiful bird started to ruffling her feathers, shaking me off as she shouted in my head, "Go, Annalise. I'll be right behind you. Now, jump!"

I hoisted myself into the exit, seeing Tailya's face dripping with sweat on the other side. I turned to greet my phoenix, but she was nowhere to be found. "Fyra! Fyra!" I cried, trying to force my feet forward against the pull of the portal. Tears welled up in my eyes when I perceived Fyra wasn't coming with me.

The exit closed up and I made my way to the other side to meet Tailya and David. Harshly moving my left knuckle across my cheeks to wipe off the unwanted tears, I allowed the guilt to eat me up inside.

Anger was turning into rage. This was starting to become habitual anytime something bad happened. "Geez, Annalise. We thought we'd never see you again," David said, pulling me toward him. I was so caught up in my fury that my arms wouldn't lift to accept his kindness. I just stood there like a bean pole.

He moved his arms and grabbed my face with both hands. "Anna, are you alright? Anna, speak to me Anna!" Tailya rushed up to my side. "Anna, can you hear us? Make some kind of sound."

Their worrying struck up a temper out of me. "Let go!" I yelled, grasping David's hands to throw off my face. "No! I'm not! Would you be alright if you just lost someone that sacrificed themselves for you?! I can't, I-I" There were no words to describe to my friends what I was going through. All I could do was drop to my knees and wail.

I cried for Fyra, I cried for my Queen, for Kedron, self-pity and for my poor father who was wasting away in the dungeon.

Tailya and David knelt down covering me on both sides with their bodies as they wrapped their arms around me and squeezed tight. "Don't cry, Anna," Tay said, lifting her other hand that was holding Fawn's wand. "Look, we can change the future." I lifted my eyes and there was a mirror image hovering in front of me.

On the inside, I looked to be a mother and wife. My right hand was being held by a little boy with blonde hair and in my left was a tall, brown-skinned man with broad stocky shoulders and dark brown hair.

I stopped weeping and Tay reassured my vision. "See, Anna. We can change it with this!" She thrust the magical stick in the air with determination. Her last word was full of zeal, and I started to let myself hope for what I had just saw.

David unwrapped his arm, brows furrowed, and lips pursed, looking like his sister when she was mad. I offended him. "What's wrong?" Tay asked him, wondering why he suddenly let go of our group hug. He huffed and then answered with a groan. "I don't have dark hair."

Tay's eyes met mine, forcing a grin across both our mouths. We bellied over on the ground not able to control our laughter. David started brooding, kicked a rock, and said, "Geez, what's so funny?"

We both gathered ourselves, saying in unison, "Nothing. Nothing." Then Tay and I pulled our lips tight to silence our giggles. It sounded like we were coughing with closed mouths for a while until the bubbles in our bellies finally subsided.

"Are you two finished?" David huffed, still expressing annoyance that he was not the one beside me in the future.

Letting both my friends pull me to my feet, I snatched Fawn's wand out of Tailya's hand. "Be careful with that, Anna," she hissed, crossing her arms, and glared at me.

When the enchanted rod touched my hand it instantaneously gleamed white. My closed palm was also lighting up and then I watched the beautiful beam turn into a deep dark red.

"Go on, take it. It's yours, girl. Remember, we can do great things together with this. Don't forget the book in her back pocket, we're going to need that too." I watched as my other hand started to move around my friend's back against my will. I felt like the voice had some kind of hold over me again. And the stick I was holding had now turned a deep burgundy, looking like the sky in Abaddon.

The hissing voice was getting louder, almost to where it was the only thing I could concentrate on. "Grab it," it said in a whisper. The book's glowing image was starting to implant itself in my eyes as I continued to listen and reach for it. "Almost there." I hesitated and it no longer hissed but roared through my head. "Grab it!"

"Annalise, stop!" Tay's shriek silenced the trance that had a hold of me. I blinked my eyes to find David with his hand fastened on mine and Tay opening up my fingers on the other to take back the danger-ous staff.

"Sis, I think it's unwise to keep these two materials with us." David addressed Tay without breaking his focus on me.

"Nonsense. We need them if we are to get to Egladon." She re-sponded.

Tailya was right. After all, what I had just gone through in the tor-tured world, the gateway disappearing and reappearing, it had become known to me that we were going to have to rely on the magic from the book and the wand.

"Here, Anna. I'll carry this burden, so you won't become tempted," Tay said, unlocking all of my fingers and removing the enchanted bar from my grasp. What felt like a ton of bricks weighing on my chest in-stantly lifted allowing me to breathe in a deep amount of fresh air again.

Snapping her fingers, she said, "Apotamievo." Just like that, the rod faded into thin air and was put away.

Returning my mind to the present, I took a glance around at the new world. My breath was stolen. Bright golden ancient-looking trees surrounded us. "Where are we, you guys?" I asked, spinning in circles completely captivated by the scene of this evergreen forest.

"I don't know. It's not like I've been here before," Tay said, follow-ing my excitement now twirling herself along beside me.

"Come on." David clasped his long fingers over my wrist and started to pull me. "Yeah, let's check it out, Anna." Tay agreed along with Da-vid, locking hold of my other wrist.

Their enthusiasm was starting to make me feel like a rag doll being lugged around by a toddler. I made my body become dead weight, so they'd stop dragging me. "You guys!" I shouted, yanking myself free from their strongholds.

"I'm just as astonished as you two but seriously I can walk all by myself, okay?" Eyes lit and wide smiles planted on their faces told me they weren't rattled so I grinned back and motioned my hand to move forward.

Up ahead was an opening that would lead us out of the holt. Walking past the last two golden-leafed trees, we stepped right into a dreamy landscape with a huge body of blush green water, surrounded by evergreen mountains, ancient grey stone rocks, and tall shrubs that put off pleasant scents of vanilla, faint lilac, and soft almond through the air.

All three of us stood there in awe, watching the light pink buds from the tree float above our heads and softly hit the ground. In this world, they seemed to have only one bright sun. There were radiant colors of lemon, violet, blush, and orangish red hues occupying the shimmery light blue sky.

My poor neck started to develop a dull cramp as I continued staring up at it. I lifted my hand to give it a rub but still wouldn't peel my eyes away. I was lost in its mystery.

We traveled the grounds taking in every piece of the colorful setting. Our journey came to a standstill when we noticed in the distance, a massive cement wall stood guarding what looked to be a village. My thought was it must have been built to keep out intruders which regrettably was who we were.

"You guys, I don't know what galaxy we're in but it's eye-dazzling here." Just as the words left my lips an ear-splitting rumble resounded above us.

CHAPTER 19

Annalise

Teeth chattering, all three of us lifted our heads as slow as a snail. David strongly gripped my fingers and Tay on the other side of me grabbed hold of my shirt accidentally pinching my skin. "Stars, Tailya!" The penetrating sting of her fingernails caused me to yelp and attract the creature's attention.

The quake in the sky caused Tailya, David, and I to tremble and swallow hard, knowing we were about to be this thing's breakfast, lunch, and dinner.

Hastily it skyrocketed down in a circular motion toward us like a vulture waiting for its prey to take its last breath before ripping it to shreds with its claws.

We stood there stupefied. Our feet wouldn't let us move. I shut out the terror, clenching my eyes as tight as I could.

The earth shook beneath us when it landed, causing my legs to wobble off balance. I could feel its stare piercing through me, and I was wondering if the beast had already ingested Tay and David.

My eyes started to water at the thought, but I was too terrified to even look.

" Hey, you there. Hey, the girl with her eyes clamped." Oh no. It's talking to me. "Don't open, don't open", I winced inside. "It ate them, and now it wanted to see what I would taste like.

"I'm bitter, I tell you, bitter!" I shouted in my head. Tay giggled and I relaxed feeling relieved that she hadn't been devoured.

Lifting my lids, Tailya was holding the wand and pointing it toward my temple. "Don't worry, Anna. The dragon's not going to eat us." "Dragon?" "Yeah, it's a real dragon!" David blurted. I turned back to Tay. "How did you know what I was thinking?" She smirked while wriggling Fawn's magical rod up and down between her fingers.

I was confused with David and Tay's excitement about the winged beast, seeing as it was now nowhere to be found. "What dragon? I don't see anything except you two." I attested, crossing both of my arms.

"If you're ready, I'll show you," Tay replied with a cautious sigh. I turned to David and the boy was just smiling away like he didn't have a care in the world. That or he was daydreaming.

"Hey, David. Snap out of it." I waved my hands from side to side in front of his face trying to wake him up and get him back to reality.

Looking at Tailya, I bobbed my head, ready to see the dragon. "Okay. I warn you he's very huge. So don't scream, Anna." She heeded while swirling the enchanted stick a few times and shouted "Vgaino!"

I addressed my focus to where the rod was pointing. A silhouette of what looked like bright rubies were appearing before me and then at one fell swoop, its whole body was visible.

I gasped but quickly eased when the mysterious creature greeted me.

"Pleasure to meet your acquaintance, girl." No words. I was standing there overlooking this magnificent being while my two friends gawked at me.

"You can close your mouth now, Anna," Tay said as she walked over to the beast. "See, it's quite friendly," she said, placing her hands on the creature's scales.

The rays from the sun in the sky split open the clouds and I could see all of its body clearly now. The dragon's underneath radiated a metallic yellow bringing back to mind those beautiful ancient trees we passed on the way.

I continued to stare as its upper body seeped into my eyes glittering blue with pink frosted colored wings that shone into my very soul as the sun beamed down on it. The astonishing beast was more than magnificent. It was dream-catching.

My mouth still wide open in wonder, I had to blink my eyes three times to make sure I was really there. That I wasn't still being tortured in Abaddon and that all of this was not just a self-conscious illusion playing in my mind.

The dragon chortled, and bits of smoke clouds hovered above my head.

"You mustn't be afraid of me. I am the guardian of this place. My title here is Yinglong."

I laughed out loud at its name. "Why in all the turtles do they call you- uh what was it again?" I asked, still giggling.

"Yinglong. It means winged dragon. I am the only one they have encountered with flying ability." "Oh…," I said, moving my head slowly up and down along with a dropped jaw. Another giggle popped out when I turned and saw David mimicking me.

David walked over to Yinglong, smacking him on his scales like he was some kind of human being able to understand his gesture. "So, uh Yinglong, what do you call this world?" "World?" replied the dragon at a loss for David's question. "Yeah, world. You see my sister, Anna, and I have been traveling through portals trying to get to a world called Egladon."

The blue shiny dragon looked puzzled, but David went on anyway. "At first my sister and I got separated from Anna and ended up here. Tailya was able to open a gate, with the wand that hid you in plain sight, to save Anna and bring her to us. So, I ask again, where are we?" In slow motion, the creature bowed its head and said, "Welcome to TungWing."

"TungWing," I thought but accidentally uttered aloud. "Yes, Anna. Tu-n-g-Wing…" David said slowly and drawn out, treating me like I couldn't comprehend. "I'm not a jobbernowl, David!" I huffed while glaring at him.

Yinglong puffed out smoke with his snorts of laughter. I guess our quarreling was somewhat amusing to him.

Tailya chimed in between us. "Don't mind those two, Yinglong. They are always going on about something." David and I stopped to glare at Tay. "We do not!" we hissed, denouncing in unison against her remark.

"Anyways," she said, rolling her eyes at us. "Yinglong, we need to find a portal out of TungWing. Can you help us?"

His golden underbelly rose off the ground showing a multicolored jewel planted in the dead center of his chest. "Do you mean this?" He asked, raising his neck high.

All three of us said joyfully with glistening eyes, "Yes, that's it!" Yinglong laid back down. "My apologies, friends. I am afraid I don't hold the key to open this gateway. You all must find the crown prince Li Che; he lives not too far from here. That way over there." The dragon moved his head to the left, showing us the direction we needed to set out on. "Li Che?" David spoke out oddly like how I had already been thinking. The man's name baffled me too, seeing as I had also never heard anything like it before.

"But how do we get past the long-stoned wall and into the palace?" Tay asked, looking perplexed herself.

Yinglong's voice rang over through the plans going on in my mind. "You have no need to go there. He reassured. "The crown prince has his own mansion over there just beyond the cherry blossom trees." I gasped. So, that's what those pink petaled shrubs are called? They smell like a sweet pastry from my kitchen back in Bristeria."

The dragon slightly bowed. "Yes, we are very fond of them ourselves in the springtime." "It's spring here?" I responded while questioning to myself of how long I've been gone and if everything was still the way I had left it. My Queen and Kedron still evil and my King being held hostage in the dungeon. I forced the painful memory back down into the pit of my stomach. The thought was provoking me into frustration and trying to change my mood. I wasn't about to let that happen, so I quickly decided to put my focus on those saccharine-smelling trees and everything else around. Yinglong was the most en-thralling thing in this land aside from the cherry blossoms and multicolored clouds.

We were not sure of the way that was supposed to lead us to Li Che's palace. "If this world has dragons, then what other creatures would we encounter here?" I thought, as we three stood there staring at all the trees. Every direction was the same and looked like it would take us far from our destination. So, we asked Yinglong to help us find the right path.

The metallic-colored firedrake raised one of his wings swiftly flapping it, causing a gust of wind to shake off some baby pink leaves. We watched as they fell to the ground. Yinglong succeeded, giving us a soft pillow like line to lead the way.

We bid our new dragon friend farewell and hurried toward the petals afraid that they might blow away or disappear.

I paced behind my two friends, swept away by the charming vision of TungWing. The smell of creamy vanilla, lilac, and roses filled my nose as I thought to myself, "If I can come back to this world, I will." "Tay, can we visit TungWing again someday?" I shouted ahead, wanting my wish to come true. She turned her head back and smiled. My chest rose high, feeling light as a feather. I felt content here. And just as I was about to ask how much further, as if they somehow knew the answer, we stopped in front of this huge eggshell color-looking palace with a brown wooden door. The entrance had some kind of weird symbols written on it that neither one of us could make out. Tay grabbed for Fawn's baton hoping it would help. She pointed at the gate and chanted, "Lysei." The letters on the door started to shift around and change into full words making the ideograms possible for us to read.

"This wand really does work on everything," I thought to myself while perusing over the sign. "Residence of Li Che, the Crown Prince of TungWing" David read aloud.

I stepped in front, shoving him behind. Pounding my fist against the door, I started to shout, "Excuse me, uh, crown prince." Tailya made her way up to the entrance, aggressively pushing her brother and me over to the side.

She started to call for him as well when the door flung open. Standing there inside the entrance was a short lady with silky black braided hair. Her bright green dress with red flowers drew me in. She stood gracefully, hands crossed over each other and placed at the center of her waist.

Her knees bent slightly, and her body lowered as she smiled and greeted us. She seemed kind but not one of us could understand her. She spoke a language that we'd never heard before. Tailya poked the girl's throat with the wand and said, "metafrazo."

The poor thing went pale, but we could comprehend her words now that Tay used the translation spell.

"Don't be alarmed, please. We simply need your help. Do you know where we can find the crown prince?" I asked, placing my right hand gently upon her shoulder.

She slouched, loosening her tension. "Why did you curse me?" she asked, turning and looking at Tay. My friend smiled. With soft eyes, she replied, "I didn't, we just needed to understand what you were saying to us. So, I used a translation spell. We come from a different world, so we aren't familiar with the way you speak here."

"I see." the young girl said, curtsying again. "So, will you help us?" Tay asked once more. "What is your name, miss?" I asked, dropping my hand from her shoulder.

She grinned softly. "My name is Lin Lan. Although, his highness calls me something different." Her eyes sparkled on the last part, and I wondered what it was. However I could see from the look of her rosy cheeks and turned up lips, she wasn't going to share.

Watching her stand there moving her body side to side and still grinning, I asked "What's so funny?" She batted her long black lashes and spoke softly. "Nothing is funny, my lady. It's just that when I think of his highness, I can't help but feel cheery. He is quite handsome, you know." She covered a smile as she blushed once more.

"Huh. What? Who's handsome?" The jealousy coming from David tickled me pink and mustard up a laugh I was trying to keep silent. "Oh, here we go again," Tay uttered which made my chortling even louder. David scowled and huffed. I turned my attention back to Lin Lan and she was in a daze still thinking about the crown prince.

"Well, we'd like to stay and watch you daydream some more about your infatuation with the crown prince," David chimed in, looking at me and sticking his tongue out like he was going to be sick. "But unfortunately, we need to press on."

He clasped his fingers around my wrist, pulling me behind him past our greeter. I turned my head over my shoulder and Tay was on our heels following speedily.

"Where are you going?" I asked David, still allowing him to drag me. He softened his grip. "We're going to find Li Che. Don't you want to get out of here?" he asked, picking up his footing.

The huffing and puffing coming out of him were quite amusing. I quickly had to raise my other hand to hide the smirk that tried to form across my mouth.

"Anna, I wouldn't mind coming back to revisit TungWing with you at all. Yes, I'll bring you with me." Tay finally answered, completely stolen away by all the landscaping inside the crown prince's palace. "Mhmm," I replied as I looked around at the beautifully kept up grounds.

David just stood there staring at a sign that read "Junjie". His eyes were squinted, and I giggled to myself silently. It was as if the harder he creased his eyes the easier he thought it would be to read.

"Hey, David!" I shouted from across the court, "You can't read it. It is in another language." I finished while sarcastically shaking my head. "Come on Tay, use the wand to change all the writing to where we can understand it. Oh, and see if you can make the prince talk to us but without pointing the wand at his throat like you did to Lin Lan. I have a weird unpleasant feeling that we could die here for such actions."

She pulled the magic rod from thin air and then gave me an assured bob as she started to wave it around and chant. Thank all that is delicious in the world that the only one around us was the girl who greeted us at the door.

I turned my focus toward her, watching her mouth pop open as her eyes dazzled at the sight of magic being swept all around her while listening to Tay speak out "Kana Gnosto" as she pointed to every plack, door, and hanging trinkets inside.

I walked my way over to gently grab Lin Lan's hand so we could enjoy the excitement together. Before our eyes, every wording in front of us, behind us, and to the sides of us started to change into our language. Lin Lan's stare was the sight of awe and intrigue.

"Who is there?" We heard a man's voice ask, coming from the other side of the court. "I looked at the maid. " Is that the crown prince?" " I said, who's there?" the man called again. Gracefully Lin Lan dropped my hand. "My lady, yes that is his highness, and he sounds displeased, I must go." Just as she curtsied to excuse herself, the crown prince stepped out in front of the door that we were facing.

Staring us down he roared, "Who are you and what are you all doing in my house? Guards! Guards!" Tailya, David, and I looked at each other as we all swallowed the giant lumps in our throats.

CHAPTER 20

Brighton

As I watched her eyes light up when she laughed, I thought to myself, "This is her. This is my princess, the one I will spend the rest of my days with." I found myself in a trance staring at her as she glowed with joy.

"So, Sir Brighton, what made you want to come to Egladon and become a knight?" My beautiful maiden wasted no time wanting to get to know me and I couldn't have been more pleased.

Milaya's eyes twinkled as she looked me over, causing me to give off a big toothy grin. I could feel my cheeks starting to heat up and I just knew they were changing color.

She giggled and I cleared my throat, brushing off these sissy stirrings that were trying to take hold of me. However, she smiled and all that I was trying to accomplish had fallen through just like that.

"Let me tell you a great story," I said, regaining my composure. Milaya scrunched her nose and bobbed her head, softly she replied, "Alright my sir Brighton."

Her gentle tone pulled at my heartstrings causing me to let out a faint satisfied exhale.

"Okay, miss Milaya. I'll tell one of my grandfather's great tales." I could see the fascination wash over my angel as her beautiful coco orbs glimmered at every word I spoke.

She stopped me mid-sentence. "Sir, I already know about the sea monster that haunts Egladon's waters." I paused in thought, staring at her deeply wondering what my lady had encountered.

Milaya gently nodded, persisting for me to keep speaking. I grinned from ear to ear. "She is still wanting to hear me talk some more". I thought as I relaxed beside her and laid back with my hands crossed behind my head, staring up at the sky.

Repositioning herself she asked, "And how do you plan to capture this sea beast?" Peering down into my eyes she waited in curiosity. I lost my wording when she started biting the edge of her bottom lip.

"A hem" I cleared my throat. Flailing my arms, and throwing my body up quickly, I almost head-butting my lady love. Pridefully puffing out my pecs I replied, "When I become a knight of Egladon's court my pegasus Arkimedes and I will lead a team over the waters to once and for all end that monster's reign."

Very calmly she took my hands into hers. "Sir Brighton, the determination in your gaze is the same my father had when he told me he was going off to slay the sea serpent."

She was becoming anxious, and my gut wrenched when I noticed my princess had wetness forming in both of her tear ducts. Just as the water was about to roll down past her cheeks to her chin, she pulled me in close, crying out, "No. No. You mustn't go. You don't understand the danger that lurks out there." I thought to myself while listening to her pleas, "If you heard Mason's tale just now, you'd know just how much I understand completely." "Oh, please Brighton, say you won't go. Stay here on land with me where it is safe." On her last words she gripped me even tighter.

My heart sank when Milaya had finished and I felt moved by her plea but even with the tugs going on inside, it didn't take away my urge to slay the sea beast.

I unlocked her arms from around me, leaning myself back enough to gaze into those chocolate-colored eyes.

With my thumb, I gently moved it across each of her cheeks, brushing off her tears while fixating myself straight into her stare. I thought, "in this moment I don't want her to speak. No, just continue focusing into my eyes and take in deep breaths in order to calm herself down". My heart ached for the torment she has been through.

"It's alright my lady. You don't have to say anything more." I said, staring intently into her eyes, pushing back a strand of her hair that had fallen down onto her sobby cheek.

Softly placing it back behind her ear, I gave her a small grin hoping it might cheer her up a bit. She sniffled a couple of times and while gathering herself she said, "I'm sorry for all of my blubbering, Sir Brighton." She sniffled twice more which I thought was adorable.

A chuckle tried to make its way out, but instead I hastily forced out a rough cough to hide the unwanted expression. Sitting herself straight and looking up at me she said, "Okay, I can tell you now." "Tell me what, my lady?" I replied, not taking my gaze off of her.

She grasped my hand. "I can tell you what happened three years ago." I nodded, agreeing to go ahead, and let her share what she has experienced.

Pulling her into my chest and stroking her brunette hair with my other hand, I said, "I am all ears, princess."

She moved her head up, locking those alluring topaz eyes with mine, and took a deep breath before speaking. I continued running my hand down her lengthy tanned locks as she began.

"Three years past, my father, Lord Timious"-
I cut her words short with a loud gasp. Scratching the top of my head I thought, "It can't be him. Willy would've said something." "Is something the matter, Sir Brighton?" my angel asked softly. Probably because I suddenly stopped the relaxation of my hand caressing her head in order to run it through my own.

"My apologies, Milaya. No, nothing is wrong. Please, I promise I will not interrupt you again." Resting the side of her head against me she started over.

"I had just turned twenty about a week before my brother, Patroklos, and my father Lord Timious were asked to go out in search of the thing that was wreaking havoc on Egladon. Before they left, they told me a fisherman went out on his boat at dawn and never returned back to shore and that both of them must go to look for him. I knew deep down they shouldn't travel at dusk, but my father and my brother were prideful, and they weren't the type of men to be told what to do. All I could do was wrap my arms around them, caution them to be safe, and bid them both farewell. When the door closed behind them, I dropped to my knees in tears, praying for All-knowing to protect and watch over my family."

Lifting her chin with my index finger to meet my eyes, I asked, "Who is this All-Knowing you speak of?" "Huh? Oh, it's the divine creator of the universe," she answered with a sad tone. "Hmmm. Well, I'd love to hear more about this wonderful being."

Milaya smiled then frowned. "It's too complex right now, maybe later." The only thing I could think of why she wouldn't share it was that her sorrow from the loss of her father had somehow hardened her heart and she was angry.

I sat there pondering over this divine All-Knowing she spoke of. I thought, "Is that the name for God here?" That was until I was interrupted by her sudden outburst. "My father's gone, okay?! Nothing's going to bring him back. Not you, not me, and certainly not the creator!"

That was the first time I witnessed the Mad Maiden Milaya that Willy and Mason had tried to caution me to stay away from.

Her shout didn't just come from anywhere. She was hurt, heartbroken, and I could also sense that she felt lost without her father. I could hear her pain coming from her broken-hearted sobs. "She'd never be called that name by me," I thought. Her spite though, caused her to jerk her chin from my finger and pull away.

In thinking of a way to soothe my princess's animosity, I took my hand from hers, gently placed my palms on her cheeks, and lowered my forehead to meet hers. Then I whispered, "My lady, I didn't mean to upset you. Won't you please pardon my curiosity?"

Milaya leaned back and looked up at me surprised. "You're-you're not going to run away?" "What, no. Why would I do that?" I questioned grinning, then grabbing her shoulders to pull her in close. I pushed her back so I could search her eyes. When they locked to mine, slowly I leaned down to brush the tip of my nose against her forehead.

She breathed in deep, calming her nerves. I told her she didn't have to finish telling me what happened since it brought up so much sadness, but she responded, "No, I am better now. I can tell the rest." I gazed into those word stealing eyes again and then smiled, slightly tilting my head in agreement.

With a faint crease across her mouth, she began to share the rest of her tragedy.

"My brother said when they reached the mountains, father told him to go off over towards the cave. Patroklos said to father he didn't think it'd be wise to split up and leave him alone. But father was stubborn and wouldn't listen, and he insisted my brother go search the cave. Patroklos said the moment he turned Artrayious around, he heard a loud splash of water behind his back."

I thought to myself while she was still telling her story, "I wonder who Artrayious is. But Brighton you said you wouldn't interrupt. That I did. I'll wait until she is finished." I could feel the movement of my inside head bob as I refocused my undivided attention back onto my lady.

I missed a little when I got lost in my interest in who Artrayious was, but I picked back up on her saying, "Artrayious swiftly spun my brother around to see where the splash landed but he said it was too dark to make it out."

Milaya shivered in my arms and sniffled as she ended her last sentence. "My father, he-he was nowhere to be found." I moved my hand down to pat her back, consoling her in her time of need. Pushing herself away from my chest, I watched her blow her nose on some old rag she had pulled from the pocket of her dress.

"I mean, surely you would think my brother could have at least spotted father's big oaf of a pegasus somewhere," she blurted and then continued blowing her nose.

My heart ached even more for my dream maiden. I wanted nothing more than to help her find Lord Timious if possible but first I needed to get out of the line of fire,-

Snot. My insides started to feel queasy just thinking about any of it landing on me.

She peeked her eyes up. Gazing into mine she pleaded, "Do you see now why I don't want you to go? It's too much of a high-risk that you wouldn't return either."

Listening to Milaya's words requesting me to stay on land was music to my ears but I couldn't let her see it on my face. I was a man and I had come here to become a knight and to slay the beast.

"Shh. We won't worry about that now. It's getting late. When can I see you again, my lady?" I asked while patting her back and watching the stars give light to the sky.

Both of us stood to our feet. Milaya picked up the cloth and began to fold it neatly for it to fit into the wicker basket. She smiled then replied, " Good Sir, I would be delighted to see you on the morrow at breakfast if you have time." When she finished, I grabbed her right hand and lowered my lips, softly pressing them against her skin to bid her a good evening before going to turn in for the night.

When I made it to my sleeping quarters, I kicked off my boots, hit the pillow, and drifted off in thought of Milaya before closing my eyes. The morning felt like it had come too soon as I rolled myself to my side to sit up and plant my feet on the floor.

Rubbing my eyes, I noticed I was the only one left in the tent. Willy and Mason had already gone to eat without me. Those good for nothing gluttons, I thought as I laced up my boots to go join them. Making my way down the path, I thought, " I hope I am able to see my Milaya." When I entered the dining hall, I found Mason standing on a table with all of the soldiers and knights surrounding him but no beautiful brown-haired maiden. I sighed.

He had their full attention, and I already knew what he was about to say. So I rushed over pushing and prying my way through the crowd. There was a chair a few inches away from Mason. I was gearing myself up to leap off of it. I had it in my mind that I was going to cover his mouth and pull him from the table. But in the midst of my planning, I was too late.

He had already begun to speak. "Listen up men. Brighton, Willy, and I have seen what the water monster is capable of, and the outcome is not pleasant. One of the men shouted, "Oh yeah? Where's your proof?" I listened as all the others roared along in unison.

Willy climbed up next to Mason, taking a puff of his medicine. "He's telling the truth, guys." They didn't seem to believe him either. So, I got off the chair, walked over, pushed my way through an opening, and yelled, "It has eaten someone's head!" The man that started the mocking was now suddenly at a loss for words and all the others fell silent in their thoughts.

I turned my head toward Mason with a half-formed grin while giving him an "I'm on your side" fist pump. He nodded in gratitude and in that moment, I realized it was better to speak up than to hide the truth.

CHAPTER 21

Annalise

Lin Lan rushed toward his highness, dropped to her knees, and lowered her eyes to the ground. From my point of view, this felt all too familiar, and I thought to myself, "The poor girl's about to get lashes." We heard her loud plea from across the court. "My lord, my lord. Please don't be angry. They have come to seek his highness' help."

She spoke fast but we could still make out every word. Li Che posted himself in front of Lin Lan like an immovable statue with his feet firmly planted, shoulders straight back, and one hand ready to unsheathe his sword.

Tay and I turned to each other blinking with our chins dropped. We were surely thinking the same thing, "we might become prisoners here". Turning my focus towards David, I saw that his posture was almost like Li Che's. I shook my head slowly, glared at him, and clenched my teeth. "What are you doing? You're going to make all of us lose our heads." I hissed at him without moving my lips for fear that his highness would see me talking and think I was being imprudent.

Shooting a quick glance at Tay, and a slight head tilt motioning her to follow my lead, I dashed over to kneel myself down in respect, following Lin Lan's body language to a T.

Tailya finally made her way over. She imitated Lin Lan just as I did. And with her head already facing the ground, she lifted her hand, and moved it in a cupping motion to call her brother over.

I didn't have to lift my head to see that she was annoyed. I could hear it from how loud she was breathing through her nostrils. I forced back the giggles that were coming from the bubbles in my tummy. "I wasn't going to be the one to anger Li Che," I thought while inhaling deep and watching David's knees hit the floor right beside mine.

Finally, the crown prince spoke. "You three do not belong her"- "I know man. That's why we're trying to leave," David cut him off. "No regard for Li Che at all. Arrogant." I thought about smacking my palm to my head.

Li Che drew his sword pridefully. David panicked, throwing his hands up in surrender. "Whoa-whoa. Come on prince. Look, you're a guy and I'm a guy, we're both fellows here. There's no need to go sword happy on us, okay?" The crown prince's blade landed in the eyesight of Tailya, Lin Lan, and me.

Strongly clenching my jaws, I pushed away any fear and peeked up to see what the reaction was on the crown prince's face.

He and David's eyes were locked on each other. I could see my friend's shirt puffing out, knowing very well those breaths of his were full of terror, but he'd never own up to that.

Creaking my neck just a hair to the other side, I watched Li Che smirk and then sheath his weapon back in its place. He reached down for Lin Lan, telling her to rise. Before he fully pulled her to her feet, she glanced over at Tay and me with a smile and whispered, "It's okay to get up now."

When I stood up, the crown prince was staring at Tay, looking like he had been bewitched. Discreetly I elbowed her in the side and leaned toward her ear. "Tailya, tell me you didn't cast a spell on the ruler of TungWing." She grinned at Li Che before darting her eyes to me. "No, of course not. Stop insinuating that I have no self-control." She hissed, turned her focus back to him, smiled, and batted her lashes.

Lin Lan put her hand over her mouth to cover a playful giggle. I found myself gazing at the crown prince also, wanting to see why my friend and Lin Lan were so smitten.

I had to admit, he was tall and dashing with long shiny midnight hair, halfway down past his lower back. The other part was rolled up into a bun, tucked into a silver crown, and held in place with a silver pin that had an emerald on its hilt.

The clothing they wore here was a lot different than ours back home. Li Che was dressed in a white and silver robe with an embroidered belt wrapped around his waist. A see-through pendant in the shape of Yinglong dangled underneath, dazzling my eyes.

I was now fawning over him just like Tay. With her lips together, Lin Lan made a sound like she was trying to clear her throat in order to get our attention. Both of us were frozen in peaceful silence daydreaming about the crown prince.

David interrupted mine by coming over and slapping his arm around me. "Ouch!" I hissed while giving him a dirty look. He didn't pay me any mind. Instead, he jerked me in close to the point that our hips were touching and lifted his chin to Li Che like I was his or something. I rolled my eyes and then noticed the crown prince smirk at David as I shoved him away from me.

My friend huffed and stomped over to his sister, who was still in a trance. With her lips sealed, Lin Lan made another sound this time a suppressed cough trying to get Tay's attention. It wasn't working.

I squeezed my eyes shut and raised my shoulders to my ears when I saw David's fingers moving toward her forehead. "Oh no. He's going to flick her, he's going to flick her", I repeated anxiously to myself.

"Ow! David get over here. I'm going to whack you when you least expect it. You just wait and see." I opened my eyes to see David laughing, carrying on hopping around sticking out his tongue with both of his thumbs pointing toward his temples waving his fingers at Tay.

"You just wait!" she yelled again with a deep glare. This time David was stunned and then swallowed hard, believing his sister's threat. I chuckled to myself thinking, "Serves him right." Then I peered my gaze back to Li Che. He and Lin Lan were watching the show of Tay and David's bickering along with me, smiling and laughing to themselves.

"Okay. You just wait, brother. I'll get you. Oh yeah, I'm going to rip you apart." Tay huffed and puffed bent over trying to steady her breathing after chasing David around the court. Lin Lan turned toward Li Che. "My lord, I think it's best to help them get out of TungWing before their odd behavior is witnessed by his majesty, the emperor."

"Mmm." Li Che mumbled with a nod. Looking at all three of us he said, "It's getting late. The moon is about to rise. You three will sleep here tonight and we will head out at dawn to go find Yinglong." Then, he moved his head toward Lin Lan, motioning for her to take us to our rooms before turning on his heel.

David shot across the yard to fall in line with Tay and me. "Got anything here to eat? I'm famished," he said, resting an elbow on the poor girl's shoulder. She gasped. "Men and women must keep their distance before marriage." Then she quickly stepped toward Tailya and said to him, "Right this way, sir." She lowered herself into an apologetic curtsy.

Tay and I looked at one another, rolled our eyes, and shook our heads. Tay said, " Please excuse my brother David Lin Lan he has no manners" "Yeah and the boy eats all the time." I mocked feeling a little peckish myself. "I know!" Tay shouted back as her stomach growled. Staring at each other we laughed and hurried behind David following Lin Lan to the kitchen.

"I don't know how much further it is but when we get there, I'm eating whatever that smell is," David said, licking his lips like a dog waiting for its meal.

After a long stretch, we finally turned the corner and entered into the delectable aroma. The kitchen had wooden trays filled with fried chicken, some kind of weird, shaped bun, that Lin Lan said was stuffed, lettuce, and clear soup with noodles that had green vegetables in it. There was also milk for us to go along with our meal. Tay and I smiled at the sweet maid then closed our eyes to take in a deep whiff. I thought, I cannot wait to sink my teeth into the dough and taste what it is stuffed with".

Our blissful inhale was ruined by the sound of smacking and chugging. We popped our eyes open. In unison, Tay and I shouted, "David!" The glutton had already dug into the chicken and was drinking up all of the milk.

I glared at him and snatched the jug out of his hand. "Save some for us doughboy." I hissed before taking a sip. "Buuuuup." The disgusting jerk let out a loud stinky hot breath right in my face. Bile started to bubble in my throat when the foul smell of sour milk and rotten eggs hit me.

"Ugh, David!" I roared as I grabbed a handful of his hair. "That wasn't funny! And now I can't even eat my meal!" "Oh, come on Anna. I was just jesting around. Don't be such a princess." He said, prying my fingers apart, untightening my firm grip. I continued squeezing my fist as tight as I could but eventually, he got it open and freed his hair.

Lin Lan stood there gaping with her mouth wide open in shock. She looked at Tay and asked, "Women. They can act like that to their lords?" I was just about to answer but Tailya beat me to it. "Oh yeah, those two? They are always like that." she said, flicking her wrist toward David and me, and I felt the need to clear up Lin Lan's question.

"We are not always like this, and he is not any lord of mine. No, we are not allowed to hit anyone. The rules are the same here as they are back home in Bristeria. But this boy right here, this boy", I repeated, "irritates me beyond belief." "Pshh, whatever." David mocked, throwing out his hand like he was swatting at a bug.

Lin Lan's eyes widened and then she mumbled, "Ohhh." followed by a giggle. After my friends finished stuffing their selves, Tailya, David, and I let the peaceful maid escort us to our rooms. I myself was ready to hit the pillow after the day I've had.

The sound of Fyra's voice pinched my heart and I felt the trickling line of a tear rolling down my cheek. Great. Not getting any sleep tonight. Yippee. The snide remarks popped in my head from out of nowhere. I was thinking back on my phoenix and then bam! Wicked thoughts caused my heart to become aggrieved, leaving nothing but the taste of venom on my tongue.

"I am really not going to get any sleep tonight." I whined out loud. Immediately my scoffing stopped as Tailya, David and Lin Lan paused in mid-step. When they turned to face me, I could see that I had puzzled them with my outburst. "Is everything alright, my lady?" Lin Lan asked. She was the first one to speak and I couldn't steer my eyes to acknowledge her.

"Annalise, breathe. Listen to my voice. That's it, deep slow breaths." Tay instructed while coming towards me lifting her palms up and pressing them back to the ground. "Is your friend, okay?" Ling Lan asked David, still confused about why I all of the sudden went from relaxed to irritated.

We stopped in front of the first room, and Lin Lan said, "Annalise this will be your sleeping chamber. "Aw... Why does she get the first room?" David groaned. I smirked and then stuck out my tongue as Lin Lan answered, "Everything here is done differently than where you all are from. Here, the first are last and the last are honored first."

"Well that's all mumbo-jumbo if you ask me" David scoffed. " The boy is such a whiner" I thought. Tailya's calming technique helped and I could feel the tightness in my chest start to subside. I found myself yearning for the long circular ball of fluff that was laid across the top of the thin white sheet covering the wood beneath.

My bed made it feel like I was sleeping in a giant box, but I didn't care. The window faced emerald mountains and cherry blossom trees. As soon as I sat down to remove my shoes, I heard the door next to mine close and then another a little further down. "Hey, Tay, is that you?" "Yeah, I'm in the room next to yours," she answered, pressing her hand against the paper wall. I could see the form of her shadow figure from the candlelight in her room. It made me feel at ease.

I laid back, resting my head against the pillow as I stared off at the night sky thinking to myself how peaceful and breathtaking it was before shutting my eyes and drifting away to the next day.

Pulled out of my slumber from a horrific nightmare, I rushed over to Tay's room to wake her up. Strongly grasping her shoulders, I began shaking her. "Tay, Tay, wake up. Come on, I need you to get up." Finally, she opened her eyes and became alert.

The door closed behind my back, and it startled me. I accidentally dug my nails into Tay's skin. "Aaah!" she screamed. I covered her mouth with my hand while looking over my shoulder to see that the person who closed the door was David. "What is going on in here?" he asked loudly. "Shh," I replied, pulling my palm away off of Tay's mouth.

"You guys, I had a shocking dream that woke me straight up out of my sleep, and I felt like something was telling me to come to warn you about it." "Oh, Anna, here you go again," Tay said, yawning and sitting herself up. I gazed deeply into her eyes and then faced them towards David. "No, I am not wrong about this. I can feel it in the pit of my stomach, you guys."

David raced over to sit beside us, asking, "How scary was it?" I turned to see if Tay was going to ask a follow-up question, but instead her reaction was blinking. "If you get your sister to stop doing that, I'll tell you." I said a little annoyed. David went to raise his fingers towards Tay's forehead.

He was getting prepared to pull her out of her stupor. Right before the flick, her eyes stopped dead ahead glaring at her brother causing him to retreat. Slowly he pulled his fingers back, not taking his focus away until she stopped scowling.

"Okay, we're ready Anna. I'm wide awake thanks to this peanut brain." She jerked her head towards David on her last three words. I took a deep breath and then began to tell them everything I had dreamt.

"Okay, listen, I was walking in the courtyard looking up at the stars when all of the sudden a bright beam of light shot straight down from the sky. I shielded my eyes with my arm so I wouldn't get blinded. My hair flew back, and my body trembled from the loud thud that landed beside me. I went to lower my shield when the scene changed, and I was now talking to my watcher, but I couldn't make out anything he was trying to say. The previous scene had switched, and what came into view was now me hovering over the palace watching as it was being surrounded by people in all black with swords and masks. From this point, my dream stays. I saw Li Che, Lin Lan, and you two come out of your rooms in a panic. Li Che called for his warriors to guard the entrance, but it was too late. I watched all of you get slaughtered one by one and then I woke up all sweaty and distraught."

David tried to brush it off. "It's just a bad dream, Anna." Although Tay, seemed to be pondering on every word. A thunderous crash came from what sounded like a short distance from the door. "What was that?!" Tay frighteningly whispered. David jolted from the bed to blow out every candle in the room, making it to where no one could see in. Slowly he crept over to the door and slid it open just enough to peek out.

Quietly sealing it back he turned his head and nervously said with wide eyes, " Anna, I'm starting to think your dream wasn't just a dream." The clanking of blades connecting to each other forced Tay and me to tremble. "It's happening, it's happening," I squeaked out. But even though I was in a bad state of shock, I still needed to see for myself what was going on. I stood up and crouched down, putting all my weight on the balls of my feet, and made my way towards the door. Splitting both sides apart to poke my eye through, I witnessed Lin Lan hunkered down, knees to her chest rocking back and forth petrified underneath a cherry blossom tree. Men dressed in all black with masks and swords were surrounding her.

I leaned my head back in and cautiously stepped away from the door. I didn't want to make any sound, so I left it cracked. Cupping my hands on both sides of my mouth I said as quiet as a mouse, "We need to get out of here." "How are we going to get by without being spotted?" David replied back, lifting both of his palms while raising his shoulders.

"We can't make a sound and we need to stay as close to the walls as possible. Follow my lead." Both of them nodded in unison and moved towards the door with me. Tay put herself in front of her brother. He slid himself over, placing his body in the middle. Tay gripped one side as I grabbed the other and we began to pull the door apart at the same time, hoping it wouldn't make any noise. Our eyes almost popped out of their sockets when a giant silver blade grazed the air between us and rested its tip in the middle of David's chest.

CHAPTER 22

Brighton

Willy and I crossed our arms and squared our shoulders while star-ing down the men as Mason began to warn all of them. "Alright, mates, listen up. The fisherman tales are real. I am a true witness." You could hear a coin drop on the floor; it was so quiet.

The soldiers weren't asking any questions. They were all ears hanging on our friend's every word. "My charge, Drake, and I were out at sea to gather food for the next two passing moons. We were pa-tiently waiting for the nets to fill when the water around the boat suddenly turned dark."

I gazed over the crowd and saw that almost every one of the men had their jaws dropped in anticipation. I focused back on Mason who was still speaking. "The water stilled and after the calm, a giant storm shot up straight from under the boat. Mates, I had never seen anything like it. This was by far the scariest creature I have ever, ever laid my eyes on, and I tell ya, I've seen some creepy things."

Willy and I could tell that all of Mason's flashbacks were starting to flood his brain. The poor guy was having a hard time controlling his emotions which were causing him to shudder again. Pinching his tongue between his teeth for a moment so he could get his bearings back, he looked out at the crowd only to see that all the men's eyes were wide open, and they were all staring at him.

He took a deep breath and then croaked, "Mates, the beast swallowed Drake's whole body." The dining hall became a room of noise as every single man gasped in fear and started talking amongst themselves.

Mason wasn't finished and he couldn't seem to talk over all the chatter. I picked up a plate and a knife and began banging them together to help get the soldiers' attention. As soon as all eyes were back on Mason, I motioned for him to continue.

He nodded and then addressed the men. "I'm telling you all mates; I know how eager you are to go slay it but take heed in going to the waters for now lest you want to end up like my charge." One of the men yelled over the crowd, "Did you get a good eye on what it looked like?"

Our friend scanned through the men trying to put a face to the voice that rang out over all the commotion.

I chuckled under my breath when Willy gripped Mason's left shoulder to prop himself up onto his tiptoes. I knew he was helping Mason scout the crowd as well but to me, he looked like a kid in a candy store trying to reach the counter.

Gawking at both of my friends, I was at odds as to why they were so attentive and keen to see who the query came from. I guess Mason wanted to make sure they believed him so no one would be foolish and lose their life.

Willy leaped off the table right as Mason was getting ready to shout again. "Make a path for our leader, men," Willy yelled out while pushing the others with the back of his hand.

All of the soldiers and knights raised their voices when he stepped in between them. "Lord Patroklos," some of them addressed. Others lowered their heads, calling him sire. Mason and I jumped down off the table to greet our leader.

"Lord Patroklos, sire, I didn't see you come in. My apologies, my lord." Mason said, as he dropped to kneel in respect. Being the newcomer in Egladon, I just stood there with my lips pressed together tightly. I was already in his good graces, so I wasn't about to speak and let myself ruin anything.

Lord Patroklos glowered at his soldier. "I have asked you time and time again to refer to me as Patroklos," he replied, standing my friend to his feet. And with his humble remark followed by his action, I was able to feel at ease.

After making his way around the crowd, Lord Patroklos readdressed to Mason what the other man had been wondering. Staring deep into my friend's eyes he questioned sternly with every word slow and drawn out, "Did you see it?"

I could hear Mason's loud gulp before answering, "Yes, sire. And it spoke to me." Our leader's gaze widened when he heard Mason's last reply. We watched Lord Patroklos raise a hand to cross over his chest. He had to have been reflecting on old memories because I could see the pain in his eyes.

The story about my lady's father was written all over his face. "My lord," I said while clearing my throat. I was going to make a vow to help him find his father, but he stopped my words by turning to meet me and said, "Please, it's just Patroklos, Brighton. You can drop the formalities."

The man's words were full of grief and all I wanted to do was bow and stay silent. The beating of my heart slowed as I remembered the look on Milaya's weeping face when she cried out that her father was gone and nothing nor no one could bring him back. With her woeful voice ringing in my ears, I thought to myself, "I had better not make promises that I don't know if I could keep."

Willy and I watched Lord Patroklos shake away the horrible memories in his head, while Mason stood at attention waiting for his next orders. "Well, Mason. Go on with it. Don't stop on my occasion, soldier." He nodded and with one quick bow Mason blurted, "Sir this monster rose up at least three to four castles high. Drake and I didn't have anywhere to escape. Not to sound like a bloody chook but I couldn't move even if I wanted to."

Our poor friend was ashamed and could not get over his guilt. We listened to him as he continued. "My eyes were frozen solid. I couldn't even make them blink. The bloody thing descended straight over Drake and swallowed him whole right in front of me. I knew my demise was coming next, but it didn't, sire. Instead, the sea beast shot back up out of the water and levitated itself straight in front of my face."

Lord Patroklos gasped and then prodded Mason to describe the fierce monster. Willy and I both placed a hand on Mason's shoulders, giving him a friendly head bob. "Don't hold anything back, Mason," Willy said as he squeezed the top of his arm.

The soldier nodded and then began. "Sire, the head appeared to be like the form of a snake. And its eyes"-

Poor Mason croaked when he spoke of the beast's scary orbs. He gulped in anticipation of bringing up that image in his head. At least that's what came to my mind about it. "Sire, its eyes were so dark that you'd think you just fell down a long black hole with no light to see your way out. Dangling from the sea serpent's nostrils were pieces of Drake's flesh. Wedged in between its sharp pointy chompers were bits of bone. When the monster said to me, "I am not here for you, Mason. You are not the one I am after." Sire, my charge's blood was dripping from its mouth."

Lord Patroklos looked worried. Turning around to address the crowd he motioned, "Let no man in Egladon step foot on the shore until I give the order." We all agreed and then he finished by saying, "Let us train tirelessly and wholeheartedly men. We will gather our strength and wits, and in two fortnights, we will be ready."

Shouts of hoorah sounded over the crowd as Lord Patroklos made his exit. With my other fist, I nudged Willy across the arm. "What do you suppose Mason meant by saying the water beast wasn't here for him?"

Thinking back on the history of my grandfather's tale and what the guys also told me, made my knees go a little weak. "Brighton get a grip.

This was part of the reason you wanted to come here", I said to myself. Then, I croaked, "Who do you think it's here for?"

Lord Patroklos graced us with his presence again. "Brighton, come with me." Mason and Willy chimed in. "My lord, can we attend also?" Their speaking at the same time caused Patroklos to cough out a laugh. He lifted his palm high, motioning that it was okay for my friends to tag along.

Before leaving, our leader stared down at the men. Volumizing his pipes so all could hear, he propositioned once more. "No man here in Egladon should by any means go near the shoreline or hike the mountains." "What, no mountains?" I thought, now terrified that this creature was able to come on land.

Mason sighed. The poor guy loved going for a hike to clear his head in the evening. At least that's what I heard from Willy. The soldier bowed his head to Lord Patroklos and asked, "Is there anything else, sire?" The fierce knight glowered and huffed. "Yes, Mason. Stop calling me that. You know my name, use it. I am just like all of you. Now let's get ready for war."

Willy and Mason frowned but still dropped their chins in respect for our head knight. I on the other hand stood there puzzled, wondering why Lord Patroklos didn't want to be addressed by his true title. All three of us turned and followed on his heels. In the short distance from the dining hall to the training grounds, my stomach started to churn from thoughts of all the bloodshed that was going to happen.

Through the gates stood mine and Lord Patroklos' pegasus, Arkimedes and Artrayious. We entered in and behind ours, Mason's pegasus, Brontes, was overstuffing his belly with all of their food.

"Brontes, you oversized bloody bludger. Save some for your mates," Mason commanded.

Brontes immediately stopped chewing. Swallowing his last bite, he closed his eyes and grinned big at Mason before turning his back toward him. "Aw, don't be like that, mate," Mason said, walking over to his pet and stroked his mane.

"Pegasi are extraordinary creatures," our leader proclaimed while making his way over to Artrayious. Brushing his hand across his pegasus' side, he continued speaking. "They are known for their celestial teleportation in and out of the mortal and immortal realms. Artrayious here, came on his own free will. Didn't you, boy?" He asked, while looking up at him and now running his fingers over one of his pet's wings. "This hoon had to be trained with tough love. Didn't ya, ya ol bludger?" Mason said in the middle of massaging Brontes' stifle areas, helping to release any tightness that would cramp him up in flight.

Brontes started to nicker, whinny, and then neigh. It became so loud it caused Arkimedes and Artrayious to follow along. Patroklos walked over to Mason and leaned into him asking with a low voice, "Are they planning to attack us?" Mason burst out laughing. He stopped rubbing Brontes' legs to give the knight a clap on the shoulder. My friend's outrageous action stunned me.

I couldn't believe that he had just treated Lord Patroklos like an equal having no rank. When the soldier was able to control his chortling he said, "I think they're snickering at us mate." They both guffawed at Mason's reply, and I played along forcing out a couple of tee-hees myself, hoping to relax my perplexed mind.

After they had calmed down, the knight noticed my baffled stare. I stood there at attention as I watched him amble his way over. Throwing his arm around the back of my neck, he asked, "Soldier, why are you so serious? At ease. We're all in the same position here." His laid-back gaze retracted my body's tension and I felt I was able to speak freely. "So, my lord. What do you prefer we address you as since you don't care to be called by your title?"

My leader put his arm down and sighed. Looking away, he said, "My name is just Patroklos. Lord is my father. I never wanted his title. The elders forced it upon me when he vanished. I don't believe him to be dead like the others. That is why I refuse to be called by his caption."

I lowered my eyes to the ground thinking to myself, "The poor guy is in denial."

"I allow my friends to call me Patroklos, brother, and mate. Like Willy and Mason do. You may do as you wish. I would rather be addressed to as family than some unfamiliar ruler of Egladon."

Willy tossed the knight an apple while saying, "See brother, we're all comrades here. There's no need to treat Patroklos any differently." "Yeah, mate. He don't care for it." Mason chimed in. I slapped my new friend on the back. "Alright. How about I stick with big brother then, seeing as I will be marrying Milaya very soon."

Willy and Mason stopped in mid-chew on their apples, dropped open their mouths, letting the leftover pieces fall out, and hit the floor as Patroklos replied, "Huh?"

When his smile turned into a frown I gulped. "Since when did you meet my sister?" He asked with an unwelcoming glare. Willy answered in my place, "He spit out some food in the dining hall and it bounced off the wall hitting the lady on the forehead." I leered at my big mouthed friend for putting in his two cents. "I see," the knight said calmly. Then he focused back on me. "And did you apologize?" I gulped. His peering was strong and uncomfortable.

Patroklos turned to look at Mason and Willy. Before I knew it, they were all mocking me. I sucked in a heaping amount of air, and then spun on my heel to blow it out. My whole body felt like I'd jumped into a pool of water at wintertime.

"I'm just pulling your chain, Brighton." the knight said, walking back my way. I circled back around to meet his view. "Who am I to tell my sister whom she can and cannot union with," he said, smacking me against my left bicep. "My poor muscle," I thought, wanting to grab the skin and start massaging it. The twitching sensation started, and I just knew it was about to spaz out on me.

"Keep your composure, Brighton. Keep your composure..." I repeated in my head while gritting my teeth. The man's strength turned my arm into a jelly roll. No more firmness around the sides with a rock in the center. Now, it was fluffy and squishy in the middle.

I became a little headstrong and decided to test this newfound friendship. With Willy and Mason, I could retaliate. So I wanted to try to do the same with Patroklos. Clenching my fist into a ball I struck him back, while saying, "That's good to know big brother." For a moment the knight looked grave. I turned my focus on Willy and Mason who were simpering. The thunderous sound of Patroklos' guffaw followed by my body being pushed forward, told me I could let myself horse around with him too.

I felt as if I had a band of brothers and knew no one could tear us apart. "Here, catch," Willy called out, tossing all three of us our pegasi brushes. We chatted for a while, grooming and girding them up for training.

Patroklos started singing the war song of Egladon. I listened as Mason and Willy sang along with him. *We're men, men of pride. We won't give up too easily or sign away our rights. We will train hard, and we will become strong. So, you'd better watch out for the mighty men of Egladon.*

After suiting up our partners, Patroklos said it was time for us to go and get changed. I followed behind Mason and Willy into where all the armor was kept. The first thing I reached for was the chain mail. I remembered it was the first thing to put on. Next, I slipped a tunic over my head, put on my chausses, grabbed a sword and shield, and then shouted, "Ready!"

"Good on ya, mate!" Mason shouted from across the chamber. "Saints Brighton, give me a hand!" Willy shouted, fighting with how to get the chain mail on. Mason put his palms together beating them loudly. We both chuckled, causing our frail friend to grimace. "Alright, alright. We're finished, Willy. Here let me help you with that." I said walking over to him, wondering to myself why he bothered suiting up in the first place.

"Willy, you know that mate isn't going to let you train. I'm afraid to tell ya but it's always going to be a no because of your illness." I couldn't look my poor friend in the eyes. I felt sorry for him, but Mason spoke the truth. There was no way Willy would ever be able to join us in the battle. When I felt his shoulders slouch, I sighed for my brother.

He didn't bother listening nor did he want to remove his chain mail. So, Mason came over to help and we finished arming him up. Willy reached for a sword and shield and then made his way out of the door.

Mason and I already had our weapons ready, so we marched behind him shaking our heads feeling sympathetic for him.

Passing the gate and into knight territory, we met Patroklos, he was standing next to Artrayious. "Wha! You can see the castle from here. I didn't know we were so close." I said, peering my eyes up toward an opening that looked to be a window.

My three brothers had coy smiles planted on their faces when I looked back down. Then they teased me, batting their eyes toward me like a bunch of school maidens. I huffed and lifted my view back up.

A small amount of air was stolen from my lungs when I noticed her beautiful face staring down at me.

CHAPTER 23

Milaya

My breath stilled making my heart skip a couple of beats when I heard his voice from the courtyard. I stopped reading, placed my book on the end table, and hurried myself over to the window. There was no way to hide the overwhelming joy forming upon my lips when I laid eyes on my handsome knight geared up in all his armor.

"Oh no. Did he catch me staring at him?" I said to myself, jerking my body away from the opening. Shyly I peeked my eyes back around allowing myself to take another glance. I took in a deep whiff of fresh air, sucked in my belly to my spine, and raised my shoulders to my ears while curling my toes.

"Ugh. The man has me smitten. What am I going to do? How will I ever be able to stay serene in front of him now? Hmt hmt hmt" I groused as I slapped a hand over my untamed mouth, begging All-Knowing not to have let Brighton hear my childish whining.

Then I giggled as I envisaged out loud, "Milaya, seriously. He can't hear you from all the way up here." I became bashful and started to blush answering my question. My tummy felt like someone was doing flips inside as I danced around my room captivated and lost in thought daydreaming about our tryst.

I put a halt on my spinning about. Slow, long, drawn-out breaths needed to be taken, seeing as I was starting to make myself dizzy from all of my bliss. Walking over toward the glass by my bedside, I chugged down a heaping amount of water, almost finishing it. "Bwaaap!" Oh goodness me. That came out of nowhere.

I stared coyly giggling until a snort forced its way out. Quickly covering my mouth, I timidly scanned my room making sure no one heard or entered in catching me in the act. When all was clear I snickered once more.

"Sir Brighton, he he he. When will we marry?" I giggled out loud, walking across my chambers to pick a flower from the vase on my dresser. Going back across the room to my reading chair I sat down, sunk in, and began plucking petals. "He loves me, hmm, he loves me not. He loves me, mmm, he loves me not. He loves me!" I blurted out while plucking the last petal from its stem. My giggles were quickly interrupted when he opened my door.

"Who loves you?" my brother asked, busting into my room uninvited. "Get out." I hissed, pointing my finger at him to leave through the same way he entered. "Not until you tell me who has stolen my little sister's heart." I huffed and puffed, trying to make it look as if I were frustrated and annoyed. But he wasn't buying into my act.

I went charging across my room going straight for my door. I thought to myself, "If Patroklos just came in, then Brighton might still be around the castle courtyard." I placed my hand on the handle just about to pull it open when my brother interrupted my happy state.

"If you're looking for Brighton"- My eyes shot over at the mention of his name. "He left before I came inside." He finished with a smirk across his face. My heart sank, turning my cheery smile into a frown. My brother tried to console me, saying, "Don't worry Milaya. He's quite fond of you too." before turning the handle to leave to his sleeping chambers.

The instant my door closed, I raced over to my bed letting gravity take me while grabbing my pillow, giggling and smiling. Patroklos peeked his head back in. "Get out!" I yelled. My brother grinned big. "I caught him staring up at you, you know?"

I leapt off my bed with my pillow still clenched to my chest. "You did? Did he say anything about me? Aw, tell me Patroklos, my most favorite brother in the world." I couldn't control my emotions. I was too excited to hear that my dream guy had been looking up at me.

Patroklos didn't answer. Instead, he laughed at me and shook his head while closing my door. I went back to my bed and laid there thinking about my dashing soon to be knight until I eventually fell asleep.

"Uh," I groaned rolling over to my side in order to deplete the rays of the sun against my closed eyes trying to force me to awaken. I grabbed my pillow from underneath me and smashed it over my head.

Another hour of slumber was about to greet me. That was until bois-terous laughter and the sound of clanking steel hitting together energized my body.

"Brighton?" I spoke out, throwing the pillow off and kicking the blanket onto the floor. I sat up quickly and scooted myself toward the edge of my bed, listening for his voice. "Mason, don't let your guard down!" I heard my brother shout. I threw myself back onto my mattress, disappointed. "Good form, Brighton. Keep driving!"

"Huh?!" I ecstatically hoisted myself up and rushed over to the window, forgetting my slippers. A deep breath escaped my lungs as I squeaked to myself, "Its him, its him." My morning felt complete as I stood there silently in my nighty watching my soldier train with my brother and the others in their armor.

I watched his every move. He was precise, controlling every single footstep. Every time he spun to avoid a plunge; I could feel my heart still. Patroklos commanded them to break and replenish. Watch-ing Brighton chug down his water, I found myself drifting off into space, running my fingers through his strawberry locks in my mind. I stood there in wonder, swaying side to side.

"Hey men, looks like we have a spy on our hands." My brother's announcement pulled me straight out of my happy place. Brighton looked up and we locked eyes. I gasped as I darted to the side. Taking a deep breath and smoothing my ratted hair with my fingers, I made myself presentable enough to peek back around. When I searched for my soldier, I found him already gazing up at my window smiling at me.

I giggled and then stepped away not wanting to interrupt his lessons. "Brighton, are you still with us?" Hearing my brother teasing my handsome soldier brought a smile across my face as I readied my-self to go wash up and get changed.

Entering my room, I thought I'd wear my light pink dress with a white sash across the top along with my creamy flats. My heart beat fast when the vision of Brighton's eyes glistening at me popped into my head.

After getting changed, I walked over to the window excited to see the look on his face, but they had all left the courtyard. I turned and headed for my door to go look for him when the breakfast bell rang. I yanked my handle and ran down the stairs making my way to the dining hall hoping to see him there.

The moment I stepped in to have breakfast, I began searching the room to see where he was sitting. All eyes were gawking at me, but the only eyes I wanted to meet mine were his. I turned around to see if he might be in the food line, but he wasn't, and I started to feel discontent.

Disappointed, I went to grab my breakfast, even though now, I didn't feel much like eating. When I circled back around, I almost dropped my plate. Brighton was standing in front of me, eyes twinkling and grinning from ear to ear. "My lady," he said, reaching out for my plate to carry. Blushing and batting my eyes, I placed the dish onto his palm. He winked at me before spinning on his heel to head back to his seat.

I gasped when his hand locked onto mine to pull me behind him.

Brighton was quite the gentleman. When we made it to the table, he pulled my chair out for me. I was a smitten kitten with no words, I just sat down, batting my lashes while showing him some teeth as he scooted my chair into the table. We were timid and shy to talk to each other once again.

Both of us sat there across from each other smiling away. That was until I blinked. "Ahem" My soldier awkwardly coughed forcing a giggle out of me. "How did you?" We both said in unison, and then we chuckled. "You go first, Sir Brighton." I said, knowing my cheeks were probably turning the same color as my dress.

"How did you sleep?" he asked while scooping his spoon into his porridge. I didn't answer right away. Instead, I began to smile, thinking about the first look on his face when he came up to me yesterday. The thought of our first meet and greet of him hitting me in the forehead with a berry caused me to cover a giggle. After gathering my emotions, not wanting my soon to be knight thinking I was laughing at him, I replied, "Uh… How did you sleep?" He stared at me a couple a of seconds perplexed. I giggled to kill the awkward silence. "Umm, what I meant was, my night was very peaceful, no complaints here ha-ha."

Looking down at my bowl and moving my spoon around in my breakfast, I thought to myself, "Great, Milaya. Make the man worry that you've gone off your rocker again. Ugh. why is my heart beating so fast? Why am I unable to muster up a conversation with him? I did so the other night just fine."

I looked back up in order to get out of my head. Oh, for all the flowers. Those viridescent eyes of his locked onto mine. I tittered, sounding like a shrinking violet and then went off into dreamland.

The activity playing like a show in my mind was enough to keep me occupied all day.

We're back at our tryst, talking and laughing. He's smiling and seems
more relaxed, I as well. The sun is shining beautifully as we're lying there under the tree looking up at the clouds. I say something and he turns his focus towards me.

"Milaya?... My lady, hello?" Flickering my eyes to the sound of Brighton's snapping fingers, pulled me straight back . "Aw. I didn't get to hear what I'd said." I whined under my breath. "What was that my lady?" "I beg your pardon?" I said mindlessly, still a bit unaware of the present. "Oh, ha-ha." I tried to act bashful while grinning from ear to ear and fluttering my lashes. Thankfully it worked. almost knight dropped his shoulders, relaxing back in his chair and contently smiled.

Finally the shy tension eased up and we were able to carry on just as we had the other evening. " Are you practicing flying on your pegasus today, or will you be doing, as my brother calls it, "ground training?" He chortled, "Honestly I won't know my lady until I'm told." He smiled again and I began to fawn over my sightly soldier as my heart said, "Thump-thump. Thump-thump."

Brighton had finished his porridge. "Well, my Milaya"-
"He-he, what did you just say?" I interrupted.
"My Milaya." He repeated as he lifted my hand and gave it a gentle peck, leaving me giddy and speechless. "I must be going, my Milaya," he said again, this time with a coy smile. I couldn't let myself get lost and turn into putty. "A lady needed to have a set of morals," I thought as I lifted my eyes, took back my hand, smiled, and said, "Sir Brighton, if you must go, then you shouldn't waste any more time."

My soldier stood up tall searching me over. I winked and then shewed him off. The poor man oddly waved as he left the table. When he turned his back I silently giggled. As I watched him leave confused,

I thought, "Little does he know we'll see each other this afternoon." Smiling at my idea, I sat there quietly and finished my breakfast. "Yuck!" I said out loud. My porridge had gone cold.

CHAPTER 24

Annalise

"Nobody leaves alive," the masked man heeded. All three of our mouths dropped in terror. We expressed our compliance with the swift bob of our heads. I heard Tay and David's hard swallows right after mine as our eyes watched the men dressed in all black fly over our captor.

Li Che and his guards had just about taken out the whole fleet of rivals. The enemy detaining us never lifted his gaze. When I focused on him, I noticed that the orbs looking back at me were softening. "No, it can't be. Wait, can it?" I thought to myself while taking a hasty breath before timidly reaching to unmask him.

"Anna, what are you doing?" Tay nervously gritted through her teeth with a fake grin. She squinted her eyes looking like she was going to lose it just as I grabbed the black cloth and tugged down.

"Ferguson!" I shrieked, putting David and Tailya into a confused state. "Shhh. They'll hear you. He whispered, sternly. " My watcher came to save us in his human form but for some odd reason, nothing inside of me was jumping for joy. It was as if he knew what was tormenting me when he said, "Stay focused. I am here now. They have no power. Just listen to my voice."

A sigh of contentment lifted off my chest and I felt my body relax. David moved back into the room giving Tay and me space to step back as well while Ferguson stayed posted guarding the entrance. Peeking our heads out the window it was like watching Brighton's fencing lessons back home, only with flips, gilding, flying, kicks, and punches.

I jerked my view toward Tay. "Did you see that?" An enemy had been kicked in the stomach causing him to spiral through the air and slam into the brick wall. "Whaa!" I could feel Tay and David's shooshes coming, telling me to calm my excitement. "Did you guys see that? Tell me you both caught that!" "What?" Tay asked, muddled.

"You didn't see it? " Ugh, see what Annalise?" Tay huffed. Li Che just hoisted himself off the ground twirling in mid-air and took out six men!" I excitedly roared and then quickly slapped a hand over my rambunctious muzzle, slouched down out of sight, and awkwardly turned my gaze toward my watcher.

I was waiting for him to scold me for my vehement behavior, but he didn't. Instead, his eyes twinkled, and he had a peaceful grin, like the chaotic scene happening outside wasn't stirring him up at all.

Lin Lan snuck through a passage behind us that we didn't even know was there. "Is everyone alright?" she asked brushing off some leftover dirt that was attached to her dress. "Yes, my watcher came to save us," I replied pointing my finger in Ferguson's direction. "I don't see anyone there, my lady." I got up quickly and moved towards the door. "Where did he go?" I inquired quietly to myself. Ferguson must have left when he felt that we were in the clear. "He didn't even say goodbye. I didn't get the chance to thank him," I muttered discouragingly.

Li Che appeared in the entrance sliding the door fully open. "They're all dead. It's safe to come out now. Let us get ready, it's nearly dawn, and we set out to seek Yinglong in one hour." The crown prince had blood gushing down one of his arms from what looked to be a nasty cut. "Lin Lan." "Yes?" she responded hurrying in front of him to curtsy. "Take these three to go fill their bellies while I go and get cleaned up." "Consider it done, your highness." The maiden complied as she bent her knees and lowered her head awaiting for him to turn and go his way.

After Li Che dismissed himself, Lin Lan spun herself back to us, and said "I bet Mr. Jie has fresh meat buns ready." Then she shyly giggled. "Meat buns?!" David astonishingly asked. Tay and I made fun of him when we noticed the drool on the corner of his mouth. "You're such an ogre." I huffed while letting my eyes go to the back of my head. "What? I haven't eaten since…"- Tay and I waited as we watched the glutton count his fingers.- "Since five hours past." He finished. Both of us snickered and then strolled behind Lin Lan. Tay and I heard her giggling to herself as she was crossing foot out of the room.

"Out of my way." David shoved me and his sister into the wall to get there first. "The food's not going anywhere." Tay and I hissed.

"Says you!" He sneeringly shouted back, turning the corner. Making our way around as well, passing a couple of doors, Tay and I walked into the kitchen to the same scene. David was pigging out on all the food and milk.

"David!" We both yelled with our hands firmly planted on our hips. He stopped his gorging and walked up to me with a closed hand and a glass in the other. "Here, Anna. I saved this one for you." My eyes looked down at the crushed bread full of meat in his hand. The food looked as if it had already been chewed. "Gross! No, thanks. I'll get my own." I began to walk over to the basket of food to get one for myself when the boy brought up a hot smelly wind, burning my poor defenseless nostrils.

After rubbing out the sting from my eyes and holding my breath so I wouldn't contaminate the kitchen with the bile bubbling in my throat, I chased the vulgar boy around wanting to unleash my fury. "Don't let me catch you!" I shouted as he taunted me around the entrees.

"You two stop!" Tay hissed and then turned to our host. "I am terribly sorry for these two, Lin Lan. They apparently don't know how to be civil." She finished while shooting daggers at her brother and me. I thought to myself, "She's not much older than me. So why does she think she has the right to apologize for my behavior, let alone portray herself as Queen Cheylenna?"

"She doesn't care about your feelings. Can't you see, she even acts like she's embarrassed by you." I could feel the persuasive tugging from the hisses in my ear. They were strong and started to empower my thoughts. Every nerve in my body began twisting up into knots and I was too weak to hold back the poisonous strike of bitterness.

"Tailya, why don't you stop trying to be our elder and mind your own business. It's not your place to plead for me. You know what?" I paused. The insulted girl stood there. I could see the water forming in the outer corners of both her tear ducts.

There was a small quiet voice repeating "No, Annalise. She's your friend." which caused a twinge in my heart. I knew why the feeling came, it was to get me to stop but the dark force had me trapped, and what rolled off my tongue next, brought Tay to full tears. "You know what? I know you're ashamed of me and you can't wait to get rid of me. Well, guess what? Your wish is granted. Give me my wand and the book. I don't need you anymore. Give them to me and I'll be on my way. I didn't want you guys to come in the first place, remember?" I felt no remorse no guilt. I just stood there with a mean glare like something, or someone had completely taken over my vessel and there was nothing I could do about it.

"Annalise!" David shouted while yanking me down onto a chair. His forceful jolt caused my anger to spill out even more. " Stars, David!" I hissed. He firmly pressed his palms down on both my arms and made me listen to his lecture. "That's enough. All my sister and I want to do is get you to Egladon safely!" I rolled my eyes and smacked my lips silently repeating his every word while tilting my head side to side.

Tailya sniffled. "Here, Anna. You can have them." Then she brushed a hand under her nose wiping away the unwanted snot. "No! Don't give those to her!" David shouted, yanking the wand and enchanted book from his sister's hands. I huffed as I turned my view to poor Lin Lan who was bewildered from my sudden outburst. I sat there sulking, watching my friend dry her eyes and trying to remember what my true self was.

David placed one of his palms on my shoulder as he lowered himself down to my eye level. "It's getting worse, isn't it?" He asked, peering into me, and swiping some teardrops off my cheeks that I didn't even feel roll down.

Tay moved her brother from my gaze. Placing her hands into mine she kindly pulled me to my feet while saying, "It's alright, Anna. I know you didn't mean what you said." Then she snickered and asked, "Would you like for me to turn you back into a fairy?"

My eyes widened as my chest caved in. "You mean be a fairy by night and a human by day again?" She smiled and nodded. I strongly shook my head. "No way!" I blurted and then quickly followed up with, "I mean I'm not a little girl anymore. Plus, didn't you say before that you don't know how to reverse it? Besides, it's more of a curse if you ask me. No thanks. It's a miracle on how it's been lifted off of me in the first place."

Tay sighed. "I was just trying to help. And yes, I did say that but now we have Fawn's book so I would be able to change you back. What do you think David? Do you want to save time on traveling by foot? I can turn you back into Starbeam." She asked turning toward her brother.

David and I looked at each other and then faced Tay. Together we replied, "Nope!" and ended with a satisfied titter. "You all can turn yourselves into different creatures?" Lin Lan asked with sparkles in her eyes. "Mhmm," Tay answered, with her eyes closed and a grin from ear to ear plastered on her face. "Wha…" The maid said awe-stricken.

Somehow my trance had ended, and I saw my friend holding our most valuable weapons in her hand. "Tay put them away. We need to go and find Li Che so he can summon Yinglong to open the portal."

She turned her focus back to me and groaned. "Anna, you're no fun." Her brother and I stared her down, so she'd listen. "Let's go," I commanded while spinning on my heels to walk out the door.

Turning the corner from the kitchen we ran into the crown prince. He was standing there patiently with one of his hands behind his back. Looking at him, I thought. "I wonder if he just heard all of that." We all paced behind him. For some odd reason, he kept looking back over his shoulder at me.

David moved himself in front of me standing up tall and poking his chest out. Li Che smirked while shifting his head to the side to stare at me some more. Turning around I asked Tay, "Did I do something?" She looked back at Lin Lan for an answer, but the maid wouldn't lift her head. Tay turned back to me and shrugged.

His highness' gawking was beginning to make me feel uneasy. I sucked in a huge breath for courage and then, exhaled loudly, "Is there any particular reason for your staring?" My sudden blurt brought the crown prince out of his daze. He walked around David causing all of us to stop in our tracks.

The man searched deep into my eyes and said, "I know you."
I gasped. "We've met before, haven't we Cheylenna?" Tay and David shot their bug eyes at me. All I could do was stand there frozen, blinking profusely while my mind began to go haywire.

Li Che waved his hands in my face. "Hello?... Hello, I'm talking to you, Cheylenna."

"Y-you know my mother?" The crown prince reached for my left wrist. "Don't try to fool me, witch." Jerking my arm back I glared into his cold eyes. "My name is Annalise. I am Cheylenna's daughter." The man gasped as he confusedly stumbled back a couple of steps.

My friends were still standing there stunned. I bet they were wondering what I was, "Are we all going to die here?" I gulped at the thought. Lin Lan hurried around Tailya. Coming to my rescue she put herself in between Li Che and me. "My lord, I believe she is speaking the truth. Look." The maid lifted my right hand and turned my palm towards the sky. "She doesn't possess the mark, see."

His highness yanked my hand from Lin Lan's grasp, pulling it up to his face. After thoroughly inspecting every crease, he dropped my fingers. "It seems that you aren't Cheylenna. Come, who are you? Why did you step into TungWing?" He asked in a harsh tone. Irritated, I responded with a huff, and then answered. "Your highness, I told you, my name is Annalise. My friends and I got stuck in your world by accident. We need to summon Yinglong to open the gate so we can get to Egladon."

As the prince stood there pondering, I thought about the same strange scar I had vaguely seen before myself. Looking at Li Che I said, "My queen told me it was a burn mark from when she was a little girl." The crown prince put his head down and shook it. Directing his view back up into my eyes he said, "I am afraid you have been misinformed, Annalise."

Li Che grabbed my wrists and walked me over to a table in his courtyard. David, Tailya, and Lin Lan followed behind us. Sitting me down the crown prince said, "Before you all leave, let me tell you a story."

My two friends and his maid gathered themselves around me. While we waited in anticipation, I pondered on what his highness was going to say about Queen Cheylenna that I hadn't already figured out for myself. I cleared my mind, ready to listen for any clues on how to help my mother and free her from her torment.

The crown prince began to pace back and forth alongside the table. I guess he was thinking of how to tell me my mother was evil, but I already knew that. Turning his focus onto me again he started to speak. "Several years past, when I was a young boy, I was told by the emperor to go and train with the guards. This was essential in order for me to become the next ruler."

David raised his hand like a student waiting to be called on by his teacher. After tittering, I couldn't help but mock him. "We're not in a classroom bonehead." My friend glared and then the crown prince marched up to me, leaned down, and said, "You may not bear the mark, but you sure do take after her." I gasped.

Tightening my lips, I dropped my head down and fell silent while waiting for him to continue. After the moment had past, and I heard nothing. I lifted my head to see that Li Che had a coy smirk like what he had just said was a ploy to quiet me. It worked. I sat there with my hands underneath me ready and willing to hang onto his every word as he continued again. "I had just finished sparring with the general's son and was getting ready to be sent into the bamboo forest for my next task, hunting my first tiger."

"Did you kill it?!" David blurted. The man bobbed his head. "But not right away. It was protecting a girl." He darted his eyes at me. "Your mother." Tay, David, and I gasped all at once as Li Che continued. "She looked wounded, and the tiger was laying over her. I sauntered toward the vicious feline with my hands raised in caution, but the protective beast wouldn't budge."

"Then what happened?" Tay's enthusiasm came out like she was a kid at a puppet show. I could see that his highness was starting to get annoyed from their interruptions, so I hissed, "Be quiet, you guys. Let him finish."

The crown prince looked at Lin Lan in frustration but when she gave him a warm smile he went back to his story. "Ahem. Where was I?" David was just about to open his big mouth and tell him until he witnessed my "don't even think about it" glare. The boy gulped and stayed quiet allowing Li Che to remember on his own.

"Oh right. Your mother was seriously injured so I slowly walked up to the tiger with my sword behind my back. When it lunged at me, I struck it across its throat. As it flew beside me, I rushed over to check on her. The skin on her legs looked like it had been chewed on. I ripped a piece of my shirt off to bandage them and then unlatched my robe, draping it over to comfort her. I began wrapping your mother up and was getting ready to throw her over my shoulder when I saw it. The mark of the sea demon my ancestors wrote about in their scrolls."

A chill rose up my spine as I continued to listen. "The evil creature that haunts the waters of Egladon-" "Egladon?!" My disruptive shout caused Li Che to pause but the crown prince didn't seem to be upset this time when I interrupted him.

Instead, he slowly closed his eyes and bowed his head in sympathy. "But, but that's our destination, right?!" I asked in a chilling tone as I peered into Tay's eyes.

Gasp. "Brighton is there!" I shouted. My heart was racing, and my mind was beside itself. I could feel the pressure in my eyes getting wider and wider at the thought of not being able to get to my brother in time.

    I had to bury the thought. I couldn't allow myself to lose control from something I didn't even know the outcome of. So, I inhaled a heaping amount of air into my lungs, forcing myself to let the tension go, and continued to listen to the rest of Li Che's tale about Queen Cheylenna.

    Turning my ears away from his voice, I thought, "I wonder if knowing any of this could help save my mother." I drifted my focus back to the prince, picking back up on him telling us about the symbol of the sea demon and how he asked his physicians to watch over the queen. "She was out of it for three full days. When she finally had awakened her memories had been wiped from her. Cheylenna couldn't remember where she last came from, where her home was, what her parents' names were, nothing. Just her name. The poor thing was pitiful with nowhere to go and no knowledge about her life. So, I allowed her to stay here in TungWing. On the day she came to, I informed her of where she was, who I was, and where she'd been staying. But it turned out that that night I was explaining these things to her she seemed uninterested and was itching to leave me. I caught her staring at my royal seal, and I started to wonder if that was the real reason for her coming here. Before I realized it, she had reached out and grabbed the emblem from my belt and then took off running. When I caught up to her, she was lying on the ground stunned in front of Yinglong. He told me she was there to open the portal. When she regained consciousness, she claimed to have had no recollection of what just happened. This time I was reluctant to believe her because the black trident symbol was glowing underneath her palm. I stretched out my hand and was going to twist hers up when I noticed her eyes."

In the last part of his sentence, he stared at me in curiosity then asked for me to turn up my right palm. I sighed and did as he said. The crown prince grabbed my fingers. "My apologies, it's just"- He searched me over for what felt like forever, making me feel a little timid- "you resemble her every feature." I sighed again and then he said, "Okay, girl. To sum up this story, your mother is evil and has been taken over by some dark powers. I tried to heal her with my inner chi by suppressing her wicked side until the day came that she was too strong, and her body would no longer allow my power to penetrate through. Your mother had completely succumbed to evil. TungWing is protected by Yinglong, so when he sensed her awakening, he knew she was a threat and could no longer allow her to stay here."

"Hold on," I said, cutting him off again.

"Yes."

"Well, you said until the day came."

"Yes, that is correct."

"So then how old was my queen when she had to leave?"

"Hmm. I'm not quite sure, but if I had to guess since she was just a little younger than me at the time she arrived, I'd have to say eighteen or nineteen."

There was a pause in my breathing when I heard my mother's age. When she went through the portal, and departed from this world, she must've landed straight into Bristeria and met my father, King Cyrus. He told me they married at nineteen.

The thoughts racing inside my head could not be tamed out of fear that my destiny had already been written. And here I was, just a puppet having its strings pulled.

CHAPTER 25

Annalise

"Hey, Anna!" David jerking my body back and forth while shouting in my face resurfaced me back to the present. "I'm awake, blockhead." "Oh. Well, you weren't a second ago, was she?" he retorted looking over towards his sister to agree with him. "No, she had her head in the clouds again," Tay replied to her brother.

I reached out for Tay's hand, squeezing it tightly with salty droplets leaking from the corners of my eyes. "Anna, what's wrong?" She consolingly asked, covering my clenched fingers with her other hand. Her sad gaze caused more tears to fall. I was beside myself, screaming on the inside like a caged baby animal crying for its mother.

How do you tell someone that you hear two voices in your head and the enticing one is becoming more and more powerful which is causing you to act out and speak what it says? It's not possible. Even I would look at that person oddly. No, I can't tell them, they would just think I am crazy or bewitched.

Another discouraging notion swam about, and it was starting to become challenging to depict what thoughts were my own.

"Don't cry, Anna. We'll make it to Brighton and then you can introduce Tay and me as his future good brother and good sister." The young man's fantasy mindset choked me up, drying up any liquid that was still on the verge of trying to seep its way out.

"What in the stars did you just imply?!" I shouted, jerking my hand out of Tay's while using my other to unblur my eyes. I needed to be able to see my target seeing as I didn't want to miss this satisfying image. Marching straight up to him with a fake smile and batting my eyes to throw him off, I balled up my fist to the side.

Just as I was about to connect my raptured strike to his left cheek, Li Che caught my thirsty bell ringer. "As amusing as it would be to watch a girl lay a guy out, I have to protest. I'm afraid time is not on our side, young ones. We need to move."

"Well, isn't that just my luck? Fiddlesticks! I almost had him." I yelled to myself still tightly clenching my fingers. When the prince let go of my hand, it was numb, and my skin was white. You could see every single blue vein poking through.

I swallowed my huge fire-burning lump of vengeance down to the pit of my stomach while gritting my teeth under a fake smile of obedience.

"You know you can get him when he least expects it." The slithering voice caused my body to react as I listened. I felt my head slowly tilting side to side like some strange energy was flowing through me and then I inhaled deeply through my nose thinking I was in Bristeria's bakery, relishing in all the sweet flavors of gingerbread, chocolate, and vanilla as they danced on my tongue.

Ashamed of becoming a slave to the voice, I timidly looked around to see if any of them had witnessed my weird behavior. I sighed in relief when I saw that everyone's eyes were forward.

Watching my feet and Tay's in front, I tried to clear my mind and refocus on getting to Egladon. "Annalise." "Yeah," I answered while lifting my head. "Huh?" Tay said, looking over her shoulder. 'Didn't you say something?" She stopped and turned all the way around to face me. " Anna, I haven't said one word since the prince caught your fist."

The puzzled look on her face was what I was trying to stay away from. "Oh. Ha ha ha. I thought I heard you call me when I was singing in my head." I replied awkwardly. "Huh-uh, Anna." She said, searching me over. "Okay then, well you better turn back around if you don't want to bump into David. I'm going to go back to singing to my-self."

My hasty reply managed to disband any concern Tay was feeling for me as I watched her spin back on her heel to face forward. Even though I put myself back in the clear, it still baffled me that someone or something spoke out my name so clearly as if they or it was walking right next to me.

I kept a sharp eyes view as we headed in toward the mountains. Tailya, David, Lin Lan, and I about tumbled into one another when Li Che stopped suddenly. "Not much further." He addressed while pointing ahead. "Stars... It feels like we've been walking forever. My feet are throbbing," I groaned.

David stepped around Tay. "Here, Anna. I'll carry you the rest of the way," he offered, grabbing my hand and pulling me up onto his back. I knew being higher up would help me be able to see better, seeing as he was six feet and some inches tall. I allowed it, clasping my legs snugly around his waist.

"Look!" I shouted pointing ahead. "Ah. He's right on time." the crown prince said as he focused his eyes on the sky. Yinglong was in mid-air flipping in circles. "What is that dragon doing?" David chortled. "I would suppose he's passing time waiting on us." The crown prince chuckled.

The closer and closer we got to Yinglong the more I started to feel like I was about to toss up my breakfast. Hopping off of my friend, I felt my feet as they began to take three giant steps back. It was as if they were being controlled.

David chuckled. "Did you fall off? Come on we're almost there," he said, locking our hands together. When he started to pull me, my body began to feel like I was being pricked with pins and needles. It was clear that some kind of force wanted me to stay away from the dragon, but I didn't care. I wanted to get to Brighton, so I endured every single prick with every step.

Li Che turned around to face David and me. So I twisted my body to see what he was looking at. There was one of those golden-leafed trees behind us. The crown prince walked over to it, and we watched as he made himself comfortable, laying his head against the stump. He spoke to all of us in mid-yawn, making it difficult for us to understand his words.

His highness sounded as if he was trying to talk while holding onto his tongue.

I couldn't help but let out a breathy laugh.

"Uh. Come again." David retorted, cupping one of his hands behind the back of his ear, and leaned his body to the side towards Li Che. "David, don't be disrespectful." Tay hissed. I giggled once more. His mockery was quite entertaining. Tay's glare that was toward her brother was now focused on me. "Shh. Don't be rude, Anna." I cleared my throat while swallowing my next laugh.

Lin Lan walked up to the three of us. "I think his highness was saying we are to camp out here until morning and then we'll make our way to Yinglong at high noon." "That is not what I got at all," David replied with a chortle while rubbing the back of his neck.

"We're just going to sleep, right here in the open. What about tigers or men with black masks? What if more come and try to attack us while we are resting our heads?" I blurted, panicking. My eyes shifted at the sound of Li Che tapping his fingers against the sword in its sheath. He widely yawned once more, and then said, "Don't worry young one. If they come, my men will be ready. If you hear tigers roaring it means they have already found their prey." I glanced around frantically before sitting down beside my friends.

My knees weren't wanting to bend, so Tay tugged my arm, pulling me into the middle of them. "Here, Anna. We'll protect you." "Hey, look over there," David whispered while nudging me with his shoulder. First, I look at him giving my attention and then I turned my eyes to the trees all around us. "Wha!" I said amazed. There they all were. The crown prince's guards were posted underneath every stump in sight. And there were even some others up ahead with fires lit to keep away unwanted predators.

Feeling more at ease, I hunched myself down in between my two friends. I heard Tay heavily yawn. "Goodnight, Tailya," I said while rolling to my side to face David's back. The crown prince started to snore, causing me to lie there half asleep. Not too long after Li Che, Tay started.

I began tossing and turning, accidentally bumping into David. "Hey!" he quietly huffed. "Sorry," I whispered in return while sitting myself up and leaning my back against the tree trunk. Twisting to my side, I rested my elbow on the wood and bent myself over David, "Psst. Are you asleep?" I asked.

My friend shook his head and then rolled over on his back to look up at me. "What's wrong? Something keeping you up?" he jested with an ear-to-ear grin planted on his face. "Yuk-yuk-yuk. I'm not amused." I replied while rolling my eyes.

"Oh, come on. Where's your sense of humor?" Pressing his palms into the grass, he sat up next to me. "Alright, Anna. I'll bite. What's going on?" "Huh? Oh, nothing. I just can't sleep with all of the grizzly growls around us." He laughed. "Yeah, they do sound like bears, don't they?"

Both of us started to snicker and in that moment, I was actually grateful for him. Talking with David seemed to be keeping me from listening to the slithering voice that was trying to talk to me in my mind. "Hey, David?" "Hmm," he answered, twisting his head towards me. As I looked into his eyes, my heart started beating fast and I felt an awkward sensation in my tummy that caused me to suck in an excessive amount of air.

I watched his long blonde lashes as he blinked his eyes and coyly smirked at me. "David." "Yeah?" "There's something that has been bothering me." "Oh, yeah? What's that?" "Well back at your house I didn't see you in any photographs. Why is that?" The boy chuckled and playfully nudged his shoulder into mine. "Maybe because I'm adopted," he whispered in my ear. I gasped as I jerked my head away.

The whiplash was so strong that I hit the side of my head against the tree bark. I bit my tongue while trying to hold back my tears of pain. David tittered when I began rubbing out the dull ache. "I was trying to keep my voice down. Geez, why are you so jumpy?" he said and then smirked.

After repeatedly massaging out the sting, I awkwardly coughed. "Okay, I'm better now. Tell me how you came to be Tay's brother." "Let's see, where to start," he answered as he lifted both of his arms. Crossing them behind his head getting himself cozy, he began his story. "Well, let's see." I watched my friend as he sat there in a daze trying to recall his childhood years.

Conflicted, he said, "Anna, I can't remember anything before being a unicorn." The poor guy looked troubled. "Don't worry, David. It's not important right now. When we get to Egladon we'll ask Tay. Maybe she knows something about your adoption." He nodded his head and then sucked in a good amount of oxygen, letting go of any anxious thoughts.

"Wow. We chatted the whole night away." I said while placing my hand above my forehead to shield the sun as it began to rise.

"Yeah. It's really bright in this world." He replied as he squinted both his eyes and tried to focus on my face.

I guffawed, waking everyone up by watching him bob and weave his head from the sunlight. "I have to say, David, I really do find you quite sidesplitting." "Hm-hm," he sneered. My friend let out a sonorous yawn while lengthening his arms high above his head. "Well, if any were still snoozing, I believe they're awake now," he said, satisfyingly scratching his stomach underneath his shirt.

"Oh, my stars," I said, rolling my eyes, and then stood to my feet. Whatever feeling that was that I was getting last night, now regressed back to the strong annoyance that I already have for him. I jerked my head towards Tay, averting my eyes from David's brazen behavior. "What?" he blurted in a defensive tone.

His outburst stirred up a giggle, but I popped a hand over my mouth to silence it. I spun back around and smiled at him with my eyes until it was safe to remove my palm. The boy had a giant toothy grin plastered across his face. I could feel my cheeks getting warm, so I quickly turned back to Tay hoping to stir up a conversation.

"When do you think we'll head out?" The girl didn't answer me, instead, she just let out the same ear-splitting yawn and carried out similar movements of her brother. "What is it with these two?" I thought while squinting my eyes, stiffly shrugging up my shoulders and sticking my two pointer fingers in both ears.

After enjoying her good stretch, she glanced around and finally said, "I suppose at any time, seeing as Li Che and Lin Lan are now awake." Looking over there to see for myself, I said, "You and Lin Lan must be in sync somehow because here she comes just as you finished your sentence."

Her rosy cheeks lifted high as she replied, "That's because smart minds think the same." Through a chuckle, I retorted, "Yeah. Okay, Tay." She snickered and then shrugged while sticking out her bottom lip. "Are you kids up and ready to set out?" The crown prince asked, making his way over. "Got anything to eat princie? My stomach is starting to sound like an angry dog when you take away its bone."

All of us guffawed after we'd heard it, but David became sore. "What? It isn't that funny guys." He tramped back over to where we were supposed to have slept and kicked the tree stump. Turning my face towards him, I pressed my thumb to the tip of my nose and began to wiggle my fingers while sticking out my tongue.

I giggled while watching him huff and puff. He was reaping from his temper. The pigment on his face looked like he had just eaten something extremely spicy. I leaned my head forward trying to make out what he was saying but he was too far from my sight. He kicked the wood again and then held the toe part of his shoe as he hopped on his other leg.

"What is that boy doing?" The crown prince asked concerned. "Your highness don't pay him any mind. He's just throwing a tantrum, isn't he Tay?" I answered, turning my head and slightly bending my knees in respect. Li Che's lips curved up a little as he watched my friend take out his frustrations on the poor innocent tree.

I stood there trying to focus on listening to instructions about the journey for today, but I couldn't seem to get my ears to tune into the crown prince's voice. David over there hurting himself was grabbing all of my attention. An uncomfortable guffaw forced its way out and caused Li Che to stumble on his words.

When everyone around me fell silent, I cleared my throat letting out an awkward cough. "My apologies, your highness." Then I quickly bowed in meekness before him. "David! Are you about finished acting like someone took your favorite slingshot? Hurry up and get over here. Li Che is mapping out our path for today." Tay's shouting was the same as a parents' or teacher's scolding.

The feeling of fear was all too familiar. It made me think of my queen and the evil in her that made her so cruel. I had to step back, spin on my heel and go gather myself. I knew if I didn't walk away at that moment, I would start to cry in front of his highness, Lin Lan, and Tay.

Explaining my emotions to them would just drudge up bad thoughts again and cause me to speak out with an untamed tongue. "Annalise!" Tay called. "Hold on, I'll be right back." I shouted. "I think I see something over here!" I lied, this time not feeling an ounce of remorse. It was as if it was becoming a part of me like some kind of natural instinct.

Not long after shouting back to Tailya, David made his way over to me. Out of nowhere he reached out his arms and pulled me into a much-needed embrace. My mind stopped racing the moment my ear rested against his heartbeat. He began patting my back. "Let it out if you need to. Just remember they are nowhere around to hurt you."

His words pierced my ears like a knife splitting the skin of an orange. Just as the juice would have poured out, so came my tears. I had no idea how he even knew what I was dwelling on but having him come to my rescue at that moment helped me to keep from changing into something I didn't want to be.

Lifting my head up, I sniffled and then said, "Thanks, David."

"That's what I'm here for." He replied self-assured.

"What gave you the idea to come over here?" I asked, still drying up my tears.

His eyes softened and for a split second, I thought I was looking into Ferguson's eyes. "I don't know. I was beating the tree with my foot and all a sudden I heard, "Go find Annalise." When I looked up, I saw your face as you were walking off. Something stirred inside of me, and I felt compelled to come over and console you. So here I am."

CHAPTER 26

Brighton

Clink-clank. Clink-clank. There was no better sound than that of swordplay. Learning how to handle one better than I have already been taught was growing more confidence in me by the minute. Slash. "Whoah. Watch it Mason, you broke through the skin!" I yelled as I watched the blood trickle down my arm from the gash caused by his blade.

Mason dropped his weapon along his side. Scratching the back of his head and looking conflicted, he said, "Crickey! Sorry, mate. I thought you were going to thrust up in order to counter my attack."

"That was the plan," I replied while shaking my arm, trying to get rid of the sting. I ripped the sleeve of my shirt to tie around the cut, hoping it would stop the bleeding.

I wanted to slice myself for being negligent. Telling myself I'd be alright not wearing my chainmail today was just flat-out barmy. "Ya alright mate?" Mason had worry written all over his face like I had made him my nemesis. "Brighton, mate?" I put aside thinking about the pain and gave him some friendly comfort.

"Don't fret, brother. It's not your fault, but my own. I should've put my armor on." I clapped him on his back, and it seemed to have helped relieve some of his tension. "Alright then. Ya ready to go again then, mate?" He asked eagerly, already getting into his attack stance.

Crossing my sword in front of me, I answered, "Hold that thought." Then I swiftly took off to go put on my chainmail. In the armory chamber, I grabbed everything that would cover me from head to toe. The cut on my arm was starting to tingle and become annoying. I wasn't really looking forward to another sparring. Pushing my feelings aside, I put on my chausses, reached for my chainmail, followed by strapping on my iron chest plate, and lastly throwing on my helmet.

Since Mason seemed to be a little off today, I was not taking any chances of being sliced across the face. Pulling one of the drapes to the side so I could leave, I took off back to the training grounds. Mason was right as I had left him flinging his sword around in every direction.

"I was gone for a while. I'm shocked you haven't worn yourself out yet." My friend spun around to face me. "Bahahaha. What made you bring out the fancies?" He teased.

"What? It's just our regular battle armor." I justified.

"Yeah, but we're just practicing mate," he replied while still guffawing.

Gritting and speaking through my teeth, I said, "The cut you inflicted is throbbing something fierce. I am not looking forward to another." I gave him a crazy-eyed look on my last sentence hoping to instill a bit of fear into him.

A deep aggravated sigh left my lungs when the guy began laughing hysterically. I got even more irritated when he started to cough because of laughing so hard. Grasping my sword as tight as I could without letting my fingers go numb, I creased my eyes and furrowed my brows. I spat to the left side of my boot and then said, "I'm going to shred you up like a cooked turkey on Thanksgiving." My friend's eyes widened and then he gulped. Satisfied with myself on the inside, I showed off a smirk. Peering my eyes into his I said, "You ready?"

He forced down another swallow, and then began slowly shaking his head while parting his lips. "Brighton, calm down now, mate. I was just pulling your chain. Get it mate? Chain..." The man started guffawing again while grabbing a chunk of my chainmail and pulling it up off the skin on my arm.

Mason's corky sense of humor was the exact reaction I needed. His joyful chortle became contagious. The heaviness in my chest started to fade, removing all of my aggression and before I knew it, I had followed in with my friend. "See, we don't have to be so serious, do we mate?"

"Hahaha, you're right, brother. I don't know what came over me." I answered back, almost completely out of breath from laughing so hard.

Lord Patroklos and Willy entered through the gate and caught us. We were still in the spirit of laughter, standing there hunched over holding our sore bellies and gasping for air.

What Mason said and did wasn't witty enough for all of this guffawing, but we just couldn't seem to slow it down. It wouldn't come to a stop. It felt as if we'd stood there chuckling for many minutes.

"Ahem." Willy acted like he was clearing his throat, trying to get our attention. Mason and I raised our heads. We stared at him blankly. Our guffawing died instantly when our eyes shifted to Lord Patroklos standing there with his feet planted, shoulders squared, and arms tightly crossed.

Judging from the way our leader's lips were pursed, I murmured, "Well this can't be good." Mason must have felt the same as me because his reaction was a gulp. The man's swallow was so loud that we all heard it. Patroklos unlocked his arms. "Slacking off will get you killed in a real battle, lads." He scolded.

I felt offended by the sternness in his voice, so I grabbed the chainmail that was over my cut. Lifting it and pointing with my other finger, I said, "I assure you, Patroklos, we have not been over here just goofing off."

"Mmm. I see. Alright then, gents, as you were." Willy picked up both our swords off the ground handing Mason his first.

As my friend placed mine into my hand, he winked and said, "Go. Show our leader what you can do." Then he smirked and winked again.

Mason and I dropped the tips of our blades toward the ground. Dragging them across the grass, we made our way into the middle of the training court. While Mason was getting into his stance, he asked, "Ready?" With a firm grip, I raised my weapon high. "Ready," I answered. I squared my foot stance and pointed my hips forward. "Nothing was getting past me." I thought, staring down my opponent, as I put myself in position for attack or defense.

Mason and I grinned as we started to circle each other. Clank! Both of our blades ferociously connected causing our balance to falter which made our feet stumble backward a few steps.

I could still hear the ringing in my ears as I repositioned. This time I got into my warrior stance lengthening out my right arm straight in front, holding my sword with its hilt directly pointed at Mason while the edges lined up with my arm and the tip faced behind me.

Twisting out my left foot while turning my right to point towards Mason, I was eager to go again. As soon as I saw the slightest bob of my friend's head, I allowed my wrist to whip my iron around. Slash! Mason jolted back, balancing on his heel as the tip of my sword cut the air across his neck.

His eyes widened as he gripped the handle of his weapon tighter. The moment he turned his head to spit, I spun around on the heel of my left foot sweeping my steel in the air across his torso. That time I accidently connected. My eyes bugged out and I gulped while thinking "Thank the stars he has on his chainmail."

When my friend looked down, he let out a huge breath of relief, realizing my sword could not cut him. "You said you were ready," I smirked. Mason replied while still trying to catch his breath. "I was, I mean I am. Where in the sea turtles did you learn to fence like that?"

I looked over at Willy to give him a wink, but he had already beat me to it. So, I just gave him a toothy grin. Turning back to my sparring partner I answered, "A friend of my father's taught me when I was little."

"Where did your father meet this man because I've never witnessed this style before!?"

"Poor Mason was befuddled. It isn't thing special, it's just a fighting tactic," I thought while trying to remember my teacher's name. "Good form, Brighton! You will have to teach me sometime!" Lord Patroklos shouted from across the grounds. When I looked over, I saw that he was grinning from ear to ear in astonishment.

I complied with a swift bob and then shifted back to Mason. "Another go?" I asked. My friend's eyes creased in concentration as his chin moved towards the ground. "Watch my feet. I'll go slow." I said smirking and getting back into warrior mode.

The man's eyes twinkled at my every action as I willed the steel to slice and dice in thin air across the top of his head, the caps of his knees, and under his chin. "Crickey. Mate, this is bloody fantastic. Where can I find this teacher of yours?" He asked while watching me spin on the tip of my right toe as my left leg extended behind, sweeping the ground while the edge of my sword sliced the air across the back of his ankle.

When I stood up and dropped my weapon, relaxing both arms, Mason reached out for my hand. "Good on you, mate!" He shouted over excitedly. The man was shaking my wrist so much that I felt like my arm was about to be pulled out of its socket.

"That is enough for today, lads!" Patroklos' grin was still plastered across his face. I could tell my leader had been very pleased with my performance and I had to admit, even though swordplay to me is a passion, I was still undoubtedly grateful he called it quits.

I needed to tend to my wound, seeing as the blood that was seeping out my gash, was now all dried up and crusty. "Yee...," I groaned out loud, thinking how my lady would react if she witnessed it this way. "Oh, come on. I want to have a go around!" Willy yelled while giving a "poor pitiful me" look to Patroklos. The knight took one glance Willy's way and worry washed over me for my frail friend's well-being.

When I saw that Patroklos was not going to budge, my heart was able to travel back down my throat to its rightful place. I sighed. Fully relieved, I said, "I'm a bit peckish, who else?" All hands rose and I laughed. "Alright then, men. Let's go ask the cook to make us something." I shot my eyes toward Patroklos giving him a look of "is that okay" and he simply smiled while giving me a humble nod.

Then I turned to Mason. "Hey, let's do it, mate," he said grinning. Throwing our arms over one another's shoulders, we picked up both swords and started walking over toward Willy and our leader.

When we made it over to them, I asked, "Lord Patroklos, could Mason and I have your consent to go and remove our armor first? This stuff sure is uncomfortable." I finished my last plea while pulling the collar of my chainmail away from my neck. When our brother permitted us, Mason and I took off down to the armory chamber.

During our jog, I said, "Hey, after we eat, you, me, and Willy need to go down towards the shore." His feet slid as he tried to slow down. I stopped myself and took four big steps back, putting my right hand on his shoulder. "Do you need to catch your breath, man?" He shook his head but still didn't speak. "Why did you stop then all of a sudden? I asked, confused. "Mate, we were commanded not to step foot on shore until Lord Patroklos says", he answered, breathing heavily. "I just thought we could catch a glimpse of what we will soon be fighting." I said, standing him back up straight. " It isn't worth it mate, trust me. Come on. Let's go, we're almost there. I can see the tent. Let go of that bad plan, Brighton." He answered, giving me a brotherly head shake, holding a hand full of my hair.

He still couldn't seem to get his head around my proposition. I watched him as he sucked in and blew out about five deep breaths. Then he looked at me and asked once again, "Brighton, what in all sea turtles were you getting at? I thought we agreed not to step foot on shore, let alone near it. Even Lord Patroklos forbids it." "Alright. Alright." I said, replying as if I was holding up my hands in surrender.

A few minutes of silence went by, then I threw my arm around my timid brother's neck and began pulling him the rest of the way. Reaching the armory, I pushed one side of the cloth as Mason moved the other. Playfully shoving him inside, I followed behind and began to remove my boots. "Hurry, man. I'm hungry. I want to eat and then go look for my lady, since we won't be stepping foot on the sand anytime soon." I said, giving him a wink.

He paused in the middle of removing his chausses and shot me a coy smile. "You really like that beauty, don't ya mate? Tell me, is she crazy like the others say?"

A titter forced its way out as I answered. "She is going to be my wife."

"Crickey. You got it bad, mate." He started laughing but I didn't care. I sat there deep in thought, drowning him out. Milaya's brown eyes, brown locks, her smile, and our conversation were all I was thinking about. I chuckled when the replay of her sudden outburst resurfaced. Her angry face to me was adorable.

"Hey, Brighton, mate. Hello? Hey!" Mason shouted while putting his hands together close to my eyes. The crackling sound caused my peaceful daydream to vanish. I shook my head letting go of my trance. "Saints, Mason. What can I say? When you asked about Milaya, well I, I…"

"Hey!" Mason snapped his fingers brushing the tip of my nose with his thumb. When I focused on him, he huffed. "Get that stuff off and get dressed, will you? Stop googly eyeing off into space."

I gave my friend a mocking big toothy grin as I stood up to remove my iron chest plate and all the chainmail. Fully clothed, Mason and I left and headed over to the kitchen.

Walking in we saw that Willy and Patroklos had already beaten us there. "What took you guys so long?" Willy asked, stuffing bread into his mouth. "Yeah, what did take you both such a time frame long to get here?" Patroklos chimed in, right after taking a swig from his silver chalice.

My mouth started to water, and I felt the saliva as it began to trickle out of the corner, leaving the gooey residue on my bottom lip. When I lifted my hand to wipe it off, Mason popped off, "Showing your skill off made you that hungry, huh?" Then he began to snicker.

I chuckled, smacking him in between his shoulder blades. With clenched teeth and a fake smile, while directing the guy to his seat, I said, "Come, have a sit, brother. The bread's getting stiff." Then I forcefully pushed him onto the chair.

He leaned to one side looking up at me and then he snickered. Making my way back around the table, I let out a sarcastic titter. "Ee he he" I mocked, getting him back as I sat myself down to try and enjoy some bread as well. "Tho wuth shu thay o eh hu eh hu eh hu."

"Brighton! You alright?" Willy asked, rushing out of his seat to beat me across my back. "Ehhu eh hu ehuhu." I couldn't stop coughing. My friend continued while scolding, "Don't talk with your mouth full."

His eyes were slit, so I knew I worried him. Saints. I had to say I scared myself as well. The moment that notion came in, I started swiftly bobbing my head on the outside and all of them stared at me. Mason touched my forehead. "Yep. I'm afraid the mate popped his cork." "Get off!" I huffed, twitching my head and swiping his hand away.

"Brighton, it's alright mate. We're all friends here." I was annoyed and I seriously had an inkling to punch that coy grin right off his lips, but when I heard Patroklos and Willy guffawing, it took away my irritability and I joined in. Not long into our laughing fit, all of us started choking on our bread.

We didn't give it one thought because us men were enjoying ourselves and having a merry ol' time. I rocked back onto my chair legs, patting my stomach, and took in this moment thinking to myself, "I could make this place home."

Thud. My chair hit the ground as I leaned my body toward the table. Everyone stopped their chatter. "Saints. I guess my weight is more than I thought." I said with wide eyes. "Crickey!" Mason chortled out. All of us stared at one another and then fell once more back into laughter.

Willy and Patroklos had their chalices to their mouths. When they pulled them away, it felt like a spritz from a watering hose hitting my face. Before I knew it, all four of us had fallen off of our chairs. We stayed on the floor rolling and guffawing for what felt like a day's past.

Mason was the first to get back up. He grabbed his chalice and smashed it on the tabletop. "Another!" He shouted to the cook.

After things had died down, I asked Patroklos, "Are we finished with our training? I want to go find your sister after I scarf down this last slice." There was a disturbance in his eyes but still, he grinned and answered. "I am afraid I forgot to tell you she's left Egladon. She had told me she was off to visit an old friend or something along the lines of that. To be honest, I didn't know she even knew anyone out of Egladon." My heart pinched as my mouth dropped. "Courage, man. She won't be long. Besides I will have plenty of things to keep you occupied." Even though my leader was jesting around, his words still stung.

"But I just had breakfast with her this morning." I said in sad tone. Patroklos gave me a concerned one eyebrow raised kind of look, so I cleared my throat and sat up straight in my chair. Slowly eating the rest of my bread, showing him I had lost interest, I started to wonder just how long my beautiful maiden would be away. "Milaya, why did you leave without coming to say farewell," I quietly said under my breath while dropping down my head.

CHAPTER 27

Milaya

Leaving the dining hall, I saw that the day had turned out to be full of sunshine. I went back to my chamber and grabbed a good book to take with me for a little light reading down by the shore. "The Maiden and Her Courageous Knight," I read the title a loud to myself while skipping my way down the mountain. This book was my all-time favorite, seeing as I could relate to the maiden's character.

When I made it to the white crystallized sand, I immediately kicked off my shoes and ran towards the water. After giving them a dip, I walked far enough up to where the waves couldn't reach me. I planted myself down, enjoying the sun rays and being swept away into an enchanted fairytale while I listened to the roars of the ocean in the background.

My face was buried, and my eyes were fixed on every word. I was about to reach chapter five when my father's voice came into my head and made me lose all of my concentration. "Milaya, my child, you need to leave." I froze in shock thinking he was near. I stopped reading and hoisted my head to scour the shore. There was nothing nor no one in sight, so I shook it off and continued back to my book. The sound of the white caps rushing in against the shoreline was soothing and I thought I would put my book down for a bit to lay in the sand and enjoy a peaceful nap, letting the heat from the sun warm my body , relax me, and put me to sleep. The moment I closed my eyes, the waves silenced, and I heard my father's voice again, "Milaya, my child, leave now before it is too late." The whisper startled me again, making me sit up and glance at my surroundings.

"Father! Is that you!?" I shouted as I rubbed my eyes trying to get them to gain more focus. "Daddy? I can't see you." Nothing spoke back and my father was nowhere to be found. "This isn't amusing!" I shouted, now feeling somewhat frightened. I took a deep breath, grabbed my book, and started reading once more keeping myself alert for any surprises.

I could hear the crashing of the waves getting louder and louder in the background as if I was right in the eye of a storm. Then there was a quaking splash that got my attention. When I lifted my eyes from the page my whole body stiffened. I could hear my subconscious scream as the water hit my face. I closed my eyes thinking, "This isn't real, it's not real, , it's not real. Please don't eat me," I cried on the inside.

The feeling of warm liquid seeped from both corners of my eyes as it thunderously yelled, "Look at me, girl!" I lifted my lids to see sharp needle-pointed teeth right in front of my nose. My heart started beating uncontrollably. Instantly I started to feel nauseous and faint. My nerves were all out of whack. Just as my eyes began to roll back, the sea monster lifted its head and slithered backward. "Humans," it murmured aloud.

"I am not going to eat you, girl. If I did, then I would have no one to bring forth my destruction." All of my muscles loosened giving me the ability to stand to my feet except my poor knees were still shaky. "Wh-who are you?" I asked, petrified. "Bahahaha, I am no one of consequence, my dear girl." I quivered from the sound of its cackle. I could feel my eyes shift as they were being pulled unwillingly.

"Mmm, yes that's better." The monster had compelled me. I couldn't look away let alone move. Lost in a trance from its hollow orbs the sea beast began giving me instructions. "Listen well, girl. Go to Brighton's chamber and bring me back something special that belongs to him. If you run into anyone, tell them you will be going to TungWing to visit an old friend and that you are just needing to get a few things before you go. Don't try to beg for help. There is no use. I have stolen your voice. Ahahaha, Ahahaha now go and hurry back." It's vicious cackle was enough to make me want to crawl in a dark hole and stay there. With no free will, my head bobbed on its own, and then I felt like an alive but dead on the inside walking vessel as my feet began to walk me off the sand and back up the mountain.

One of my brother's soldiers passed by me staring, I started to walk towards him to ask him to go and get my brother, but he swiftly took off kicking dust. So, I unwillingly continued to the castle.

When I got up to my room, I shoveled through all of my father's belongings hoping to find something to break this force hold. There was a knock at my door. "Milaya?" It was my brother, but I couldn't speak to answer him. He pried open my door to see my chamber turned upside down. "Sister, what are you doing?" he asked, shocked. I opened my mouth just as tears streamed down my face, but what came out was not what I wanted to say.

"Hehe, oh you know me, just looking for my favorite dress."

"Okay then," he answered with an odd chuckle as he began to rub the back of his neck.

"Brother, I need to go and grab something before I leave for TungWing."

" TungWing? And what? You're leaving?!" he said abruptly.

"Mhmm. I am going to visit an old friend." The awful creature was using me as a puppet and speaking with my voice. I couldn't control anything. He started to speak again but the monster interrupted, "Not to worry, I know, I know, I'll be safe, and I'll be back within a day or two." It was as if the monster knew I was about to start wailing for help because what rolled off my tongue next scared my brother, and he's never been afraid of anything. "Get out of my way Patroklos or I will devour you just as I did your father." I watched his eyes widen and then quickly go docile.

After that my brother gave me an odd look and then moved aside. The sea beast put him in a trance along with me, and he wasn't able to see that I needed him. I don't think he even noticed I was crying. Instead of questioning he just said, "Safe trip, sister," as my controlled vessel left. When I looked back over my shoulder, my poor brother was standing there frozen solid. "You didn't have to do that to him," I hissed on the inside. "Silence!" it shouted back, and I felt like I was really going crazy.

"That's it, almost there. Yes. Bring me back what I want." I could hear the beast's whispers so clearly and it only made me want to scream out more. After grabbing a picture drawing of a boy and a girl on their horses riding through a forest from Brighton's end table, my body started to jerk in place. My feet began to pivot and before I knew it, I was down the stairs getting ready to leave the castle.

I stayed focused on the drawing. It seemed as if it was drawn by a child. I started to wonder if my dashing soldier had already been wed. When I looked up from the picture, the sea monster had already brought me back to shore. Fog was all around me and I couldn't see any part of Egladon.

A symbol in between the monster's forehead glowed red. In mid-air right at the shoreline, a doorway appeared. It commanded, "You are to go and find a girl named Annalise. Show her this picture so she will trust you and bring her and her friends back to me. If they ask for your identity, I will speak for you. Now go. Oh, and one more thing, if you fail, I will eat you whole. Ahahahaha..." My feet began moving towards the gateway as I heard the beast cackling over and over in the distance. I thought, "Who are these people and why do I have to be the one to fetch them? Then my body went through the opening.

CHAPTER 28

Brighton

The last two nights of training were starting to take a toll on Mason and me. Sitting up on the side of my mattress, I started thinking of Milaya and the glistening glow on her face when she smiles. I knew Patroklos said she went to a place called TungWing for a couple of days to visit an old friend but if she didn't come back today it would be going on three. I ran my fingers through my hair while staring at the floor in deep thought.

"Milaya, when will you return?" I exhaled out in dismay. "Get a grip, mate. She's only been gone for a couple of days." Mason said, hurling one of his boots toward the foot of my bed. "What in the stars is all the commotion so early in the morning?"

Willy was now up and yawning while shaking his breathing contraption in one hand and scratching his head with the other. "Saints, Willy, it's almost breakfast time. It's not early." I answered tossing Mason back his boot. "Brighton's just over there devo about Mad Maiden-" "Don't call her that! And I'm not devastated!" I huffed cutting him off. "Milaya," he finished as he winked at me.

"Oh. Not to worry brother. I'm sure she'll be back soon. Lord Patricklos isn't worried so you shouldn't be either," Willy said trying to console me and my racing thoughts. I stood up to get dressed and Willy did the same. After fastening my boots, I noticed Masons were across the room by the window. "Hey, mate. Toss me my daks, will ya?"

I laughed while walking over to pick them up. "What did you just call your breeches?" "Ha-ha," Mason sneered. "Don't be a drongo, mate. Just bring them over." As I tossed them to him, I noticed Willy rolled his eyes. "Who plucked your chicken?" I asked abruptly. "It isn't good to mock others' ways of speech." He growled. "Oh, I was just simply jesting. You know that don't you brother?" I answered looking in Mason's direction.

"Yeah, mate. I didn't take it to heart. Willy, mate, I'm not a bloody chook. I can speak for myself. Brighton didn't offend me." "Oh," Willy answered, dropping his head, more than likely feeling sheepish. "Well now that that's settled, let's go eat and get to the training grounds to figure out what Patroklos wants us to do today," I said, throwing my arm over Mason's shoulders and directing him outside as Willy followed on our heels.

After leaving the dining hall, Mason and I went to suit up in the armory while Willy stayed behind to help wash dishes.

"Pass me those chausses." I said to Mason as he was putting on his chainmail.

"Here you are, mate. I wonder what our sire is going to train us on today."

"I don't know brother, but I hope it involves flying," I replied while putting on my last piece of armor.

"This helmet seems as if it's been tightened somehow."

"No, mate. Your head's just grown bigger, hahaha." My friend continued to guffaw as he forcefully pressed the iron down on my head. "Yuck, yuck, yuck," I replied while he was fastening it. "Don't be a dog, mate. It isn't your style." He said smacking my chest plate and guffawing. I began to chuckle as well. After all, he was quite humorous.

Still laughing I pulled back the drape saying, "Let's go Mason. We don't want to be late." We left the tent and hurried to meet our leader. "Strewth! Willy, mate, how did you make it here so fast?" Mason shouted. Up in the distance, we could see Patroklos and Willy waiting for us. Our leader had Artrayious standing right next to his side, and he was stroking the underneath of his chest.

My heart started to dance inside as I began to think what I desired was going to happen. We were going to get to train on our pegasi today. I picked up my footing on every stride excited to hear our instructions. Finally, coming face to face with them, Patroklos said, "How did you two sleep? I hope you got plenty of rest because your task today will not be easy." I gulped.

"Go and get your pegasi and then report back to me, quickly lads." he commanded. Mason and I took off to the stable cave to get Arkimedes and Brontes. I didn't care how hard the challenge was going to be, I was just ecstatic that we got to fly. "Mason, did you remember to brush Brontes last night?" He stopped dead in his tracks. "Crickey! That bloody beast is going to trample me." He answered, wide eyed and rubbing the back of his neck. My friend stood there for a second. He was probably contemplating how to butter up his pet. I stared at him, chuckling.

"Come on, man. He can't be that upset." I threw my arm over his shoulders and began to pick up the pace, pulling him alongside me. He let go and started running on his own. Reaching the cave, Arkimedes was already stepping out to greet me. "Brighton. Are we taking flight today for training? Oh, I mean neigh... neigh."

Letting out a half-winded laugh, I reached out my hand to stroke his side. "It's alright boy. I know you can talk." Arkimedes cleared his throat "Ahem. Since you are fully aware now, I would much rather prefer to be called by my given name and not this boy you speak of. I am not some furry hound creature."

Mason started guffawing and I tried to explain. "Arkimedes, boy isn't bad. It's just a way of saying I care. You know, like another pet name." He started to whinny, and it ultimately turned into a nicker. "Sir Brighton, I am over four hundred years of light. I have not been a colt for quite some time now, so no more calling boy. My name will do quite nicely sir if you please." He finished while bowing his head.

I turned to look at Mason and I caught him lifting his hand to his mouth to cover a smirk. "Okay, Arkimedes it is then," I answered with a titter. Mason was still trying to keep his composure by acting as if he was clearing his throat. With a suppressed chortle he called out, "Brontes, ya best be in your stall and not in the food supply area."

We heard him blow out and we immediately knew that's where he was. "Brontes ya big glutton. We're flying today. Stop stuffing your face!" He shouted as he took off into the cave.

"Come on, let's go Arkimedes. They'll catch up." "Oh, I do hope so sir," he said as he bent his two front knees to the ground while also lowering his right wing for me to climb upon. As soon as I settled my-self, he began to walk us back to the training grounds.

"I must say sir it has been rather long since I've taken to the clouds. Pardon, but I could be a bit rusty."

I guffawed as I reached my left hand down to pat his neck. "I'm sure we'll be fine my friend."

"Do hold on sir Brighton for my reassurance, will you?"

"Sure, thing Arkimedes." I answered and then swallowed hard thinking, "Saints, this beast might drop me."

"Whoa Brontes. Slow down, mate!" I heard Mason yell from behind us. Twisting my body to look over my shoulder, Mason was hanging onto one of Brontes' wings for dear life as they tried to catch up to us. I turned back around, shook my head, and laughed at the sound of Mason's squeals.

"I do wonder if those two will ever get along," Arkimedes said while entering through the gate. "Hey, Willy. Check out Mason." I shouted, busting a gut. Not long after Patroklos, Willy and Artrayious joined in. "Yuh, yuh, yuh, yuh." That was the only thing we could hear out of that poor man as Brontes began to circle us slowing himself down. Mason lost his grip from the speed of his pegasus and was now dangling a quarter of the way down from the ground.

Brontes fully stopped, bent his front knees, tilted to his side, and shook Mason off his wing. The poor guy went tumbling and we watched as his body rolled over the grass. "Crickey!" He shouted from a distance, while standing up, and wiggling his body. He looked at us and then began to check himself for any abrasions. Walking over, he brushed the grass and dirt from his arms and elbows while giving Brontes a heavy scowl.

Making his towards us he said, "Patroklos, I'm not flying on that hoon. He's trying to kill me." Willy and I guffawed. "Maybe next time you'll remember to groom me," Brontes blew out as he nickered. Poor Mason didn't have a comeback. He just dropped his chin and said, "My apologies, mate." Brontes bowed his head accepting our friend's amends.

"Alright, now that all has been settled, let us begin today's drill," Patroklos voiced out. Squaring his shoulders and uncrossing his arms, he started pointing in different directions of the grounds. "Brighton, you and Arkimedes are over by the castle wall. Mason, you and your pesky pet are over by those trees. Artrayious, Willy, and I will go to the middle. Willy, you stay on the ground. When I take flight you two follow, and when we're all in the air I'll give further instruction, agreed?" I felt bad for Willy, but I knew it was because his lungs wouldn't be able to take it. Mason and I looked at each other and then faced back. With a quick bob, we both said in unison, "Agreed." We all about-faced and headed to our places. Just as Arkimedes and I made it to the castle's south wall, I noticed Patroklos and Artrayious had already taken to the sky.

Leaping up onto Arkimedes' wing, I heard our leader begin to shout out instructions. "Alright, men. I need you to treat this training day like your life depends on it because when we are fully ready to take on that sea beast, these skills will be the only thing that could save you from being eaten."

I gulped. Making my way up my pet's wing, I thought, "Am I really ready for this? What happens to Egladon if we lose?" Gasp. "Milaya! What happens to my beautiful angel?"

"No!" I roared out loud frustrated over my anxious notions. I wasn't going to give them any room to fester and cause me to lose sight of what was important. Training to kill that vile sea creature.

"Did you say something, sir?" Arkimedes asked as he flapped his wing to give me a boost onto the top of his neck. "Thanks," I said slightly winded as my stomach plunged into his withers. "My pleasure, sir," He answered, not paying any mind to my excessive coughing.

"Okay, I'm ready when you are, my friend," I said after gaining some much-needed oxygen back into my lungs and setting myself upright. "Yes, sir. As soon as Artrayious gives me the signal, I shall take flight," He responded.

Across the way, I saw Mason climbing up Brontes. He gave me a coy grin and wink after he had reached his position, and I wasn't sure, but I think I saw Brontes show his teeth to me as well. "Hey, Arkimedes. Do you think Brontes has other arterial motives?"

"If he does, they are not towards you sir. If I'm not mistaken, his father was eaten by the sea monster. Oh, when was it, ah yes a little over three years ago."

My eyes widened in shock. "You mean when Lord Timious disappeared?"

"Precisely," he answered with a sharp bob.

"So that means Brontes' father was Lord Timious' pegasus?"

"Yes, Sir Brighton, you are correct." As he replied, I was thinking, "Milaya never said anything about her father having a flying partner, I wonder if he's still out there somewhere."

"Brighton!"

"Huh? I mean yes sir." Patroklos' yelling pulled me straight out of my theories. "I called your name three times, where did you drift off to? Also, don't call me that." I looked over and Mason was leaning back on Brontes guffawing.

I cleared my throat. "Ready!" I called out. "Ready for what? I haven't told you anything yet. I just got your attention." He sternly shouted back and staring at me strangely. A few seconds of awkward silence went by and then Patroklos said, "Alright then. Now that all eyes are on me, Brighton, I want you and Arkimedes up in the air to practice dives."

Next, he turned toward Mason and Brontes. "You two will start here on the ground and go over takeoffs. Remember they need to be quick like the blink of an eye." Mason nodded in full compliance. "Men, Artrayious and I will fly up higher to observe. Once we see that you have your first task down, we'll resurface, go eat and come back for flight fighting."

I watched as Brontes began to bend his knees getting ready to hoist off the ground as Arkimedes and I were about to take our first drop. I squeezed my eyes closed and grabbed a huge chunk of his mane for dear life.

"You ready, Sir Brighton?"

"Uh, sure," I replied, allowing my right eye to peek open. "Alright then, gather yourself cause here we go..."

"Ahhh...! Yeah! Wah Hoo...!" The force of the wind against my face was causing my eyes to water and blur my vision. So, I couldn't enjoy the scenery around us but from the thrill of the dive, I didn't care.

We were descending closer and closer toward the ground. When the grass came into focus my stomach started to churn. I thought Arkimedes heard the bubbles forming because he shouted, "You might want to close your eyes if you're feeling ill, sir!"

I chuckled remembering this magnificent creature was in sync with me and could read my mind. I shut my eyes while swallowing down some unwanted stomach acid.

Boom! "Am I dead?" I asked under my breath while peeking open one eye. "Sir, we are not dead. We've just landed."

"Oh. Ha, you heard that, did you?" I timidly chuckled. "Saints Arkimedes, your hooves hitting the ground sounded like a crackle of thunder." He blew out his nostrils and then began to whinny while prancing in place.

'I do say Sir Brighton you are a smash to be around ahahaha. Ready to go again?" he asked, excited. Curling his mane around my fingers, I clenched my thighs tight and answered, "Oh yeah." In what felt like a flash we were already in position for another nosedive. "Alright sir, I'm going to go faster this time, are you ready?" It was a friendly warning not a question as he brought his wings into his sides, and we began to free-fall like a raindrop from the sky.

"Saints, there goes my stomach again," I thought as I held my breath and folded over.

After five rounds, I couldn't hold back the chunks any longer. So needless to say, my breakfast was all over the ground. Patroklos and Artrayious descended and landed as I just finished wiping my mouth. "Good start to the day brothers. Now let us go replenish," he yelled, sliding down his pegasus. I shouted, "I cannot eat anything right now!"

Mason and Willy walked up chortling. Willy was laughing so much that he had to take a puff from his breathing contraption. "Brighton mate, hahaha, you better get that under control before the real deal." Mason teased. I spat. "It's not that funny."

"Uh pardon me sir but it is rather humorous," Arkimedes chimed in. I sneered, and then heaved once more, listening to their guffaws in the background.

"Alright you three, let's go." Patroklos was ready for some grub, so I swiped the back of my palm across my lips, and we all followed as he began heading toward the gate. I let the air out of my cheeks and thought to myself, "I hope my stomach allows me to eat something even if it's just a piece of bread." Then I belched.

"Mmm..." I said, patting my full belly. Right as we reached the dining hall the queasiness subsided, and I was able to sit with my brothers and enjoy our meal. We made it back to the training court and Patroklos was ready to give us our second set of instructions. Mason, Willy, and I followed him around to the front of the castle. Near the closing gate, was a metal chest filled with wooden swords and shields.

"Listen up Mason and Brighton, these are what you will use in fighting skill today. When I feel confident enough that you two won't slice each other up, then I'll allow you to use your real swords."

Mason guffawed. Smacking our leader across his back he said, "You're jesting right? Come on, mate, you can't be serious." Patroklos chuckled. "Oh, I'm very serious mate," he said, returning Mason's playful gesture. "Now grab your weapons and let's go," he said, spinning on his heel. I picked up a small wooden carved sword that looked fit to be a toy for a youngster like my brother Kedron and then shrugged at Mason and Willy.

"Watch out mate, I'm coming for ya," Mason said, pointing his small weapon at me. All three of us busted out in laughter. After gaining our composure we hurried over to meet up with Patroklos.

CHAPTER 29

Annalise

"Are you better now?" David asked, searching me over. "I think so. Ferguson, is that you?"

"Huh?" He replied confused. "What? Sorry, did you say something?" I swiftly countered trying to sway him away from what I'd just asked. "Oh, ha ha never mind. I thought, well I don't know what I was thinking."

"Uhh… okay then," he said, perplexed. "Hey, I think they're waiting on us. Look they're staring over here," I said while pointing at the others.

"Yeah, we better go then. Any more waterworks forming?" I giggled and shook my head. My friend pulled me to my feet, and we headed back over to hear the crown prince's instructions for today. When we were within earshot range, we could hear him already going over his plan with Tailya and Lin Lan as his army stood at attention behind them.

"Listen up. Yinglong is still about a two-day's journey, so we'll make our way up the mountain this morning to gather some berries, eggs from the eagles' nests, and water from the falls. There should be enough to keep us nourished until we reach the dragon."

All three of us bobbed our heads at the same time as his soldiers shouted behind us, "Yes sir!" We broke off. Tay, David, and I went to the right as Lin Lan, of course, went with Li Che and his army towards the left. As we made our way up, Li Che yelled, "Beware of tigers! They are very active this time in the season. Here take this David!" He tossed my friend a sword. The tip almost hit my foot causing me to jump back a couple of spaces. "Thanks, princey!" David shouted back. Li Che smirked, "Don't mention it!" Tay and I rolled our eyes.

"What do you think?" He asked with a prideful grin plastered on his face. Tay sighed. "Oh, come on, sis, I'll protect you ladies," he replied, swinging the blade from side to side. That thing came right up to my eye level. "Hey! Watch it!" I blurted. "Sorry Anna." He said frowning as he dropped it to his side.

It already felt like we had been walking for the entire day. "Ugh, are we about there?" I groaned, stomping the tingles out of my feet. "Shh...," David sounded looking at me with an intense stare. "Did you guys hear that?" he whispered, panic-stricken.

Tay and I stopped moving to listen. David gasped, "There it is again." He blew out as he wrapped his fingers tightly around the hilt of his sword. I shot my eyes over to Tay and she was holding her breath. "Listen. It's coming from over there. Over there!" I shockingly gasped while pointing at the bush just near a tree with blue leaves.

All three of us watched closely as the red berries on the bush began to slightly move. David moved closer to it while Tay and I backed up slowly. "Be careful David," we both whispered. He nodded and continued to tiptoe. When he was almost within reach of touching a leaf, the berries stilled, and the bush went silent. David spun around to face us. He looked like he was about to say something while shrugging his shoulders. Tay and I stayed focused waiting.

"Raaa!"

"David watch out!" I shouted. "Ahhh!" he screamed as a giant tiger pounced on top of him. Tay and I froze in terror, eyes bugged, and hearts racing like a jockey on a horse trying to reach the finish line. I was breathing so fast that I started to lose air and my head began to feel fuzzy.

"Raaa!"

"Erg. Grr. Ugg." David was rolling around all over the ground trying to slay the vicious feline. "Ahhh!" He yelled as the cat sunk its teeth into my friend's left shoulder. A teardrop leaked down as I stood there thinking David was about to be eaten.

"Now David!" Tay shouted at the top of her lungs. She startled me with her yell causing me to jerk my head towards her. When I looked back at David he was being dragged across the ground by the tiger.

"David!" I cried out. The boy turned his head and winked at me as if he wasn't the least bit scared or in pain.

I began to take a cue from Tay and held my breath. The tiger stopped and extracted its sharp fangs from David. The cat stared into my friend's eyes like it was asking him, "Any last wishes?" However, David didn't falter. It was as if he was waiting for this opportune moment. Without the fierce tiger noticing, David savagely thrusted his blade into its stomach. "Roar!" It wailed out and looked like it was getting ready to chomp David's face, but the plunge was too deep, and my friend was able to roll the tiger off of him.

Standing himself up, he looked at his sister and me then said, "What, you two weren't worried, were you?" I huffed and shook my head. "You're so full of yourself brother." Tay chuckled. Coming from a distance we heard, "Are you three alright?"

"Yeah, my brother just gutted a tiger!" Tay shouted back.

Walking over the hill was the crown prince, Lin Lan, and another girl. Her dress was the same color as the cherry blossom leaves and it glimmered in the sunlight. When they had made it to us, Li Che said, "Girl, this child says she knows you. Have you ever seen her before?"

I stood there looking her over while Tay blurted, "No can't say I have."

"I wasn't asking you. I was asking her," Li Che replied pointing at me. "Oh, well you can see how one can become confused when you say girl seeing as we're both girls," Tay retorted with a slight bend in her knees.

Lin Lan covered her smile that was caused by Tay's sarcasm. The crown prince chuckled and didn't seem to mind as he said, "I can see now how that could be puzzling, miss. My apologies." My friend crossed her arms. "Thank you," she replied mockingly. "Ahem. As I was saying, you girl," he stated pointing to me once more, "Do you know this person?"

I stood there, my eyes moving from head-to-toe thinking, "Okay, Anna, where have you met this girl?" But staring into her eyes, I couldn't recall a time or place, so I answered, "No your highness I don't know her, nor have I ever met her." Li Che's eyes creased as he glared at the unidentified girl who had just shown up suddenly.

"Guards! Guards!" he roared. As soon as they came over the hill, he commanded, "Take her to the prison for questioning and if she doesn't confess why she came to TungWing then she will be sentenced to death by noon tomorrow. Go and tell my father." Two men went to grab her when she reached out and clasped her hand around my right wrist. "Annalise, Annalise. I know Brighton!" She yelled. "Wait!" I shouted. "Your highness, she said she knows my brother. Please release her." The crown prince searched me over and then turned to his maid who nodded on my behalf which I was grateful for.

He lifted his palm, waving it through the air for his men to unhand the poor girl. She dropped to her knees and began to weep. Tay and I locked eyes while David blurted, "Hey, I just fought a tiger. My shoulder is bleeding, do you have anything for me to wrap it with?"

"David," I hissed. "Can't you see the poor thing is fear-stricken? Leave her alone." Tay chimed in after, "Geez, brother show some compassion." I bent over to pull her up and when she looked up at me there was torture in her eyes. I thought to myself, "I've seen this look before, but where?" In a deep stare, she squeezed my wrist. "Help me," she whispered.

Tay heard her and blurted. "Help you with what?" The girl's saddened gaze changed as she began to glare at my friend. To break the ice I asked, "Where did you say you knew my brother from?"

"Huh? Oh, I met him a couple of days ago in my world." Tay placed her hands on her hips and spouted off, "Uh, and just where are you from?"

I giggled not being able to control myself. I knew she was protecting me, so I let her have her fun. The girl paused like she didn't know what to say. "Well, if you're finished talking, I guess we'll just hand you back over to his highness then." The two men from before began to reach out and the girl shouted, "Wait! I have something for you."

From the pocket of her dress, she pulled out a folded piece of paper. "That's not good enough," Tay hissed. "We want to know where you came from."

"Wait, no look. I am from Egladon," she yelled, unfolding the piece of paper. Holding it up in front of my face she said," See. Here, I am not lying. If I were, how could I manage to have this?"

In her hand was the picture I had drawn for my brother when I was little. Both of us on Nicodemus and Ghost in the forest back home when he was teaching me how to ride. "How?" I was at a loss for words. "Children as touching as this is, we still have a task to tend to," Li Che spoke out after clearing his throat.

"Oh right. Sorry, your highness. Let's not split up this time though in case we have another run-in with another tiger, we need your warriors to protect us and our new friend. Uh, I'm sorry, what is your name?" David popped out his chest. "I'm all the protection you need. I did kill the first tiger, you know."

"Yeah, but not before getting dragged around like a ragdoll." I snickered. He scowled as the girl giggled at our tiff. Then she answered, "My name is Milaya."

Everyone began making their way up the mountain towards the falls. I was glad because I was extremely thirsty. "Milaya," I said, walking beside Tay. "It's a pleasure to meet you." She smiled and then shifted her eyes forward. "Children, we're almost there. Just a bit further up the hill and we should reach the freshwater along with the jujube and kumquat trees." The crown prince announced as he put a little more speed in his stride.

"Thank the stars!" David shouted back. Li Che looked back over his shoulder and snickered at my friend. We picked up our pace as all of our bellies started to growl in neglect.

"Wha!" I yelled, completely astonished. We reached the falls and right near it were the fruit trees. I ran over to pluck one from its leaf. "What does this orange one taste like?" I shouted as I bit into it. "Pa, pa, pa. Ew, what is this?" I groaned. The orange berry was so sour I had to spit it out. After that, my lips began puckering from the strong taste. Lin Lan made her way over to me giggling and I noticed that Tay and Milaya were following behind.

David was over by the water hole slurping it up like it was going to disappear. I shook my head and laughed. "Here, try these, Annalise." Lin Lan held out her open hand filled with red shriveled berries. They didn't look very appealing, so I was hesitant to grab some and put them in my mouth.

Walking up to his maid and taking a couple from her to pop in his mouth, Li Che said, "These are one of our delicacies here. They are sweet, savory, and it'll get rid of sourness from the kumquat." He winked at me and then started chewing. "Mmm. Very good," he said while pointing towards Lin Lan's open palm.

I sighed and then said, "Alright, since I am really hungry, I guess I will just try this one also." I picked the smallest one I saw hoping they weren't trying to jest me. I clamped my eyes closed, stuck it in my mouth, and started to chew it slowly.

The moment my teeth pierced it a gooey sweet apple flavor hit my tongue. "Mmm!" I sounded allowing my eyes to open and look at everyone. "Where is the tree, I want some more," I said while chewing up and swallowing the last bit.

Li Che guffawed, "Over there by your friend lapping up water." I looked over and saw that David was still in the same spot drinking the water like a thirsty dog. I giggled at the sight. "Tay, Milaya, and Annalise let's go gather some jujubes." Lin Lan proposed Tay and I nodded while slightly bending at the knee, but Milaya was nodding her head like something was talking to her.

She didn't even realize Tay and I had already started to leave until I grabbed her arm to pull her along.

CHAPTER 30

Annalise

"David, you've been over here drinking from the falls long enough. Geez brother we've only been without for a night. You can't possibly be that thirsty." Tay scolded as she picked some jujubes from the tree. David stood up and walked over to his sister, Milaya, and me. "Bwaaap! There I feel better now."

"David you obnoxious little goon!" Tay continued to yell out unpleasantries toward her brother as she waved the hot stinky air from her smell zone.

Milaya guffawed and it was the first time we witnessed her becoming more relaxed. "So," I said, stuffing my mouth. "How did my brother Brighton know to find me here?"

"Huh?!" she blurted looking like she was on the defense to answer me. "Oh, well. Umm…" she spoke again in hesitation.

Tailya, my protective bodyguard, skeptically stared her down. David and I kind of just stood there a little baffled. Tay squared herself right in front of the poor girl's face. "Tell me, Milaya, why are you having trouble answering Anna's question?"

With the way she acted, looking at the ground and spinning her thumbs around one another, it was starting to become a little difficult to trust her. All three of us watched her suspiciously. She looked nervous about something and to us, that threw up a red flag. I thought, "Does this girl really know my brother? I'm going to test her some more."

"Ahem," I cleared my throat and deeply peered into her eyes. I sternly asked again, "I said, how did Brighton know where to find me?" Raising our voices, I and my two friends began to shout for the guards. "Guar"- "No! Please, I'll tell you, I'll tell you." She pleaded. We looked at each other and nodded, giving her the chance to explain for the third time. " Annalise, when your brother told me himself, I thought it to be silly. Please believe me it is the truth." She said raising her palms faced in the air trying to calm us.

We closed our traps. Tay and I firmly planted our hands on our hips while David squared his shoulders, spread his feet wide, and crossed his arms like a judge getting ready to sentence the guilty.

Milaya took in a huge breath and then began to give us more of her explanation. "When I met your dashing brother a couple of days ago, we made up a time to get acquainted. At our place on the mountain to start the conversation, your brother Brighton began telling me a story about how he journeyed to my home, Egladon."

We were all still considering her words, but neither one of us spoke. We just stood there and listened as she went on. "After finishing our shy meet and greet, we lied down looking up at the clouds and that is when he told me about how he went through a world with unicorns and met an enchantress who he said wasn't trustwor"-

"Wait," I cut her off. With what she had just said I didn't want to control my tongue. "Hold on, go back. What did you just say?" I turned to Tay. Her eyes and mouth were wide open. I could see that she was about as shocked as I was. David must have been also, seeing as his arms had dropped and his brows were now raised in suspicion.

"Wait, did you say unicorns?" David asked, with a little shakiness in his voice.
"How…, how is that even possible?" I asked confoundedly.
"Yeah, how is that possible?" Tay repeated.
"You three think you're stunned now, wait until you hear the rest."

The girl continued but while she was speaking all three of us were confused and in deep thought because we knew what she was talking about. It was still odd to me though that my brother saw unicorns when David and that witch Yurika were the only two. I pushed the racing thoughts to the side for now and continued trying to listen. "Your brother and his friend Willy had to go through a portal that led them into this miraculous world, that's how Brighton put it anyway. This is where I became a bit lost as he said he saw you and was waiting for you to come to Eg"-

"Woah, Woah, Woah." I interrupted again. "That was really him!" Tears were starting to stream down my cheeks as I asked, "How old is

Brighton, and what does he look like?" I thought to myself as I waited for her answer. "Was that really him that I saw from a distance through that window?"

"Brighton is tall, about six foot something, I'm guessing. His hair reminds me of almost ripe strawberries, you know when they have a little white on top of the red?" She began smiling from ear to ear as she described my brother to me, and when she finished last with his age, my body sank down toward the ground in despair.

Turned out that we both had aged in that life-taking world. It really was him that I saw staring back at me in the window of Fawn's hut. Milaya said she thought he was twenty-four or twenty-five. She said he looked the same age as her brother, and I had already come to the realization that she was speaking the truth, so I stuck out my hand. "Stop, just please, stop. I believe you; I just need a minute." I put my head to my knees and let the tears fall as I thought about all the time I have lost with my big brother. When everything was dark, my memories started playing a slideshow. In the first image, I looked to be five or six and I was in the forest curled up on a tree stump. This was when my mother had just reprimanded me, and I ran away to hide. Brighton came looking for me with a cookie in his hand.

The next picture forged into focus, and I remembered this one like it was yesterday. Brighton surprised me in the kitchen after being gone and I leaped into his arms for a tight squeeze. My tears became heavier on the last memory. Brighton was laughing at the name I picked out for my horse. I could hear it so clearly as if he was right next to me. It caused me to lose all control as my body sank into itself and began to jerk in a hard cry.

I heard David's heavy footsteps coming toward me as he dropped to one knee and began to pat my back. "Come on now Annalise. It can't be that bad. It's not like he's dead." I looked up and shot him a glare. Directing my eyes toward Milaya who was oddly staring off into space, I sniffled while asking, "Has my brother fulfilled his dream?"

"Huh, she answered, coming back from la-la land. Then she looked at me funny and said, What? Oh yes, he is training with my brother to become a knight right as we speak."

Her reply was strangely fast spoken almost as if it had been rehearsed or something. Tay must've thought the same too since I caught her staring at Milaya with distrust. I looked at my friend and shook my head motioning for her to let it go for now. When or if I really get to see my brother, I will sort everything about Milaya out then.

She nodded, complying with my request. I stretched my arms out in front of me. "Alright, I'm better now. David, can you help me up?" My friend brushed his palms together, getting the dust off from the dirt, stood up, grabbed my hands, and hoisted me to my feet.

Li Che and Lin Lan came over to us. "Have you four gathered your fruit and drank plenty of water?" his highness asked. When I looked toward the crown prince, he immediately rushed to me and cupped my face. Searching my eyes and swiping a water line that was still visible under my bottom lashes, he asked, "My dear girl, who made you like this?"

I was a little thrown off by his compassion for me, so I moved his hand, bent my knees while leaning into David, and said, "Thank you for your concern, your highness but everything is fine here."

The man wasn't convinced, and he continued to stare at me. "Hey!" I blurted, "Did you not just ask if we've replenished? Well, we have, is it time to go back down the mountain?" My enthusiasm threw him off, causing him to break his gaze and hopefully keep him from speculating any longer.

I gave the man a toothy grin and waited patiently for his reply. David wrapped his arm around me acting like a jealous suitor. "She asked you a question princie." I awkwardly giggled toward his highness.

Leering up at David, I gave him a coy smile. Through my teeth, I said, "If you don't remove it, I'm going to bite it and draw blood." The boy tilted his head, smirked, and unattached his arm. I smiled at Li Che again. "You were saying."

The crown prince chortled. "Come on children. Gather as much fruit as you can carry and let's go." The moment he turned his back I immediately started grabbing jujubes and chunked four of them at David while hissing, "Gross, gross, gross, gross." He dodged every one of them while tittering like a little schoolgirl. "Ugh, stand still and let me hit you," I huffed. Tay and Milaya were picking from the other side guffawing hysterically.

"Na na na na." David was still taunting me. "Erg. Stand still! Ugh, I'm such a bad aim," I grumbled as I smacked myself on the forehead. I noticed Tailya and Milaya had finished picking their red berries, so I grabbed a handful for myself from the ground, glared at David, and said, "Let's go."

The boy followed behind me at a distance. I could still hear his guffaws in the background, and it was making my blood boil. I looked over my shoulder, stuck out my tongue and then mocked him, imitating his actions. After rolling my eyes I turned my view back forward to see that Li Che and Lin Lan were picking kumquats from the other tree.

When we reached them, I thought to myself, "Ick" as I remembered the strong sour taste. The crown prince shouted ahead, "Alright, children, it's time. The sun is now in the middle of the sky which means dark is approaching. We need to get down the mountain before we lose light, or we will be offering ourselves up as cat food."

Both of Tay's and my eyes got wide. In unison, we shouted, "Will we make it?"

"If we leave right now, yes we should," he replied in haste. "Well, what are we waiting for then? Come on. I am not up for wrestling another one of those vicious felines." David blurted, and we all ambled our way down the hill back to our camping spot.

I could see the bottom and the stump that David and I had stayed up talking at. Li Che's army had already made it there and they were getting into their guarding positions. They pulled their swords from their sheaths, laid them across their shoulders, and began to pace back and forth.

"Men, go to your posts and stay alert." The crown prince demanded when we got there. "Yes sir, your highness," they obediently complied. I watched as each of them went to their spaces.

The crown prince's positions he had them get in, formed a huge circle around us which actually made me feel safe. "Huh, maybe there's hope that I'll get some sleep tonight after all," I mumbled. Li Che wasn't lying when he said the sun was leaving us soon. I went to sit down by Tay and when I looked up, I saw that the stars were already filling the sky. "Wha… Tay look!" I said amazed, elbowing her in the side.

"What?" she hissed, rubbing her ribs. With my finger still raised toward the sky I pointed up again and said, "Look." She lifted her eyes replying, "Wow, they sure are bright. Then her eyes dazzled as she said, "And they sparkle too."

"What's sparkling? I want to see."

Tay and I sighed as David spoke with his mouth full again. "Nothing David," I answered, rolling my eyes.

My attempt to brush him off didn't even phase him as the boy wriggled himself in between his sister and me. "Ouch! Watch my hair," Tay hissed. "Well move your tangly mop," David scoffed back. I began laughing. That was until the big oaf leaned back, yanking mine as well. "Ah! David, get up!"

After the three of us got situated, we were able to sink back into the tree bark, look up and enjoy the little balls of light. "Get some rest, children," Li Che commanded.
Awe for all the beanstalks," I groaned as I began to lie my head on the tree stump.

"The brightness of the sun penetrated through my lids letting me know I slept all night. Reaching my arms out in front while flexing my feet, which didn't help much since they had shoes on them, I began to stretch while making my high pitch screeching sound. "Emmmahhh!"

"Geez Anna. Do you have to be so loud?" Tay scowled while letting out a deep yawn.

I began to rub my eyes to help wake them up. Everything would be blurry to me if I didn't. Prying one open and then the other, I saw a silhouette of a face almost nose length away and I thought it was David trying to annoy me already, but it wasn't.

Gasp. "Milaya, can I help you?" I asked, a little disturbed. The girl sat there on her knees staring at me like she was bewitched. "Hello"… I called, waving both my hands in her face. She blinked twice and then said, "Oh, hello, how did you sleep?" I didn't answer. Just thought, "Stars, my brother sure can pick them." Then I smiled at the poor thing.

David got up next. "Morning Anna, sis, weird girl," he said, tipping his chin. I awkwardly coughed while turning my face toward Tay to hide a chuckle. Milaya showed no recollection of David calling her weird as she replied, "Good morning" a bit too gleefully for my taste.

Not long after David, everyone started to rise. Li Che got up and stretched while shouting, "Let's get ready children!" What he didn't notice was we were already up and getting prepared. "I get to see Brighton soon". I shot to my feet at the thought but then worry started to overcloud my excitement as I also thought, "Will he even know who I am?"

David got up and nudged me. "Hey, what are you thinking about?"

I looked at him, scrunched up my nose and answered, "How do you know I'm thinking and not just patiently standing here?" He chortled.

"Oh, come on Anna, you have that I'm off in la-la land look. You can't fool me."

My friend was spot on, and he was right, out of everyone here, he's the only one I couldn't get anything past.

I inhaled deeply and then blew out in one sentence. "Do you think Brighton will be able to recognize me now?" I bit my bottom lip waiting for his reply. The boy grinned. "You worry too much, come on." He looped his arm through mine and began tugging me over to where the others were.

"Wait, you didn't answer. Do you think-" He cut me off. "Of course, he'll know Anna. You're his sister, now stop being anxious." I wanted to pop off something at him, but I let it go because even though I didn't want to admit it, his chide did make me feel better. "Okay," I replied, dropping the stress off my chest.

"What are you two so deep in conversation about way over here?" Tay asked with concern in her gaze. So, I replied, "I was telling your brother he needs to put some water on his head to tame that mop." Then I quickly slid my eyes to the side and winked at him hoping he would get my hint. Thank the stars he did because he answered with a whine. "Sister, your friend's making fun of me again." Tay sighed and shook her head. I winked at him again, thankful we were in the clear and I didn't have to bring it up again. While no one was looking, I let out a strong exhale and rolled my eyes as I thought, "I hate doing that."

CHAPTER 31

Brighton

"Listen up you two. It is time to show me what you can do in the air with your fighting skills." Mason chuckled. "With these," he mocked, holding the wooden toys up to our leader. "Precisely brother," Patroklos chuckled back, not being one bit bothered by Mason's sarcasm. I just stood there listening and eagerly waiting to spar.

"What about me?" Willy called out while petting Artrayious' wing. Patroklos looked his way. "Willy, you will stay on the ground with me." Our poor frail brother wasn't at all happy with the answer our leader gave back, but he obeyed anyway knowing it was probably for the best.

I didn't agree though. I knew he had a hard time catching his breath sometimes, but he did have a breathing contraption for when that happened. So, I spoke up. "Lord Patroklos." I used his title. I wanted to let him know that I was being serious. "I don't think it's best to keep Willy from being trained. I mean, what will he be able to do in the battle if he doesn't know how to fight?"

"I do know how to fight, Brighton." Willy chimed in.

'I'm talking about in the air on the back of a pegasus."

Willy's mouth started to curve down until Patroklos said, "You do make a good point, Brighton. Willy, go and grab one of those swords and shields for yourself and then go get Sorbit." Our brother was thrilled. As he took off, he shouted back, "Thanks, Brighton! Thanks, Patroklos!" I couldn't help but smile from his excitement and my other two brothers apparently couldn't either, seeing as they were both showing teeth as well.

The stocky knight faced Mason and I, giving us our first set of orders. "You two get ready. I'll call out to you the fighting skills I want you to practice first. Okay, Mason, you go to my left, and Brighton you go to my right," he instructed while leaping up onto Artrayious' wing. Mason and I headed in the direction of the places we were once in earlier.

Arkimedes and I were already at the wall and set to take flight. Mason was having a time with Brontes though. "That pegasus has a mind of his own."

"He sure does, sir," Arkimedes answered, and I thought, "Saints I said that out loud." Then I laughed at myself.

Brontes finally stopped eating the grass and followed Mason over to the tree. Patroklos guffawed. "I think you'd better spend more time with your pegasus, mate." Mason snickered as he began to climb up Brontes' right wing.

"Alright. Alright. All jesting aside, let's get you four in the air. Ready?"

"I am!" I shouted back.

"Let's do it, mate."

He chuckled at Mason's reply and then said, "Great. First, I will have you two work on balance."

He had a coy smile when he said it and I was a little perplexed on what he had meant until Brontes and Mason took to the sky. I looked up and saw Mason begin to stand up on his pegasus' back.

"Sir, I will do my best not to drop you. Shall we give it a go?" I sneered at my pegasus even though he couldn't see me. "Well, Arkimedes, you telling me this makes me all the heebie-jeebies in my gut falter away ," I replied while shaking my head. "What are you two waiting for?" Patroklos yelled. "Okay, I guess I am ready Arkimedes, let's go." I took a giant breath in as we hoisted off the ground up toward Mason and Brontes.

Standing up on Arkimedes back was definitely trickier than I thought. I couldn't keep my feet still and they kept wobbling off balance. It was starting to become tiresome really fast. Just when I would think I had had it I'd fall right back on my rear end and have to start over. "Ugh, I'm never going to get this!"

Mason was chortling the whole time while watching me. Finally, he helped out by saying, "She'll be alright, mate. Take your feet and spread them a little further than your shoulders and you should be able to get your balance."

"Thanks, brother. I'll try it!" I shouted back.

"Okay, Arkimedes here goes nothing." I stood up slowly this time, spaced my feet apart just like he suggested, and low and behold, I was fully standing. "Look, I'm not swaying anymore. Thanks again, Mason!"

"I do say, well-done sir. Shall I ascend higher now?"

Arkimedes began to stretch out both of his wings, and I shouted. "No, wait! I'm not- Ahhh…" Thud. I fell again and this time it actually hurt since I had been standing all the way up and not just squatting like before. As I rubbed out the ache, Arkimedes said, "I do apologize sir. I thought you to be ready."

I didn't reply. The pain in my rear had taken all of my attention. As it continued throbbing, Mason shouted, "Try again mate and this time tighten your stomach muscles!" I chuckled under my breath saying, "Saints, brother, I've tried over five times now." After rubbing my backside and groaning a while, I decided I'd give it another go around.

Feet spaced and planted, stomach tight, and this time knees not locked, I felt ready. "Okay Arkimedes when you're ready."

"Yes sir," he answered fervently. We began ascending and my body started to sway a little, but I didn't let go of my stance. I flexed my stomach muscles as tight as I could and kept my knees at a slight bend.

"Hold on sir we're almost there. The toughest task hasn't even begun yet." His words went in one ear and out the other as we flew higher. The altitude made it hard to hear his voice. My ears weren't picking up anything except the loud whisps of air as we swiftly ascended. I was in awe when we had finally stopped. Egladon's view was amazing to see up high. I could see every piece of the land from up there and it was incredible.

Mason and Brontes glided over to us. "She sure is a beauty, isn't she?" I wanted to laugh at my brother for calling this world she, but I swallowed instead and answered, "She sure is." Then I chuckled.

"Okay, Arkimedes let's go down so I can hear Patroklos."

"Do stand firmly sir. It's going to be a bit unpleasant the first time."

"A bit whaaaa!"-

"Hahaha, she'll be alright mate," Mason yelled as Arkimedes swiftly descended.

I could feel my feet start to move so I bent my knees even more and stuck my elbows into my sides. I was able to stay steady after that and the ride started to turn into a thrill. I looked over my shoulder and saw that Mason and Brontes were gaining speed on me and Arkimedes.

Turning it into a race, I shouted, "Faster Arkimedes faster!" Mason caught my drift as I heard him yell, "Strewth! Pick it up Brontes. They're going to beat us!" Almost within view of the castle, I started wondering how many times Patroklos was going to have us do this. As fun as it has turned out to be I was eager to start sparing.

"Woah! Look at that!" I could see Willy and his pegasus standing by our leader. Thud. I fell on my poor sore rear again as Arkimedes' hooves hit the ground. "Bahahaha, don't worry Brighton my brother you'll get the landing down once you do it about ten times over." Looking over at Patroklos with wide eyes, I gulped.

"We almost had you two, mate," Mason said while sliding down Brontes' wing. "Yeah, yeah. Sure, you did," I replied with a smirk. "Whaa..." Willy's pegasus was remarkable. I bet he named him Sorbit because of his body's beautiful bright yellow coat.

His wings were jet black like a lump of coal and his eyes were solid white with grey rings for his pupils. He looked the oldest out of all the pegasi and when he spoke, it confirmed the theory in my head because his voice was raspy just like an old man.

"Hunt hum." I guess I got lost in admiration because Patroklos started coughing in order to get my attention. When I peered my eyes toward him, he said, "Yes, yes, I know. Sorbit is eye-catching but we need to get back to drills before we lose our light." Mason and I nodded then spun on our heels to go climb up onto our winged horses.

After I'd made it up, I heard Patroklos say, "Willy get ready because you are going up too." Then he asked him, "Do you have your inhaler on you?" My friend pulled it from his pocket and answered, "Never leave my room without it." I smiled.

"Alright then, up you go," Patroklos said as he took in a deep breath. I knew he was worried, but I felt that Willy could handle this. Plus, I knew my friend was stronger than everyone thought him to be.

Mason and I waited to leave the ground until Willy had fully climbed up Sorbit and was situated. When he gave us a thumbs up, I patted Arkimedes' head and said, "Ready when you are." Then I heard Mason say, "Let's go mate" to his pegasus Brontes. Sorbit took his cue from Brontes and all of us held tight as we lifted off into the air.

"Alright. Mason and Brighton, you two are to descend ten times without any breaks. I gulped and then thought, "My poor stomach." Patroklos finished with saying to our frail friend, "Willy, you and I will test some rounds of what your lungs can handle."

"Okay," Willy replied as he grabbed a chunk of Sorbits' mane.

Arkimedes and Brontes were on fire. Mason and I had just finished our tenth dive and my stomach never got the least bit queasy. I whined to myself for no reason. It was remarkable to me that I even managed to stay on my feet and stick the landing by the seventh time.

Feeling pretty good about myself I shouted, "Hurry up Willy. I'm ready to sword fight!" Our leader guffawed and then said, "All in due time Brighton," as he and Artrayious landed. "Willy, how do you feel? Do you think you have enough energy to still spar a little?" Patroklos asked, concerned. Our overjoyed frail brother shot his eyes at me and answered, "Saints yeah." We laughed as our meek friend was over the moon in excitement.

Patroklos chortled for a while longer at Willy's zealousness and then said, "Brighton, Mason, if you two get this down before the sun sets, I'll hold a coronation this time tomorrow and dub you both knights of Egladon."

"Hey, what about me?" Willy whined. Patroklos laughed once again and without a second thought he replied, "You can be their squire." Our friend was just excited to be a part of anything and shouted back, "Yes sir!"

"Ha ha ha, alright then let's get our battle formation down first." Following our leader's command, we all gripped our wooden toy swords and shields as our pegasi hoisted us up into the air.

"Alright listen up carefully, brothers. I want some good clean sparring. When you walk off your pega"-

"Wait, what?" I blurted, cutting him off completely baffled.

"Here I'll show you mate," Mason said as he walked straight off Brontes' backside and stood in front of me in mid-air.

I sat there gaping in amazement. "Yes, just like that," Patroklos finished. "How-how is he doing that?" I asked, tilting my head and stuttering my words from a state of shock. "On guard, mate," Mason said, fooling about but I couldn't even muster a chuckle. I was still beside myself.

"Ahem," Patroklos cleared his throat to quiet my friend and his taunting. "Now, as I was saying, your pegasus will be able to gravitate you in the air while fighting. When they spread out their wings, they can produce gravity from the rays of the sun and use their brain waves to keep you floating. Be on guard though because if they get injured their hold will falter and you will plummet to your death."

Gasp. I took a hard swallow on his last instruction. Grabbing my wooden weapons and standing up I said, "I'm trusting you Arkimedes." Then I began to walk across his back to meet Mason. Before stepping into thin air, I gulped once more. "She'll be alright mate. It's just one foot in front of the other." Listening to him and staring at the man blankly, I thought, "Gee Mason I feel much safer now."

"I wonder if you'll still be this calm when I start to fall to my death," I grumbled as I lifted my right foot off Arkimedes and planted it right smack on top of Mason's. "Hey, stand in your own air space, mate " he growled, pushing me off to the side.

"Woah what!" I started to scream until I realized I wasn't falling. "Whaa…, would you look at this?" I said jumping up and down as gravity held me.

"Alright, Brighton, now that you've established you can't fall, let's get started." I followed Patroklos, Mason, and Willy to the middle of our pegasi while swinging the little wooden sword from side to side.

Getting into our stances, Patroklos began demonstrating to us our first attack move. "Alright men slice, spin, and thrust. It looks something like this." We all watched as our leader slashed his sword like he was cutting it across someone's neck. After that, he ducked down while spinning on his left heel, sliced invisible shins, and hoisted up while plunging his blade into thin air. "Woah man. If that was a real body you would have made a fatality," I blurted.

"Precisely," he said while breathing heavily and sheathing his weapon back to his side. After catching his breath, he said, "You, Willy, and Mason practice doing five rounds. Control your breathing better than me because if you can handle five then I'll have you finish all twenty then we can move on to jump kicks."

We nodded in agreement and began our drills. "Saints. I know why you made us use wood instead of the real ones," I yelled out as Willy plunged his weapon into my left armpit. Even though it was wood the pressure from it still stung.

Finishing up the last round I noticed Lord Patroklos was on to something when I started to feel the burn in my lungs as my heavy panting became stronger and stronger. We took a short break to catch our breaths and regain some strength. When we were ready our leader said, "Only fifteen more to go." Then he chuckled. I sighed and, on the inside, I was telling myself, " Come on Brighton, it's not that hard."

I finished off round twenty with barely any air left in my chest. I about fell over when Patroklos said, "Well done. Time for jump kicks." I wasn't alone in my groaning that time. Willy and Mason were just as worn out as me.

After learning our leg technique, it was time for air fencing and I thought, "Saints, is this day ever going to end?" Patroklos stood in the middle of us. "Brighton you and Mason are a team. Willy, it's you and me brother." With our swords ready we thrust them up over our heads and shouted, "For Egladon!"

Mason and I were jesting back and forth having a great spar when he said, "Hey mate isn't Mad M"- I scowled when he started to address my angel with that foul title. "Milaya," he finished with a gulp. When he said her name, I was no longer able to focus on our swordplay at hand. I got lost in thought wondering when my lady would return.

CHAPTER 32

Annalise

"Okay, children just a little further along, then my men and I will have you safely to Yinglong, through the gate, and on your way to Egladon."

"Many thanks, princie."

"David," I sighed, irritated, because he wouldn't drop that ridiculous name. "What?" he answered like he'd said nor done anything wrong. He leaned over to Li Che and smacked him across his shoulder blades.

"Besides, I bet you're used to it by now, aren't you princie?" David was treading on thin ice as Li Che deeply glared at him while removing the arm that he had draped around his neck after his extremely offensive behavior.

"David, get over here," Tay hissed through her teeth and then embarrassingly smiled at his highness. "I am truly sorry for my brother's actions. Really, he didn't mean any harm."

"It is alright, girl. I too would react the same if I thought some other guy was trying to court my lady."

After he'd finished, he looked at David and then directly at me. Tay and Lin Lan giggled. I shifted my eyes to David and then back to his highness saying, "Who, me?" Looking at David again I rolled my eyes while saying, "In your dreams, blondie."

The crown prince, Tay, and Lin Lan busted out laughing hysterically. David began huffing and puffing as I followed along. "Ha! In your dreams," he mocked back. The four of us stood there and had a long good chuckle while David scowled, stomped his way over to where we'd stopped, and began brooding.

"Annalise." Tay hissed.

"What?" I answered looking at her confused.

"You didn't have to be so blunt, did you?"

Deeply annoyed I exhaled. "Weren't you just laughing with me like two seconds ago?"

She sighed. "Yes, but... Well, look at him over there."

I shrugged while saying, "You go over and cheer him up then. I'm staying right here." My friend shook her head and walked toward her brother.

"Children we really do need to set out," Li Che said while pointing at the dragon in the sky. All three of us looked and he was doing flips in mid-air up ahead. It was as if the poor thing was bored or something waiting for us to arrive. "It's still about a day's travel. Can you three make it?" I did a meek bow and answered, "Yes we can your highness." but I was really thinking, "Are you serious? Another whole day?!" I faked a smile and then twisted my body while shouting, "Tay, David stop talking and let's go! Didn't you two hear what Li Che just said? We still have a full day to get to Egladon. David, stop sulking I didn't mean it, honest, now come on!" I wanted to reunite with Brighton badly, so at this point, I was willing to say anything.

Knowing my tongue was spouting off lies, I began to feel little tugs on my heart to come clean. To tell him the truth that I was just saying all the things he wanted to hear in order to get him to stand up and move. Just as I was about to walk over and apologize, the hissing started. My feet stopped in mid-step like they were being controlled as I heard, "Don't go apologize. He doesn't care if you're sorry. He doesn't even want to hear your voice. Just stay away."

Since the voice hadn't spoken in a while, it was as if I no choice but to listen. The feeling of shame drenched over me like a wet blanket as I twisted back around to Li Che and Lin Lan. About five minutes later, Tay and David stopped talking finally, made their way over, and then we all followed his highness in silence.

Half a day had gone by, and my friend still had his back to me. He hadn't turned around to look at me once nor say anything. A whisper in my head said, "You really hurt him this time," while the hissing voice followed with, "He deserved it. You don't need him anyway." I sucked in a deep breath as I started to become overwhelmingly drained. From then on, the hissing never let up.

I rubbed my forehead as my mind very quickly became distraught. I couldn't seem to control my own thinking. My eyes darted over to look at Milaya and it just so happened that I caught her sneering at me like she was plotting to do something evil. Her piercing glare gave me the shivers. It was like something wicked was staring at me through Milaya's eyes. I jerked my head towards my feet as the hissing voice continued torturing my mind.

"Ahahaha. Everyone hates you. They are all in deep thought on how they are going to get rid of you. Don't you see? Your own brother left to get away from your constant whining. And your mother, she can't even stand you. Kedron, well let's just say your little brother now despises you."

My head started to throb and there was nothing I could do to escape from the oppressive hissing. Feeling low about myself I allowed the salty droplets to fall. I needed someone to turn around and say something, anything to silence the thoughts, but no one did.

"Look!" Tay shouted while pointing toward the sky. "We're here children." Hearing my friend's and the crown prince's voice aside from the awful one in my mind, I shot my head up. Li Che was pulling his royal seal from his belt. David glanced at me and said, "Finally."

The hissing voice started to fade as I lifted my eyes to look at Yinglong. "Oh, great guardian of TungWing, I have brought the gate key for these children to pass," Li Che called out while holding up the royal token.

The dragon stopped summersaulting in the air and said, "There are four of you now" while looking straight into Milaya's eyes. They shared stares until I shouted, "Please, Yinglong! We need to get to my brother in Egladon."

The giant creature turned his focus to me and then spread his wings to descend to the ground. Every one of us began to wobble as our feet vibrated from the great dragon's landing. "My apologies," he said as he brought his wings back into his sides and raised tall.

The crown prince chuckled. "It's quite alright, old friend." The dragon bowed and then shifted his eyes to me asking, "Are you ready, girl?" David answered for me. "Oh, she's ready." Tay chimed in." She really wants to see her brother, Mr. Dragon." Yinglong stared at Tailya for second and then blew smoke from his nostrils. "Mr. Dragon," he said gleefully. "I don't think anyone has ever addressed me so formally." Then he laughed again.

"You there," he called out while looking at Milaya. "How did you get here?" The girl yelled back, "I came through a portal from my world. I was told to come and find Annalise to bring her back to Egladon." Yinglong stared into her eyes suspiciously and then turned his focus to me calling out, "Beware girl. I sense trouble coming your way." Immediately the hissing voice countered with "Don't listen to that dumb creature, he is lying. There isn't anything that you need to be aware of."

After that, he laid on the ground, lifted his upper body, and began to open the gateway on his chest. I shook off the evil voice as I watched the multicolored jewel began to glow. Then I looked over at Milaya and saw her eyes change from amber to deep green. I gasped, thinking I was in some sort of déjà vu, remembering that Wesley's did the exact same in the other world.

Both Tailya and David rushed to grab my hands eager to get me to Egladon, leaving me no time to react. I wanted to warn them about Milaya, but she already had crossed through. Before I let them pull me in, I quickly spun around to give his highness and Lin Lan a thankful nod and bow as I took one last eyeful of their remarkably colorful world. I smiled and winked at Lin Lan while saying, "Save me some of those jujubes. I'll be back."

She giggled as a tear fell down her cheek. I thought, "I'll miss you too shy girl." Then I let them lead me through. It seemed that every time I would step into one of these gateways, I would always see clips of strange things. This time to my right was a picture of a colossal red dragon with seven heads and ten horns and seven crowns upon its heads.

I squeezed my eyes shut as the image gave me a terrorizing chill, but it didn't help. I couldn't seem to get those yellow glowing eyes out of my mind. Then I heard an impish snicker. As the figure of the red monster began to fade away the black shadow with yellow eyes stayed put and continued to stare at me.

There was no way for me to escape. If I opened my eyes, I saw frightening things. While all that was going on, I still had something dark haunting me even in closing them. It was like being fully awake but yet trapped inside a nightmare.

"Annalise, you can open your eyes now. We're here," Tay said softly as she loosened her grip. "No unwanted stops," I replied, peeking open one eye. David chortled. "Not this time."

"Oh, thank the stars," I blurted while opening the other eye.

"Whoa! Look at the ocean!" David shouted while running toward the cliff. "What in the seashells is that?!" he shouted pointing his finger down at the water. Tay and I walked up to the edge of the cliff to see what he was going on about.

My baffled friend was pointing at a long dark shadow beneath the water. "Whaaaa… you can't even see the end of it!" David yelled. I looked at the boy, shook my head and said, "Let's go find my brother, maybe he knows what it is. Then I followed with, oh yeah, did Milaya say anything to either of you before she went through the portal? Did you two happen to notice anything strange about her?"

Both stood there in deep thought for a minute and then at the same time with no words my friends shook their heads cluelessly. I wanted to tell them what I saw but if they didn't see it, I thought maybe my eyes were just playing tricks on me, so I followed with, "Well, surely she has to be close by here somewhere. We weren't that far behind I don't think." They shrugged at my assumption. "Stars, you two are no help," I hissed while scouring the grounds around us.

"What is that?" I asked shocked.

"What are you pointing towards, Anna?" Tay answered, squinting her eyes, trying to focus on the blurry speck below us. "Doesn't that look like it's a person standing near the water", I asked. When Tay leaned over a little further, I said while grabbing her hand, "It might be Milaya waiting for us. Come on let's go." I spun on my heels, dragging Tailya behind me. I realized we had left David by his self in the midst of rushing down the mountain.

"Hey wait for me!" He yelled coming up beside us. Halfway down all three of us discovered that the blur was Milaya, and we looked at each other puzzled when we noticed her lips moving. She was speaking but there was no one around.

Reaching the bottom, I yelled out," Milaya, who are you talking to?!" She jerked her head back at me and then began running towards us. We stopped walking and waited for her. "I was wondering when you three would arrive," she said with a smile planted on her face. I stared into her eyes, but they were no longer a deep green. They had completely changed back to amber.

Gawking a little too long, Milaya asked, "Annalise, is there something I can help you with?"

"Huh? Oh, I thought your eyes had changed to green. My mistake." She smirked at me, and I felt a shiver run up my spine. "Yeah, I noticed it too. They did turn green in the forest when we were getting ready to go to sleep last night," Tay blurted in suspicion along with me.

"I never saw them change," David grumbled like someone had just stolen his last cookie. "I thought while glaring, "You two said that you didn't notice anything funny about her." After the thought I laid my glare solely on Tay. She stared at me and snickered. I just sighed and let it go. I was over it and anxious. I just wanted to find my brother and put all curiosity to a standstill for now. "Milaya, I don't care if your eyes turn into rainbows, would you please just take me to Brighton?" I said, wanting to get a move on.

Tay and David guffawed as the girl smiled and said very weirdly, "Right this way" while motioning with her hand in the direction to go. My friend's and I stared at her for a few seconds, knowing there was something definitely off about her. However, I knew she was the only one I had to take me to my brother, so I motioned for all of us to follow. As we cut through the trees, I got lost in thought. "It sure is quiet around here. I wonder where all the villagers are. Ugh, I am so exhausted. Will we ever get to Brighton?

Milaya stopped suddenly causing Tay, David, and me to stumble into her. She turned around in a panic and cried out, "Annalise, help me! She won't let me go!" Tay and I stared at each other bewildered. When we looked back at Milaya her eyes were starting to change again.

"See, David, your sister and I weren't lying!" I shouted. Before her eyes fully turned green, she warned, "Run, run you three before it's too late." Then she calmed back down and smiled, which shot chills all throughout my body.

I gave Tay that same look from earlier. What we were thinking was in fact right. There was something definitely off with Milaya. Tay agreed with a nod not even needing to say anything. She pulled Fawn's wand from thin air, and I said shockingly, "You still have that thing?"

David answered, " Well, I think it's a good thing that she does." I sucked in a deep breath and then said, "Alright Tailya let's do it." Poor Milaya stood there shifting her eyes back and forth completely lost as to what was about to happen.

I watched as my friend began to twirl the rod in the air. She quickly pointed it at Milaya and shouted, "Apokalyto." What came from the girl's mouth made us freeze. A loud pitch cackle followed by, "So... we meet again you three."

Suddenly an image of a jet-black-haired lady in a torn purple dress with yellow gunk on her teeth appeared in my head. "Y-Y-Yurika," I stuttered. "Aa hahahaha, very good, you do remember me," she cackled. I looked at Tay and my friend was already circling her wrist and beginning to chant.

The witch peered her eyes at me and said, "I'll see you soon, Annalise" and then Milaya's eyes changed. I began gasping for air in a state of panic. "What-What just happened?" she asked groggily. Then she looked at all three of us startled. "Wh-Who are you all?" Tay hastily put the magic rod away and walked over to our confused friend.

"It's a long story but to give you a short version I'm Tailya, that's my brother," she pointed to David. "And this is Annalise, Brighton's sister."

"You're Brighton's little sister! Are you alright!?" she shouted in disbelief. The poor girl stared at me blankly while I stood there bent over trying to catch my breath. Since she couldn't remember anything, I knew had to ask again. So I took a couple more deep inhales to calm my nerves. "Do you know where I can find my brother?" Her eyes twinkled as she smiled at me. "Oh, yes please follow me, miss Annalise."

As we started walking again, I thought, "Where did that witch go? How is she still alive? Didn't she evaporate into thin air the last time we saw her? How is it that she can possess bodies? Gasp. Can she do that to me too? And what did she mean when she said she'll see me soon?" The what ifs of fear started to cloud my mind and the feeling of excitement of getting to see Brighton was being overtaken.

The hissing voice also started. " You know he will call you crazy. And you are a foolish girl to think that your brother will even believe you. Bahahaha, he will call you a liar and disown you. Don't try and tell him the truth, you will just fail."

"Anna, look!" I heard Tay's voice calling me. Thankful to be pulled away from the worrisome notions and that tormenting hissing, I looked up. "Miss, here we are," Milaya said softly. Gawking at me a few feet away was a tall stalky redhead with bright green eyes. He was staring at me like he wasn't sure who I was.

"Well, what are you waiting for?" David said, nudging me in my side. "Yeah, go over there," Tay agreed as she gave me a friendly shove. I smiled at them and then I took a deep breath, balled my fists, and headed towards him. Just as I was about to say the first word, he creased his eyes and said, "Lissy?" I became mute as my body froze. Overjoyed, my eyes began to fill up and my body started to shake. There was no forcing them back that time. Searching him over and over, grateful to see him again,

I stood there allowing myself to turn into a blubbering mess.

CHAPTER 33

Re United

I thought both of us would run into each other's arms for a much overdue long embrace but that didn't happen. My brother was in a state of shock with how much I had changed, and I was feeling regret from having Tailya use that awful spell to grow me. "So much time, lost," I thought as we just kept to our places; Brighton was blankly staring at me while I was still in tears.

After a few minutes, which felt like a whole day gone by, I wiped my face and decided to speak first. Through my sniffles, I said, "Bubba!" But he stood there with no emotion on his face. My poor brother was doing exactly what I thought would happen. Over my shoulder, I looked at Tay and David in sorrow. Then I dropped my eyes to the ground and shook my head.

I was telling them without words that all of my fears were happening. Even though he said my name he still didn't believe it was me. David, my strong-minded, nothing can scare him, prideful friend, stepped in front of me and started to address Brighton for me. My eyes widened as I began to lift my hand to cover his mouth. I wanted to be the one to break my brother's confusion, but I wasn't fast enough.

David draped his arm around my shoulders while looking directly into Brighton's eyes. "Listen up." He said. "This… is your long-lost sister, Annalise…"

"David," I hissed while elbowing him in the side. "He's not a simpleton. Did you have to say it long and drawn out like that?"

After I scolded my friend, I awkwardly gave Brighton a big toothy grin. My brother directed his gaze over to Milaya. The way his eyes softened when he looked at her, I knew she had to be someone special to him. Finally, he spoke but it wasn't to me. "My lady, it's so good to see you return. Shall we alert your brother of your arrival?"

The girl looked at me and smiled bashfully. My blood started to boil as my sorrow turned into anger. Ill-will thoughts started popping in one by one. "Why is she so special? I'm the one who's supposed to be special. What makes her so great that he has to ignore me? Ugh, why can't he see that it's me?" I was so jealous and my nine-year-old miss prissy self-came out.

"Bubba! Look at me. Hello…" I began to stomp in place while flailing my arms as I stuck out my bottom lip. When he put his focus back on me, he busted out in laughter. "Lissy, of course, I know it's you. How could I forget my little sister? Now get over here and give me a hug." "Uh. But. You…"

I was so dumbfounded by his playfulness that I couldn't move or speak right. I just stood there trying not to hyperventilate. He eventually came to me with his big, long arms spread wide. Standing right in front of me he said, "My, you've grown." Then he looked at David. "Ahem. Do you think it would be alright if I could hug my sister?" My friend cleared his throat while dropping his arm and moving to the side. I giggled at my brother's sarcasm as I thought while looking at David, "How does it feel to get a taste of your own medicine."

Brighton grinned really big and then wrapped me up tight. "Why does it feel like it's been a year or two since we've seen each other but we both have the appearance as if nine years have passed?" he whispered to me as he let go of our embrace. I searched his confused eyes and answered, "Bubba, allow my friends and I to get something to eat, get settled in, and I promise I will tell you everything I know."

He smiled and then looked up at Milaya asking, "My lady, could you please take Lissy and her friends to the dining hall?" Looking back down at me, he placed his palms on my shoulders and said, "After you and your friends fill your bellies, "not to full,"- he chuckled,- "I'll find you and her a chamber to share, but this one," he said lifting his eyes to David, "This one will stay with me and my two brothers."

"Brother," I sharply replied. He chuckled and said, "I have some things to relay to you as well." I sighed and rolled my eyes.

My brother dropped his hands and walked over to grab his maiden's. She shyly smiled while saying, "Right this way please." Tay, David, and I followed on their heels toward the eating courters.

As we entered, there was a table in the middle surrounded by very loud spoken men. After getting my food, I began to make my way over to see what all the fuss was about. I was just about to make a right turn when David asked, "Where are you going?"

Holding my tray, I lifted my elbow while tilting my neck. "Over there for a moment, I'll be right back." He nodded and went toward Tay, my brother, and Milaya. Reaching the table, all the men were chattering at one time, so I coughed loudly to get their attention.

Two men with their backs faced toward me twisted their heads around. One man leaned to the right while the other leaned his to the left creating a hole for me to see through. All the men surrounding the table paused in mid laughter and began to stare at me in a way that was saying, "can we help you with something miss?"

I felt very uncomfortable as my heart started to race and all of the saliva in my mouth started to dry up. Sitting at the table was a dark brown-haired man with tan skin. He was the only one in a chair. I thought, "This guy must be the one in charge."

A man next to me said, "Lord Patroklos, I think this girl is waiting to say something." "Lord," I thought as their leader began to lift his head. When he turned his neck to the left to look at me, our eyes locked.

He opened his mouth, getting ready to say something but my heart fluttered causing me to drop my tray, spin on my heels, and hastily head back to my brother, friends, and Milaya. I could hear the men guffawing behind my back and I thought, "Way to go, Annalise. That was amazing." Then I huffed, looked down at the floor, and shook my head.

Plopping down in my chair, feeling completely humiliated, I got angry with myself. I snatched David's bread from his plate and began ripping pieces off to shove in my mouth. I was surprised I didn't bite a hole in my tongue from how hard I was chewing.

My jaws slowed down as I began to think about his beautiful eyes. They were as blue as the sky in TungWing. Inside his bright blue were specks of gold and circling the bright blue was a yellowish green. I felt my chest rise as I inhaled deeply through my nose feeling completely captivated.

"Brighton, who are these three?"

"Yeah, mate. Who are these two beauties?"

I could hear them, but I didn't pay any mind because I didn't want to come back to reality just yet. While in my state of dreaming, I heard my brother speak. "Patroklos, Mason, this is my sister, Annalise, and her two friends."

"Patroklos," I gasped on the inside.

Next, David said, "Anna, stop chewing like a cow eating hay." This pulled me straight from my fantasy and into choking on my bread. When I lifted my head, I shot a cold glare at David. He of course smirked and then pointed his finger to my right. "Someone is talking to you," he said through his teeth, grinning big.

I leaned across the table to look at Brighton thinking it was him trying to get my attention, but it wasn't. My brother's eyes went wide as he began motioning his head to the right. I twisted in my chair and the man stretched his hand out and said, "Hello, Annalise, it is a pleasure to meet you." Gulp. My heart felt like it was about to explode.

Staring into those bright blue eyes of his, I became speechless again. I just sat there staring then giggled and then I awkwardly smiled.

The other man standing next to Patroklos asked my brother, "Brighton, mate, is your sister a little bit, you know," he whistled while twirling his finger next to his head. My brother guffawed, which caused me to come to and blurt out, "I am perfectly sound, thank you."

"So, you can talk," Patroklos said with a smile from ear to ear. I took in a deep breath as I thought, "This man is so handsome."

Apparently, I stunned the other man because what came from his mouth was a very odd-sounding word. "Crikey. Not afraid to talk to him," he said. I replied back to the dirty blonde sun kissed man, "Uh, what?"

With a huge toothy grin, he answered, "I said Crickey, miss." I laughed; I had never heard a word like that before. I asked, "What in the stars does that mean?" Everyone began guffawing at the table from how shocked I was as he answered, "It means you surprised me."

"Oh, okay," I giggled once more.

"Ahem." Patroklos interrupted with a fake cough sounding as if he was becoming agitated. The man and I controlled our titters and put our focus back on everyone at the table. I started to twist my body back to face Brighton but noticed Patroklos was still stretching out his hand to greet me.

In a super-fast-paced motion, I stuck out one of mine. When I went to retract, he had already wrapped his thumb over the top of my palm. I didn't struggle but I did melt as his eyes softened and his pouty lips curled up into a beautiful smile.

Staring at him, my heart pitter pattered as I drifted back off into fantasy land. "Lissy." In my daze, I heard Brighton. I shook my head and focused back in on my dream. Patroklos and I were walking together on the shore. I bashfully giggled as I looked up into his eyes. "Lissy." Rats, Brighton, just a few more minutes. "Lis...sy..." "Go away," I say through my teeth while smiling at Patroklos in my optical illusion.

Soon after that, I felt my body move which was weird because I was next to Patroklos staring at the ocean. "Lissy, Lissy, Lissy!" I unlocked my grip, threw my hand back down, and frustratingly shouted, "Stars Brighton, what!" My dream faded as I blinked my eyes and came back to reality.

"Lissy," Brighton said with a smile," Can you let go of the knight's hand now?" I looked up at the man realizing that everything I had just done or said in my daydream, I subconsciously acted out in front of everyone. All of them started laughing hysterically and my eyes widened so big that I thought they were about to pop right out of their sockets.

I gasped and then dropped his hand feeling mortified. He didn't seem to mind. He just laughed and said, "You're very interesting, miss." Then he smiled. I couldn't help but laugh at his encouraging comment. My uncontrollable chortling caused everyone at the table to keep on as well. I was no longer shy toward my handsome knight. Everything around me except him started to disappear as I stayed focused on his gaze.

My brother cleared his throat, breaking up our connection. Both of us blinked our eyes and deeply inhaled through our noses. Directing my view toward Brighton, I saw he was already in the process of giving me that "don't even think about it" look. However, I wanted to get to know Patroklos more, so I gave him back my "but bubba" eyes and he caved. Discreetly he said, "We'll discuss this later." I smiled big and sat back in my chair.

David overheard him and stopped laughing. "Discuss what?" he concerningly asked. "Huh," Tay chimed in.

"Nothing you two. It's between my brother and me," I replied with creased eyes. "Oh," they both said in unison.

Patroklos chuckled and then looked at Brighton. "Brother, this has been fun. I jerked my eyes toward Brighton, thinking, "Brother" " Don't forget training starts soon and after that you are going to become a knight of Egladon." He finished. Before spinning on his heel to leave, he looked down at me, smiled, and winked while saying, "Till next time, miss Annalise." When he turned his back, I sank into my chair. "What's wrong with you?" David huffed as he crossed his arms.

CHAPTER 34

The Coronation

Our chamber was dazzling. From the shimmery see-through curtains hanging over the bed to the wooden wardrobe full of dresses near the golden bookshelf. It was glistening from the sunset peeking through the shimmery curtain. The object quickly became my favorite thing in the room. After gaping at it for a long while, I ran over to the giant mattress, hoisted myself up, laid my head down, told the ladies good night, which Tay was already snoring logs, and went to sleep. Waking up to the irresistible smells of honey and cedar, reminded me of the white flowers with little green balls on the ends just on the outskirts of my forest back in Bristeria. I couldn't believe it, but the aroma was actually making me miss home.

I planted my feet on the hard wood floor, stood up, stretched and then made my way over to pick out a borrowed dress from Milaya. I yelled across the room, "Tay, wake up, it's already mid-day and I don't want to miss my brother's coronation!" Rolling herself out of bed she yawned while asking, "What's for breakfast?"

"Didn't you hear what I just said? It's already time for lunch. You missed breakfast."

"Well stars Anna, why did you let me sleep so late?"

"I tried three times to get you up, Tailya," I replied, crossing my arms.

"Wow, I guess I was more tired than I thought," she said back while bending over to stretch her back.

"You must have been because I tried shaking you, pulling the blanket off of you and I even allowed your brother to come in to shout at you. That was around sunrise." She laughed and then made her way over toward me to grab a dress for herself.

Just as I was about to open the door, Tay whispered by the window, "Anna, come here. I see Milaya and your brother." Rushing over I looked down and they were holding hands walking and talking. Tay and I looked at each other. "Aww," we said in unison and then we giggled.

"Hey, Anna, isn't that?" I directed my gaze to where she was pointing. When I saw him, I repeated over and over in my head, "Please don't, please don't, please don't."

"Lord Patroklos!" she shouted for all to hear. The dark brown-haired knight lifted his eyes and I dropped down so fast pulling Tay with me like we were being shot at with arrows.

"I can't believe you did that," I hissed while breathing heavily. She snickered and then replied, "Isn't it bizarre how he looks just like the man you were holding hands with in that image I showed you?"

"What, no. That wasn't real and no one can see the future, Tay," I said, staring into her eyes, thinking this girl had lost her mind.

Biting down hard while trying not to appease her with a glare, because I knew she was just trying to get a rise out of me, I said with a fake smile, "How am I supposed to go down there now?"

"Yeesh, Anna." She replied. "You really shouldn't show that many teeth when you're angry. You look like an alligator getting ready to have its dinner." Her whole body did a fake shiver causing me to burst out in laughter.

'Come on, let's go," she said, grabbing my hand to pull me up while grinning from ear to ear. Down the steps we went, and at the bottom, Milaya, my brother's brown-haired beauty, was waiting for us. "Are you ladies ready for the coronation?" she asked excitedly. "I know I am. Brighton has dreamt of this day probably since before I was born." The maiden smiled. Tay and I followed on her heels as she led the way.

"Where is your brother?" I whispered. Tay shrugged and then giggled. "I bet he got caught trespassing in the women's wing trying to come and get us. He's probably being redirected by one of the men as we speak. Or he could just be already waiting for us in the corridor." I laughed and shook my head at all of her assumptions.

"Just through these doors, ladies. Someone will be there to take you to your seats," Milaya gracefully motioned us in as she smiled, spun herself about, and then headed off to search for my brother.

A blonde man was making his way toward us through the crowd. When I was able to recognize his face, I yelled while waving him down, "Mason!" Next to me, I saw Tay showing all of her teeth as her cheeks raised high and her eyes rapidly fluttered. I gasped then elbowed Tay in her side. "Look. There he is."

"Ouch. There who is, bony girl?" she answered with a glare and rubbing the sting from her ribs.

"Lord Patroklos, see him?" I whispered while tilting my head and shifting my eyes toward where he was standing.

His bright blue eyes were looking everywhere amongst the crowd. When ours finally locked, I immediately shot mine to my feet and then I smiled thinking, " He is so captivating. Twisting my body from side to side, I giggled as I began to daydream about Patroklos reaching for my hand to place in his. My fantasy ended just as Tay nudged me. "Mason is approaching us." She shyly whispered through her teeth.

"What?" I said rubbing my left arm. "Look over there," she said, pointing toward the stage. My brother was kneeling in front of Lord Patroklos in all of his knightly armor but as proud as I was for him, I still couldn't take my eyes away from my beastly knight. I stood there searching him over, from his forest-green robe to his tree bark-colored shoes.

"Oh, how I want to be wrapped up in his silver cloak." I whined with a winded exhale.

"What did you say, Anna?" David asked, standing to my right. "Gasp. Where did you come from? Stars, David." I hissed.

Leaning over to Tay and ignoring her brother's question, I whispered, "Where did he come from?"

She snickered and shrugged while saying, "Why, afraid you won't be, how did you put it, wrapped up in his cloak?" Then she began teasing me, wrapping her arms around herself. "Yeah, yeah Tailya, go ahead, give yourself a big hug cause you're going to need it when I get through with you," I said, cracking my knuckles. She burst out laughing and I followed not long after while poor David stood there looking like a lost puppy.

"Ahem. I don't know what's up with you two, but we need to go and find our seats. The ceremony is about to begin, Anna," David said after clearing his throat. Then he reached for my hand. "My lady," Mason said to Tay as he also stuck his hand out for her to grab. I leaned over toward her right ear, "Well he just walked up from nowhere, didn't he?" She gave me a wink and then giggled.

My friend placed her palm in her escort's hand and then immediately looked my direction. Even though she acted calm I could see the screaming of excitement from the glimmer in her eyes. I smiled and gave her that "stay calm" look as she allowed Mason to lead her across the room.

"Shall we," David asked, grinning with all of his teeth. I sighed, smiled, and then let the prideful boy accompany me to my place. Getting ready to plant myself, I bunched up pieces of my grassy green dress on both sides as I stared at my knight smiling away while thinking, "I wonder if he smiled at me because we are both wearing the same color, or he thinks I'm pretty. Hmmm, I hope it's written in the stars." On my last thought I cooed out loud, never taking my gaze off of him.

"Are you thinking about me again, doll?" David said with a coy grin and a very displeasing wink.

"Hmmm, what can I say, you're all I think about." Then I stuck my finger inside my mouth while sticking out my tongue, acting as though I were gagging. "Hahaha," he said, shifting away from me in his chair.

I deeply inhaled, satisfied with myself and then I put all of my attention back on my knight and his almost new royal subject, my brother. " People of Egladon. May I have your attention," Lord Patroklos spoke out, his voice elevated trying to address the entire crowd. As soon as a hush fell over the room, he started his speech.

"It is my honor to announce the next subjects to the knighthood round table of Egladon. Men, would you come and kneel beside Brighton?" he said looking at two other men, one being Mason. I glanced over to Tay and the girl was without a doubt carried away as she sat there letting her teeth sparkle for all to see.

I covered up a giggle and continued listening. "These three men have been trained hard all hours of the day and I couldn't be more thrilled to have them as my new brothers. It is going to be an honor to have them fighting in any battle right alongside me."

He pulled the sharp shiny steel from its sheath saying, "And without further ado, by the power of my father, the true ruler of Egladon, Lord Timious." The crowd bowed their heads in respect saying, "Lord Timious, may he rest in peace."

Tapping his blade on each side of the first man's shoulders, he said, "I dub thee with courage, dedication, and brotherhood. Arise, Sir William." Mason was next and I saw Tay move to the edge of her seat from my peripheral. I chuckled and shook my head.

"To the one who was afraid to address me by anything but my title for the longest time." I could see the simper across my brother's friend's face as Lord Patroklos said, "I dub thee with honesty, enthusiasm, and brotherhood. Arise, Sir Mason." Everyone clapped and cheered until Lord Patroklos put his palm up high for them to quiet down.

Kneeling last was my brother. "Poor guy," I muttered under my breath. I could see his anxious perspiration from where I was sitting. My handsome knight was getting ready to speak again and I was all ears. "Last my people I am truly honored to introduce this man to you. He has been with us for a little over two fortnights and he has excelled in every one of his tests and has even taught me a new style of fencing. Mighty subjects of Egladon, I am beyond thrilled to dub thee with strength, honor, persistence, and brotherhood. Arise, Sir Brighton of Bristeria." As my brother stood, my tan-skinned man placed one of his hands on my brother's shoulder, turned him toward the crowd, raised his voice, and said, "Welcome to knighthood at Egladon's table, Sir Brighton."

I watched as my brother searched the crowd for his lady. When he found her, he smiled and winked. Then he met my eyes and grinned from ear to ear. I just kept clapping and cheering, thinking, "smooth..." then a giggle forced it way out. Needless to say in that moment I was overjoyed for him.

Milaya and Brighton were hand and hand as they made their way across the room along with Mason and the other new knight on their heels. Walking up to me he said, "So, what do you think Lissy? Pretty spectacular, isn't it?" I hoisted off my chair and wrapped my arms around him. "Bubba, I am so over the moon for you. You are finally living your dream." He chuckled, "Yeah." Then he bashfully rubbed the back of his neck while looking over toward Milaya who might I say was showing all of her teeth as her eyes glistened.

The ceremony room began to clear out as everyone started to make their way toward the dining hall. "Oh, we're never going to eat," David whined, placing his hand on his stomach and moving it in a circular motion. "We are all headed there now, David." I huffed. My brother guffawed. "Lissy, you know this boy?" he asked while trying to regain his composure. I looked David up and down, shrugged, and answered, "Yeah, I'll claim him, I guess. Then I winked at David while saying, "Bubba, he's the one you made go with you to the men's sleeping courters last night. You just don't recognize him because he is all cleaned up." My friend scowled as Tay, my brother, his lady, and I folded over in laughter.

After we entered the eating hall, I heard behind me, "What is all the commotion over here?"

"I know that strong voice," I said to myself, as I felt my tummy start to flutter. I looked up. Gasp. It was him, my brown-haired, tan-skinned, bright blue-eyed, beastly knight. He gave me a half-grin and my heart said, "Take- take, take-take."

Staring into my eyes he said, "What was that, miss?"

"Huh?" I answered, confused.

"You just said take. Take what might I ask?"

I sucked in a giant amount of air as my eyes widened. I thought for a moment they were going to burst out of their sockets. I slapped a hand over my mouth and spun around feeling sheepish and red-faced. Under my breath I muttered, "Take me away forever is what I want to say." Then I giggled.

"Pardon?" he asked, placing a palm on my shoulder. I just about went weak in the knees until David chimed in, "Hey, Lordy, I don't think that is very appropriate seeing as she belongs to me."

Right after the one too many knocks in the head boy's assumption, my brother said sternly, "She belongs to who?" Patroklos chuckled and my friend gulped as he answered, "I was just jesting S-Sir Brighton sir." I had to cover up a smirk and force back down the bubble of laughter trying to burst out.

Tay and I watched as David filled his plate. I leaned toward her ear, trying not to laugh in it, asking, " Do you think he'll save us some?" The girl tittered and answered while grabbing for her dish, " I hope so." When she was finished filling hers it was time to reach for mine. " Will you allow me carry to your plate to the table, Annalise?" I forgot my handsome knight was still standing behind me. I turned and he had a giant toothy grin planted across his face. The only thing I could get out was, " Uh huh." He chuckled and his beautiful eyes twinkled. My knight grabbed my hand and lead to where the others were sitting.

The awkward dinner was over and before Lord Patroklos got up from the table, he looked at my brother and his other knights then said, "Brighton, Mason, Willy, I trust that you three will explain my order to the ladies and this gentleman about Egladon." After our instructions were told to us about no one being able to step foot near the shore, everyone started to stand and stretch their legs.

It was now just Brighton and me as all of the others had returned to their chambers for the evening. Happy to finally be by myself with him, I was able to explain on what the reasoning was behind our strange but very real-life changes. I was just getting ready to part my lips, but he beat me to it and started first. "Lissy, what in the stars is going on?" I took in a deep breath as I thought, "Geez bubba real subtle."

He was conflicted and I could see this was not going to be easy. Looking into his eyes I swallowed the huge lump that was lodged in the back of my throat as I began trying to explain in the best way I could. I placed my right hand on his arm, not letting up from my gaze. "Bubba, right after you left, scary things started to happen and I'm not just talking about my annual beatings from the Qu"-

In shock from my words, he cut me off.

"Wait, what? You're saying mother, our mother, mistreats you?"

I could see the dismay all over his face as I answered, "Yes, bubba, but listen. I don't believe it to be her." My brother let out a disturbed breath as he leaned back on his heels.

"You don't?" he replied while lowering his brows confused.

I shook my head. "No. Something is controlling her, something evil and it wants my head on a platter. Brighton, I got so scared when I heard mother talking to it in her room that I ran away. That is when I met Tailya, Tay for short. His eyes glistened after the last thing I said, and I knew he was forcing back a smile. "She was a fairy when I"-

"A what?!" he shouted, cutting me off again.

I gulped and then answered, "Yes bubba, fairies are real. Tay helped me escape the darkness by turning me into a fairy so I could hide in plain sight. A Human by day and a fairy by night. The day I left Bristeria, Kedron was still five and I was still nine. You had just gone after teaching me how to ride Ghost. I followed Tay to her coronation and then went through a portal in her new tower." My poor brother was beyond words and couldn't believe what I was talking about, nor what he was hearing. As I kept going, his mouth dropped wide open along with his brows raised. "Bubba the rooms"-

I lost all train of thought on what I was saying and paused for a moment, thinking about the rainbow walls in one of them. Quickly I waved my hands, causing my brother to chuckle and then continued. "No no, we'll get back to that. Okay, where was I, oh, right, so we entered into this mystery world with unicorns and magical creatures, but I came to find out that my friend's gift had actually turned out to be a curse. She wanted to take me to meet someone who could teach me spells to save our mother from the evil that traps her. The enchantress's name was Fawn"-

"Wait, what did you just say?" he interrupted perplexedly.

"Fawn, bubba, keep up, will you?"

"Wait, shhh... hold on, I know her," he said, straightening his whole body to attention.

"I know you do bubba. I saw you in the same world just in different time frames."

My brother shook his head. "Huh," he said, completely baffled.

"I mean, you were you, just older than when I saw you last." He let out a breathy "okay", while rubbing the back of his neck. "That world ages you without you even being aware of it, bubba. Tay of course helped me along with mine, unwillingly though that is neither here nor there. " Huh?" he said upsettingly. I ignored it and went on. "Anyways I met David there and he was one of the unicorns you probably saw."

"Yes!", he blurted. I giggled and he cleared his throat. "Ahem, I mean yes Willy and I did witness unicorns, a baby, and a mama." I could see that my brother was finally up to speed and happy not to be so lost anymore.

I nodded as I answered ,"Mhmm. That baby was my friend David."

He smacked himself on the forehead and then said, "Lissy, this is too much. Just skip to the end."

I sighed, still wanting to tell the rest of my story. Peering into his eyes, I finished with, " Brighton. Mother has gone full evil and has taken our little brother with her. They have overcome King Cyrus and have locked him up in the dungeon."

My brother's eyes widened, and I started to weep while saying, "Bubba I was there. I was there. I tried to free him, but I just wasn't strong enough. He was so frail. So frail. I don't even know how long they've had him down there. An… And now we're older an-an." Full-on bawling, I screeched out , "I don't even know if he's still alive."

He began patting my back to calm me while using soothing words. "Lissy, he's not dead. You can't think like that." I looked up, wiping the dribbles from my mouth as I sniffled, " Bubba, I came here to find you so we can go back and fight them together." Then I blew my nose on the skirt of my dress.

He chuckled, "I forgot how graceful you are." I hit him on the arm. "Oh be quiet." We both guffawed and then fell silent. I thought, "It amazes me how he can still make me laugh even in times of sorrow."

After a few moments of gazing at the stars, my brother broke the silence. "Well, Lissy, I better be going to sleep now. I have an early day of training ahead."

"But I thought you were finished. That's why you're a knight now."

He looked at me with trepidation saying, "Lissy, there is something I need to warn you about and that you need to tell your friends about as well." " Is this the thing Patroklos was talking about, and you wouldn't let Mason or Willy tell us at the table?"

"Yes." He replied giving me that stern "You better pay attention" look and all of a sudden, I became a little frightened. With a deep breath leaving his lungs, he said, "I am training for battle, sis."

"Battle," I replied abruptly. "What battle is there here in Egladon?"

"There is a sea monster that haunts the waters."

Gasp. "I know. I know," I interrupted sarcastically.

He peered into my eyes. "You know? How do you know?" "It left its mark on our mother when she was a little girl." My poor brother was at a loss for words, so I kept talking. "When I was in the world TungWing before I came here, I met a crown prince named Li Che and he thought I was Queen Cheylenna." "The man thought that you were our mother? Saints. What in stars would make him think that?" "Calm down bubba. He happened to share a lot. He told me about how she arrived and how he tried to subside the evil inside her until Yinglong the dragon made her leave." "Ying what? Dragon?"

At this point, Brighton just stared at me in shock. I grasped my other hand over his left arm and said, "Oh come on bubba, yes, I said dragon. Weren't you the one who was just warning me about a sea monster? Now try and keep up. You see our Queen has never been her real self. "Oh no." "Huh uh. I have a letter and everything to prove it, but I'll give it to you later." He gave me that serious look of " You better."

I smiled big and then changed the conversation. "So, when do we get to go fight the sea monster?" Brighton chortled as he swooped his arms around my hands and replaced his on top of my shoulders while sternly saying, "Oh no no no, not we." I gave him a pouty lip as I dropped my chin. "I and the other knights of Egladon will be going to battle. You will stay put in your chamber and wait for my return." He said with a " You'd best do as I say" gaze.

I shook my head not agreeing to one word as I replied, "My friends and I have been in a fight as well and we are all still alive so we can help too. My friend Tailya has a book with enchantments along with Fawn's powerful wand."

My brother dropped his hands from my shoulders, sighed and then grasped my right hand as he gazed into my eyes, and scolded me, "Don't ever let me catch you using that thing. It's dangerous and I don't want to see you hurt." Then he huffed and puffed a few times. "Yes, bubba. Don't worry, I can't seem to touch it without it turning red anyways."

"What!? It turns red on you?" he shouted.

"Mhmm, that's why Tay has it and not me but apparently I'm its rightful owner."

He searched me skeptically and then said, Okay, Lissy. That is enough catching up for this evening. Let's turn in. I'll meet you in the dining hall in the morning. Oh and by the way, that thing does not belong to you." He hugged me and then spun on his heel.

Since I was already close to my chamber, I decided to take a stroll down by the shore. Knowing fully well I was told to stay away, but I decided not to care. Plush I really needed the fresh air. During my walk, I started to ask myself, "What was that strange look he gave me?" Gasp. "Does he think I'm evil? Pshh, ha, surely not. That's absurd Annalise what are you thinking?"

So lost in my head I nearly ran into a tree. "Crapes!" I shouted as I sharply tapped the trunk with my finger. "Stars, Annalise, pay attention," I said aloud while rubbing a hand across my forehead. I looked back up and I could see the ocean. It was nice and peaceful. The water was still, and you could hear the whispers of the wind through every tree . As I got closer and closer toward the water, the sounds of the wind started to fall further and further away until it was completely silent.

I felt on edge and all of the joints inside my body began to tighten causing the hair on my arms to raise. Suddenly the temperature changed, and I felt like I was freezing as my teeth began to chatter. Then I heard it plain and clear as day. "Well hello there, Annalise. I told you we would meet again." Gasp!

CHAPTER 35

Brighton

I couldn't believe that we had encountered the same thing. The whole story was completely out of this universe. I just stood there staring at and listening to my sister while she was having her fun treating me like I was a simpleton wondering if there was some kind of grand reasoning for all of this. I had left my dragon training and went home right after the nightmare. All I remembered was clenching my chest and screaming out her name during it. When I awoke, I was ready to pack up and head my way back to Bristeria. Watching her flail her arms at me and begin to get little annoyed, I forced back down a chuckle, standing there nodding and smiling as she went on and on, while thinking to myself, " Yes sis, I know what a dragon is. I have ridden one. Though I thought it was pretty amazing she herself has had the opportunity to encounter one as well.

I was so thrown off track by her outrageous tale that the moment she turned her back, I thought, "Did I tell her to stay away from Lord Patroklos?" The man was too old for her in my opinion. Standing there for a moment, I contemplated on everything we had just spoken about. "Saints, we talked about everything else but that." I said aloud. Then I started to ponder on her words. My sister, a fairy?... However, she is also acting like a witch. I wonder if this evil thing has overtaken her like our queen. The restless notions in my head were starting to torment me. I was becoming anxious. "I better go and warn her before she gets to the no men allowed chamber," I said out loud as if someone was listening then I took off in a sprint.

Near the mountain before the path that leads to her room, I saw her. "Lissy, Lissy!" I shouted but got no reply. She didn't even turn around to see that it was me who was calling out to her. I began following her quietly through the trees, wondering what in the stars is this girl up to. Then I noticed what her destination was. "No, Lissy. Don't go down there!" I yelled as loud as I could but still nothing. Racing down to the shoreline I growled, "Come on feet don't fail me now."

Never taking my eyes off of her for one second, I screamed, "Lissy, Lissy, stay away from the water!" It was no use, I told myself, picking up my speed. "Must go faster." I began trying to encourage myself in order to take my mind off of the horrifying racing thoughts of my sister getting swallowed up whole by that vicious sea beast.

Smack! I ran into nothing, but it felt like my head slammed straight into a wall. The hit was so strong that I fell backwards and landed right on my tailbone. I stood back up rubbing the ache from my rear. Stretching my hands out in front of me and slowly moving them from side to side, I started pushing trying to feel my way for a clear opening.

"No way through, not one", I huffed. There wasn't anything visible and it felt like solid rock against my palms. "Saints, what is going on here?" I hissed still pressing to find a way through. Feeling helpless and overly frightened for my sister, I began to yell at the top of my lungs, "Somebody help! Can anybody hear me?! Please help my sister! Annalise! Annalise, can you hear me?!" I stood there distraught, beating the invisible stone watching as my little Lissy stepped closer and closer toward the water, not able to lift a finger to save her.

My anxiety was at the level of my body about to give out. I saw Lissy standing so still almost like she had been frozen solid, and I remembered something Milaya told me. Something about God, or "All-Knowing" as she would call Him. So, I lifted my voice as high as my pipes would carry and cried out, "Please God in heaven, I know I don't know you like I should and I probably have no right to ask You this but please God I'm begging, will You save my sister? Please!"

All of the sudden a wet sensation leaked from my eyes and began rolling down my face. Sweeping a finger across my cheek I brought it up to view and said, "When did I start crying?" I began drying my eyes when a lightning bolt flashed landing on the white sand just behind Lissy.

Gasp. "Lissy, look out!" I shouted. She finally turned around. I started jumping up and down, flailing both my hands trying to get her attention but she still couldn't see me. All I could do was stand there and witness as the beam of lightning moved closer upon her.

"Patience, friend." Gasp. "Who was that?" The whisper came from out of nowhere startling me. Then I heard it chuckle and say, "Yes, my way can make a lost lamb jump at first, but I assure you, I do not bite do not be afraid."

The voice went from a whisper to a man's and my body un-clenched from his sense of humor. Suddenly I felt light-chested, and it was easier to take in regular breaths again. "Thank you, whoever you are," I said out loud to an empty forest. "It is my pleasure, Brighton. " What did you just say?" But all I heard after that was a chuckle and then he said, "Now off you go. Go and get some rest. You have an early morning ahead of you, didn't you say?" Gasp. "You-you're the All-Knowing God." He let out another breathy laugh and then said, "I Am."

The moment I heard Him said those words, my entire body filled up with this overwhelming energy that brought me to tears. The feeling was something I couldn't explain even if I tried. Let me put it this way, I wanted to run, jump, shout for joy, laugh and cry all in the same. I didn't want to leave so I said, "Please, can't I stay? I must speak to you more." The all divine being chuckled once more and said, "I am always around. Seek and you will find, Sir Brighton. You don't need to worry any longer. I'll watch over Annalise. You are free to go now."

Lost in His mystery, I sat there in silence for a few minutes. He gave me peace and comfort. I knew Lissy was in good hands, so now without a care in the world, I stood up, dusted off my knees, took one last look toward my sister, and then spun on my heel while shouting, "Hail to the All-Knowing God, who delivered me from my pain and suf-fering!"

Making my way back to Willy and Mason, I ran into my beau-tiful, brown-eyed angel standing right outside the men's sleeping quarters. Walking up to her I thought, "Saints, I'm tired but she's so pretty." I whined that last part out when she locked her eyes to mine. What can I say, the fair maiden had me all tangled up. "Hello, my lady. What brings you out so late?" I asked with a slight yawn.

Her eyes twinkled as she giggled. "Sir Brighton."

"Please, Milaya my love, it's just Brighton to you."

She giggled again. "Uh, Brighton, I was wondering where your sister has gone. She hasn't returned to her chamber, and I was becoming out of sorts for you," she said, sweetly as she clasped her over my arm and stared into my eyes.

I chuckled, "Don't worry, the one you call All-Knowing said He would watch over her."

Milaya's eyes widened when I said His name. "You spoke to Him," she gasped.

"Yes, I did. It was easy just as I am speaking to you. Only, I can see you, but I couldn't see Him, only hear His voice." Also where I am from, we address Him as God. She stood there looking like she was in deep thought so I finished by saying, "It doesn't matter that I couldn't see Him."

"Oh," she blurted. "Why is that?"

"Because I could feel Him."

"How could you feel Him?" she asked, looking confused.

"I don't really know. Let's just say unspoken energy came over me and I felt like I could leap up into the air and run on the clouds. It could've been His presence."

She frowned. "I remember that feeling very well about three years past." I couldn't contain my zeal. I had to know more so I took her in my arms and said, "Don't let what happened in the past destroy the outcome of our future. You are the only person who has mentioned the All-Knowing God to me which means you are fully aware of who He is. I have only heard of Him by name. Please enlighten me, my angel."

She started to sniffle and rub her nose against my shirt. I didn't even know she was crying. Regret from pushing her began to set in until she lifted her perfectly shaped head and looked at me with those alluring amber eyes of hers.

My heart stilled as she said, "He is a wonderful friend to talk to. You never feel alone when He is by your side." She sighed deeply and then said with a self-reproachful tone, "I don't know why I ever left Him. When my father disappeared that is when I really needed a friend to talk to but instead, I let my anger get a hold of me and I closed myself off shutting Him and everyone else out."

I ran my hand down her hair. "From what I've just encountered I'm sure the All-Knowing God is just patiently waiting for you to return." My angel rubbed her brown eyes trying to stop any more liquid from forming then said, "Do you think He would ever forgive me?" Looking down at those little puffy cheeks I smiled and said, "From what I know just now He is compassionate and also full of kindness. I believe He wants a relationship with all He has created. So yes, my sweet angel I believe if you are truly repentant for shutting him out, He will forgive you."

Milaya sniffled a little more while nodding her head. As soon as she fully regained her composure I asked, "Can you please teach me more about the All-Knowing God. I want to know Him." She smiled real big saying, "Patroklos would be able to tell you more than I can. He has been studying and pursuing All-Knowing since He was of age to read."

Standing on her tiptoes while looking over my shoulder she called out, "Annalise."

"Where?" I said, twisting my head. My sister was safe and sound smiling at us from across the yard. No breath of relief left my lungs, only a huge grin appeared on my lips as I heard Him whisper, "What you asked of Me has been given."

Feeling completely content I smiled, embraced my lady, and bid her goodnight. Watching her as she spun on her heel, I thought "Saints, I am one captivated knight." Then I headed inside to get some small talk in with my brothers before lights out.

Through the foyer, I could hear Mason's loud obnoxious self-speaking about something along the lines of beauties. When I got to the door, I swung it open and said, "So what beauty are you talking about?" He chortled, answering, "All of us mate." Squinting at Willy I said, "Huh?"

Mason guffawed even louder then stood up and clapped me on the back saying, "She'll be right mate. You'll learn sooner or later what I'm saying." Then he turned to Willy with a smirk and whistled while flattening his palm downward to run over the top of my head.

Willy burst out. The frail guy was laughing so hard he had to pull out his medicine and take a couple of puffs. I glared at Mason then sardonically laughed while jerking away and saying through my teeth, "Get off of me."

Mason's coy grin dropped leaving him to look like a kid who was just told that Santa Clause and his elves weren't real. "Aw, come on, mate. I was just fooling about. Don't be such a"- He beat his chest with his fists, finishing with, "gorilla." I chuckled. "Am I really that stiff?" I asked, turning toward Willy. My friend shrugged silently almost as if he didn't want to answer.

I deeply inhaled and then looked at Mason saying, "Saints, brother, I guess I'm more on edge about this battle than I thought."

"She'll be right, Brighton," he replied, patting me on the shoulder. I clapped him on his back saying, "I'll try to loosen up a bit more from now on, alright. Let's turn in now. We have a big day ahead of us."

Both my brothers fell back into their mattresses and before I could get my boots off to do the same, they were already snoring. I glared at both of them mumbling under breath, "Saints, this is going to be a long night."

CHAPTER 36

Annalise

"Y- Y- Yurika." My voice trembled as I tried to speak. The water started splashing up against my feet sending more chills up my spine from its icy cold temperature. Then it felt like I was in Bristeria Bellarium's Tower of Enchantment listening to one of my teachers scratch their fingernails against the chalkboard when her voice rang through my ears saying, "Join me, girl. Join me and I promise we'll do great things together."

I began humming as loud as I could over her so I could gather my thoughts. I said to myself, "Okay, Annalise, think. Where have you heard that before?" I started to bite my bottom lip and then it came to me as I blurted, "It was you! You're that hissing voice I keep hearing.

What do you want from me? Why can't you just leave me be? Get out of my head!"

All the witch did was cackle, and I couldn't have felt more afraid than I did when I was little and staring at the yellow eyes as I hid under the table in Renard the Tard's store. "There is no need for you to look around for a rescuer, girl. No one is coming to save you. Now be a good little blind following puppet and come fully into the water."

I gasped as my feet started to move one following the other. The only thing I knew to shout, I did. Raising my voice to the top of my lungs, I cried out, "Ferguson! Help, Ferguson!" Not a moment too soon a huge lightning bolt landed right behind me causing the ground to shake under my feet.

Turning my head and watching him make his way up to me, I cried, "I don't care what I have to do, just please get me out of here." He turned his back to me looking over toward the trees, but no one was there. So, I anxiously shouted, "What is so important right now for you to be looking over there? Please help me!" My watcher didn't say a word, just smiled, grabbed my hand, pulled me into his wings, and hoisted us into the air.

I could hear Yurika's ear splitting scream, "Nooo! She is mine!" as we ascended. Then all of a sudden, the water had motion. The waves began to roar as a ginormous snake-looking fish shot straight up out of the deep blue. I clamped my eyes and said out loud, "Not real, not real. It's just my imagination, only my imagination." Then Ferguson looked down at me with all of his eyes and said, "Afraid not, Annalise." My whole body quivered from his answer.

"Hey, how come you're just now talking? Why didn't you come sooner? Aren't you supposed to be watching me?" Crash! We landed at the doorstep of my chamber safely. He chuckled at my questions then he answered, "Yes I am assigned to you, but I too have a King that I follow commands from, and He told me to wait and let things play out, so I obeyed. Trust me you were never in any real danger. With Him around, they have no choice but to bow down."

"They? Who are they and what in stars do they want?" I asked as I cracked my neck looking up at him. He didn't answer, so I instead I asked, "Ferguson, can you please change? My neck is starting to ache from trying to look up at you." My watcher chuckled. "Close your eyes then," he said as he started to glow. I did as he said while still thinking, "What does he mean by they?" Then I opened my eyes back up when he said, "It is done, Annalise."

Excessively rubbing my lids trying to get rid of the spots that kept on appearing every time I opened my eyes caused from Ferguson's bright beam of light as he changed, my watcher stood there in human form chortling at me. "Alright now," he said, still coughing out giggles.

I shook my head as I made a bewildered sound trying to regain my focus. Once all the color spots were gone, I whispered, "Okay, I can see now."

"Why are you speaking so quietly?" he whispered back, poking fun at me. I pointed over his shoulder with wide eyes toward my brother and Milaya.

"Can't they see you?" I asked a little panicked. He laughed, "Only if I'm assigned to them, can they see me. They might think you are out here talking to yourself."

"Ha ha ha, very funny. Okay, well you had better be off then. Thank you, Ferguson, for saving me. I"-

He cut me off sternly saying, "I did not save you, Annalise. I was sent by my king so don't give praise to me for I am but a servant."

I nodded my head but still felt confused as to who he was implying. The moment he began to flicker, getting ready to change back and leave I asked, "Well might I ask then the name of the person I should thank for my release from Yurika's grasp?"

He smiled as his heels touched back down on the grass and said, "My king is more than just a person, Annalise. Ask your brother in the morning. He might have some answers for you."

I turned my head to the side as I lifted my hand to shield my eyes when Ferguson began to lift off the ground and change back into his celestial self. Before going up into the sky, he called down to me. "Seek and you will find! Knock and the door will open! Ask and it will be given! Remember my child, you are not alone!"

Then I watched as he ascended into the stars leaving me to ponder on everything he had just said. I thought, "I know I've heard that before but where? I remember them coming from a still small voice but for the life of me I couldn't remember."

I began to get frustrated until my brother's lady came running toward me shouting, "Annalise, you're okay! Oh, I knew you would be." as she draped her arms tightly around my neck. Tay stuck her head out of the window. "Anna, is that you? Where in all of the stars did you run off to? I've been worried sick!"

I rolled my eyes thinking, "Yeah. Uh huh, sure you have. That's why you're in your nighties with a book in your hand." I didn't say that though. Instead, I yelled back, "I'm alright, Tay. Just took a stroll down by the shore."

"The water, did you go near the water?" Milaya asked while shaking me.

"Yes. Yes, as a matter of fact I did," I replied as I moved away from her grasp.

Looking up at Tay I yelled, "I have a lot to tell you. We're coming up!" Then locking my fingers onto Milaya's I said, "You need to hear this too, let's go." I pulled her inside, up the stairs, and into our room.

"What is so important, Anna?" Tay hissed, tossing her book onto the table.

"Tailya," I said her full name, causing her to give me all of her attention.

"What, what's going on, Anna?" she gasped.

Sucking in a timid breath, I began to tell her everything I had just come across. "Tay, it's Yurika. She's the sea beast." Of course her being in complete shock, she cut me off. "How in the stars is that even possible, Anna?"

I could see the confusion written all over her face so I said, "Well if you let me talk, I may have a theory." The baffled girl glared and then nodded as the other one continued to squeeze all the feeling out of my left hand.

"You know how Yurika was a unicorn when we met her?" She didn't answer with any words, just nodded again. "Okay, so think about this. If she can be a unicorn then change into an enchantress, then speak through Milaya, and now become a sea beast, do we think she is really a she and that it's just a witch haunting us?"

Tay got up out of her chair silently and slowly walked over to her bed. I believed she was lost in deep thought. I knew poor Milaya was because when I turned to look at her response she was looking up and tapping her chin.

None of us spoke the rest of the evening. I mean, what was there to say? We all knew that we were dealing with something extremely wicked. Tay and I knew we had already defeated it once, at least we thought we had. Before closing my eyes to try and get some rest, I leaned toward Tay's bed, whispering, "We need a master plan on how to defeat this thing again."

"I have something already in mind, but you and I are the only ones who can know about it because it is very risky. You could lose your life," she whispered back as Milaya blurted, "Go to sleep now, ladies. Tomorrow morning I'll take you to meet your pegasus."

"Pegasus!" Tay and I mystifyingly shouted at the same time.

"Mhmm," she answered, rolling over and giving us a big smile. Tay looked at me and said, "We need to tell David."

Through my teeth and with a glare I sharply replied, "No." My friend smirked. Then both of us rolled back onto our pillows.

Not long after closing my eyes, the hissing started. "Come to me. Take the wand and burn it. That thing has no power over me, girl. I...I can give you all the power you need. So come on, they don't care about you anyway. Don't you know that are nothing to them but a nuisance. You're Queen even said that you were a mistake. Honestly girl, why do you even bother fighting?"

"Leave me alone!" I screamed out loud while sitting up onto my elbows but unfortunately all I heard was an impish cackle which caused me to huff and throw my head back on my pillow. I cried on the inside as I became very restless and started to toss and turn.

The sun rays shone through our room, and I realized that the evil darkness made sure I didn't get any sleep. Milaya rose up off her pillow. "Good morning, Annalise," she said while reaching her hand up in the air.

"Is it?" I growled back.

I wasn't meaning to sound so hostile, but I didn't sleep one wink last night. I was tortured in my mind which caused my body to weaken mentally, physically, and emotionally. Let's face it, I felt like a walking time bomb. Anyone says or does the wrong thing and Boom! Instant rage. "Hey, Tay, wake up it's time for breakfast and then we get to go meet our pegasus. Hurry up!" I shouted a little to abruptly.

She sat herself up and did the same as Milaya. Getting dressed I thought, "I could spit nails right now."

"Anna, what is with you this morning? Didn't you get any sleep?"

Tay's question was just like adding fuel to a fire and I snapped, "What does it matter!? You two slept well, didn't you? Don't worry about me. It's not like you really care anyway."

"Crapes," Tay said while looking at Milaya wide-eyed. "What got into her?" she asked her.

Milaya shrugged. "I am just as puzzled as you are, miss Tailya."

"Yee… Please. Please don't call me that. It sounds too formal. Tailya or Tay will be just fine." She said while shivering and shaking her head.

"As you request," Milaya answered with a gentle smile.

I just stood there by my bed huffing and puffing wondering to my-self why in the stars I couldn't seem to calm down. "Are you ready, Anna?" Tay asked while coming over to gently wrap her fingers around my palm. The heaviness in my chest subsided and all three of us took to the stairs heading toward the dining hall.

Walking in straight away I didn't waste any time scouring the crowd in search of my knight, but he was nowhere to be found. Disappointed, I dropped my head. "Who are you looking for, Anna?" David asked, walking up to tease me. As I sighed not caring about him at the moment, I answered in a low tone, "No one."

Just as I was about to start an oh woes me party in my head, a deep voice spoke out behind me, "Apologies, miss, but you are holding up the line."

Eeep! I didn't need to turn around. I already knew it was him, my handsome bright blue-eyed dreamy man. Plus, I remembered his scent, how could it ever leave me? Aromas of pomelo, coriander, and green leaves danced through my smell zone as I daydreamed about strolling through the forest, looking each other in the eyes and holding hands.

A giggle left me and then I heard, "Are you alright, miss?"

"Yes, Lordy, she is perfectly fine." I burst out laughing when David tried to deepen his voice. Yanking my arm, he hissed, "Come on, Anna. Let's go." I was already feeling sheepish from my lost in space giggling, so I allowed my jealous friend to pull me away.

When I turned back to look over my shoulder, Lord Patricklos was smiling at me. Contagiously, I smiled right back.

After staring across the room at my knight and not even touching an ounce of my porridge, Milaya announced that it was time for us to go meet our pegasus.

Making our way up to an extraordinary-looking cave, I started to think of a name for my newfound pet. Walking in, immediately we saw a beautiful white one with ice blue wings. I began to get lost in its cloudy color eyes. "Wha!.. Tay, look at this one. The shape of its eyes is in the form of icicles!" She plugged her ears from the echo of my screaming, and I chortled. "Sorry," I said, still over ecstatic.

"Hahaha, you like this one, do you?"

Gasp. "Patroklos," I said on the inside. Spinning around to face him, I was surprised to hear myself say, "Yes, very much. Is this one spoken for?"

My dream guy chuckled, "No, miss, he is all yours if you want him."

"Oh, yes please," I replied hastily.

Looking my beautiful creature over, Patroklos asked, "Might I know what you are going to name him?" "It's a male?" I asked while smiling from ear to ear and taking in a nonchalant sniff of his charming scent. " Yes, miss he is." He replied. I giggled under my breath and then answered, "Rain, I will name him Rain."

"Oh, might I ask how you came up with that?" he asked while searching my eyes.

I fluttered my lashes and answered, "His eyes remind me of what the clouds look like before it rains."

He laughed while saying, " It seems you and your brother have the same mind."

I looked at him like "Huh?" but didn't say anything. Even though I could stand and talk to him forever I had to say farewell for now so Tay and David could go find their new flying horses as well.

After smiling and waving, I spun on my heel, realizing I had just left Rain behind. "Stars, Anna, get it together," I grumbled as I smacked myself on the forehead. Behind me, I heard chortling. I turned to look and saw Brighton, Milaya, Willy, Mason, and of course because he never left my knight. At that moment I started to feel very green.

"Do you always talk to yourself, Lissy?" Brighton asked guffawing. I couldn't get angry. My brother's laugh was always contagious. Since the nausea quickly subsided, I joined in saying, "Yes and sometimes I even answer myself." All of them including me bent over in laughter after that.

"Hello. It's our turn. Can we get a move on please?" David scowled.

"Pipe down, little one," Patroklos said while pressing his palm toward the cement. I giggled when David started to turn into a tomato as he shot daggers toward my knight.

"Hahaha. Come on, David, I was only jesting. Here, follow me, I have one down the way that I think you will love," Patroklos said walking up to my friend and tossing his stocky muscular arm around his neck. All of us pace behind them as Tay and I turned our heads right and left looking at all the magnificent creatures.

"Look!" David shouted just a few feet away. "I want this one, is he taken?"

My knight laughed, "No, he is all yours."

When Tay and I reached the stall of her brother's new pet our eyes widened at the sight of this galaxy-looking winged horse.

"Woah, David! Look at his eyes!" I shouted astonished at the color and shape. It was as if we were staring into a flame becoming mesmerized. The shape of its eyes was in the form of swords. Now I knew why David was in awe with this one. The pegasus had snowy white wings and a body as black as soot from a chimney.

"So, what's his name, David?" I asked as I swayed my body side to side while staring at Patroklos.

"Draco."

"What", Tay blurted while laughing.

"I said Draco," he growled.

"Okay, okay. Draco it is. Geez, I was just teasing you."

"Come on, you two. Don't start quarreling," I pleaded. "Besides we still need to meet yours, Tay."

She smiled at me replying, "I've already picked mine out."

"Huh?" I questioned, puzzled. "When?"

"When you took off over to see David's, I saw mine, and I've already named her," she said with a satisfied grin.

"Okay, let's see her, and then I want to know her name," I said following behind towards the stall of her new flying horse.

CHAPTER 37

The Final Battle

Staring at my friend's pegasus in its eyes, the shapes and colors were incredible. I was becoming impatient and wanted to know Tailya's pet's newfound title. "Come on, Tay, what's the creature's name?"

The simper on her face just made my anxiousness even more prevalent.

"Ugh," I growled.

"Alright, alright," she said guffawing. "Geez, Anna, you have no patience in you whatsoever."

"Nope," I said with a playful toothy grin.

"Thundra!" she shouted, causing me to take a step back.

"Geez, way to kill the excitement out of it, miss cranky," I groaned.

Tay's pegasus had all kinds of amazing features to her. She had a violet body, white wings, yellow eyes that could strike fear into anyone, and diamonds for the shape. "Wow, Tailya, she really is something but what made you want to choose a female?" I asked while walking over to brush my hand across Thundra's wing.

Tay walked up beside me. While running her fingers through Thundra's soft snowy wing, she said, "I didn't pick her. She nudged the back of my head when I was standing with my back to her stall. So, I believe she picked me, didn't you, my violet beauty?" The last part came out as she started petting Thundra's leg while I still stroked her fluffy wing.

All the men came walking up and it was to my understanding that they were ready to go.

"Mi"-

"Please call me Annalise or Anna," I blurted, cutting off my knight. He never finished his sentence, but he did smile at me which made my knees buckle a bit. "He is so handsome," I thought as I sighed contently.

"Uh, Lissy. Lissy." Stars my brother was trying to get my attention. Well daydream, you'll just have to wait. I growled on the inside.

On the outside, I gave Brighton an irritated grin and answered, "Yes, bubba?" Then I fluttered my lashes playfully.

He just smirked, not saying one peep. He knew, but of course Tay didn't care. I just knew that this girl was out to get me. In front of everyone she said loudly, "Anna, you have a little bit of drool coming out."

"Huh," I wiped my mouth so quick I almost gave myself a busted lip. "Stars, way to get him to notice you, Anna," I hissed under my breath. I looked up and David had a big smirk plastered on his face. He rolled his eyes at me then grabbed my hand and said out loud where everyone including Patroklos could hear, "You don't have to wipe your drool off for me sweet thing." Then he winked, threw his arm around me, and proceeded to say, "I'll take you just the way you are. No need to try and impress me." After my friend had finished teasing me, he winked again and walked me toward the entrance of the cave.

I was so embarrassed my nerves started to stiffen and I didn't want to control my actions so the moment we were away from everyone I let him have it. "Who in the stars do you think you are?! What makes you think you even have the right to humiliate me like that?! We're friends David, just friends. You don't belong to me, and I certainly do not belong to you! You got that?!"

I threw his arm off of me. He tried to reach for my wrist, but I yanked it from his grasp and stormed off thinking, "How in all the stars can I ever face him now? I bet Patroklos must be thinking I'm some kind of a joke." Kicking the dirt in my path I said aloud, "Crapes, as grumpy as I am, I'm not going to be much help in anything today."

"Yeah, you could say that."

Gasp. "Brighton, what are you doing here? Shouldn't you be in locked arms with Milaya, talking up a storm?" I couldn't even look up from my snide comment. I was afraid if I did, I might snap at him too.

"Lissy…," he said in his "I'm going to speak and you're going to listen" kind of brotherly way. I thought, "Uh oh" and immediately stopped my pouting. Lifting my eyes to his I grumbled, "What, bubba?" then waited for the scolding to start.

My brother chuckled as he said, "I was coming over here to tell you not to be ashamed."

"Huh," I replied as my spirits lifted a little.

"No one laughed and my leader is quite taken with you."

"He is?"

"Yes. He said, "your sister is something spicy.""

"What?" I couldn't help but giggle from the way my knight described my attitude.

Brighton sighed and said, "Oh saints, Lissy," as he smiled at me.

"Are you ready to go back now? There are a few things I'd like to show you before we set out for battle," he asked while giving me a slight nudge on my arm with his elbow. I took in a deep breath, nodded my head, and answered, "Ready" then we took off to meet up with the others. "Wait. We left David", I said through a staggered breaths. "Oh him? He left a while back after you yelled at him. Now come on, pick up your feet." I gave my brother a quick bob while swallowing hard trying to produce some saliva to coat my throat. The dryness was starting to make me cough and gag a little.

As we got closer and closer toward the cave, we could see everyone, and my lips curved up so high that my eyes creased. My heart started beating rapidly and my tummy fluttered when I heard Patroklos say, "There she is" with his bright baby blues locked on mine.

Brighton and I began making our way over. I kept muttering under my breath while flapping my elbows, "Okay, Anna, don't say anything off the wall. It's easy just smile, nod, and maybe giggle a little. Now come on let's air out some".

My brother stopped in his tracks. Staring me up and down he started guffawing. "What in the saints are you doing, Lissy?" he blurted.

"Shh. Keep your voice down. I whispered, still trying to get rid of the perspiration. "I'm airing out a bit. I don't want to go over there all sweaty. I might smell and that would be a disaster."

He pinched two of fingers together and ran them across his lips like he was sealing them shut but he was still coughing out laughs in the process. "Alright already," I hissed.

"Hello," I said while fluttering my lids at my knight. He didn't reply. For once I think I had stunned him. I covered a smirk and then looked at Tay.

"Where is your brother? Brighton said he left shortly after I scolded him. I thought he'd be back by now."

"Oh, he's probably still sulking by the tree outside. Didn't you guys see him when you came in?"

I shook my head and then sighed as I replied, No Tay that's why I just asked you" and then I looked at Brighton. "Did you see him?"

"No, Lissy. I don't recall anyone being out there," he replied in deep thought.

"I'm right here," David shouted walking into the cave. I dropped my head as he passed me feeling a little regretful for the way I handled things.

"What?' he asked his sister because she wouldn't stop staring.

"Nothing, just making sure you're okay." She replied.

The boy shrugged while saying, "So, we bickered, what else is new? Right, Anna?" I guess David was deciding to sweep my outburst under the rug and forget about it and frankly I couldn't have felt more re-lieved. Of course, that didn't mean I would allow, nor let him continue on controlling me. That part I would stick to my standards. I bobbed my head at the thought as everyone stared at me oddly. I crossed my arms saying in my mind, "Way to go, Anna, you nailed it." Then I rolled my eyes thinking, " This is exactly what I didn't want to happen."

Shortly after standing in silence, I swallowed down my embarrass-ment and then we all geared up our pegasi and headed toward the training grounds. "Oh my stars! It's beautiful over here," I said as we went through the gate. Patroklos walked up from behind me. "Oh, you like this courtyard, do you? Perhaps you'd care to join me on a stroll this evening after dinner."

Walking alongside him, I thought, "Is he trying to court me? Yeep!" Not saying a word for fear of ruining this wonderful moment, I turned toward him and swiftly nodded as I blinked my lashes rapidly which of course caused him to chuckle. I watched as my knight puffed his chest out, showing off, and said, "Alright men, let's show them some fighting techniques."

Brighton looked at me while getting ready to climb on his pegasus' wing. "Better stay grounded, for now, little Lissy. I gave my brother and eye roll and he tittered. "These guys can be a touch frightening getting on the first time." He finished. I smiled at him and then looked at Tay and winked.

She smirked while pulling Fawn's wand from thin air. "What is that?" Brighton asked, a little shocked.

"That, oh, that is Fawn's magic rod," I answered with a coy smile. "My friend here is about to show you, men, how it's done." My brother looked adjugated as Tailya began twisting it in circles over her head. He gave me a stern look and I dropped my gaze quickly as I told myself quietly, "bubba , you just don't understand."

Tay pointed the stick toward me. Circling her wrist, she shouted, "Ti einai."

They all watched as my feet left the ground and got placed safe and sound on Rain's withers. Mason blurted, "Hey, how about doing that for me?" Tay tittered and then granted his request. But my brother just shook his head as if he wasn't pleased with any of it.

"Hahaha, alright, all playing aside, we really should get to the sky," Patricklos said. I watched as he and his mystical steed ascended into the air, then my brother, and then Mason. "Come on, you two, let's go."

"Uh, hello, what about me?" David shouted from the ground. Tay and I laughed then she used Fawn's wand to lift him onto Draco.

In the air right next to my brother I said, "Hey, what is his name? You never told me." I could tell he was still upset so I tried striking up a conversation. He stared at me for a minute, sighed and then spoke.

"I didn't?" he answered.

"No, bubba. I bet you were thinking to, but my outburst must've made you forget."

He chuckled, patted the withers of his pegasus, and said, "Lissy, meet Arkimedes."

"Oh, hello there. Yes, miss, it is a pleasure to meet you."

"Oh wow, you can talk."

Hearing Arkimedes speak made me miss Fyra even more now. Leaning down to mine, I said, "Rain can you talk too?"

Arkimedes chimed in, "I am afraid he can't hear you too well, miss. You see there was a terrible explosion in our world, and it caused a lot of our pegasi to lose their hearing. I'm afraid Artrayious and I are the only two that came out with our hearing still intact."

"Oh, okay, so who is Artrayious?" I asked thinking, "where in the stars did this creature learn to speak so proper?" Then I laughed at the thought.

"This is Artrayious," Patroklos said, flying up next to me. "And that is Brontes," he said, pointing over to Mason. When I looked toward him, I noticed that Milaya, and Willy weren't with us. "Where is your lady friend?" I asked Brighton. However, before my brother could answer, my handsome knight said, "My sister doesn't like to use her pegasus for fight training. So, you probably won't see her until dinner."

"Hmmm," I replied with a quick bob.

Ugh, endless training for what felt like hours on end. I flew over to Tay and David. They were practicing dives. Mine was balancing although it felt more like how many times can one fall on their rear end before they can't get back up. "Tay, I'm tired of this."

"Me too," she replied.

"Let's just use magic to make us warriors." Even though I knew my brother would be against it, I just wanted to stop plummeting on my poor tail bone.

"I'm right there with you," she answered as she began to lift her hand to bring forth Fawn's wand.

It was starting to surface when my brother shouted, "Lissy, get back over here. You're not done."

I looked at Tay, sighed, and then shrugged while saying, "Well, it was worth a shot." Then Rain and I went back toward my brother and Patroklos.

Our training was finally over. My legs and arms felt numb from all the jump kicks and swordplay. I couldn't wait to get Rain back to his stall for the evening because I was starving, and my stomach felt like it was trying to eat itself.

"Help!" I heard someone scream as we got up to the cave.

"Shhh. Did you two hear that?" I asked shifting my eyes back and forth from Tay and Mason. They were in the middle of chatting. "Help!" Gasp. There it was again. "Quiet you two. Did you hear it?"

"I heard it."

"Yeah, me too," David and my brother both said walking up beside me.

Mason spun around to look at Patroklos who was trailing behind him and Tay. "Hey, mate, did you hear someone shouting?"

The stocky knight stopped to listen. Once all of us closed our mouths, we all heard it. "Please somebody help me. I can't, it's got me, help!"

"Listen, it's coming from over there," I blurted pointing toward the sand. All the knights eyed one another. My brother looked at me and sternly said, "Annalise, put Rain up and you and your friends head back toward the castle."

"But bubba, where are you going?" I whined.

"My brothers and I are going to head to the shore and check it out," he said, not at all looking my way but still nodding at them to go.

I let my brother leave letting him think I would obey. However, as soon as they had all cleared from the entrance, I looked at Tay and said, "This is it. We can't back out now. Time for your master plan."

She peered her eyes into mine with a look of "I am ready." I furrowed my brows. "Weapons ready?"

"Ready," she said, grabbing for the magic wand.

"I didn't dream of being in a war so soon. I haven't even had the chance to get to know Patroklos let alone go on a date." The thought brought out a disappointed sigh as I watched my friend spin the witch's magic stick in the air.

"Uh, guys what master plan? How come I wasn't in on it?" David had a little frustration in his tone, and I thought, "That's exactly why we didn't tell you."

He scowled and crossed his arms, "What's going on?"

"Come on David, I'll fill you in when we get there," I said trying to get him to move but knowing I had no intentions of telling him anything. I turned back to Tailya. "You and David keep a hold of your pegasi."

She bobbed her head as she swirled Fawn's wand and chanted, "P'ano."

Once she was positioned on Thundra's withers, I said, "Hey, what about a little boost for us too."

She giggled and then hoisted us up onto our pegasi. "Oh, and Tay," I said, getting situated. She looked at me as I began to bend my elbow like I was holding onto a shield. "Yes." she answered. "We are going to need some real weapons."

"Got it," she replied, already in motion as the wand glowed in her hand.

"Wow! Thanks, sis!" David shouted as he looked over his shiny metal blade and shield. Not too long after she granted me the same. "Stars, Tay, it's like you're a human genie. Do you think that thing could be of use to us in the fight?"

My friend smiled and shrugged then said, "I only know what I know."

That one went over my head, and I thought, "What in the stars did that mean?" However, we had no time for my curiosity. We needed to get to the ocean, so I said sternly, "Tay, David, gird yourselves well. We have the battle to get to."

Draco, Thundra, and Rain flew us into the trees just above the shore. We could see my brother, Patroklos, Mason, and it looked like Willy had come to join them after all as well. "Brighton!" I yelled but he didn't even turn around. He and his brothers were just standing there staring into the water.

Wait, I knew this scene from earlier.
"Ferguson! Ferguson!" I started to cry out for my watcher and Tay and David, both gave me a "she's lost it" look. I knew why all of them were frozen. They were in the same trance Yurika had me in.

The closer we got to them the more activity there was in the water coming toward them. I shot my eyes at Tay and shouted, "She's coming!" David rode up next to me and shouted, "Who's coming?"

I shook my head and then turned my attention forward. "Ahhh," David screamed when he witnessed Yurika shooting up out of the water. "Wh-what is that?" My poor friend was beyond fear-stricken as he had finally laid his eyes on the massive snake-like fish head with hollow black eyes. "The sea monster looked like it was getting into position to devour all of them," David cried as Yurika's sharp-edged teeth began to part, showing drips of blood from her last meal.

"That poor man who was shouting for help," I thought. I looked over and Tay gave me a swift bob. She was ready and so was I. David on the other hand not so much. I felt the same as my friend. I was and have been for a while now hoping that this was all just some kind of morbid dream, and I can't wake up till it's ran its course.

I took in the deepest breath I could suck into my lungs and then started to cough as I blew it out. Yurika's body was now hovering over my brother's and Arkimedes' heads. I turned to Tay and cried out, "Make this shield fly swift and true, hurry!"

"It won't do anything, Anna," she said with disbelief.

"It will. It will break her concentration long enough for us to get down there. Please, do it now!" I shouted.

"Okay. Rain, fly. Fly like you've never flown before, please…" I pleaded, stroking his side. Suddenly my pegasus took off and we ascended into the air. Before I knew it, he had me within throwing distance. I reared my arm back and then chunked my shield toward the sea monster as hard as I could while Tay shouted, "Ptisi!" My metal shield spun wildly toward Yurika, and I watched it closely, hoping it would penetrate her skin.

I wanted to look over my shoulder and see if Tay and David were on my tail, but I was too afraid for my brother, so I yelled, "More speed Rain!" Crash! We landed on the sand right behind Brighton and the others just as my shield sliced the beast in its neck causing it to drop back into the water. I said to Rain, "I think it worked." Then Tay and David, who were up in the air next to me, shouted, "We don't stand a chance on the ground!"

"I know!" I yelled back. All of the guys were awake from their trance. Brighton turned around and said, "Lissy, I told you three to stay put."

Rain and I lifted off the ground and flew above his head. I shouted back, "Bubba if I had listened to you, you all would have been eaten just now. Come on and get up here. And please stop arguing with me. Now let's go get this monster!" My brother shook his head. The water started to form ripples and I knew we needed to move. "Let's go! Let's go! She's coming!" I shouted. Looking up toward the clouds I saw David and Tay already in position.

"Brighton, you all come on, we need to get up there with them right now!" The ripples were moving faster, and I started to panic until Brighton looked at Patroklos, Mason, and Willy saying, "Alright you heard my sister, what are we waiting for?"

Their pegasi leaped off the ground and began to follow me. I looked over my shoulder as Yurika sprung her giant body up from the water heading straight for my brother with her mouth wide open. "Brighton, look out!" I yelled. Right as I shouted his name my brother's friend came to save him savagely swinging his sword.

A relieved sigh left me when I saw Brighton was in the clear. Just as I turned my head back toward Tay and David, I heard, "Nooooo! Willy!"

Tay gasped and David's mouth dropped. I twisted my head and saw Willy and his pegasus' body were dangling out of the sea monster's jaws.

Brighton jetted up to us passing his two other brothers and shouted, "That beast is mine!" I watched as Yurika finished off poor Willy and his pet. All six of us were finally in formation and ready for the unexpected. I wiped the tears from the corner of my eyes after watching my brother's friend get devoured.

"Here it comes. Get your weapons ready," Patroklos yelled while gripping the hilt of his sword and raising it to his shoulder. Their pegasi formed a circle and Tay, David, and I watched as my knight, Mason, and my brother leaped off of their pets and began standing in mid-air.

"What in the stars?" David said with his head shifted to the side. My jaw dropped wide open, and I was baffled as I watched all of them walk across the sky just as if they were on solid ground.

Looking back up, Yurika was zigzagging toward us just like a slithering snake would when hunting for its prey. "Get ready!" I shouted. Brighton, Patroklos, and Mason still wanted us to stay back and let them handle it. This time I gritted my teeth and tightly squeezed Tailya's hand as they began to attack.

Yurika cackled and then struck at Mason. He jumped to the left and plunged his sword toward her eye but missed. The giant fish-like serpent reared back and tried attacking my handsome knight next only to miss as he dropped down to spin on his heel while sweeping around on his other leg for a connected kick to Yurika's body.

Patroklos' blade plunged up into the creature's gut causing it to strike down and sink its teeth into the arm that was holding the sword.

My stomach churned as my heartbeat rapidly for his survival. "Mason, look out!" Tay shouted. Her chest was rising and falling as she anxiously watched him try his best to connect a plunge.

"It's too strong," Brighton yelled. "Retreat. Retreat," he called out heading back toward Arkimedes. When Yurika saw that my brother's guard was down, she looked over, and winked with one of those soulless eyes. Her massive head swayed side to side as she stuck out her lizard tongue and reared herself back like a slingshot. "Brighton, watch out!" I shouted.

He was able to dodge, and I sighed in relief. I watched as he started to crawl up Arkimedes' wing. His pegasus gave him a friendly boost by flipping up his wing to send my brother up onto his withers. Mason and Patroklos were already on theirs as they made their way over to my brother to check on him. "Brighton...!" I screamed for my brother. That horrifying witch was getting ready to strike again. "I got you, mate!" Mason shouted as he swung his blade toward the vicious sea creature so my brother and Arkimedes could get safely up in the air.

"Okay, Mason, let's go." Brighton said.
Gasp.

"Mason! Mason!" My brother looked over his shoulder to see his friend being eaten sword and all as his pegasus Brontes descended toward the ground. More tears began to form for the loss of both his friends. Patroklos yelled out to my brother, "He wouldn't want us to stop fighting! Don't let his death be in vain!"

Brighton rolled and slid down Arkimedes' wing in rage.

Gasp.

"Tailya," I cried out. She shook her head. "Tailya, they're going to die!" I shouted. I knew why she was hesitant. I knew I might not come out of this alive, but still, I was not going to allow myself to just sit by and watch as my brother or my knight got devoured along with all the rest.

"Tailya, please!"

"It's too risky, Anna."

"What is going on?" David chimed in. I didn't answer.

"Fine, you won't help me? I'll just do it myself."

"Uh, what is she doing?" David confusedly asked, staring at Tay.

"She's trying to end her life is what she's doing," Tay hissed.

"Ugh! I don't have time for this!" I hissed back.
 Rain spread his wings getting ready to move as David and Tay shouted, "Annalise!" in unison.

We flew over to my brother and Patroklos so I could get the evil witch's attention and when I got within earshot of her hideous form, I began to entice her, hoping it would be enough to draw her away. "Hey, you evil beast, look over here. I'm the one you want, the one you've been after. Come on, come see if you can get me." My brother's eyes widened as Rain, and I took off.

"It worked. She followed me and left Brighton and my knight alone." I thought. Zigzagging toward me she got herself within striking distance. "Okay, Rain, it's time to show me how good those reflexes of yours are." As I said it, Yurika struck, causing Rain to hoist up and me almost to fall off his withers. "Watch out, Lissy!" My brother shouted from below.

Yurika slowly pulled away from my head and then cackled, "You wretched girl, you all can't defeat me. I am going to swallow every last one of you starting with him," she roared out the last three words as she nose-dived toward Lord Patroklos.

"Patroklos!" I shouted in the midst racing down to him as fast as Rain could descend with his wings tucked in. Tay and David came speeding down to us and when I got just above my knight and his pegasus I hoisted myself off of Rain.

"Lissy, no, what are you doing!" Brighton screamed. "This is my fight bubba. She wants me." I said under my breath as I took my last living steps. I couldn't let Yurika take Milaya's only brother.

My plan to draw the witch away wasn't working this time. She reared back getting ready to attack my knight. Rain dashed in and hooked his teeth to the top of my dress, popping me up high. "Guess you didn't care for my plan either," I thought as I landed on his withers. "Quick, boy, we don't have much time," I said as we gained speed toward my handsome knight.

"Bahahaha, two for the price of one," Yurika hissed as she struck. Thank the stars Rain darted to the side and Patroklos did the same as well. I gulped as she began to position herself again. "This time I'll swallow you two whole," she growled while striking. "Noooo!" I screamed as she almost sunk her teeth into my knight.

"Ahhh." Her vicious strike came unknowingly and caused me to fall off my pegasus.

"Annalise!" David yelled as he and Draco dove down to catch me.

Falling to my demise while staring into his eyes as he stretched out his hand for me, I smiled and closed my eyes. "This boy really does care for me," I thought. I lifted my lids back up to look at him one last time. I was getting ready to stick my hand up when her massive body hovered right above his head and mouth began to open. "David! Noooo!"

My friend smiled at me one last time before Yurika closed her mouth. "David!" Tay shouted. Thud. Rain swooped underneath me, and I landed hard on his back. I wailed as I watched Yurika furiously chomp down on my friend and his pegasus' body.

"Tailya!" I screamed.

That's all I needed to do. She was already in motion spinning the wand and pointing at me. Poof! "Yes, it worked," I said, fluttering alongside Rain the size of a speck of dust with my blade ready. "Okay, boy, you distract her. I've got other plans." I sniffled and wiped away livid tears with my empty hand.

Tay watched as I flew around to the back of Yurika's head. When I was in the clear I raised my weapon as high as I could. Looking down at Tay showing her I was ready, she winked. Poof! She switched me back to my full-size. I plunged the tip of my blade into the sea monster's skull, wedging it in deep until my steel hit bone. Then I immediately shouted, "This is for David...!"

The giant beast roared in agony and started to flail. "Ahh!" I screamed. I could feel my body raise as she continued to jerk around. I looked down to see that my shoe had somehow got stuck in between one her ridges. "Tay I can't hold on much longer!" I yelled.

"I'm coming, Anna!" she shouted racing toward me.

"Ahhh, she's sinking!"

"Let go, Anna!" Tay shouted.

"I can't! My foot is wedged too deep in one of her scales. Tay, I can't get loose."

"Annalise!" Tay's scream faded as Yurika began to speedily sink down. I reached up my hand for her rescue, but I watched as my fingers went further and further out of her reach. As I felt the icy cold water touch my legs I heard Brighton scream, "Lissy!"

I took in a heap of air, closed my eyes, and thought," this is it", as the feeling of pins and needles penetrated my body and was being pulled down into the abyss of the deep blue.

To all of my readers. I would like to say thank you so much for all of your support. It really means more to me than you could ever imagine. I hope you all can see that this is a story inside a story and a beautiful one at that.

Tales Of Bristeria is my first novel and I am having so much fun writing it. I never dreamed I could write let alone have the imagination for a full novel. I guess that's what happens when we listen to the lies that are spoken from others. We don't realize it, but we allow them to identify us and then there is no room left for possibilities. I am grateful for a God that can change my perspective and transform my mind into His image. Thanks again and I hope you all stay tuned for Book 3 when we will find out if Annalise is still alive or if some kind of crazy twist happens.

Acknowledgements:

First, I want to thank the one who is the center of my life. Thank you, Daddy. You are the sole purpose for how this story came to life. All glory goes to God.

Secondly, I want to thank my amazing husband, better half, and the best friend that I have always wanted. Patrick, you are my everything and I couldn't have got through this without you or without your awesome encouragement. Thank you, my love.

Thank you to our wonderful son Justin Smiley for his love and support. I love you kid!

Thank you, Tim Barton, for believing in me, encouraging me, and always being there for guidance. Love you dad.

Thank you to my girl Angie Fashik who has always lifted me up and encouraged me.

Thank you Thokozani Houston for being there to give me advice, lift up my spirit and encourage me to keep going throughout the whole process when all I wanted to do was throw in the towel so, so many times. :)

Thank you to my incredible editor/publicist Shannon Whittington. You are always so patient with me and for that I am grateful. And lastly, thank you to all of my friends, family, and fans for making Tales of Bristeria thrive.